A Call to Arms
Book One of the Chronicles of Arden

First Edition

Shiriluna Nott & SaJa H.

'A CALL TO ARMS'
Copyright ©2015 by Shiriluna Nott

All rights reserved. No part of this work may be reproduced, either physically or digitally, without the express written consent of the author. All characters are creations of the author's imagination and any resemblance to persons living or dead are purely coincidence.

Edited by Karen Robinson of INDIE Books Gone Wild
Proofread by Jennifer Oberth of INDIE Books Gone Wild
Cover Design by Dennis Frohlich

Dedicated to my loving parents, who instilled within me a passion for reading and creativity, and who always encouraged me to follow my dreams.
—*Shiriluna Nott*

For my mother, my first true hero, the one who always believed in me.
For my children, in hopes that one day there will be no need for heroes.
And for those who still cannot speak for themselves for fear of oppression.
—*SaJa H.*

If you would like to receive notifications regarding upcoming releases in the *Chronicles of Arden* series, please sign up for Shiriluna Nott's mailing list here; http://www.shirilunanott.com/mailinglist.html
We only send updates when a new book is released.

Links to other books in the *Chronicles of Arden* series:

NIGHTFALL: BOOK TWO
http://www.amazon.com/dp/B00X1UTEBW

TABLE OF CONTENTS

Chapter One 7
Chapter Two 18
Chapter Three 34
Chapter Four 53
Chapter Five 67
Chapter Six 83
Chapter Seven 104
Chapter Eight 122
Chapter Nine 151
Chapter Ten 172
Chapter Eleven 181
Chapter Twelve 208
Final Word 234

CHAPTER ONE

"Feels cold enough for a hard frost tonight, don't you think, Gib?"

Gibben Nemesio paused in the middle of his labor, brown eyes shifting toward his younger brother, Tayver, who had also ceased his work. The two boys had been outside all day and made admirable progress with the harvest, but cutting down and stacking wheat was a slow and strenuous task. With only two pairs of hands working, it would take the two brothers three full days to reap the entire field. With a heavy sigh, Gib relaxed his grip on the handle of the scythe and lowered the tool until it rested against the pile of wheat he'd just finished bundling.

He raised his head to gaze at his surroundings. A fog was rising from the creek that wove its way along the farthest corner of the field owned by Gib's family. The mist was thick and dense, the kind that swallowed everything in its path. It was quickly enveloping the entire farm, dwarfing the already slight amount of land that Gib could call his own. His brow creased as he noticed a harsh bite in the air. The sun was still well above the horizon, but already the chill more commonly associated with darkness or winter had begun to seep through both clothing and skin.

Gib pursed his lips and his face fell into a pained grimace, but he was careful not to show his displeasure to his younger sibling. There was no reason yet for alarm, and Gib didn't want to worry his brother unnecessarily. As the eldest of the three Nemesio boys, worrying was *his* job. Tayver and Calisto had given up enough of their childhood due to their impoverished and unfortunate circumstances. Protecting them from the distress of adult responsibility was the very least Gib could do—for as long as he could manage anyway.

Recomposing himself, he turned toward Tayver. Flashing a meager, forced smile, Gib replied, "I don't think it'll freeze tonight. It's still a sennight until the harvest festival begins. The cold usually stays north for a while yet."

Gib bit his bottom lip, taking a moment to plead in silence to the Goddess of Light. If ever she were to listen to the requests of a poor farm boy, this would be an ideal time. *Daya, be merciful. We'll lose half the field if there is a hard freeze tonight.* This would surely spell disaster for his family as it had already been a rough year on the crops. With too little warmth and

7

so much excess rain, the fields had resembled a bog for the better part of the season. The spring crop had yielded less than desirable results and now the autumn wheat was not growing as high or heartily as it should.

Tayver raised an eyebrow dubiously. "Nothing has been 'usual' about this year so far."

Gib reached up to sweep a hand across his forehead, brushing the mop of unruly mouse-brown hair away from his eyes. He was in desperate need of a haircut but the harvest would likely keep him far too busy to make the journey to Willowdale to see a barber, at least for the foreseeable future. He might have to grit his teeth and allow one of his brothers to take a pair of shears to the locks before then.

Gib smiled, attempting to reassure his brother. "Well, then our fate lies in the hands of the Two. By the grace of the Goddesses we've made it this far. Surely they must care to some small degree."

An imploring snort came from the younger boy. "If Daya and Chhaya cared about the lives of the simple folk, surely They would have blessed us with sunshine this growing season instead of showering us with rain and hail." Tayver groaned as his hands worked to tie off a bundle of stacked wheat. "We didn't even have enough barley to sell at market this year. If the wheat doesn't yield results, I'm not sure if we'll make it through the winter."

Gib shot his brother a stern look. "We'll be fine. Really, Tay. If the need arises, I'll slaughter one of the goats for meat. Remember the drought two wheelturns ago? We made it through that all right, didn't we?"

"I suppose we did."

"And the blight that ruined our entire potato crop last fall—we came outta that just fine."

Tayver was shuffling his feet in the dirt, chestnut eyes cast downward. "Or like when Pa died and Liza was already gone. Cal, you, and I were alone. We got through that too."

Gib blinked in surprise. Their father's death had always been an uncomfortable subject among the brothers, and Tayver usually didn't initiate any conversation pertaining to the matter. Gib found himself hesitating, wondering if he should press his brother or not. Their father had been dead for two years and Tayver had never opened up about the loss. Others had told Gib to give Tayver space and as much time as he may need but it had been hard. Only eleven at the time, Gib had suddenly found himself the head of the household. He had two young ones to care for and an absent older sister who had joined the Arden sentinels to bring a scanty purse home to the farm as time permitted.

Gib busied himself with slicing down the next batch of wheat, unsure how or if to proceed with this conversation, while Tayver followed behind.

They worked in relative silence for a short time until the younger brother spoke again tentatively. "It's supposed to get easier over time, isn't it? Shouldn't the pain fade after a while? Why do I still miss Pa so much?" He stopped working and wiped at his eyes.

"We all miss him, Tay." Gib set down his scythe and put an arm around his brother's shoulders, not knowing what to do next or how to offer comfort, but knowing it was what their father would have done. Gib looked around desperately, wishing for something to say that wouldn't cause further tears. "There's nothing wrong with missing Pa. Or even Ma. It's normal and right to miss them, but we have to go on. Neither of them would want us to give up."

Tayver sniffed sharply and rolled his reddened eyes. "I know that but—when is it going to get easier? When will we be whole again? Is Liza going to come home? And is Pa ever going to have justice? Doesn't anyone care?"

Gib looked away and winced, hiding his expression. He'd hoped his brother would be too young to see the apparent injustice of their plight. Tayver and Calisto needed to be able to mourn the death of their father and move on. By now they should be able to simply go back to being children again—but it seemed that such luxury was not meant to be theirs. Tayver dashed Gib's hopes with each question.

He took a deep breath and pushed onward. "It's not as easy as that. Pa's been dead for two years. It would be next to impossible to find the thief who killed him now."

Tayver yanked away from Gib as though scalded by his touch. Balling small hands into fists, Tayver shot back, "But it's wrong to kill! The sentinels should have found the thief and killed him! He doesn't deserve to be out there still, killing other people like he did Pa."

"I agree. I wish the killer had been tracked down too, but there just weren't any witnesses. The Willowdale marketplace is busy. The thief was fast and knew what he was doing." Gib reached out a tentative hand and touched his brother's hair with gentle affection. "There wasn't enough information or guards to find him. It was an accident, Tay. Pa was in the wrong place at the wrong time. It doesn't make any sense and it hurts but there's nothing to be done for it now."

Another tear slipped down Tayver's dirty cheek. "That's not good enough." He took in a choppy breath and wiped at his face again. "Pa is gone. Liza is out there in danger. And we've been left all alone."

Gib nodded and took up his scythe once more. "I know, I know. Pa *is* gone but he taught us right. We know how to work this farm and are strong enough to survive. He's given us all he could and we can do no more for him than prove that we can do this, that he didn't fail us."

He set himself back to work and hoped his brother would follow along again. Getting their feelings out into the open was good, but the crop wouldn't harvest itself. Feeling the need, however, to assure Tayver that their elder sister was in no immediate peril, Gib added, "Liza knows what danger she's in out there, but she's smart enough to keep herself out of harm's way. She chose to become a soldier because it's the right thing to do. She's a sentinel of Arden so that she can help others like us. She keeps people safe—people like Pa who might find themselves at the mercy of a thief."

A long moment followed while Tayver seemed to debate all Gib had said. Anger flashed in Tayver's cold, dark eyes, but he was managing his emotions as stoically as could be expected of a young boy. After another deep breath or two, the younger brother picked up his own tools and set back to work. "I miss Liza. She should be here, at home with us."

Gib nodded. "Yes, but we're not alone. You, Cal, and I have each other. We're together and we're going to stay together. I promise."

Tayver grunted and their conversation faded into silence. All that could be heard were the soft, steady swishing of their blades and their footsteps as they worked. Then the wind began to pick up, carrying the sound of whistling crickets. Shortly after, a choir of frogs joined in as well, lending their harmonic voices to the nature-borne song. Evening was settling in all too soon around them. Gib refused to say anything more on the subject, but his mind wandered back to the possibility of frost as he hoped against it.

The first stars had begun to peek out of their daytime hiding places. The sky was a glorious mix of rich reds and deep blues, and the stars twinkled against the dusky canvas as though they were dancing for the brothers, enticing them to halt their labor and admire the beauty painted in the heavens before them. Under any other circumstances, Gib would have gladly obliged, but the threat of a freeze was a serious concern. He couldn't stop, not until darkness had stolen all trace of daylight from the land and it was impossible to see, let alone reap the wheat.

About half a mark later, Gib heard a harsh scraping noise in the distance followed by the bustle of small feet scampering toward them. The first sound was unmistakably the door to the family's cottage. The hinges had been deteriorating for the past several cycles and would be rusted over entirely in a matter of time. Gib made a quick mental note to look at the door when the light of day returned.

"Gib! Tay!"

The quietness was broken by the spirited voice of Gib's youngest brother, Calisto, calling to the older boys from the edge of the field. Gib sighed and rolled his eyes but couldn't help the smile that played at the corner of his mouth. Cal was out here for one of two reasons. Either he was hungry or something had gone wrong inside the house, and Gib was almost positive it was the former.

"Let me guess," Gib called back across the field, his tone playful despite his weariness. "Dinner is ready."

Even through the growing darkness, Gib could see his brother's lips curl upward into a fully fledged grin. Calisto nodded his head with vigor. "Yep, sure is! And that's not all! Guess what! Liza's here!"

Gib nearly dropped his scythe and was certain that his jaw almost hit the ground. "*Liza?*"

Tayver was likewise flabbergasted. His eyes darted toward Gib. "I thought you said she wasn't supposed to come home until Midwinter."

Gib's mind was racing with questions. The last he'd heard from his sister, she'd been stationed in Silver City, a three-day journey by horseback from the farm. In her letter, Liza had stressed how busy she'd been, especially with the constant threat of war breaking out on the eastern border. Surely she hadn't been given a leave of absence with so many duties to fulfill and the rising threat to the country. What was of so much importance that Liza had been given permission to return home?

"Come on," Calisto was pressing in a gleeful voice. "Come to the house and see her!"

Brown eyes hopeful, Tayver looked to Gib for permission to quit working, and with a sigh, he nodded. He couldn't force Tayver to stay now that their sister was here. "I'll finish up. Cal and Tay, you both go on ahead." Both boys raced toward the house without another word.

He wanted to drop what he was doing and follow behind his brothers but knew he could stack several more bundles of wheat before calling it quits for the night. Gib worked with renewed vigor despite his aching back and shoulders. It took every bit of self-control within him not to throw his scythe aside and sprint toward the cottage. As excited as he was by the arrival of his sister, her unexpected visit troubled Gib—and he wondered if it had anything to do with the conflict on the border. His stomach flopped as the realization dawned on him that perhaps Liza had come to tell them she was leaving for war. After all, she'd mentioned in her last letter that the High Council of Arden had been pushing for battle against Shiraz for some time now. What if the declaration had been made? What if Liza left—and never returned?

Gib swallowed his emotions, reminding himself it was ridiculous to jump to such conclusions. Liza had also assured Gib in the same letter that the King of Arden was doing all he could to avoid conflict with Shiraz. The King didn't want to resort to fighting if he could help it. Gib didn't pretend to know much about the policies of the country, but he was pretty sure that only the King could declare war on another nation, so although the High Council seemed to be pressing for battle, unless the King gave the order himself, Arden would not march.

No, it was more likely Liza had been relocated to one of the settlements on the western border—Ostlea or Greenbank perhaps—and she was simply stopping by on her way through to inform her brothers of the reassignment. The threat had to be all in Gib's head. No war was coming. That couldn't be the reason his sister was here.

True darkness had fallen across the field now and Gib had no choice but to cease his labor. He stored away his tools in the shed which also housed the family's livestock—a pair of goats and a few hens—and then followed along the path toward the house. The outline of the cottage was visible against the darkened sky as he made his approach, and smoke was rising in gentle wisps from the vent at the peak of the thatched roof. Relief washed over him in a wave as the boisterous laughter of conversing siblings could be heard from inside the house. It felt good to be home.

Gib pulled the door open, cursing under his breath as the hinges groaned in protest. He'd little time to dwell on that, for almost as soon as Gib had closed the door, Liza swept up—seemingly out of nowhere—and all but threw herself into his arms.

"*Gib!* You finally decided to come join us!" Liza taunted in playful jest as her arms closed around his shoulders. "You're shaping up to be just like Pa, you know that, right? He wouldn't stop working until it was so dark that he almost broke his neck trying to get back to the house!"

Gib chuckled and returned the embrace. Liza smelled of leather and scented soap. Her mouse-brown hair was tied with a ribbon at the nape of her neck, though a number of rebellious ringlets had escaped during her travels and were now congregating around her ears. All the Nemesio children had the same curly brown hair and large chestnut eyes. Liza frequently reminded them they had inherited their looks from their mother. Gib would have to take Liza's word on that because he could hardly remember what his mother looked like now.

"You look taller," Gib remarked, holding his sister at arm's length.

Liza smirked, eyes glittering with mischief. "You don't."

Gib's head fell back as he laughed. "Well, damn." He could hear Tayver snickering from the far corner of the room.

"What about me, Liza?" Calisto asked as he pulled on the frayed edge of his sister's tunic, not wanting to be left out of the conversation. "Have I got any bigger since you were last here?"

Liza leaned down, pretending to scrutinize him with a withering gaze. She was quiet for several moments before nodding her head in approval and replying, "Hmm. I think you have, Cal. At this rate, you'll surely be taller than Gib by this time next year." She gave the youngster a wink and Calisto grinned proudly.

Gib snorted but couldn't think up any other form of rebuttal. He extended an arm to gently poke his brother in the ribs and force a change in the topic of discussion. "Hey Cal, didn't you say dinner was ready?"

The young boy's eyes widened. "Oh, right!" He scampered toward the open hearth, which was situated against the far wall of the room. A large kettle of pottage simmered above the fire pit. The flames had long since burned low and now only glowing embers remained to keep the stew warm and illuminate the cottage. Calisto used a ladle to stir the contents of the pot while Tayver brought over wooden bowls.

"We only have enough bowls for three of us," Tayver muttered as he handed the utensils to his younger brother. "The other one is full of water from the leak in the roof, up in the loft."

Gib was certain Liza would have something to say about that, but fortunately she was merciful and kept quiet. Fixing the thatching on the roof was yet another project Gib just hadn't had time to get to yet. He and Tayver had been so busy with the crop and he couldn't ask Calisto, only nine, to climb up there and risk falling.

"You can have my bowl, Liza," Cal offered, always a hero.

Gib shook his head, getting a word in before his sister had the chance. "No, you go ahead, Cal. I'll wait to eat. I'm not even that hungry." As if to mock him, Gib's stomach gurgled in protest a moment later and he held back a grimace. He was starving. But he was the head of the household now and it was his job to see the family had full bellies at the end of each day—and so he would wait.

Gib scraped the last bit of food from his bowl, savoring the taste. Pottage was best when it was fresh but by tomorrow the leftover vegetables would already begin to mush together in such a way that it was like eating slop meant for a pig.

The fire pit crackled with renewed life as Liza added another log, this time not for cooking but for warmth. Tayver and Calisto had long since retreated to the loft. The boys always slept up there, except during the colder months when it was impossible to ward off the bitter winter air except by lying directly in front of the hearth. Gib had vague memories from his childhood of the entire family bundling up and spending the long winters sitting around the fire, telling stories and sharing merriment despite the fact they were always cold. Things had been different in those times. The walls of the cottage had resonated with the sound of laughter. Now only silence remained. They had no time for play or merriment, only survival.

Liza sighed in a weary sort of way, pulling Gib away from his dark musings. He raised his head in time to see his sister sit down beside him at the table and watched as she extended her hand to take hold of Gib's forearm.

"You've done an admirable job with the upkeep of the farm," she said in a quiet voice. "Pa would be proud of you, Gib." Liza squeezed his arm and her grip was firm, strong like their father's had been. A pang of sorrow stabbed Gib in the chest.

Gib forced a smile, but he didn't feel proud. He felt tired and stretched past his limit. Truth be told, he wasn't sure how much longer he could run the household by himself. It was such a monumental task for a boy of thirteen.

He knew he was being silly, even selfish. Thirteen was practically manhood in a poor family where a child was fortunate to survive birth and damned lucky to see his tenth winter. In another few wheelturns, he would be expected to marry and start a family of his own—more mouths to feed and worry about when he could barely ensure that Tay and Cal kept from going hungry. It all seemed like a cruel joke. How could anyone keep their right mind with so many responsibilities to fulfill?

"I don't know how Pa did it," Gib admitted. "I don't know how he managed to keep four children clothed and fed after Ma died. He's more of a hero than he'll ever know."

Liza's smile was stern as she squeezed her brother's arm again. "He did what he had to do. As will you." Her brown eyes shifted toward the loft, perhaps to reassure herself that the two younger boys were sleeping. The firelight illuminated her face and for the first time that evening, Gib noted the worry lines surrounding Liza's eyes. She had seen only five winters more than Gib, but Liza appeared as worn down as Gib felt. Was the stress of her sentinel job already taking its toll on her or was something else eating away at her conscience?

Liza lifted her face and the smile that had been present the moment before was gone. "I have news for you."

The sentence was simple, but Gib could feel the weight of the words pressing down on his chest, threatening to suffocate him. He'd known. Little chance existed Liza was here for pleasure. She was here to deliver bad news, he was sure of it. Gib held his breath and waited for her to continue. The silence was insufferable.

She seemed to sense his dread and glanced back toward the loft as if to be sure the younger boys were out of ear shot. Her mouth pressed into a thin line as she reached into a deep pocket on her uniform. Gib winced at the sight of a small scroll sealed with the royal emblem of Arden—the rising phoenix. This wasn't just something bad, it was something important.

Liza reached out to hand the document to Gib, but his arms were suddenly as heavy as lead and he couldn't lift them. Instead, he felt his mouth open and the hushed words spilled out without consent. "Is it war then? Are you going to leave us as well?"

She flinched as if she'd been bitten and withdrew the scroll, holding it in her lap. "You know I would never willingly leave any of you, don't you?"

Gib lowered his head, feeling foolish. "I'm sorry. Of course I know you don't have a choice. I just—what am I going to tell Tay and Cal?"

Her dark eyes met his in an unknown emotion, and Gib's guts turned to ice. Liza's voice trembled. "This conscription isn't for me."

Oh Gods. He couldn't breathe. His lungs had collapsed and his throat closed up. *No air.* He slammed his eyes shut, shaking his head. This couldn't be happening. It couldn't be for him, could it? He was the eldest son of his family but did that matter when his elder sister had already joined the sentinels? He didn't know. The laws concerning the entry of women into the military were still so new and unrefined.

"Uh." His lungs shuddered back to life and he gasped for air. "It's a draft notice? For me?"

Liza couldn't meet his eyes. Her cheeks were an ugly red. "I tried, Gib. You have to believe me. I tried to convince my sergeant it was unnecessary for you to be drafted seeing as I was willing to go to war. He wouldn't listen. You know how they are! He feels that it's still 'a man's responsibility' to go to war for his family." She turned her face away from him and spat. "Fools, all of them. Who are they to decide who is *worthy* of going to war and who isn't?"

Gib nodded, knowing it was true. A lot of hard feelings were going around about the recent changes that had given women permission to join the army. Indeed, Liza was the only girl from their entire village who'd ever gone to Academy to become a soldier. It had earned the scorn of many of their neighbors at the time, and some of them, especially the women, would still give Gib a sideways look in the market. It was widely whispered that his sister didn't know her place and that she tempted fate by remaining away from home and not marrying.

She set down the scroll, still rolled tightly and sealed, and took his hands in hers. He wondered distantly when his had grown to be the same size as hers. "It's not war yet." It was meant to be a comfort, but it did little for his trembling nerves. "And if the King and Queen have their way, it will never come to that. It's the damned High Council—"

Gib understood. "They're still pushing for war."

"Over a ridiculous land dispute." She sighed. "Be that as it may, you've been called and you have no choice but to answer."

"Yeah." His voice sounded distant even to himself. He didn't remember taking his hands from his sister's but the next thing he knew, he was picking up the parchment and clumsily peeling at the wax seal. It fell open easily, as if it didn't carry the command for him to drop his life where it was and march to Arden's aid. How could something so harmless looking be such a threat? But it could be the very thing to seal his doom. It was calling him to a war he may not come home from. A shiver raced up his spine.

The text was laid out in fine, unsmudged ink, and it was obvious that whoever had written it was well schooled. The letters flowed together and the line of script was straight and appealing to the eye. Gib squinted, wishing that any of those things would make it easier for him to read it.

Raising two brothers and working the farm had left little time for proper schooling.

Liza reached forward to help him. "Here, let me. We had to do some basic schooling at Academy." She took up the scroll and scooted closer to the fire, her dark eyes reflecting the guttering flames.

"Let it be here-by known," Liza began, her voice choppy as she picked away at the message. Gib was proud of her. The women from the market who thought little of her surely couldn't read at all. "By dec–declar–ation–declaration of King Rishi Radek, on behalf of the country of Arden, one Gibben Nemesio has forth–with–forthwith been called upon to aid the army of Arden."

She swallowed and Gib felt like he couldn't breathe once again. They both took a short break there, letting the severity of the situation settle over them before she pressed on. "Soldiers are to report to Silver City for training. Failure to com–comply will be judged treason."

The air around the two siblings was heavy with their shared silence. No words could describe the rolling pain in his guts as his mind ran swiftly with all the possibilities of death and hardship that might befall him. The full realization of what he needed to do crashed over him like a wave.

"How can I go, Liza? What about Cal and Tay? They're not old enough to take care of the farm on their own! The field is still two days away from being fully reaped. I have to fix the door and the damned roof is leaking—who will take care of them if we're both gone? They'll never make it through the winter. I can't leave."

"Gib." Liza's voice was stern, steady, a grounding force within the chaos. "You have no choice. You have to go. Before I came home I stopped across the road to see the Fadells. Baria said she would keep an eye on them like she did when Ma died."

"Baria is old! Hell, Abbas is old. Their son Altair is going to be married come spring. They're not going to have the time to see to it that Tay gets the fields planted." Gib collapsed onto his back heavily and looked up toward the ceiling, at a total loss. Could Tayver plant the fields on his own? Cal was still too small to put in a whole day in the fields. Gib had no other options though. No money was available to hire help, and no other kin remained to divide the chores between. "I don't—I don't even know what to do with them. They can't come with me, can they?"

His sister didn't meet his eyes and he knew before she answered. "No. The academy will only provide housing for the student." Gib threw his hands into the air, but she pressed on, shifting closer to him. "Wait, just listen to me. Nothing can be done for them this winter. I'll help you get the wheat in tomorrow and Altair said he'd come by to help once his chores are done. You know Abbas will take our portion to the market for the boys. He and Pa were friends for years. He'll do right by them and make sure they get the money—"

Gib gripped either side of his head, clenching a fistful of curls in each hand, and slammed his eyes shut once more. "I know that! Abbas and Baria have been nothing but good to us, it's just—" He stopped to take a breath, but his chest felt tight and his eyes were burning. "How am I supposed to take care of them if I'm not here? Ma and Pa are both dead. It's my job to make sure the rest of us survive. I can't let the young ones down, Liza. They could die if I fail them!" He gasped for breath and the tears won. He felt like a child again. He was supposed to be the adult.

Liza swept in, wrapping her arms around him and pulling him close to her body. "I know it looks bleak, but it's going to work. The boys only have to get through this winter and then they can come to Silver in the spring. Tayver will be old enough to apprentice to someone and Cal can go to the workhouses until he comes of age."

"Pa always said the workhouses were dangerous."

Liza sighed and bowed her head. "They are. But Cal is a good worker and he can keep his nose out of trouble. I'd be more worried to send Tayver in there. He'd talk back once and—I don't know what else to do for them, Gib. The boys can't run the farm on their own forever, you're right. They'll have to go somewhere."

He wiped at his closed eyes. It felt as though the entire world were spinning out of control. "I'm supposed to care for them. I promised I would."

"You've done well. The best you could. I dare anyone else to do what you have with as little. But this is out of your control. You have to report to Silver. If you don't, you'll go to prison and then what good will you be to Tay and Cal?"

Gib sucked in another shallow breath and willed his nerves to calm. Liza was right. Nothing else could be done about any of it. "How long before I have to leave?"

She smiled against the top of his head. "*We* leave. I'm going with you. Three mornings from now we ride out at first light. That should give us enough time to harvest the wheat and get the house in shape for winter."

His mind was racing with all the different tasks he would have to do. Two days didn't seem enough. The field and the home repairs, firewood to be collected, animals to be cared for, two boys to be seen to—it all seemed too much. And tomorrow he would have to break their hearts. "I don't want to have to tell them."

"I will, if you want."

One more tear escaped as Gib looked into the fire. "No. I'll do it. It's only right."

CHAPTER TWO

Three mornings later, a deluge of rain saw Gib and his sister off. It was cold and miserable and completely fitting with their circumstances. Calisto had clung to Gib, crying unabashedly, while Tayver pretended to be devoid of any emotion at all. Gib knew his brother was every bit as sad as Cal, but Tay was putting on a stoic face for the sake of the family. He was already trying to step up and accept the responsibility of adulthood. He had no choice.

Liza had given both boys a hug and showered them with kisses, telling them to be strong. Then she and Gib had climbed onto her horse, a silver palfrey named Lilly, and left the farm behind. Gib hadn't looked back—it would have undone him. He was grateful the rain was coming down steadily enough to mask his tears. If Liza noticed his quiet sobs, she didn't say a word about it.

By midday, the rain had passed and the sun came out long enough to dry their soaked clothing. When the pair stopped to set up camp for the night, Gib took the clothes from their dampened pack and let them dry as well. They had one change of clothes each. Liza had insisted it would be best to pack light as the crown of Arden would provide him with everything he may need. It wasn't like Gib had many personal belongings anyway. His tunics were frayed around the edges and the only pair of boots he owned were far too small for his growing feet, but nothing could be done about any of it now. Perhaps the crown of Arden would be generous enough to replace his worn clothing. Only time would tell.

They traveled south for three days, following alongside the Tempist River. Liza explained to Gib that the Tempist ran parallel to the trade road all the way to Silver City, so during the times when Academy was on interim, all he needed to do to get home was follow the river north. Gib barely heard her speaking. His mind was preoccupied by the thoughts of leaving his brothers to fend for themselves while he traveled to an unfamiliar place. No neighbors would lend him a helping hand and no family would comfort him. A cold lump formed in the pit of his stomach.

As they journeyed farther south, the flatlands gave way to high, rolling hills of green that seemed to reach up and collide with the skyline. The number of travelers using the road increased dramatically as well. Some people were on horseback like them—but the road also had pedestrians, carts being pulled by teams of oxen, and even a line of caravan wagons. Gib's eyes burned from the dirt being kicked up along the path, but he couldn't seem to look away. He'd never seen such things before.

The sun was still high in the sky when Liza announced they would arrive in Silver City within a mark. Gib straightened in the saddle, curious enough to lean out and look around Liza's body. They were in the midst of climbing yet another rolling hill, so he couldn't see what lay ahead.

Gib's stomach was fluttering as though he'd swallowed a bug. "Where is it?"

Liza pointed forward. "Just wait until we reach the top of this ridge. You'll be able to see the entire city from there." She gave Lilly a jab in the flank, coaxing the palfrey to move faster. The horse snorted imploringly but obliged.

As they climbed the hill, Gib's anticipation rose with it. His heart was pounding in his chest and he forced himself to take slow, steady breaths of air. *You'll be okay. You can do this.* Lilly was moving at a full trot by the time they reached the crest of the ridge, and all at once, Gib was able to see everything for league upon league ahead of him. He let out a strangled gasp at the sight.

The royal city of Silver sprawled across the valley below. It was the largest thing Gib had ever seen in his life, stretching as far as the eye could see in either direction. A wall made of smooth grey stone wrapped around the entirety of the city, roof peaks of the tallest buildings just visible and lending the impression of tightly packed houses, all shimmering in the bright afternoon sunlight. The Tempist flowed through the middle of the city, an iridescent line of blue that cut the city in half. Gib knew he'd remember this sight until the day he died. He stared, eyes wide and mouth gaping.

Liza smiled broadly. "Welcome to Silver."

Another mark later, the travelers stood at the gates of the city, waiting to be allowed passage. The wall spanning the perimeter was at least three times as tall as Gib and made of the finest limestone he'd ever seen. Liza explained that heightened security meant all travelers going into the city must now be questioned. Gib swallowed nervously and wondered what kind of people the sentinels were attempting to keep out as he caught sight of an archer patrolling the wall, nearly invisible in the shadows.

When it was their turn to approach, Liza reached into her pocket to pull out a copper emblem with the golden inlay of a phoenix carved into the metal. Her badge identified her as a sentinel and would help her gain entrance to the city. From the corner of his eye, Gib warily watched the pair of guards working the gate. Both men looked gruff and threatening clad in full chainmail armor, with sheathed swords longer than Gib's entire arm.

The older of the two guards measured the riders with a shrewd eye. "State your names and your business in Silver," he demanded, nothing playful about his tone. This man would slice open any person suspected of being false.

Liza cleared her throat, declaring herself: "Liza Nemesio, sentinel of Arden, returning from my family's homestead and reporting for active duty." She set a hand on Gib's shoulder and he jumped. "And this is my younger brother, Gibben. He's to go to Academy for training. He received a conscription notice from the King and is here to fulfill his duty to Arden."

Gib held his breath, but after a moment, the guard nodded and motioned for them to pass. Gib didn't dare speak again until Lilly had carried them well away from the wall. He leaned in close to his sister's ear. "That was a little scary."

Liza laughed. "Yes, the worst part of all was my fear that you weren't going to be able to hold down your breakfast."

They shared a chuckle before Gib's attention was drawn toward the interior of the city. The houses just inside the wall were small and compact, resembling shacks rather than true houses. Most of them were made of cheap materials—wood, clay, even mud. The people who lived here were dressed in shabby clothing, some of them in nothing more than rags that hung from their bodies. The disheveled, dirty peasants paid no attention to the travelers as they passed. A distinctive clicking noise rang in Gib's ears, and at once his gaze fell upon the ground as Lilly's horseshoes hit the pavement. Somewhere between the wall and here, the dirt pathway had given way to stone. It was the most peculiar thing Gib had ever seen. The village near his home would never have been able to afford the cost of laying cobblestone.

The streets seemed to wind back and forth rather than being a straight line. Liza told him the city was designed that way intentionally, so if the walls were ever breached, the royal palace wouldn't be so easy a trek for the enemy.

The farther into the city they went, the grander the houses became. The clay huts hugging the city walls gave way to two-story homes, and even those houses were dwarfed in size by the manors further along the street. These households were the size of small mountains and each had their own gated courtyard.

"Do royalty live in these houses?" Gib asked in astonishment.

"Not even close. These are the homes of the nobility—rich merchants, guild masters, and the highborn mostly," Liza explained, and

Gib could only shake his head in awe. His sister snorted. "A big waste of space if you ask me—oh, we're almost to Traders Row, the trade district of Silver. If we weren't already sharing a horse, I would warn you to stay close. It can get hectic here."

Indeed, the streets were becoming so congested that the flow of traffic was bordering on a standstill. There were people *everywhere*. Gib could not find a single area of unoccupied space. He clung to Liza, fearing that if he were to fall, he would be lost in the sea of people. Liza turned in the saddle and gave him an encouraging smile.

"It's a bit overwhelming the first time, I know."

Gib's head was spinning. "There are so many people—"

"Aye. Traders Row is the busiest area of the city. It's where all the merchants live and sell their products—and where the city folk come to make purchases." Liza patted Gib on the knee when he couldn't even manage a nod in response. "It won't be so bad once we cross the river and get onto Academy grounds, I promise."

His sister pulled on the reins, maneuvering Lilly through the horde of swarming bodies. The mare seemed at ease with the commotion surrounding her. Even when a pair of children darted in front of the horse, chasing a chicken that must have escaped them, Lilly showed her dissent only by laying her ears low and issuing a snort.

Great, Gib lamented to himself. *The horse is better socialized than I. I'm doomed.*

Somewhere to his right side, he heard the bleating of goats as two old men bartered back and forth, trying to negotiate a fair purchase price for the animals. A robust woman in an apron hollered across the street as she waved a loaf of bread high in the air, and somewhere behind them, a baby wailed to be fed. All the voices blended together to create a dull humming sound in Gib's ears.

Gib closed his eyes in a desperate attempt to escape the situation. If he didn't have to see the insanity surrounding him, he could imagine he was back on the farm. He could pretend he was lying in the soft hay of the goat pen, just waking up from a nap. His brothers were boiling a stew in the cottage, their laughter carrying through the open doorway. His lips curled upward as he smiled. They sounded so happy, the way children should sound. Inhaling deeply, Gib could almost smell the aroma of spiced meat in his nostrils—

Liza's voice cut through his wistful dream like a knife. "We're almost there."

He opened his eyes and at once snapped back to reality. A narrow bridge lay before them. It spanned the width of the Tempist River. Out in the countryside, the river was treacherous, a swallow of dark water wide enough for a ship to navigate if some captain was foolhardy enough to attempt the feat. Here in Silver, however, the river flowed sluggishly and was only as wide as two rowing boats placed bow to stern beside one another.

Lilly's hooves clattered against the cobblestone path as Liza guided the horse onto the bridge, and Gib was drawn to the multitude of cracks within the stone masonry where moss had tried to creep through only to be smothered by the constant barrage of horseshoes and footsteps.

"This isn't the only bridge in the city," Liza explained. "The one that serves as the gateway to and from the royal palace is much grander, but this bridge is closest to the sentinel training grounds and the academy, so you'll want to use it as you come and go." She motioned for Gib to look ahead. "Speaking of which, here we are."

Gib could feel the color drain from his face. A massive collegium rose in the distance, casting an imposing shadow across the path. It was constructed from the same grey limestone as the city wall and was equally as stunning to behold. At least three stories tall, the building loomed above all other constructions in the area like a mountain of solid rock.

Gib was momentarily unable to find his voice. "I—is this—?"

"Yes," Liza confirmed. "Academy." She pointed to the left. "And that wooden building across the way is the royal stable, where all of the horses which belong to the Crown are kept. The sentinel barracks are on the other side of the stable."

"That's where you'll be, right?" Gib asked, needing the assurance that his sister wouldn't be far away.

Liza nodded. "Unless I'm assigned elsewhere in the moonturns to come, then yes, I'll be in Silver." She clasped Gib on the shoulder. "Come on, let's turn Lilly over to the stable master and then we can figure out where you need to go."

Gib walked in silence up the corridor which he'd been told led to the dean's office. The passageway was so congested he dared not take his eyes from his sister's back. All around him were boys and girls his age and a little older. They had their own bags of belongings with them. Some had little like himself and others had entire cases full of possessions. Parents were present as well, mostly with the well-dressed children, fawning over them and giving words of advice or encouragement.

Laughter drew his attention as they passed one boy who looked to be about Gib's age but was a spectacle to behold with pale white skin and hair. Beside him, a well-dressed man was beaming proudly, as any father might, and Gib was struck with yet another pang of wistful yearning. If events had played out differently, his own father might have been here too, seeing Gib off to his classes.

His longing drew short when he collided with Liza's back. She looked over her shoulder at him and smiled.

A giant door made of solid oak and taller than the highest point of Gib's entire house loomed ahead. His mouth went dry. Was this where he was meant to go?

"This is Marc Arrio's office. He's the Dean of Academy," Liza informed. "We're in luck. There's no line."

Gib glanced around. Liza was right. *Am I late? Is that why there are so many people in the corridor but no one ahead of us? I won't be arrested if I'm late, will I?* "Sh–should I knock? So they don't think I didn't come?"

Liza chuckled. "No. The closed door means there's someone already in there. We'll wait for your turn." She looked him over narrowly and Gib fidgeted with the attention. Her hands, roughened by the work of a sentinel, ran through his mess of curls. "You'll do well, Gib. You always have."

He opened his mouth to say a word of thanks but nothing came out. Before he could try again, the door opened and he closed his mouth, stepping aside. With wide eyes, he watched a tall man with fair skin and dark, short-cropped hair with only the slightest trace of silver flecking his temples step past the threshold. He was talking to a young girl about her classes. His loud voice carried well but wasn't offensive in tone. "All right, your classes have been set. You're sure you don't want to rethink them?"

The new student's voice was gruff for a girl, and she didn't smile as girls were encouraged to do. "I've had thirteen years to think, Dean Arrio. I know what I'm doing."

Gib winced. Surely she shouldn't speak to the dean in such a way. Her dark skin and features suggested she was not highborn but the mark on her brow, a simple red mark in the shape of a diamond, could mean she was foreign. If she was foreign, perhaps the girl didn't know she was being impolite.

The tall man only laughed, loudly and infectiously. "Have it your way. If anyone has the right spirit for the job, it's you. And remember to call me Marc—Dean Arrio sounds too formal."

The girl bowed to the dean before turning to leave. Rounding fast, she almost ran straight into Gib. He noted with despair that she was nearly half a head taller than him. *Daya, will I ever grow?*

Her mouth set into a thin line and she nodded at him, wild raven hair tumbling about her shoulders and down her back. "Apologies."

Gib opened his mouth to assure her of no harm done but she was already on her way past him. He watched as the girl wove through the congested hallway and wondered where her father was. Things must surely be different here in Silver. Back home, girls were meant to be polite and soft spoken, and they weren't typically allowed to wander off on their own—though she didn't appear to be wandering.

"Liza Nemesio? Are you here to see me?" The dean was speaking. He sounded genuinely surprised.

Liza turned a quick smile on him. "I am, Dean Marc. Or rather, my brother Gib is." She grabbed Gib around the shoulders and pushed him forward. Gib was intimidated by someone so tall and with such authority. He opened his mouth, but again his voice failed him.

Dark, clever eyes sparkled down at him and smiled on their own before the dean's mouth followed suit. "Another Nemesio, eh?" He clapped Gib on the shoulder so hard Gib feared his knees may buckle. "All right. Let's head inside and get you set up." The dean whirled around and re-entered his office. Gib shuffled along behind him.

Inside the office a wide desk made of red oak was polished to a smart shine. Dean Marc sat on it and leafed through a couple of documents, gesturing for Gib and Liza to take a seat in the plush chairs in front of the desk. The fabric on the chair was some of the finest Gib had ever seen, and he winced at the idea of sitting on it, fearing the dirt on his clothing may rub off.

Stiffly, Gib chose to rest only the smallest amount of himself on the edge of the chair. His legs would be screaming at him soon but he didn't want to risk any harm to the fine things in this room which he could surely never pay to replace. Liza came over a second later and flopped down in the opposite seat. He gave her a sideways glare but a lazy smile was all she paid him in return.

"All right," Dean Marc declared at length, never looking up from his papers. "Are you a volunteer or a draft—" He glanced up then and knitted his well-tamed eyebrows. A lopsided smile crossed his mouth as he looked over Gib. "Afraid of the chair?"

Gib's face burst into flame as he struggled to find something to say. "I, uh, it's a nice chair. I didn't want to—my clothes might be—sorry." His head swam as he tried to re-collect his thoughts.

Again came the laugh that beckoned others to join. "I have sentinel trainees in and out of here all the time. I think you'll be all right. Unless that is how sitting is done where you come from."

A smile threatened to curl one corner of Gib's mouth, but he wasn't sure if it was allowed or not. He tried to think of something to say but came up short.

The dean pressed on, opting to speak to Liza instead. "Doesn't talk much, does he? You'll have to teach him how to sit properly when you get the time."

Liza laughed heartily, and the ice in Gib's gut receded just a little. Perhaps this wouldn't be as bad as he'd originally envisioned. The dean seemed friendly, not at all how Gib had imagined everyone in Silver City would be. His Pa had warned him of city people sometimes being cold— mean-spirited even—but thus far it didn't appear to be true.

Gib found his voice at last. It was weak and choppy but audible. "Sitting doesn't happen much where I come from. Forgive me, Dean Marc. Perhaps I'll have to take a class on it."

Marc tipped his head back and laughed some more. The sound echoed off the high archway ceiling filling their space. The dean was smiling so broadly that small creases had formed around his eyes and mouth, and Gib wondered if the dean was older than he'd first appeared.

Highborn or not, the dean seemed genuine, and Gib had just begun to relax when a new voice cleared its throat testily. Marc grunted and his smile fell away as he turned to look over his shoulder. Gib jumped when he realized someone else was in the room with them.

Sitting in a dark corner with a writing slate and parchment in his hands, another man glared back at them. His facial features were cold, and the stranger's thin lips were pulled back into a sneer. Gib's stomach flopped. Perhaps his father hadn't been wrong after all.

"Could we wrap up these informalities so that we may continue about our day, Marc? Some of us have other, more pressing obligations." Effectively having sapped all the merriment from the room, the stranger straightened his pristine white robes and fetched his quill from an inkpot by his feet. He pressed a blond wisp away from his face and refocused on writing. "This one's name is—?"

Marc nodded but seemed to be merely obliging his companion rather than agreeing with him. The dean turned back to Gib and Liza with a dim expression. "Allow me to introduce Diedrick Lyle. He's our Instructions Master. It's his job to see each student gets the classes he needs."

Diedrick snorted shortly and continued to scribble on his parchment. "I asked for *his* name, Marc, not to be introduced."

Gib blurted without thinking, "Pleasure to meet you, Master Lyle. I'm Gibben Nemesio."

The Instructions Master reacted as though someone had just slapped him across the face. He floundered, clearly offended by something, and Gib was sure he shouldn't have spoken directly to someone so lofty. He knew better. His father would have scolded him for such "sass" but in the moment it had seemed like the best thing to say. What right did this Diedrick Lyle have to talk down to someone he didn't know? *The right of privilege, idiot, something you don't have*, Gib thought to himself with a grimace.

Liza's eyes were wide and Marc coughed so as not to laugh. The dean drew enough attention away from the offence that Diedrick lost some of his rigidity and opted to slink back into his chair, glaring at the lot of them. He said not another word, only scratching his quill against the parchment in front of him.

Marc cleared his throat to ground their conversation. "All right, Gibben, did you say you were a volunteer or drafted?"

Gib instinctively reached for his rucksack and the conscription notice within. "Uh, I got this—I'm drafted? I guess?" He was blushing again. Every word from his lips seemed to land without grace. Why did he have to sound so dimwitted? He found the scroll at last and offered it with a shaking hand. Marc accepted and his smile felt warm and reassuring.

The dean read over the scroll once and nodded. He asked if Gib's name was spelled correctly on the scroll and then relayed the letters to Diedrick. "You've seen thirteen summers then?"

"Thirteen wheelturns. Yeah." Gib fidgeted with his hands, unsure if he should offer more.

Marc graciously didn't wait. "Just old enough then. You'll need to be trained in basic hand to hand combat as well as Ardenian law and policies."

Gib nodded, head swimming again. *Laws? Policies? I hope this will all be explained.* He tapped his fingers on his knees and tried to focus.

Diedrick spoke again, addressing only Marc. "That's all the recruited need. Anything further would be a waste of funds. He'll pay back his debt to Arden by having extra time for chores."

Gib winced but kept his treacherous mouth closed.

It was Marc who came to his defense, as Liza seemed to know when to keep quiet and had offered to say nothing since they'd first arrived. The dean held up a hand, signaling for Diedrick to pause. "Can you read, Gibben? Or write? Calculate?"

Gib swallowed, but his mouth felt bone dry. "I, uh—I can read some. And write my name, some small words. There's a bit of calculating to be used for farm work but nothing grand."

Diedrick snorted again as he continued to scribble.

Without any trace of scorn or pity, Marc came to a quick decision. He glanced over at Diedrick again. "Add him for basic literacy skills and arithmetic."

The Instructions Master looked up, his face drawn and eyes fierce. "Literacy and arithmetic? What *exactly* do you think he'll be reading and calculating on the battlefront?"

"I said to add him to the roster. Do it," Marc reiterated.

Diedrick Lyle set his quill down and gave the dean a withering glare. "This will be considered a waste of funds and will have to be approved by the council—"

"I'll speak to King Rishi. Don't concern yourself."

The argument ceased there and the only sound in the room was the rapid scratching of quill on parchment, along with muttered curses and various inquiries as to what a common peasant could possibly learn from further classes. Gib tried his best to ignore the ranting.

Marc clapped his hands together. "All right, Gibben. Let's take you to your room, shall we?"

Diedrick Lyle may have had something venomous to say about that as well, but Gib leapt from his seat and was out the door so quickly that if any words were spoken, they were lost in the bustle of movement. Liza and the dean followed and the three of them put the office behind them.

Once the door was closed, Marc let out a deep sigh. "Thank the Two Goddesses for midday meal. It will be a while before I have to go back in there."

Gib thought to smile, but all at once an arm closed around his shoulders and Liza was pulling him in close. He looked up at her, wondering why she was hugging him, but he should have known already. The look on her face caused a cold knot to form in his gut.

"I have to go, Gib. I need to report in."

He grabbed her hand. "You have to go now? I mean, don't you want to know where my room is? In case you should need to find me?"

"I know where the new recruits' wing is. I'll come find you as I have time."

Gib swallowed. "Are you sure you know where to find me? You would have stayed in the girls' wing, right?"

She smiled and nodded as if to assure him but before she could say anything, Marc cut in. "Actually, I think I'm going to take him over to the eastern wing. There's an older student there who has an empty bunk. This draft has filled my halls so full that I'm going to have to get creative."

Gib's insides froze, but Liza smiled. "Eastern wing? That's fine. I know where it is. I'll come see you when time permits. Probably in the evenings, after dinner." She hugged him again, squeezing him so tightly Gib found it hard to breathe. "You'll do well, Gib," Liza whispered into his ear. "You always have."

Gib wanted to say something—anything—but his voice had vanished. He managed a nod before Liza turned away, but not before her tears got the better of her. His sister all but ran down the corridor. He was comforted by having been witness to her tears. Liza's grief made his tears more acceptable. Marc's hand rested on Gib's shoulder, and he allowed himself to be guided away.

By the time they arrived at the room where Gib would live for the next two years, he'd been led through so many different corridors that he had no idea where he was or where he'd come from. He wasn't even sure if he was in the same building anymore. Somewhere along the way, the grey limestone used to construct the walls near the front of the collegium had shifted to a pearly-colored marble. The arches in the doorways were also free of cracks and showed no sign of erosion, suggesting this section of the building had been erected much later.

Marc must have noticed Gib eying the architecture as they walked, for the older man cleared his throat and struck up a conversation. "You lucked out, Gibben. This wing of Academy is a lot newer than the side my office is located on." The dean's voice seemed to boom after such a long period of silence.

Gib wasn't in the mood to chat, but he felt he owed it to Marc for being so kind. "Was this dormitory built recently?" Gib asked in a soft voice.

"Recent by a historical standpoint, perhaps. I was a boy—younger than you are now, I would wager—when the late King Eitan Viran suggested the academy building at the time be expanded to include a larger dormitory so more trainees from outside the city walls might have a place to live while they studied in Silver."

"King Eitan was the ruler of Arden before King Rishi Radek?"

Marc nodded. "Aye. His daughter, Jorja, who was queen until her death, married King Rishi, who has since been remarried to Dahlia Adelwijn. Anyway, after the plans were laid out, the dormitory was built over the next twenty wheelturns. When Eitan died, King Rishi made certain the project was not abandoned." The dean rolled his eyes with distaste. "As you can probably imagine, the High Council balked about the additional expenses throughout the entire process, but—" He reached forward and touched his fingertips to the fine marble as he walked. "—I dare say it was worth every copper spent, if only to see the privileges of the few be extended to the less fortunate. Now we have the means to offer residence and education to young men and women as far away as Port Ostlea."

Gib swallowed thickly as he digested everything he'd just heard, and then he came to a simple conclusion: he liked the dean. Marc Arrio seemed genuinely kind, the type of person who wouldn't judge another based on their social status or whether or not they were educated. He wanted equal opportunities for everyone, not only the elite. It was admirable, yet Gib still couldn't help but fret. The dean had shown compassion—but would Gib find it anywhere else in this city?

"Ah, here we are," Marc proclaimed, coming to a halt. Gib looked around. They were in a hallway lined with doors made of soft maple wood. "Most of the students on this floor are in their third or fourth year of study. We normally try to house the youngest students together, but due to— recent developments, we're short on space. Don't worry though, since you're new to Silver City, having an older roommate will be beneficial."

Gib wasn't entirely convinced. He'd never lived with anyone other than his two brothers and sister. *What if I'm roomed with a highborn? Someone like Diedrick Lyle who will judge me the moment I walk through the door. Will I be laughed at? Scorned? Ignored? What if my roommate hates me so much I have to leave? What will I do then?* Gib's head spun as he tried to steady his gasping breaths. "Am I to meet my roommate now, sir?" Gib managed to ask. He could scarcely hear his own voice through the pounding of his heart in his ears.

Marc rapped a fist against the door nearest to where they had stopped, the sound of it resonating down the empty corridor. "Indeed. Let's hope he's here."

Gib held his breath as they waited. For several moments nothing happened. The door didn't open and he could hear no movement coming from within. Perhaps his roommate had gone to eat lunch. Or maybe somehow, he'd gotten wind of Gib's arrival and was purposely avoiding answering the door.

As more terrible scenarios traversed through Gib's mind, finally a shuffling sound came from inside, followed by the jiggle of the brass door handle as someone from the other side pulled on it. The door slid open and Gib found himself staring at the marble floor, unable to raise his eyes.

He heard Marc speak in a casual tone. "Oh good! You're here."

A lofty tenor voice responded at once. "Marc? Is everything all right?"

"Mind if we come in?"

The other voice hesitated. "We?"

Marc touched Gib's shoulder and he jumped. "I found you a roommate. This is Gibben. He's new to Academy and to Silver. I think the two of you will get along."

The dean gave Gib a gentle push forward. His stomach was churning and he was pretty sure his face had turned a horrific shade of crimson. He could feel Marc and the other boy staring, waiting for words or action. Swallowing the nerves down, Gib managed to raise his head just enough to be able to make eye contact with his new roommate.

A youthful boy stood in the doorway. The boy was tall and slender framed, with raven-colored locks that fell past his shoulders in gentle waves. His skin was light, untarnished by sunlight or malnourishment, and his facial features were soft.

He was well-groomed, clad in a flowing white robe embroidered with golden lace and intricate beading. A sash made of fine blue silk was wrapped around his waist and small precious jewels hung from his fingers and ears. Gib's stomach flopped. This boy was most certainly highborn.

Two silvery blue eyes observed Gib warily, but the smile playing on his thin lips suggested the boy was attempting to be polite, if not friendly. Again the delicate voice came. "Hello, Gibben. My name is Joel."

Gib's voice was caught somewhere deep within his throat. His stomach was in knots. He shuffled his boot against the floor, barely able to hold the other boy's gaze. Gib felt inadequate standing beside this wealthy boy in his fine clothing and jewels that probably cost more than Gib's entire farm.

The boy named Joel was still staring at him, expecting a response no doubt. Gib parted his lips, meaning to say something—*anything*—but no words came forth. It was as if some invisible force had fluttered by and stolen his voice away. Joel's smile was troubled as he turned to Marc for help and Gib let out a strangled noise, mortified. He was making himself appear an idiot!

Marc stepped in to put an end to the awkward lull. "Sorry, Joel. I must have interrogated him in my office for so long earlier that his voice has gone hoarse." The dean gave Gib a light tap on the back. "It's my fault, really. You know how much I enjoy talking people to death."

Joel's smile was wistful. "All too well, Marc Arrio. Your wife must have the heart of a saint to deal with such a scamp for a husband."

Gib was taken aback as he listened to their banter. Should a student be speaking so casually to a figure as important as the Dean of Academy? His head spun when Marc didn't reprimand or scold Joel for talking in such a way. In fact, the dean was chuckling.

"Your wit almost exceeds that of your father," Marc replied, an amused grin playing on his lips. "And for the record, my wife happens to be quite the intellectualist herself. She can appreciate a man who likes to talk."

The older boy let out a snort and Gib felt as though he were witnessing a conversation between two lifelong friends rather than a teacher and his pupil. Joel turned his piercing eyes on Gib and gave him an apologetic smile. "I'm sorry for my behavior, Gibben. I don't normally speak to Marc so informally while in the presence of other students as it tends to give them the impression that the dean isn't worthy of respect. That, of course, is not the case. I'm allowed to make jokes with him only because Marc is a very close friend of my family." Gib nodded, unsure of what else to do. Joel took a step back, white robes cascading around his feet. "I'm afraid I've forgotten my manners. Please, come in."

Gib wasn't sure whom the young noble was inviting inside—Marc, himself, or both of them together.

Fortunately, the dean answered before Gib was forced to ask for clarification. "I'm afraid I have to take my leave now. I regrettably have a very temperamental Instructions Master awaiting my return." His dark eyes measured Gib. "You'll be all right. Joel will help you unpack your things and show you the grounds. Isn't that right, Joel?"

The older boy gave a stiff nod. "Of course. But Marc, before you leave, may I request a word with you outside the room?"

The dean's voice was hesitant. "Yes, all right. But just for a moment. I'm really running behind schedule."

Gib clenched his jaw as any hope that his highborn roommate might accept him came crashing down. Here it was. Seeing how lowly Gib was Joel was now going to beg Marc to reassign the vagrant boy somewhere else. Gib's face burned with shame and he longed to be back on the farm, away from these city people who passed such harsh judgment. Where was he to go if no student would take him as a roommate?

Marc and Joel were speaking in the hallway. Gib didn't want to listen, but the door had been left open a crack and their hushed voices carried back into the room.

"Are you sure this is a wise decision?" Joel asked. "I thought I wouldn't be sharing a room with anyone again, given the circumstances, and especially after—what happened before. My family has already been put through so much for it."

Marc issued an imploring snort. "That wasn't your fault. You know that. I know that. Anyone who matters knows that." The dean's voice had a sharp bite to it.

"People will talk."

After a pause of terrible silence came Marc's response. His voice had lost all of its rigidity. "I'm sorry for what you've endured, Joel. It's not fair, I know. But you've shut everyone out for too long. It's time you learn how to feel again. This will be good for you."

"I hope you're right."

"Trust me. Everything will work out, you'll see."

Receding footsteps sounded against the marble floor, and a short while later, Joel came back into the room. His face was drawn but as he raised his head in Gib's direction, the young highborn gave him a half-hearted smile. Gib didn't know what to make of the conversation he'd overheard, but his mind was such a whirlwind of confusion that it hardly mattered.

"I'm sorry for the mess," Joel said as he moved through the room and began to pick up what Gib assumed were the highborn's belongings. "I was under the impression I wouldn't be sharing a room." His voice was flat.

Gib winced and at last he managed to find his voice. "I—I'm sorry too."

The older boy shrugged as he reached to pick up a crate filled with scrolls and unused parchment. "It's not your fault."

Gib bit down on his lip and took advantage of the silence to get a better look at the room. It was of modest size, though bigger than the loft which Gib had shared with his brothers, and crafted from the same white marble as the corridor outside. Two small beds sat on wooden frames, one in each corner of the room, and someone had taken the liberty of laying fresh linens and a wool blanket on the edge of each mattress. In one nook of the room stood a desk and stool for writing, and there was even a large window situated along the back wall. The wooden shutters were pushed open, allowing a breeze to flow through.

"So, I think I recall Marc saying you've never been to the city before." Joel sat down on one of the beds and began sorting through his things.

Gib nodded. "That's right."

"So you must be a first-year student."

Gib wasn't sure if the words were meant to be a question or not, but he felt obligated to respond in some way. "I was sent a conscription notice. I'm meant to receive sentinel training here in Silver."

Joel pursed his lips but didn't look up. "I see."

Gib could hear the pity dripping from the boy's words but tried to ignore it. "A–are you a sentinel trainee too?"

The highborn boy did glance up now. He had a bemused look and the corner of his mouth acted as though it wanted to curl upward. "No. I'm afraid I wouldn't even know which end of a sword to use if I ever were unfortunate enough to be handed one. I'm a mage trainee." Gib felt as though he'd missed something that should have been obvious. He probably had. He didn't know the first thing about magic or magery.

He'd never met a mage in person before, though he'd seen one from a distance in Willowdale. When the well that supplied water to the entire village was contaminated, a mage was sent from Silver to purify it. Gib and his father happened to be there to see the spectacle while selling that year's barley crop at market. It would have been hard to miss such a sight, as nearly every resident of the town had gathered to watch as the mage rode in.

The mage marched up to the well, uttered a few words, and then touched his fingertips to the stone foundation. A moment later, the mage turned to the lord of Willowdale, smiled smugly, and announced the water was purified. Just like that. Gib's father told him the mage had used magic.

Studying Joel from beneath thick lashes, Gib swallowed. He wasn't sure how he felt about magic. Since childhood, he'd been using his own two hands to make his way in the world, and the idea of manipulating some invisible form of energy to complete a task made him wary. It sounded dangerous. Still, Joel was being cordial, so Gib made the decision to reserve judgment as well. After all, he knew nothing about his roommate.

"I've never met a mage before," Gib offered timidly. "I suppose that makes me sound like an idiot, but I grew up on a farm. I'd never been more than a dozen leagues from home before I got my conscription notice." He wrung his hands and hoped he wasn't annoying the older boy. "So, you can use magic?"

Joel laughed. "Yes. The ability to wield magic is a requirement for one to be trained as a mage." He turned to face Gib, as though the trainee had finally decided the lowly farm boy was worthy of attention. Joel's crystal eyes were intense but not denouncing. "I suppose you must be feeling pretty lost."

Gib lowered his head. "Yeah. I have two younger brothers who I had to leave at home. I miss them—and I'm not sure I'll be able to fit in."

Joel nodded. "Well, the good news is you're certainly not the only new recruit here, and tomorrow you'll meet the others. Probably the majority of them will be—" He paused as if searching for the right word.

"—from outlying lands, such as you."

"Lowborn. You can say it." Gib laughed with a snort.

Gib wasn't sure if his new companion would accept the slight. However, Joel seemed not to find offense. He nodded amiably. "Forgive me. I would like you to know I hold no ill will toward the common-born. I may come across as apathetic at times but I assure you this is from ignorance, not malice."

Still feeling overwhelmed, Gib managed to accept what he was hearing. "It's okay. When I ask stupid questions about you being a mage you can feel free to ask stupid questions about me being a farmer if you want."

A genuine smile graced the mage trainee's lips and Gib's stomach flipped in a peculiar way.

"Fair trade, Gibben," Joel replied in a lighter tone.

Gib found himself chuckling, which was also strange. He'd been sure just a short time ago that he might never be merry again. Perhaps this Joel fellow would be a good thing. They may even grow to be friends. Gib's stomach twirled again and he rested his hand over it, confused. "Huh."

Joel's dark eyebrows knitted together. "Are you all right?"

"Yeah, I think so. My stomach keeps doing this odd thing." As if to confirm the story, a rumbling growl issued from Gib's empty belly. "Oh. I guess I'm just—"

"Hungry." Joel finished the sentence and leapt to his feet. "Forgive me. I should show you to the dining hall. And after that, I can take you to the training arena and anywhere else you may need to become familiar with."

Gib nodded. He didn't want to be a bother but it was nice to have someone extend such hospitality to him. "Thank you."

Already standing beside the door, Joel had an open, if not overly friendly, look. "You're very welcome. Follow me." He was honest, Gib was sure and took comfort in that. With any luck, camaraderie would come later.

CHAPTER THREE

The rest of the day was a whirlwind of events, and Gib found himself swept up within the immensity of his new world. It was as though he were dreaming, merely bearing witness as some other boy stumbled through this strange place in utter confusion. Nothing felt real.

Joel showed him to the dining hall, a large open room filled with rows of long tables lined with benches. The mage trainee explained to Gib that he would be taking his three main meals here. The variety of foods offered had been overwhelming. Freshly baked bread still steaming from the oven, vegetable stew spiced to perfection, warm apple cider, and meat were all on the menu. Chicken was roasted and rolled in butter until it was gleaming, blackened pork bathed in salt, and even sliced beef—an expensive commodity which had never been available at the farm.

Gib tried a little bit of everything, and it all tasted like something prepared for a royal feast. The meat was so tender it seemed to melt in his mouth and the cider to wash down the meal was a perfect balance of spicy and sweet. Gib made sure not to overindulge. He was hungry but didn't want to be seen as greedy. Joel watched him as he ate, asking questions warmly. The mage trainee seemed to be entertained by Gib's astonishment.

When his belly was full, Gib followed Joel around the rest of the campus. It quickly became apparent that the grounds belonging to the academy were much like a self-contained city within Silver. Two dormitory wings, each of them stacked three stories tall, faced each other and were separated by a long narrow stretch of the building where the class halls were located. In the space created in the middle of the three-sided building was an open courtyard with an alabaster fountain and various shrubbery. Joel pointed beyond the courtyard to an open field where much of the physical training took place except during inclement weather.

By the time Gib returned to his room, exhaustion had seeped into his bones. He'd crawled into his bed, noting with a pang of guilt that the mattress was more comfortable than the straw mats his brothers had to lie upon. The thick, wool blanket scratched at his skin, but it provided adequate warmth, so he was able to ignore it. Gib shut his eyes, wondering if Tayver and Calisto were thinking about him. He hoped they were all right and wished he could have been there to say goodnight to them.

Sleep took him quickly and entirely because the next thing Gib knew he was being shaken awake. He sat up, blinking and sputtering, and it took a moment for him to remember he was no longer on the farm.

Joel's face was cloaked by shadow. "Time to get up," the mage trainee said.

Gib yawned as he stretched both arms high above his head. "How early is it?"

"Still a mark before dawn," replied the other boy. "Enough time for you to have a bath, eat breakfast, and report to the courtyard for morning chores."

Gib noted that Joel was already dressed in a fresh set of robes and his raven hair appeared to be damp. How long had he been awake? "A bath?"

Joel raised an eyebrow. "Would you prefer not to have one?"

"No! I mean—it's just that—that—"

"It's not custom to bathe where you come from?"

Gib locked his jaw and willed himself not to say anything he might regret. He enjoyed a good bath, maybe not as frequently as these pampered nobles, but he did try to stay clean. "I wasn't aware such luxuries were available to us. Could you show me where to go?" If his voice clipped, Joel either didn't notice or didn't bring attention to it.

After showing Gib where the bathing chamber was, the older boy excused himself. A steaming trough of water stood in the center of the room, fed by a narrow wooden conduit that came in through the window. A young attendant directed Gib to a shelf stacked with buckets and told him to fill one of the pails with water from the trough. He was also shown to the place where he could find a cloth and bar of soap for washing, and then Gib was left alone to scrub himself clean of the grime and dirt from the journey to Silver. The hot water left his skin scalded but spotless.

After his bath, Gib meandered down to the dining hall and stuffed himself full of eggs, bread drizzled with honey, and fresh goat milk. He then followed behind a group of students who were making their way to the courtyard, wondering what kind of work he would be given.

Upon arrival, a red-headed woman assigned him his morning chores. Today he was to help the kitchen staff clean and dry the dishes that had been sullied during breakfast. Gib worked diligently, keeping to himself, but many of the other trainees—highborns mostly—complained about the labor being too hard. Gib wanted to laugh. If this was hard then The Two forbid any of them ever have to bring in a field of crops.

The sun was shining brightly by the time he returned to his room. Joel was just on his way out, a bundle of scrolls in his arms. He did, however, stop long enough to ask Gib if he would be able to find his way to his first class.

"It's my sentinel training class," Gib said.

"You'll want to go to the field beyond the courtyard. Weapons Master

Roland will be expecting you."

Gib grinned weakly. "Thanks."

Joel smiled as he passed by, and Gib's stomach began to flutter again. He didn't know what to expect at this first class. Would they expect him to know anything about combat or wielding a sword? If they did then certainly he'd be laughed off the training grounds. It was with a grim sigh that he went to meet his fate.

He headed to the courtyard for the second time. Once outside he didn't see a single student and began to fear he was running late. Indeed, the only person he passed was a worker pruning the shrubbery. He glanced at her and she pointed toward the training area. Gib nodded a wordless thanks. He could have found it himself, but it was nice to see at least one more smile before he went to make a fool of himself.

As he crossed the barren yard, he began to pick up the sounds of his classmates. Voices called out merrily and laughter carried on the breeze. That, coupled with the sunny day, should have lifted his spirits, but he found no such comfort.

At the far end of the field, students were gathering—too many to count. Boys his age or just a little older swarmed back and forth, playing rambunctiously. The general chaos and disorganization put him on edge. Gib thought of Cal and Tay as he watched the strangers scuffle. It would have been fun to join if he'd known any of these boys. He wondered briefly how many of them he would get to know and then the thought crossed his mind that many of them might die if they went to war. His stomach ached as he found the far edge of the field and took sanctuary under a large oak tree.

Gib stared out into the distance, feeling more homesick than ever. Surrounded by countless trainees, he never would have thought he could experience such loneliness. His bottom lip threatened to quiver, but he bit down on it, determined not to be undone.

"It's big here, isn't it?"

Gib blinked and turned to see where the voice had come from. When he found no one, he thought to question his sanity. "H–Hello?"

"Up here."

Gib tipped his head back. Sure enough, a pair of bare feet dangled above his head. He smiled despite his mood and stepped out from under the young man in the tree. "What are you doing up there?"

The boy nodded vaguely toward the rowdy cluster of boys. "Trying to not get rolled up in that."

A quiet chuckle escaped Gib's lips. "You'll have to come down when the class starts."

The new boy sighed heavily and began lowering himself. "I suppose you're right. I guess now that there are two of us we'll stand a better chance of not being yanked in." When he met the ground and stood to his full height, he was just a hair or two taller than Gib. The boy's jet black locks, hunter green eyes, and brown skin suggested his common-born status as much as his shabby clothes and lack of shoes. Gib was suddenly thankful for his boots, even if they did pinch his toes.

"I'm Gib Nemesio of Willowdale."

"Nage Nessuno, Silver."

Gib bit his lip and tried to keep his features neutral. He'd never met an actual Nessuno orphan before. Willowdale was so small that any orphans born there typically didn't survive long enough to be taken to the closest orphanage. "So you're a local?"

Nage shook his head. "I work in the mines by the lake."

"Mining? I wouldn't know much of that. I have a farm."

"A farmer? So you're from outside the city?" Nage glanced over his shoulder as if he could see the farm from here. His smile was wistful. "I've never been very far outside of the city. Of course, I've never been this far *into* the city either."

Gib chuckled but his response was interrupted.

"*Oh no.* Here he comes." Nage ducked low.

Gib was instantly on full alert. "Who? The Weapons Master?"

"No. My roommate." Nage blushed a little and scuffed his foot across the ground. "He's a good enough sort but—he's highborn."

"Oh, I see. Mine is too." Gib craned his neck to look for this roommate but had no clue what he looked like. "He also means well but he's odd. He thought I didn't bathe."

"At least he didn't assume you were a waif. Mine kept asking me why I didn't have any shoes and wanted to have his father buy a pair for me."

Gib cringed. "That's awful."

"This is him." Nage had lowered his voice so much Gib almost didn't hear it.

An instant later they were joined by a third boy. Although he was taller than Gib remembered, he recognized the boy immediately as the pale youth outside the dean's office yesterday. Today he wore a wide-brimmed hat which helped conceal his pale head and equally blanched skin. Despite the warmth outside, he also wore long sleeves and full-length breeches. His fancy training clothing, with brass buttons and embroidered seams, was out of place compared to the rest of the boys.

"Nage, you found a friend?" the newcomer asked in a deep tenor voice.

Nage shook his head. "No. We just met."

The tall boy smiled even wider than before and took Gib's hand even though it hadn't been offered. "My name is Tarquin Aldino. Nage and I are roommates this year."

Lucky him. Gib smiled and chose to say, "Nice to meet you. Gibben Nemesio."

Tarquin released Gib's hand and an awkward silence rose between them. Gib didn't know what to say. What could he possibly have in common with a highborn? By the looks of his clothes and feel of his smooth hands, Tarquin had never done a day's work in his entire life. He'd probably been in school longer than Gib and all three of his siblings combined and possibly already owned stock in the mines where Nage would never be able to earn a decent living.

"So," the highborn offered after a minute or two. "Were either of your fathers soldiers?" When Gib and Nage both shook their heads and didn't attempt to pick up the conversation, Tarquin took the plunge on his own. "My pa is head of the Armorer's Guild and my older brother just finished schooling to be on the High Council of Arden one day. I volunteered to join the sentinels myself. I want to be a captain someday. What do you guys hope to accomplish?"

It seemed such a silly question that Gib had a hard time not laughing. What did he hope to accomplish here? In his worn out tunic and too-tight boots? With his conscription notice still in his rucksack and two little brothers left to fate? He opened his mouth and the words fell out like lead. "I hope to survive."

Tarquin floundered, obviously at a loss. He faltered as if to say something but when it became apparent they had nothing to say to one another, Gib thought to look for an escape. They were saved a moment later when another young boy hailed them from across the field and Tarquin's attention flitted away. Nage tapped Gib on the arm and nodded toward an unoccupied area beside a large shed. Without the need for words, Gib nodded in agreement and they took their leave while Tarquin was still distracted.

Nage groaned as soon as they were far enough away. "See what I mean? Not a single real thought tumbling around in that head."

Gib tried to contain a laugh. "At the very least, he did seem well-intentioned enough. I had sort of figured when I got here, no one would want to speak to me. They'd be offended by the filthy farmer."

"Yeah. Did you meet the Instructions Master yesterday?"

"Yes! What a foul man. Master Diedrick Lyle was everything I expected a highborn to be."

"I know. When the dean asked me if I could read or write I had to tell him no and that bastard laughed at me." Nage rolled his eyes. "I told Tarquin about it and he became offended for me. He said his father doesn't like Master Lyle either. I tried not to laugh because what do I care about what his father thinks? And I'm sure his rich father doesn't care for me either."

They laughed between themselves and leaned against the shed that ran along that side of the training field. Long moments passed while they stared out at the other boys, but the quiet never felt awkward. Indeed, it wasn't until the peace came crashing down that either of them thought to look up.

Only a few paces away, a small commotion broke out. A cluster of older boys surrounded one who was much younger. With a red face pointed downward, the boy in the middle looked to be about the same age as Gib and Nage. The older boys circled and taunted the boy, asking snidely if he was ready for his first day of real work or not. One of them even called the young boy a "spoiled brat." He talked back to them with defiance, claiming he was going to tell his father about their behavior. This only elicited a larger response from the perpetrators.

A knot formed in the pit of Gib's stomach and he glanced around, looking for an adult. Surely a teacher was around somewhere. Where was the Weapons Master to shoo these older, frightening boys away?

"Father can't always protect you," one of them was saying. He was tall and well-built with dark hair, olive skin, and almond-shaped eyes. His smile was smug.

"The real world is about to jump up and bite you in the ass, boy," taunted a second one who was pale but just as tall as the first. The two of them seemed to be the leaders of this group of bullies and were certainly the most intimidating of them all.

Nage kept his voice low so as not to draw their attention. "What's their problem? Why're they bothering that boy?"

Gib swallowed a lump in his throat. The harassment seemed so much louder for the sudden drop in the surrounding noise. Every other student on the field had quieted and turned to look at the spectacle. "I don't know but this isn't right. Someone should say something."

"And have our teeth kicked in for our troubles?" Nage retorted. "I'll pass. Besides, look at them. Every single one is a highborn, I'd reckon, even the young one. We don't need problems with their fathers."

The young boy who was being taunted was trying to walk away from the bullies now. "Stop it! Leave me alone. Haven't you had your fill yet?"

The others continued to laugh at him. Gib clamped his hands together and looked desperately for help once more, still not seeing any adults. He knew he didn't stand a chance on his own, especially when even Nage was unwilling to help. He thought about standing down and turning his head the other way, but he couldn't do it. It wasn't right. Someone needed to say something.

"Stop." Gib's voice carried further than he'd thought it would. His insides shook but he took a timid step forward. "Leave him alone." This time he was louder still and several people looked his way. His face went warm, but he could hardly stop now.

"*I said to stop!*" Gib's legs trembled. He'd no idea how he was still standing. It got worse when the bullies turned to look at him, their eyes piercing and critical. Gib sucked in a sharp breath. Would they come for him next?

The taunting subsided and whispers were shared like a single ripple through the group. Gib's attention was caught by the tall boy, who was obviously the leader, as he narrowed his eyes. When he swept closer, the others all followed.

His dark, slanted eyes shone coldly and his smile sent a chill up Gib's spine. The leader was well spoken with a soft, haughty voice. "What was that, Little One? Did you call to us?"

Gib swallowed and took a step back. None of them were his age. They were all taller and broader than he. They each wore a sword on their hip and swaggered as though they knew how to use such weapons. He wasn't even a threat to them.

"Spirit will only take you just so far," said the second, louder boy in a nasty voice. "Better hope ya grow a bit more, boy." He tousled Gib's curls as he sauntered past. The others said nothing as they went along but each looked Gib in the eye, smiling victoriously. He tensed, prepared for a blow of some sort, but none fell. Indeed, they continued on their way and never looked back.

Taking a deep breath, Gib straightened his hair and willed his nerves to calm. Overall, that had gone better than he'd planned. Every single one of them could have hung Gib by his feet but none had. They hadn't even offered. In hindsight, it felt odd that they should let him off the hook so easily.

The boy who was being bullied made his way over to Gib. "Thank you."

Taller than Gib—nearly everyone here was—the boy's highborn status seemed confirmed. If Tarquin Aldino's garments had been pleasant to behold, this boy's were pristine. The embroidered embellishments running up either sleeve were of red thread and stood out on his crisp white tunic. The sleeves were meant to resemble wings but seemed such a waste of time and money, something these highborn children of Silver City apparently had to spare.

Soft, dark locks gave way to large, expressive eyes. He wore a coat of arms, stitched into the front of his tunic and held in place by golden thread. Gib didn't recognize the seal but remembered many of the wealthy families in Arden had such symbols so they could easily be identified. This boy must be the son of some rich lord, Gib guessed. Out of the corner of his eye, he noticed the other students in the class observing their interaction.

The young lord offered one of his hands and Gib took it, startling when he felt callouses on those long fingers.

"I mean it," the boy continued in a soft voice. "I've never seen one as young as we stand up to my brothers like that."

Gib stiffened. "Those were your brothers? All of them?"

The boy blinked as if confused before responding, "No. Not all of them—Tell me, where do you hail from? What is your name?"

"Gibben Nemesio of Willowdale." Gib released the hand hoping to hide how badly he was still shaking. "Pleasure to meet you—"

When Gib deliberately left off in search of a name, the boy smiled. "My name is Didier. Please, call my Diddy."

"All right, Diddy." Gib glanced around once more. "Do you have any idea why everyone is staring at us?"

Diddy's smile was genuine, even charming. "I suspect they've never seen such blind bravery."

"I doubt that. My knees are knocking so bad that I can hardly stand."

Diddy opened his mouth as if to say more but before he could reply, a horn was blown and everyone around them jumped to attention. Gib followed behind the other boys as they made their way toward the middle of the field where the entire class was gathering.

A man's voice boomed over them all. "Line up. Face north."

After some confusion about which way was north, the crowd of sentinel trainees did as was told. Gib realized he couldn't see even one person that he knew and felt lost. He was surrounded by people taller than himself, so he could barely make out the silhouettes of two grown men standing at the front of the group.

"First years move to the front. Second years in the back, you know how this works. Help out the younger ones!"

In the shuffle of taller versus shorter bodies, Gib decided he was going to have to be in the front line if he was going to be able to see anything at all. The other boys were sluggish and no one wanted to get out of his way, but he refused to settle for a spot where he would be blind to what was going on around him.

"Gibben Nemesio. Come stand in front of me."

Gib huffed a sigh when he recognized the voice of Nage's pampered roommate. It could be worse. Standing in front of Tarquin meant not having to look at him. Lack of eye contact would hopefully mean no forced conversation. When a pale hand was offered, Gib took it and allowed himself to be pulled through to the front line.

"Thanks," he muttered, choosing not to look the highborn in the eye.

An elbow knocked off Gib's and he turned to see Diddy. Beyond the young lordling was Nage, who nodded with a lopsided grin. Gib breathed a short sigh of relief. At least he wasn't alone.

Gib noted with some confusion that Tarquin and several other trainees kept casting dubious looks toward Diddy, and the ones standing closest behind the young lord were doing all they could to distance themselves from him without breaking formation. If Didier saw their sideways glances, he paid no attention, but Gib noticed. Diddy seemed nice enough for a highborn. Why was everyone acting so strangely around him?

Before Gib could dedicate any more thought to the matter, two grown men swept forward to stand in front of the class. The hush that fell over the crowd was all the information Gib needed. These men were important. He would have guessed as much on his own based upon their height and dress, with authority emanating from their stature.

The first man was broad-shouldered and imposing. His facial features were hardened, with rough skin and peppered brown hair. He was wearing light armor: a plated doublet over chainmail and protective leather coverings around his arms and legs. One large gloved hand rested on the hilt of a sheathed longsword as though he might draw the sword at any given moment.

The man's hazel eyes were stern as they passed over each of the gathered trainees. "Welcome to your first day of sentinel training." His voice carried across the entire field as he addressed the group. "I am Weapons Master Roland Korbin. Some of you know of me already. For those who don't, you soon will."

He began to stroll down the line of students. "I have only three rules in my class. First, you show up on time each day in *proper* attire." The trainer's eyes skewered the group. "And by proper attire, I don't mean golden buttons, ruffled sleeves, and jewel-encrusted embroidery! What you choose to wear outside my arena is none of my business, but here you'll dress yourselves accordingly. After today's class, all students will be measured and fitted for simple linen tunics and boots meant for the physical demands of this class." Several of the highborn boys in the group sighed.

"Second, you'll give your fellow students the respect they deserve. Let me be clear. There will be no favorites here and most certainly no belittlement of your peers." Gib stole a glance in Didier's direction, wishing Roland had been present only moments before when the young boy was being taunted.

"My last rule is that you don't quit. Every soldier has his strengths— and his weaknesses. You'll experience failure in my class. I guarantee this. You'll leave the arena with bruises, broken bones, and crushed spirits. You'll want to quit. But only when you fail will you learn. You can't learn if you quit."

Gib swallowed his dread. He wanted to remain hopeful. Weapons Master Roland's rules seemed reasonable, but what if the physical training was too much for Gib? Most of the other students in the class were bigger and stronger. *What if I can't keep up?*

Roland cleared his throat pointedly and bowed his head in the direction of the second man, who until now had stayed in the background. "Seneschal Koal Adelwijn will now have a word with you before we begin today's lesson." All eyes fell upon the other man as Gib's breath left him in a whoosh of air. Seneschal? *The* seneschal? The right-hand man of the

King himself and second most powerful man in all of Arden? Gib couldn't help his gaping mouth.

Seneschal Koal was trim and had short raven hair flecked with grey that fell just below his ears. His fair skin was free of worry lines or blemishes. His mouth was set in a firm line, but something about the seneschal's demeanor suggested he was not there to cause malice or intimidation.

His outfit was as elaborate as Roland's was practical. He wore a magnificent silver tabard with sapphire-colored lace woven into the seams, and a ceremonial dagger was strung through the belt at his waist. An impressive red cape hung from his left shoulder and continued to cascade down his back. The detailed golden lines and arches stitched into the cape were constructed to resemble the crest of Arden, the phoenix. A light breeze rustled through the fine silk, and for a moment the phoenix seemed alive, fluttering in the wind.

The seneschal gave Roland a nod before taking a step closer to the gathered students. His eyes matched the blue embroidery on his clothing. He smiled, not unhandsomely, and spoke for the first time.

"On behalf of King Rishi Radek, I, Koal Adelwijn, Seneschal of Arden, extend his majesty's gratitude to the young men and women who have accepted the country's recent call to arms." His voice was smooth and articulate—the well-trained voice of a diplomat.

Koal clasped his hands together behind his back. "Furthermore, I applaud your bravery. The life of a sentinel is not for the weak-hearted and courage can be hard to find in the face of adversity. Rest assured Weapons Master Roland will do all he can to best prepare you to protect yourself and defend your country, if the need arises. I expect all of you to uphold the values of our beloved nation and to represent Arden with honor and integrity." The seneschal's eyes flitted past Gib and the young boy flinched.

"If you must draw your sword, do so only in the name of justice," Koal continued. "Your job is to protect those who can't defend themselves, not to oppress them. You serve *all* the people of Arden, not only those who are in power or well liked." He made eye contact with Roland. "I leave you now in the hands of our finest defense expert. I have full confidence in Weapons Master Roland and if I hear of any impudence directed toward him, such behavior will be dealt with swiftly. Carry on, Master Roland." With that, the seneschal turned on his heels and marched away without so much as a farewell.

Roland was quick to redirect the trainees' attention. "All right, today we're going to learn the basics of sparring, so find a partner and line up in front of the utility shed to retrieve practice swords. Boys with boys, and girls with girls."

Diddy turned to look at Gib even as he was doing the same. "Do you want to work together?"

Gib smiled with relief. "Yes, please. That would be great."

As the two boys navigated their way toward the shed, Didier smiled. "So what did you think of Seneschal Koal?"

Gib looked over his shoulder to be certain no one of importance was standing nearby. "The seneschal was intimidating," he admitted in a hushed voice. "I guess I never envisioned myself standing so close to someone that high in rank. It was like being in the presence of royalty."

Diddy's eyes danced playfully but before he could utter a response, Roland's rough voice cut through the air. "*Tarquin Aldino!* Do you not have a partner?"

Gib glanced over in time to see Tarquin's fair cheeks turn pink with color. It was clear he was embarrassed, as he seemed to be the only boy who hadn't been able to find a sparring partner. Even his roommate Nage Nessuno had been able to find someone. Gib's lip threatened to twitch.

Tarquin's face and neck were a fantastical shade of crimson as he replied, "N–no, sir. I believe there are an odd number of us—"

Roland waved his hand in the air. He pointed at someone out of Gib's view, farther down the line of trainees. "Kezra! Get over here. Looks like I found you a partner after all."

Tarquin let out an imploring groan, his eyes widening. "But she's a girl!"

Even before Gib could see her, he was certain he knew who it was. The girl from yesterday with the wild hair and diamond on her forehead stormed over to the highborn boy. Her dark face was contorted into a fearsome frown as she came upon him. Voice low and clear, her words travelled across the field. "All the more fitting for when I kick your whining ass, Aldino."

Tarquin opened his mouth as if to protest further but Roland stepped in immediately. "Enough. I don't care who either of your fathers are or whether you like it or not, you're partnered. If I hear another word on the matter you'll both be running circuits. Is that clear?"

Gib didn't watch any more. The line was beginning to move as a couple of training assistants opened the shed and directed students on which tools to take. "Will they help us if we don't know which one to choose?" he asked Diddy.

His companion nodded. "I believe so. If they're busy, you want to go for a sword that's not too long for your arm." At Gib's dubious look, Diddy smiled, elaborating further. "You should be able to hold it down by your side without the blade tip touching the ground. Likewise, it shouldn't rest above your ankle."

Gib hoped he could remember that in the future. Diddy must have picked up on his tense shoulders or stance because he was jovial and casual in conversation. "I believe Master Roland may have been singling me out a little with his speech about no jewel-encrusted embroidery. I tried to tell

Mother I would have no need of such finery, but she insisted I look my best on the first day. I shall revel in showing her my training uniform."

"I'm excited too," replied Gib. "I'll actually have a pair of boots that fit." He laughed to show that it was acceptable. "Will we have to pay for them somehow?"

"I–I'm really not sure." Diddy paused as if to think. "I would say not. Surely if you're training to defend Arden then it would be in the palace's best interest to provide quality gear. I'll have to ask Father."

Their conversation lulled and the quiet instantly sought to undo Gib's hard-earned peace of mind. "Is your father on the high council?"

Diddy flinched and Gib wondered if he'd said something wrong.

His companion recovered quickly however, flashing a smile. "You could say that."

Roland's voice boomed above the line of trainees just then as he bellowed at some poor fool who had knocked over a row of practice helms. Gib leaned a little closer to Diddy so no one else could hear. "Weapons Master Roland sure is different than the rest of the highborns here."

Diddy snorted. "What is that supposed to mean, exactly?" He feigned offense for a moment before laughing. "Besides, the Korbin family isn't highborn anyway."

Gib frowned. "What? How is that possible? Roland is a master, after all."

Diddy's eyes widened just a little as he put the pieces together. "Oh, I see. Roland Korbin was a farmer once too, just like you. He was drafted or came here on his own, I'm not sure which, and has worked his way through the ranks."

A creeping sensation began to blossom somewhere in Gib's gut. "You can do that? You don't have to be highborn to hold the title of Master?"

"It is unfortunately rare, but yes. Lowborns can ascend the social and political ranks."

It seemed vaguely familiar now that it was being said. He was sure he remembered his pa going on about this once. They'd been hauling water from the well and his father had been speaking of King Rishi and the changes that were coming to the country. *"You can be born poor, Gib, but you don't have to stay that way anymore. Arden finally has a good king who sees everyone's value."*

A slow smile crept across Gib's face. "It was King Rishi's doing, wasn't it? My pa always used to tell me stories about the good changes he'd made. King Rishi must be a decent sort. I mean, his laws have made it so that commoners can rise in the ranks and my sister, Liza, was able to become a sentinel. He seems like he must be wise."

Diddy didn't respond, but he had a huge grin on his face. Gib couldn't figure out why. They were next in line to be fitted with the wooden blades that they would bash each other with. No doubt they would leave the field today with bruises the size of small houses and here Diddy was, smiling like a loon.

Gib grudgingly accepted the shortest sword the attendants could find—and it was still just a bit too long—and then the pair of students headed out into the field to await further direction. They didn't say much as Gib was still preoccupied with the grand idea of living in a fine house one day if he worked hard. Diddy, likewise, was quiet.

Tarquin Aldino's voice cut through the air. "We could stand next to Gibben."

Gib shuddered but had nowhere to go. The highborn fool was making his way closer and the girl whom he'd been partnered with, Kezra, followed. Her frown remained constant, and Gib wondered if she knew how to smile at all. He didn't have long to dwell on the thought because Tarquin stood nearby, glancing awkwardly at Diddy. What *was* Tarquin's problem?

Kezra caught up and kneeled to tighten one of her bootlaces. Dark green eyes leveled her partner from behind wild onyx hair. "Are you sure they're the ones you want to stand next to? I'd rather spar where we'll draw less attention. This will be entertainment for all here. One of the only three female recruits right next to the pri—"

Roland's voice washed over them like a wave of thunder. "*Soldiers, to the north!*" Instantly Diddy, Tarquin, and Kezra turned to face north. Gib scrambled to follow.

"Base stance!"

Gib watched as the others around him spaced their feet and took up their swords in fighting hands. He followed along, wishing he knew what was going on. Should he already know these commands? He'd never run practice drills on the farm before. How was he supposed to keep up when everyone was already so far ahead of him?

"Good!" Roland was moving through the paired trainees. "Most of you already know basic commands. If you do and you realize your partner does not, help them out! If I catch anyone slighting their partner, they'll be running circuits. Five or six laps around the field might make you feel a little more generous!" Mutters rippled through the line of trainees.

"Speaking out of turn—another excellent way to earn circuits. If I hear talk about anything other than our drills and how to perform them, then every student in that area will run. The innocent can pay proper thanks to the one who felt the rules applied to everyone but himself!"

Gib locked his jaw. What if he had to sneeze? Was that allowed? He could feel the panic tingle down his spine. As Roland commanded them through basic formations and then had them square off against their partners, the Weapons Master's voice was the only one to be heard.

They were told to focus on defense and to take turns switching between assaulting and blocking. Gib was grateful that Diddy was a bit more reserved in his swipes and blows. When Gib missed a block, the resulting tap was hard enough to discourage him from being distracted again but not so heavy he feared real damage. Tarquin, on the other hand, winced each time Kezra caught him off guard. The thud of her sword against his arms, legs, and chest could be heard by everyone. Gib hoped he never had to be partnered with her.

Roland was moving through the pairs of students, sometimes giving advice and other times merely observing. Gib watched out of the corner of his eye as the Weapons Master closed in on them. Gib tried not to hold his breath and to keep his focus, but he was so nervous. The trainer's eyes bore into the back of Gib's skull, scrutinizing his every move.

"Widen the space between your hands on the hilt." Roland was beside them now, speaking to Diddy. "You'll have better control over your blade. There, yes. Keep your hands like that. Very good, Your Highness."

Gib nearly dropped his own weapon. *What?* He was pretty sure his ears hadn't deceived him. Had the Weapons Master just referred to Diddy as—as—?

Diddy's face flushed as he responded to the trainer in a quick, hushed voice. "Please, sir. Just 'Didier' while we're in class. You said yourself, no favorites or titles."

Roland hesitated for just a moment before conceding. "Fair enough." He gave Diddy a small clap on the back. "Carry on then, Didier."

Gib was pretty sure some form of exasperated groan left his mouth. His hands suddenly felt clammy as his nerves spiked. Tarquin was grinning up a storm beside him, and Kezra took it upon herself to lay a hearty thwack against his ribs while he was distracted. Gib felt like he'd received the blow. He was such a fool! No wonder all the other students were giving him sideways glances! He'd been talking to the Prince of Arden all this time and hadn't realized it! *Great going, you idiot. You've made yourself look like a bumbling fool.*

The Weapons Master moved past them. Gib knew he was supposed to be continuing the exercise, but he couldn't raise his hot face from the ground to meet Diddy's eyes. The prince, likewise, hesitated at first. It wasn't until one of the assistants came by with a shrewd look that both boys fell back into their routine. They continued on in marked silence until the class came to its end and they waited to put away their weapons.

"I'm sorry I didn't reveal myself," the prince whispered. Diddy's voice sounded dim as he shuffled a foot across the ground.

Gib shook his head, words lost to him. What could he say without making a further fool of himself?

"I sometimes wish I could just be like everyone else," the prince continued with a sigh. "I didn't think it was important that you knew who

I was."

Gib grimaced. "If I'd known, I–I would have spoken to you with more respect, uh, Your Highness—"

"That's exactly it," Diddy cut him off. "I don't want to be given special treatment. I don't want people to be so afraid of my title that they won't speak to me. I just want—" He swallowed and glared at the ground. "I want to be perfectly insignificant, if only for a short while."

Gib nodded, but he didn't understand. The prince was speaking as though he was discontent with his life. How could anyone dislike being royalty? Sure, he probably had a book's worth of rules and proper decorum to follow, but if being scrutinized by the public eye was the sole cost of living in luxury, surely it was a small price to pay. Diddy would never have to experience the pain of an empty belly or worry over whether he was able to purchase textiles to clothe himself. He wouldn't grow cold during the long winter nights, and even if war were to break out between Arden and Shiraz, Diddy would certainly be one of the best protected warriors riding into battle.

A sudden thought occurred to Gib and the bottom of his stomach dropped out. "Wait. Those boys from earlier—"

Diddy bit back a smile as he examined his sword. "For them to have paid you so little mind, I'm sure they realized you didn't know me or them."

"I'm a fool."

"Not at all. I'm sure they appreciated the rare anonymity as well."

Gib nodded. After they put their weapons away they were immediately lined up in front of several tailors and measured for their uniforms. Didier excused himself, explaining that he would be measured later and needed to be elsewhere now. Gib didn't want to pry, so he didn't ask where the prince was going. Before leaving, Diddy extended a wish for them to be partners again on the morrow.

Waiting in line to be measured, Gib realized no one had said where he was to report next. Judging by the midday sun, he would guess it was time to take his meal but wasn't certain. Looking around for anyone who might help, he discovered Kezra being measured beside him. They'd never formally been introduced and he was afraid to get her attention, but he didn't want to bother an instructor. Hopefully she wouldn't beat the hell out of him like she'd done with Tarquin.

"Uh, do you know if we go straight to the dining hall from here?"

Kezra didn't respond at first. In fact, Gib realized she didn't know he was speaking to her. She blinked a moment later and frowned. "Oh. Where you—? Yeah. Midday meal next then whichever class you have after that."

He nodded, a shuddering breath escaping him. "All right. Thanks."

She still didn't smile, but the more he saw of her the less intimidating she seemed. "You remember where to go?"

"Yeah. I think so. But do you know where I would go for the Ardenian Law class after midday meal?"

Kezra shrugged. "That's where I'm going after I eat. You can follow me if you don't find any of your friends at the dining hall."

The knot in his stomach released a little. "I—thanks. I'm not even really sure who my friends are. I mean, I've met so many people so fast I can barely keep the names straight."

As they headed off together, she nodded. "I'm Kezra Malin-Rai. And you're Gibben, right?" A sly but genuine smile finally graced her hard features. "Aren't you the boy I almost ran over yesterday?"

He heard himself laugh. "Gib, yes." They shared a chuckle as they made their way to the dining hall, and despite the uncertainty of what lay ahead, Gib felt his mood lighten. Between Nage, Diddy, and possibly even Kezra, he felt like he'd as good a chance for success as any of them.

Lunch went by quickly, but plenty of food was available and he managed to find Nage once more. Unfortunately, he was with Tarquin. Diddy was nowhere to be seen, but Gib supposed that made sense. The prince was busy and probably took his meal with his family.

When finished eating, Gib nudged Nage and they both hunted down Kezra. She gave them a shrewd look, but when Nage confessed he also didn't know where to go she relented and allowed the two boys to follow her. She'd suggested that they wait for Tarquin, but both Gib and Nage had assured her that he would find his own way.

Their classroom, an audience hall, was bigger than any room Gib had ever seen. A stage in the center was surrounded by tiered benches. When Kezra picked a seat close to the front, Gib hesitated. He wasn't even sure if she would allow him to follow her or not, but Nage made the choice for them and they stumbled in beside her. She glanced their way when they were all seated but didn't tell them to leave.

As time stretched on, more students filled the seats. Gib craned his neck to see everyone. "These aren't all sentinel trainees, are they?"

Kezra shook her head. "No. Everyone who will serve Arden in any way must take this class. In the next few days you'll see different uniforms. Mages wear white robes, blue jerkins for the healers, black tunics for the older students interested in law and academics, and our grey soldier garb." She stuck her nose in the air and put on a lofty sounding voice. "As well as the finery of the highborn classmen who wish to pursue a political career."

Gib rolled his eyes. "Do we all sit together or will we be separated?"

"Why? Afraid you might have to sit next to an arrogant noble?"

He huffed a laugh just before Nage sank low in his seat. "Tarquin."

Gib bit his bottom lip and looked over his shoulder. Tarquin was wandering through the aisles, appearing to be at a loss as he looked for a seat. Gib fought the urge to also slide down and go unnoticed. As the highborn's search continued, however, a familiar pang of despair settled in Gib's stomach. "No one is letting him in."

"Do you blame them?" Nage groaned. "He never shuts up. He's always going on about his family and estate and whatever else."

Kezra sighed, rolling her piercing green eyes. "He means well. He's not a braggart, just an idiot. Our fathers work together and he doesn't have any friends that I know of."

"Why not?" Gib asked.

Kezra fixed him with a skeptical look. "Isn't it obvious with that mouth? And—his look is odd." Her mouth slanted into a thin line.

An uncomfortable silence rose among the three of them as they watched Tarquin's plight. As the young highborn continued to search for an empty seat, his face and neck grew progressively redder. No one would slide down and give him a seat. People gave him narrow looks before waving him off. Gib swallowed. He knew better than to treat people this way.

"Sorry guys, I have to let him in here." Kezra's apology was hushed but not ashamed. Gib nodded, relief flooding his insides and Nage let out his breath. Apparently they'd all rather listen to the fool chatter about nothing than watch him be rejected. Kezra stood and waved. "Tarquin! Over here."

Tarquin zeroed in on them in an instant, and the relief that passed over his countenance wrenched at Gib's guts. They each shifted down a seat as Tarquin climbed in beside them.

"Thanks, guys. I, uh, it was starting to look like all of the seats were full. I guess I'll have to be faster tomorrow."

The highborn sank down and took off his hat, pointedly ignoring how others stopped to stare at his washed out complexion and odd pale eyes. Gib wouldn't ask, but the more he looked at Tarquin the more the highborn boy seemed not merely fair skinned. He'd also changed his tunic, still long sleeved, but this one was much less elaborate. Gib felt the sinking sensation worsen as he remembered thinking ill of Tarquin's fine clothing earlier. Had someone said something to him? Or worse, had no one said anything at all? Had the desperation to fit in pushed him to change? Gib's cheeks grew uncomfortably warm.

"So how are your ribs feeling?" Gib asked.

Tarquin smiled so hard it almost looked painful. "Kezra is a tough match. If you don't believe it, you'll have to trade with me tomorrow."

Gib forced a soft laugh. "No. I think I'll just stand back and watch. I heard how hard her blows were landing."

Tarquin gave a hearty laugh. "Yeah." He fidgeted with the sleeves of his tunic. "Thanks again. Really. For letting me sit with you."

The highborn didn't make eye contact and Gib was grateful. He didn't feel like looking into the face of someone he'd wronged. As he remembered how quickly he'd been judged by the Instructions Master, Diedrick Lyle, Gib came to the conclusion that perhaps he'd done the same to Tarquin Aldino.

Gib stumbled back to his room. He was exhausted. Both of his afternoon classes had seemed to stretch on for marks. The professors were nice enough, but it was obvious right from the beginning that Gib's reading and writing skills were lacking. He would need to find extra time outside of class to work on improving his literacy.

Extra time—when he woke before dawn to perform his chores and then was in class until nearly dinnertime, directly followed by evening chores? When was he going to find extra time to study? And with whom? Almost all of his new friends were well schooled already, but he didn't feel confident enough to ask them for assistance. Surely Tarquin and Kezra were just as busy as he. Gib's head was spinning as he reached his room.

As he raised a hand to push on the door, quiet laughter rose from within the room. Apparently Joel had company. Gib hesitated, caught somewhere between knocking and turning to leave. He was sure it would be polite to wait outside until he was invited in, but this was his room as well. Surely he could come and go as he pleased.

Gib tapped his knuckles against the maple door just once before pushing it open. He was shocked to see Prince Didier perched on the edge of the bed. He'd changed outfits sometime after the morning sparring session, trading the elaborate winged tunic in favor of a more practical jerkin with a silver chained belt. Gib's roommate, Joel, was sitting across from the prince and the two had been conversing. Both boys looked up as Gib blinked in shock.

Diddy's eyes widened and his lips curled into a smile of surprise. "Gib Nemesio?"

Gib sputtered. "Uh, h–hello, Prince—I mean, Diddy. What are you doing here? How did you find me?"

The prince laughed and looked over at Joel, whose crystal blue eyes were likewise clouded by confusion. "I didn't know Gib was your roommate! Joel, this is the boy I was just telling you about. The one from Roland's sparring class."

Joel chuckled in a light manner, eyes dancing. "I should have guessed by the way you described him."

"Wait," Gib interrupted, scratching his head. His gaze fell back to Diddy. "You're not here to see me?"

The prince smiled sheepishly. "No. Joel is my cousin. I came by to deliver a message to him."

Gib's eyeballs nearly burst from their sockets as he jerked around to face his roommate. "*You're* related to the royal family?" *Why?* Why did everyone insist on keeping such important information from him?

Joel shrugged, playing with the sleeve of his pristine mage robe. "You could say that. Didier's mother, Queen Dahlia Adelwijn, is my aunt by blood. My father's sister."

Gib nodded, still trying to digest this news when something else struck him. *Adelwijn.* That name was familiar. "Queen Dahlia Adelwijn? Like Koal Adelwijn, the seneschal of Arden?"

The cousins glanced at one another before Joel lowered his crystal eyes. A faint rosy color stole over his cheeks and he was only half successful in keeping the laugh out of his voice. "Yes, like Koal Adelwijn. My father."

CHAPTER FOUR

"How are your studies faring?"

Gib glanced up from the manuscript he'd been trying to decipher and smiled as Joel came into the room. Joel Adelwijn—son of the seneschal of Arden—Gib reminded himself. The shock of learning this information had been given adequate time to settle, and the two roommates had transitioned past the awkward silence. Joel continued to be aloof and they were not what Gib would call friends, but their relationship was amiable enough.

Gib had, however, forged friendships with Nage, Kezra, and even Tarquin. They were an odd quartet, but having such companionship helped Gib adjust to his new life.

Prince Didier was another constant in Gib's new world. Although the prince was often busy outside of class, the two had time to chat in the mornings before training with Roland commenced. Diddy was surprisingly humble, despite his privileged upbringing. He was curious about Gib's life, often asking the strangest questions, but without hint of mockery or scorn. The young prince's innocence about the outside world was genuine. In a way, Didier reminded Gib of his young brothers back home. He missed them despite his newly forged friendships.

Liza stopped by to see him twice in the sennights since Gib's arrival. She even brought fresh parchment on her most recent visit, and the two siblings sat down and wrote to Tayver and Calisto. Simple words were all they could manage, but it was enough to assure their younger brothers that he and Liza were all right. Gib hoped the boys were safe too.

Gib set the book aside to answer Joel's question, letting out a frustrated sigh. The words had begun to blur on the pages. "I'm doing okay. My professor says I'm a natural with arithmetic, but not so much with reading. I'm still struggling with the letters." He motioned to the frayed tome. "Hence the extra studying, though I'm not sure I'm doing myself any favors. I think I'm just making matters worse."

Joel stood before the window, locks of his raven hair rustling in the light breeze that came through. He didn't speak for a long moment, but finally, soft words flowed from his mouth. "I should take you to the library. I could sit with you if you'd like—if you need some help with the words, that is."

"Oh, uh, I mean, I wouldn't want to be a burden," Gib replied, feeling strangely flattered that his roommate—always so distant and reserved—was offering assistance. "You're probably busy with your own studies." Gib closed his mouth as a means to end his rambling.

Joel didn't look away from the window but shrugged his shoulders. "I have more free time than you might imagine."

Gib wrung his hands. "I figured you would have a full schedule, being the son of Seneschal Koal and related to the royal family. Surely you must dine with the royal court on occasion."

The mage trainee let out a sharp snort. "The court is full of petty, hateful nobles with nothing better to do than spread rumors and prey upon the vulnerable. I'd sooner dine with pigs than the likes of them."

Gib was taken aback by Joel's outburst. Something had the young man terribly upset. "Surely they can't all behave that way."

"They do."

"You're not like that."

After a stifling pause, Joel turned his crystal eyes toward Gib, shock registering on his fair features. For a split second, his eyes flashed with pain. Gib could see the isolation and fear. A strange sensation made its way from the pit of Gib's stomach to his throat. Never before had Joel seemed so genuine, so real. In his state of vulnerability, he at last seemed human.

And then the trainee seemed to remember himself, and the mask of a smile was restored. Joel's voice was hushed. "I suppose you have no idea who I really am."

Gib bit down on his bottom lip. It was true, but that was hardly his fault. He'd tried to talk to Joel, but it wasn't easy.

"And that is entirely my fault," the mage continued with a sigh. "I'm sorry, Gibben." Joel took in a breath of frantic air, and Gib was certain his roommate was about to say something important, something groundbreaking.

An abrupt knock sounded on the door. Both boys jumped and turned their heads toward the sound. Gib was suddenly aware of the rapid pounding in his chest. He'd been so absorbed in the conversation that he hadn't noticed his quickening pulse.

Joel was on his feet a second later, his robe sweeping across the floor as he went to answer the call. Gib ran his fingers along the binding of the tome which sat before him, a prickle of defeat tickling his heart. It was unlikely Joel would choose to open up again.

"Hello, little brother."

Gib glanced up in the direction of the new voice in time to witness Joel's eyes cloud with resentment.

"What are you doing here?" the mage trainee asked, posture rigid as he glared into the corridor.

The other voice was smug, dripping with haughtiness. "Oh, did I come at a bad time? I'm sure you're still content to practice such shameful acts behind closed doors. I can return later if you have company."

Joel narrowed his eyes further, face bathed with color and hands balled into fists at his side. "If you've come here to berate me—"

Smug laughter cut the mage trainee off mid-sentence. "Relax, little brother. I bring news from our father." A moment later, the unidentified man stepped through the threshold and into the room.

The similarities to Joel were undeniable. The newcomer was tall and lean, with the same fair skin and blue eyes. His hair was just as dark as Joel's and almost as long, but the locks of stark onyx were noticeably straighter, while Joel's fell in gentle waves around his shoulders. His eyes were cold and humorless, though he might have been handsome if his mouth hadn't been pulled down, contorting his fair features into an ugly sneer.

Gib sank down in his chair at the weight of the newcomer's eyes. The young sentinel trainee instantly knew the look. He was being judged.

Joel was leaning against the wall as though he might topple over without its support. "Gibben, this is my elder brother, Lord Liro Adelwijn, mage and understudy to the High Councilor of Arden." The mage trainee sounded ill. "Liro, this is my roommate, Gibben Nemesio."

Liro barked a sour laugh. "A roommate? They allowed you to have another one after what happened before?" His eyes speared Gib. "Surely you mustn't have told the poor fool your secret then."

"It's not a secret," Joel replied, keeping his reddened face fixated on the floor.

The older brother rolled his eyes. "Unfortunately not. Now it is but a thorn in the side, a family disgrace that cannot be undone. I hope you're satisfied with yourself."

Gib had no idea what the two brothers were talking about. He fidgeted with his sleeve and kept his mouth shut until Liro demanded in a sharp tone, "What's your name, boy?"

Gib narrowed his eyes. Joel had already introduced him once. "Gibben Nemesio. I was drafted as a sentinel trainee—"

Liro waved a hand high in the air. "Nemesio? Not a name I've heard before. Are you common-born?"

Joel made a noise as if in protest, but Gib replied first. "I am. Is there a problem with that?" He didn't mean to growl the words like a challenge.

Liro went eerily still. Gib held his ground, though his legs were quivering beneath the writing desk. The older Adelwijn brother straightened to his full height and a dark smile spread across his lips. "Not at all, though I'm certain you'll know your lot in life soon enough. When war inevitably breaks out, you'll be sent to Shiraz to die alongside the rest of the peasant army. Your name will be forgotten."

"*Enough*, Liro!" Joel finally found his voice. "Tell me whatever it is you came here to say, and then get out."

Liro turned his attention back to his brother. "Father wanted to be sure to extend an invitation to the twins' Naming Day dinner. If I were you, I would check with their father first. Our uncle seems to be one of the only sane members of our family left. I'm not sure he would be comfortable with your presence."

Joel locked his jaw. Gib could feel tension rising in his gut. He had half a mind to leap up and tell this Liro to leave but had no such authority. At long last, the younger Adelwijn brother found his voice, shaken and weak as it might be. "I'll speak with Father later."

"Do not keep him waiting." Without a further word, Liro let himself out. He glanced back just before he shut the door and his lips lifted into an eerie, forced imitation of a smile. "I shall pray for your damned soul as always, brother." And then, with a slam, he was gone.

Gib swallowed at the sudden silence. He looked to Joel but couldn't make eye contact while he was busy glaring at the floor with eyes that glimmered wetly. Gib cleared his throat and looked away out of courtesy. "Are you all right?" It was all he could think to say.

No immediate response was given. Joel sat on his bed and such a length of time passed that Gib went back to trying to read, sure that Joel wouldn't answer at all. When the mage trainee finally did lift his voice, it was flimsily held together. "I apologize. I'm sorry my brother was so rude to you."

"Seemed to be the only way he knew how to communicate. He was worse to you than to me." Gib paused to work up the courage to go on. "Joel, I don't know what he was talking about, but he was clearly hurting you. I just—I want you to know that I think you're a good person. I don't know you well, and it's all right if you want to keep it that way, but I do think highly of you. Don't let that swine tear you down."

Joel lifted his face and blinked, a single renegade droplet on his cheek. "Diddy was right about you. Yours is possibly the most open and compassionate heart of any man." He took in a deep breath. "Thank you, Gibben."

Gib's face flushed and his heart hammered all over again, though he didn't know why. "Gib. Please, call me Gib."

A brief while later, Gib excused himself to go to the midday meal. Joel, as always, lingered behind. His custom was to dine exceptionally early for breakfast and late for both midday meal and supper. Gib initially figured it was merely an odd habit, but the more he grew to know his roommate, the more Gib realized Joel was avoiding the people there. With the pieces of the puzzle coming together, Gib was bothered and wanted to find some way to remedy the situation.

The dining hall was packed when he arrived, which made finding his friends all the more difficult. After his plate was full, Gib wandered through the tables where they typically sat and was eventually flagged down by Kezra. He took a seat between Tarquin and Nage.

As they settled back down to take their meal, another voice spoke up. "Hello everyone. May I join you?"

Gib startled, his mouth half full with bread. "Diddy? What are you doing here? I mean, yes. Sit down. You know you don't need to ask."

The young prince laughed lightly and took one of the empty places across from the four of them. "I try to remember, but you have to understand that my manners have been ingrained in me. Mother is very strict about that."

"Speaking of which, how did you manage to get away from her on our rest day?" Kezra chided him between bites.

"Very carefully," Diddy admitted with flushed cheeks. "I suspect Father is being chastised now for aiding me in my escape."

A round of laughter rippled through them. The Queen was apparently having a difficult time allowing her son to grow up. It was only within the past couple of sennights that she'd relinquished her grip enough to allow him to dine in the academy hall. And this was the first time Diddy had managed the feat on their day of rest, which was allotted every seventh day. Gib used the rest day as an opportunity to catch up on his reading.

Gib shook his head good-naturedly. "It's so strange to hear you talk about them. I know they're your mother and father, but they're the King and Queen to everyone else."

Diddy smiled as he picked at his dish, lifting some potato onto his fork. "I shall have to have you over to meet them one day, Gib."

It was in jest, but even the suggestion made Gib's stomach churn. He realized that was the intended effect, but it still unnerved him to consider it. Meeting Diddy had been bad enough. He couldn't imagine meeting the King or Queen of Arden.

"Hey. What is that?" Nage's voice was so loud and unexpected that Diddy stopped with his fork halfway to his mouth. "On your potatoes. What is that?"

The prince glanced downward and seemed to be at a loss. "I don't see anything. A bit of gravy, nothing else—"

Gib jumped at that as well. The two of them must have looked quite a sight as Nage fumbled on in his delight. "*Gravy?* Actual gravy?"

Upon closer inspection, Gib nodded. "It is! I had some once when I was young. Pa had dipped a roll into it. It was delicious."

Nage was already on his feet. "I've never had any. I have to go get some."

Gib held out an imploring hand. "Grab a dish for us both. And some bread."

Nage nodded as he raced off, his back disappearing into the crowd. With no distraction, Gib noticed the utter silence surrounding him. Each of the others trained their eyes on him. His face instantly flushed. "What?"

This only earned him laughter from everyone involved. Gib lowered his head and took up his fork once more. "Shut up."

Kezra was laughing so hard her face had gone red, and Tarquin gasped for air. "I forget how different life is for both of you," he managed to choke out between fits. "Gravy has never been so exciting."

Kezra nodded her head but was still unable to speak. Even Diddy covered his mouth, trying to disguise his merriment.

Gib slunk down in his seat and assured them of how entertaining they all were.

When Nage returned a few moments later, with a bowl full of gravy and three small loaves of bread, he looked around at them all. "What's so funny? Did I miss something?"

Gib said, "Nothing. Go ahead and sit down."

They both dug into the gravy with their warm bread and grinned from ear to ear as they ate, oblivious to the stares their friends gave them.

After the commotion died down, they received a pair of unexpected guests. Two older boys dropped their plates on the table loudly, one on either side of Diddy, and plopped down. "Hey there, buddy," one of them said loudly.

Gib recognized both of them. They were the bullies from the first day of class. Diddy had called them his brothers. Gib swallowed. *More royalty? Perfect.*

Diddy groaned as they deliberately invaded his space. "Oh, for the love of The Two. What are you doing here? There must be someone else for you to bother."

"But we like you," the leader from that first day spoke up. He was just as lofty and well-spoken as ever. His dark, almond-shaped eyes shone with smug mischief as he plucked an apple from his plate and took a dainty bite. "Didn't you miss us?"

"I can't miss you if you won't go away." The prince's decorum slipped for the first time. His voice hissed through clenched teeth much like any little brother speaking to his irksome elder siblings.

"Now, now, Didier. That's not very becoming for a prince of Arden," said the second boy with a voice so loud it carried across the room. He trained his voice to sound formal, like how the Queen might scold her son.

Diddy's face screamed of his discomfort. He looked as though he wanted to crawl under the table and disappear. "Please go away."

The boy with the almond-shaped eyes stuck his nose in the air. "You hurt our feelings. You'll never make a good ambassador like that. And you haven't even introduced us to your friends."

The agony in the prince's eyes made Gib wish he could come to the rescue once more but he'd have no excuse this time. He knew who the two older boys were now and had no permission to speak lightly to them.

Diddy sighed, lifting one hand, and signaled to each of his friends in turn. "Tarquin Aldino, Kezra Malin-Rai, Gibben Nemesio, and Nage Nessuno, this is my brother, Hasain Radek, and cousin, Nawaz Arrio."

Gib blinked and looked at them both. Diddy's brother looked nothing like Diddy, but his cousin could have been a mirror double. Nawaz shared the same fair skin, dark hair, and wide, expressive eyes—though his were a shocking blue as opposed to Diddy's brown. Nawaz also had an odd lock of silver growing over one temple.

Hasain shared the dark hair, but his was thicker than Diddy's or Nawaz's. His shrewd eyes and thin mouth made him look calculating. His soft voice carried well even in such a loud space. "So these were the ones who took pity on you and decided to give you a chance at being 'normal.'"

Gib gritted his teeth but kept his mouth shut. He wasn't sure how he felt about Hasain. Nawaz narrowed his eyes, causing a knot to form in Gib's stomach. Had he said that out loud? He didn't like the way those intense eyes focused on him.

"Hey." Nawaz's naturally loud voice seemed to boom all around them. "Aren't you that boy who mouthed off to us on the first day of class?"

Gib's stomach sank, but Diddy jumped in to save him. "He didn't know who either of you were. Rather, he didn't know who *any* of us were."

Hasain frowned and stuck his nose in the air. "Where are you from? It would seem your schooling is lacking."

Nawaz laughed and slapped a hand on the tabletop. "Did you shit your pants when you found out the truth?" He cackled openly, and Gib thought he heard Kezra and Tarquin snort.

Taking a slow breath, Gib waited for Nawaz to stop laughing before he responded. "Not quite, but I was startled." Nawaz laughed some more. Gib turned to look at Hasain. "I'm from Willowdale and you're right. My schooling is lacking. I was busy raising my brothers on our farm before I was called here."

Any merriment either of them may have been enjoying up until that point slipped away. Nawaz sneered and shook his head. Hasain went rigid. Gib prepared himself for more poisonous words and accusations of worthlessness. Both of these older boys seemed not so different from Liro Adelwijn.

Hasain's next words startled Gib. "I'm sorry to hear that."

Nawaz shook his head and leaned back from the table as if put off from his meal. "That damned draft has gotta go." He was talking to Hasain but gestured toward Gib and Nage. "Look at them. They're boys. A farmer and a Nessuno. Chhaya's bane, it's not fair."

Hasain nodded. "I've heard talk of taking two men from each family, not just one."

"Horseshit. Arden's army is well trained and large enough without forcing new recruits. These old laws need to be struck down."

"The King has been trying to get the drafting age raised for years, but the country is torn in two about it. The High Council is overrun with fools." When Tarquin balked at that, Hasain conceded slightly. "Forgive me, Aldino. Not your father so much as—" He gave Kezra a narrow look. "—some others."

Kezra folded her arms over her chest and met his gaze without hesitation. "You're not telling me anything I don't already know. My father *is* a fool."

Gib was thoroughly confused by all of this, but Diddy showed some mercy. "Could we please talk about something more pleasant? After all, my friends don't need to burden themselves with all of this."

Both of the older boys shifted back to nitpicking Diddy for his troubles. While this may have been irksome for the young prince, it made for lighter conversation, and an entire mark later, they were all still sitting together. Their plates had long been empty and most of the other students had left the dining hall.

It would soon be time for chores, but Gib didn't feel like excusing himself. The conversation had remained light since the redirection, but he was itching to ask more about the draft. King Rishi wouldn't call for two men from each family, would he? If Tayver were drafted as well, who would look after Calisto? Gib's insides knotted up at the thought, and he stared at the tabletop until he heard his name.

"That's right. Gib is Joel's roommate," the young prince was saying.

Gib glanced up to see both of the older boys looking at him. Shifting in his seat, Gib tried to think of something to say. "Dean Marc thought that Joel would be able to help me learn my way around here and all. He's been a lot of help." He fished for something more but could think of nothing, especially under their heavy looks.

"How do the two of you get along?" Hasain asked.

Gib thought it an odd question. "Well. He's a good roommate."

Nawaz nodded, tapping his fingers on the table. "How's he doing? With school and friends?"

Another odd question, and a bit intrusive. Gib felt like he was being interrogated. "Uh, fine I guess? I mean, we're not really friends. He's two years older than me, after all. But he doesn't seem to have a lot of people over." He thought about it for a minute. "In fact, other than on the first day when Diddy paid him a visit, the only other person I've seen Joel speak to was his brother."

The older boys shared a dark look. Hasain sighed. "Liro visits him?"

"Only earlier today. Or at least, that's the first I've seen of him."

Nawaz grunted his distaste. "That's enough."

Gib nodded. Without thinking, he offered more than he meant to. "Yeah. I didn't care much for him." He winced at his own forwardness and immediately tried to correct himself. "I mean, I'm sorry. I suppose Liro is *your* cousin as well."

Hasain smirked darkly. "No need for apologies. None of us like him."

"He's damned miserable," Nawaz added.

A couple of young girls came into the dining hall from the kitchen and began wiping down the tables. Gib sighed, readying himself for the inevitability of his own chores. "Yeah, I would agree with you. It seems odd that two brothers can be so different as Joel and Liro."

The girl who had been wiping down the table next to theirs turned to look at them. "Joel and Liro. Speaking of the Adelwijns, are you?"

Nawaz instantly groaned as though he knew the girl. "Damn it, Annwyne, go away."

She frowned curtly at him and stuck her nose in the air. "Some of us have responsibilities. We can't all have rich stepfathers now, can we?"

Nawaz drew back in disgust. "What do you want?"

A smug smile formed on her lips. "I was merely doing my job when I heard the mention of Liro and Joel Adelwijn. Naturally, the discussion drew my interest. Tell me, has Joel dishonored his family yet again? Though I can hardly imagine how he could top his last offense."

Gib looked at her narrowly. More of this? What were they on about? What could Joel have possibly done that was so shameful?

Hasain was already leveling her with a glare. "That will be enough from you. Go make yourself useful somewhere."

Annwyne laughed and touched her bosom as though his words delighted her. "And what will *you* do if I don't, Radek? Your father may be a king but you're a bastard with no authority."

Diddy gasped, but Hasain merely clenched his jaw. "Leave. Now."

She waved him off flippantly and went back to washing the table. "I have a job to do."

Gib felt someone tap his shoulder and turned to see Kezra giving Annwyne a dirty look. "Let's go. We'll have chores soon enough." Gib rose with the rest of his friends.

As they climbed off the bench, the foul girl waved her rag in the air and called to them. "Oh, don't let me break up the little party. If you're going to go on about the queer, then by all means continue. I enjoy a joke as much as anyone else."

Gib wasn't familiar with the word and Nage looked equally confused, but the reaction from everyone else was instant and fierce.

Nawaz's voice rose above the others and his face had turned an angry red. "You keep your filthy mouth shut! Joel Adelwijn is no concern of yours."

Annwyne laughed, clapping her hands like a giddy child. "Oh, what *fun!* I forgot that you were one of the ones to try to protect him. There's nothing any of you can do. He deserves to be ostracized, lest his perversion infect the rest of us."

Hasain stepped forward and pointed savagely at her. "Joel is far braver than most men I know and you'll not speak so lightly of him. He has committed no crime and has never been anything but a decent person, something you would know nothing about."

She cackled and went back to scrubbing the table. "He's queer. He'd rather lie with a man, be his whore, than have a normal, respectable relationship with a woman."

Gib's head was spinning. The entire world seemed to tilt on its side, and he grabbed the table for support. He barely grasped what was going on here, but her words hit him like a kick in the gut. He was vaguely aware of a commotion. Kezra was shouting some sort of profanity and leaping over the table. He managed to look up, wanting to see where she'd gone, and was shocked to realize that Nawaz had taken Annwyne by the front of her frock and lifted her clean off the floor. She was shrieking at him to put her down and he was yelling at her to shut her mouth. Kezra, Tarquin, and Diddy were all pulling on his arms, trying to get him to put her down as Hasain paced back and forth behind them.

This wasn't good. Someone was bound to hear. Just as Gib thought to run and look for an adult, for anyone who could bring sense to this nonsensical situation, the shrieking stopped. Nawaz had set Annwyne down, and she was flailing backward, spewing all sorts of horrid names at him.

Hasain came forward at that point and she cringed back. He glared down at her, his voice so low Gib could barely hear it. "If I ever hear such foul things from you again, I'll have you removed from Academy. You may think I hold no sway, but I assure you, I know my father well and I'll make this happen. Snakes such as you need to be weeded out of the general population."

Annwyne remained defiant. "It must be a comfort for you to have fallen into such a lofty position. You go ahead and try to protect Joel Adelwijn and other perverts like him. One day you'll see. *They* are the ones who will be weeded out. And then the rest of us will be safe."

Nawaz smiled eerily. "Joel isn't the one you'll need to remain safe from if you don't keep that forked tongue in your mouth." She glared back at him but didn't say anything more.

Hasain turned back to the others. "Let's all take our leave. Now. I feel we've worn out our welcome."

With numb feet, Gib followed the others. He was grateful when Diddy hung back, so they both could leave the hall together. As they stepped out into the sunlight, the fresh air caught Gib and he felt as though he could breathe again. What had happened in there? They'd been eating and talking then all hell had broken loose. And what had that girl been going on about? What was this about Joel? Was any of it true? Nawaz and Hasain had both leapt to his defense, but neither of them had denied any of the accusations. Gib shuddered. She'd been so cruel about it. Why should she care even if it was true? He was only vaguely aware of Diddy's arm going around his shoulder.

"Gib. Are you all right?" The prince's dark eyes were concerned. "I'm sorry you had to see that. Are you going to be all right? Please, speak to me."

Gib swallowed. "Uh, sorry. My head is kinda full. I just—what was she talking about?" He regretted it as soon as the words escaped his mouth. "No. Wait. I mean, you don't need to tell me anything."

Hands wringing, Diddy replied, "Joel is a wonderful person. You've been his roommate for several sennights now. Have you ever once had any reason to distrust him?"

"What? No. Of course not. I'm sorry I asked. It's really none of my business. I don't even know if she was speaking the truth or not. She seemed hysterical."

The prince pressed his mouth into a thin line and looked at the ground. "You're right. It's not our place to discuss such things. I would only ask that if you do feel inclined to distance yourself from Joel in the future, do it civilly. *Please*. He's been through so much already."

Gib nodded but wasn't sure what he was agreeing to. But he had to go do his chores. The chores would take several marks, and he would be too busy to think about any of this. He could look forward to that. But at some point he'd have to see Joel again. The thought alone made Gib's mouth dry. He didn't know how he was going to look his roommate in the eye after all that had been said.

Gib closed his eyes and willed away all thoughts on the matter. He had chores to do. He'd have to focus on that now and make up a plan for later when later arrived.

After Gib had changed out the bedding in all of the stalls of his assigned section in the stable—and then volunteered to help water and feed the horses that were not his charges as well—he meandered back to his room. He'd concluded that he wouldn't discuss the events from midday meal with Joel. It would be best to pretend as though he'd never heard the heated conversation between Annwyne and the other students. Gib could spare his roommate from having to talk about the controversy by feigning blissful ignorance.

Hoping for Joel to be gone, Gib reached his door and squeezed his eyes shut. He entered after a quick knock. His stomach clenched. Joel sat upon his bed and read from a scroll in his lap. He looked up briefly and a small smile flitted over his features—a warm welcome by his standards. "Hello."

Damn it. Despite his best efforts, Gib froze in the doorway. He recovered as quickly as he was able and stumbled through, closing the door a bit too hard. He winced at his own buffoonery and tried to think of something to say. As if on command, his mind went blank. "Uh, sorry."

Inquisitive blue eyes narrowed ever so slightly, and Gib knew he was being judged. He tried to breathe and remain as casual as possible. He'd go to the desk and sit down. At least he could pretend to be reading. Except his feet were like lead and his legs paid no heed to his wishes. He managed to trip on his way there and nearly knocked the chair over before he sat down. The binding on his study manual was also getting the best of him, and he was red faced by the time he found where he'd left off earlier. With all the grace and poise allotted a common sack of manure, Gib finally sank down and pretended to read.

A short while later, Joel lifted his delicate voice. "How was your meal?"

Oh damn it. Damn it all to hell. Gib was content to ignore him at first. He glared down at the manual and willed his hands to stop shaking, but it wasn't easy with Joel staring. Gib wanted to stare back, not openly, but with the same dignity of any decent peeping tom—from over the top of his book.

A long stretch passed and the silence grew, the weight of it threatening to crush both of them. Finally Joel sighed and pitched his scroll aside. He brought his hands to his temples and slammed his eyes shut. "Who told you?"

Gib couldn't breathe. His lungs had frozen. Mouth ajar, he tried to force something—anything—to come out but failed.

Joel's voice was pained. "*Who told you?*"

Gib jumped in his seat and the book slipped onto the floor with a loud thud. "T—Told me what?" Even to himself, his voice sounded foreign. He wasn't sure Joel could even hear him from across the room.

The mage student's fair face twisted into an ugly mask of strife. "Don't play stupid with me, Gibben Nemesio. I can see it in your face, the abject horror, the disgust and disbelief. I know you've been told."

Gib swallowed and forced a small half-nod. "All right. You're right but it's not—I don't think—I don't even know if it's true—"

"*Which part?*" Joel's voice was caught somewhere between being stone cold and deceptively calm. "The part about me preferring men? Or the part about me bringing shame to my entire family?" His voice broke just a little, and a single teardrop escaped from each of his eyes.

Gib tore his gaze away, face hot with a mix of shame and pity. "Both. But it's not like you make it sound." When Joel glared, Gib lifted his hands to signal his peaceful intentions. "I mean it. I'm not horrified or disgusted. I don't think any less of you. I just—I'm terrible at keeping secrets. I meant to not burden you with what I'd heard. I'm sorry. I should have just been honest."

Joel's face fell into an unreadable mask. He looked away. Gib didn't push, but he likewise didn't close himself off. He didn't pick up his book and pretend like nothing had happened.

After a few tense moments, Joel slouched and a small sob shook his shoulders. "I'm sorry. I didn't mean to yell at you. I just—I'm so tired of being everyone's topic of conversation." He covered his face with trembling hands.

"Understandable. I'm sorry it was brought up."

Joel shook his head and wiped at his damp cheeks. "I should have told you myself, but Diddy spoke so highly of you and you've been nothing but wonderful. I haven't had many friends since—it's difficult to go from having many to having so very few and I didn't want to chase you away."

Gib frowned but nodded. He thought he understood. "It's still a fresh wound, isn't it? This isn't something that was discovered long ago."

"Just last Academy season. I mean, I'd known a bit longer than that but—I only grew the courage to speak of it last year. I was a fool for being so open. I'd thought I was in love and didn't wish to hide. So I told my family and spoke openly of it at the courts—I was an idiot. I should have known better. The scandal and shame has torn my family apart."

Rubbing the back of his neck, Gib ventured on with uncertainty. "For what it's worth, I met Hasain and Nawaz today. And they were both right there to defend you when—when it happened. Diddy too. They're all your family, aren't they? They weren't ashamed of you."

Joel's laugh sounded forced. "I know. But not everyone is as forgiving as they."

"I'm sorry." Gib didn't know what else to say.

"I don't need your pity."

"What you did took a lot of courage."

Joel had wrapped his arms around himself and was glaring out the window. "I was selfish. I spoke without regard for my family. I brought shame to them and that is something I'll never be able to undo."

"Horseshit. You did what you felt was right. Your family will come around."

Joel shook his head. "No. Father is getting flak from the other councilors, Mother cries every time she returns from court, and Liro can hardly stand to look at me. We used to be so close. It breaks my heart—" Another treacherous tear slipped down the mage trainee's cheek. "I'm sorry. You shouldn't have to listen to all of this."

"If not me, then who? I don't mind listening if you need someone to talk to. It seems like you could use a friend."

Those crystal blue eyes widened. "Friend?"

Gib smiled slowly, shyly. "If you would have me as one, then yes."

Joel stared out the window for a long time, his mouth set in a line and brows furrowed. Then at last, the mage trainee sighed and turned his eyes toward Gib. "I'd like that very much."

CHAPTER FIVE

"Can you at least tell me where we're going?" Gib huffed as he tried to keep up with his roommate.

Joel's smile was an enigma, as always. The mage trainee sighed as he waited in the corridor ahead for Gib to catch up, pristine white robes hidden beneath a heavy fur cloak. The halls were cold enough that both boys had donned protective outerwear before leaving their shared room. Gib was grateful his mop of brown curls was now long enough to cover the back of his neck from the frostbitten air, and he was also thankful to be wearing the mage's cloak from the previous year. It was a bit worn and hung too long past Gib's knees, but it was warm and kept him protected from the cold.

Gib raised an eyebrow as he caught up with his friend. "You know I don't like surprises. Can you give me a hint at the very least?"

The older boy laughed, his blue eyes sparkling with mischief. "All right, one hint."

Gib couldn't help but smile. Since Joel's secret had come to light nearly a moonturn ago, Gib had noted an improvement in his roommate's mood. Joel was no longer so aloof, nor was he prone to choosing solitude over companionship. The mage trainee had allowed himself to open up, to laugh and make jokes, to forge a real friendship with Gib.

"Well?" Gib asked, trying to catch his breath in the thin, chilled air.

Joel's eyes danced. "We're going somewhere that will aid with your studies."

"Are we going to the library?"

The other boy sighed with dramatic intent. "Well, my best attempt at surprising you just went flittering out the window, but yes, I'd planned to take you to the library."

A hearty chuckle made its way from within Gib's throat. "Oh, you've been *full* of surprises, my friend, let me assure you." When that earned another smile from his roommate, Gib felt his face go warm. He didn't know what to make of it, so he pressed on. "If you'd like, I can act surprised when we arrive regardless?"

Joel snorted as he led the way through the corridor but said nothing more, so Gib allowed his mind to wander. He kept his eyes fixed on the mage trainee's back, lest the two of them become separated. The halls were not as busy as they had been the only other time Gib had been to this area of the building—close to where Dean Arrio's office was located—but the pair of boys passed by several students as well as a handful of professors as they walked. Most were hurrying, eager to be out of the cold. Gib hoped the library had a fireplace.

Less than two moonturns until Midwinter, it hadn't yet snowed, but already the cold winds had blown down from the northern lands and engulfed Silver City in a blanket of frost. The flora lining the courtyard of the academy which had been so beautiful upon Gib's arrival was now shriveled and brown, and though no snow had fallen from the sky yet this season, Joel predicted it wouldn't be long. This made Gib antsy. Academy was to release for the Midwinter festival in another six sennights, and he was hoping to be able to go home to see Tayver and Calisto. If it snowed, would the roads be deemed too dangerous for travel?

The sound of a door flying open startled Gib from his thoughts, and he jumped at the sudden calamity of angry voices. He leapt back even as Joel did, pressing himself against the side of the hallway.

Diedrick Lyle's voice rose high and loud. "You'll return to my office at once and have a proper discussion with me—"

"*Or you'll what?*"

Gib sucked in a sharp breath as he recognized Kezra despite her disheveled appearance and rigid tone. Hair a mess and eyes livid, she looked like she'd possibly been yelling for quite some time already.

"Will you force me out of my career path as well?"

Diedrick came at her fiercely but stopped short of physical contact. Even from a distance, he looked a coward and Gib frowned as he watched. The Instructions Master's voice shook and his face was an ugly red. "I will do no such thing! I have made suggestions I feel will help advance you in the future."

"*Like hell they will.*" Everyone in the hall was staring now, but Kezra didn't seem to care. She kept her voice high and loud. "I'm training to be a sentinel for Arden. How will embroidery and homemaking help me become a better soldier? Pray tell. If there is something I've overlooked, let me know."

The Instructions Master locked his jaw and the color in his face went darker still. "You are a woman, are you not? One day you'll have a husband and home—"

Kezra balled her fists and took a step toward him. "*Over my dead body!*"

Gib smiled when the Instructions Master fell back, but Joel's face was etched with worry.

"I'm training so that I may have a job and stand on my own two feet. I'll be damned if I'm to be tied to a husband for my entire life!"

The silence that met her defiance was suffocating. No one in the hall—teachers, students, highborn, or low—dared speak. Diedrick Lyle looked as though he would burst, and Gib readied himself for the master's shouting.

A softer, gentler voice picked up instead. "Kezra Malin-Rai, we all have our place in this world and it is time you should consider yours."

Gib swallowed as he peered down the hall even as Joel flinched. Liro Adelwijn stood behind Master Lyle and addressed Kezra.

Kezra gave Liro a shrewd look. Her eyes were narrowed into ember slits and her chest was heaving. "My place? I have no worries about finding my place, Liro Adelwijn. And when I do, it won't come from kissing the ass above me."

Joel clapped a hand over his mouth, and Gib found it impossible to breath. No one in the hallway spoke or moved.

Liro frowned, tipping his head downward. His voice followed suit. "I suggest you come back with us now unless you want further trouble."

His words felt threatening, and Gib found himself wanting to jump to Kezra's defense. The mage trainee put a firm hand on Gib's chest.

Kezra stuck her nose in the air, her persona emanating defiance. "I suggest you leave me to go on my way. No amount of persuasion is going to change my mind. There are so few women soldiers and you two have already shamed one girl sentinel trainee into leaving. My roommate and I are the only ones left and I'll be damned if I back down because of the likes of you."

"*The likes of us?*" Diedrick Lyle's voice had gone shrill. "I'll teach you your place!" He came at her and Kezra faltered back a step, panic flitting across her hard features.

"Don't touch me! Get back!"

She'd never sounded so vulnerable, Gib thought to himself. He watched in horror as Liro also advanced.

Joel seemed to break free of whatever chains were holding him back. "This has to stop."

Not a coward like Diedrick, Liro grabbed Kezra's arm. "Stop your petulant whining now. You'll come with me and be sent to the classes that suit you."

The look in Kezra's eyes was feral. Her voice dropped so low it was more a growl. "Let go of me, or they'll be sending me to the stockades rather than class."

Liro's voice finally spiked as his eyes widened into vicious sapphire orbs. "Are you *threatening* me?"

Kezra met his gaze. "When they've cleaned what's left of you from the floor, they'll see to it that I 'learn my place.'"

Gib stumbled forward, following Joel as the mage trainee swept toward the showdown. Gib didn't know what the two of them were going to do once they got there, but they couldn't just stand there and do nothing. Liro lifted his hand as if to strike Kezra, and Gib gritted his teeth, ready for what might be his last act of bravery. He and Joel both braced themselves to make a lunge when another familiar voice boomed down the corridor.

"What is the meaning of this? Liro Adelwijn, release her!"

Marc Arrio stormed from his office toward the Instructions Master and Liro. Gib barely recognized him as the once jovial Dean of Academy. Any humor in his dark eyes was gone, replaced by a terrifying fire. The same mouth that so enjoyed laughing and smiling was set into a fearsome snarl and he'd seemingly gained a foot in height from authority alone. As Marc broke through the surrounding crowd, Liro did as instructed and threw Kezra's arm aside.

Kezra yanked back but didn't flee. She stood tall and waited for further instructions from the dean. Gib hoped Marc would realize she was not to blame here.

"What is going on?" Marc demanded. "And *why* is it happening out here?"

Diedrick Lyle lifted his voice. "I was merely suggesting beneficial classes for her, as I would any student. She became irrational and came out here to make a scene."

Kezra locked her jaw but kept her mouth shut until she was called upon to speak. Marc didn't immediately turn to her. Instead, he had his own questions for Diedrick.

"Suggesting different classes? Why? Is she falling behind in her studies?"

The Instructions Master's face pinched. "No. I had only suggested classes which may be beneficial to her future. It's my job to oversee the students in Academy and help them succeed."

Marc pointed at Kezra, a signal for her to speak. Her voice was low but carried well in the silent hall. "The benefit of my future would only seem to matter to Master Lyle if I were to conform to his idea of what I should be. I'm not going to be anyone's brainless, spineless, helpless housewife, so I informed him I will not need to learn embroidery or housekeeping. He didn't seem to like my answer."

The dean froze for just an instant, and Gib was positive he saw the corners of the dean's mouth quirk up.

"Really?" Marc coughed and proceeded without laughing. The dean turned back to Diedrick. "Well, I suppose there you have it. She has no plan on being a housewife and therefore declines your suggestions. How about we all move on now?"

Diedrick looked like he'd been sucking on a lemon, and Liro's carefully constructed mask was fooling no one. They were both irate. Kezra, however, had a larger smile than Gib had ever seen before on her face. Part of him wanted to congratulate her on her victory, but he hung back when Joel touched his shoulder.

Joel's voice was cautious. "We should leave."

Gib nodded. He'd momentarily forgotten what his roommate could risk by angering his elder brother. It would be best not to cause any more trouble for the family. Besides, Gib could speak to Kezra later. As it was, she walked directly past them on her way through, and he gave her a small smile. She didn't halt in her pace, but the fierce glint in her eye was enough to let him know she'd seen him.

Gib turned back to his roommate. "All right. Where's this library of yours?"

"Follow me."

Joel led them through the network of corridors and doorways until Gib was thoroughly lost. He hoped one day he'd be able to navigate the building by himself, but the more he saw, the more he began to doubt it. There were times, in these great and beautiful halls, when he missed his home with a fierce heartbreak. What were his brothers doing now? Was their tiny home still standing and keeping them warm? They would survive until he returned to them, wouldn't they? Would it even matter if one or both of them would be sent to war anyway?

"Joel, do you think the council will manage to pass the law that will call for two men from each family to join the sentinels? My brother, Tay, will be old enough next year. If he's drafted, I don't know what will become of him."

Joel's eyes were distant. "I'm not sure. I know my father and the King would never allow it to pass without a battle but—it does seem these days the fight is less and less in their favor." The mage trainee stopped there and Gib felt his stomach drop. "I shall have to find my cousin, Hasain Radek. He's the King's son and sits in on the council meetings already. King Rishi is training him to one day hold a chair there."

Gib nodded. "Yeah. Hasain is the one who brought it up in the first place, that day when he and Nawaz joined me and my friends for our midday meal." Despite his burning face, the question poured from his lips before it could be prevented. "If Hasain is being trained to take a seat on the council and he's the King's son, why isn't he a prince?"

Joel lifted his hand to his mouth to hide a smile. Gib was sure he'd asked something he shouldn't have. Perhaps, despite her insanity, Annwyne had spoken nothing but truths that day in the dining hall.

Joel kept his voice low, hesitating as he spoke. "Hasain isn't a prince because his mother isn't a queen."

Gib's face grew warmer. *Oh.* So that must mean King Rishi had been "entertaining" women before he'd been married to Queen Dahlia. Gib coughed. "I shouldn't have asked that, should I?"

A soft chuckle danced around them as they continued on their way. "In the future, it would be more polite not to ask," Joel replied.

Gib scratched his head and followed along. He supposed he would never learn everything in this big, new world. It was becoming apparent, though, that when in doubt he should remain silent. His thoughts drifted so far away that he bumped into Joel when the mage stopped. Joel laughed in jest, but Gib found himself blushing all over again. "Sorry!"

"No need. But here now, I have something to show you." The mage trainee pulled back the heavy door before them and motioned for Gib to follow him inside.

Gib's jaw dropped at the sight of the library. It was much larger than he'd envisioned—as spacious as at least two of the classroom halls joined together—and row upon row of shelves, twice as tall as Gib, were brimming with books.

"I never imagined it would be so big."

"This is nothing compared to the library in the palace," Joel remarked as he slipped into the room behind Gib and closed the door. "The Royal Archives are at least ten times this size."

"How can there even be so many books in existence to fill a space larger than this?"

"Mmm, many of the books at the palace are political or historical in content while the ones here tend to be educational. But there is also the restricted section at the palace."

Gib raised a curious eyebrow. "What's in the restricted section?"

"Oh, you know, anything that may be controversial or considered too dangerous for the common folk to get their hands on." The mage trainee led Gib toward an empty table as he spoke in a delighted tone. "When I've finished my schooling and apprenticeship, I'll be allowed access to the ancient magery tomes kept there. I've been dreaming of reading such texts since childhood."

"I have no idea what any of that means," Gib replied. "But I'll take your word for it."

Joel chuckled and then pointed at the chair. "I'll save my breath and your time. Trying to explain magic to the ungifted is like trying to row a boat upstream directly following a springtime thaw—futile and tiring. Sit here. I'm going to go find some reading material for you."

The mage trainee darted away and Gib was left alone to take in his surroundings. The room was dimly lit by lanterns strung along the marbled walls—lanterns blazing with an odd-colored fire. No, not fire, Gib realized as he examined the strange source of illumination. Fire wouldn't have been so well contained. These orbs were perfectly circular in shape and glowed an eerie shade of sapphire. It had to be some sort of magic.

Though no hearth or fireplace was visible, the entire room was bathed in drowsy heat. Gib wrinkled his nose as he tried to find the source of the warmth, but the longer he searched, the more convinced the sentinel trainee became that the temperature of the room was also being manipulated by magery. He would have to ask Joel—

"Here are a couple books to get you started." His roommate returned at that moment, carrying no less than half a dozen books in his arms.

Gib's eyes widened. "You want me to read them *all*?"

Joel grinned as he took a seat and spread the gathered books onto the tabletop. "Well, not all at once. Pick one."

Gib studied each of the books in turn. The bindings were all worn and fraying, and a few of them were so faded by age it was hard to read the titles. He squinted his eyes.

"May I make a suggestion as to which you read first?"

Gib nodded so Joel reached out and pushed one of the books toward the younger boy. It stood out from the rest immediately. The cover was dyed in shades of deep reds, sunlit yellows, and shades of blue that reminded Gib of the sky. Whimsical drawings were etched into the front panel, creatures he didn't recognize and surely were not anything of this world. His eyes scanned the title that was crafted in shimmering gold lettering. *Tales of Fae.*

"Is this a children's book?" Gib asked as he ran his fingers along the stonewashed binding.

"It's a collection of fables about the Old World," the mage trainee replied. "Legends and myths about the shaping of the world and how the human race came to be. My mother used to read it to me when I was still very young. It was one of the books I was given when I first learned how to read, so you should be able to pick through it with little trouble." Joel motioned for Gib to open the book. "Go on. Give it a try."

Gib felt ridiculous being asked to read a book meant for a youngling, but Joel's smile was soft and reassuring, so Gib made the decision to give it his best attempt. Anything to please his roommate. Carefully opening the cover, Gib focused his eyes on the first page.

In the beginning, there was only darkness. The Gods lived in the Void of Nothing for ten thousand millennia. They lived without purpose, without identity, without thought. And then two of these deities all at once did think, and they thought to leave. The Goddess Daya and her sister Chhaya separated themselves from the Void and forged a realm. It was a world without rain, without sun, without any kind of natural law. But it was something other than darkness.

As time passed, Daya and Chhaya filled their new world with things. Great mountains made of crystal, seas of black velvet stretched into infinity, and air with no wind but crackling with storms. For a while, only the Two inhabited this world, but after many centuries, Daya and Chhaya began to miss the siblings they had abandoned within the Void, so they thought to create a sentient race to inhabit their realm.

The Two forged a beautiful creature in their own image, sculpted by magic and set down into the world. He was their son and they loved him. For a time, the child of the Two was content to explore his new realm, but soon he began to long for companionship.

And so Daya and Chhaya created siblings for their firstborn, one thousand brethren total, all beautiful and as unchanging as the world around them. They were immortal, borne of magic, perfect.

For many ages, the Children of The Two existed in harmony, but they had not the control or wisdom of the Gods and so they began to fight among themselves, allowing emotions such as greed and jealousy to govern their lives. Daya and Chhaya saw their children at war and it displeased them, and so the Two sought out their most precious son, their firstborn, and asked him to go out into the realm and bring peace. The son did as he was commanded, but it was to no avail. His siblings would not listen to him.

Daya and Chhaya became angered at their children's defiance. They thought to undo the entire race, to send them back to nothingness, but their firstborn son begged for the lives of his siblings, and The Two loved him so much they agreed to be merciful.

Daya and Chhaya saw the error of their way. The magic of the world had made their children powerful and arrogant. And so The Two set out to create a second realm, vowing not to repeat the same mistakes. They gave this new world water, wind, earth, and fire. Daya gave the world a sun while Chhaya painted stars across the sky. Together, they crafted trees, mountains, grass, rivers, and oceans. And then they gave life to it all, but no magic. This world was to be governed by the laws of nature.

The Two began to populate the world with creatures. Magnificent lizards with leathered wings, hoofed animals with horns of ivory, enormous birds of prey that circled on high, and thousands of others. But Daya and Chhaya were still saddened by the betrayal of their children in the Otherealm, so they made new children in their image to fill the young world. The human race was born. To be certain that humanity would not befall the same fate as the Children in the Otherealm, Daya and Chhaya infused the new world with consequence. They gave the humans something to fear and respect. Death. For this world was bound by the rules of mortality.

The Children in the Otherealm were filled with jealousy when they heard of this newly created world. Many of them felt betrayed, abandoned by their Mothers. Some begged the Two Goddesses for forgiveness while others simply wanted to defy them further.

It was not long before the Children of The Two discovered a way to escape their birthplace. Defiant and curious by nature, they traversed the plane which divided the immortal and mortal realms and infiltrated the new world, bringing the magic of the Otherealm with them.

The Two Goddesses attempted to contain the magic, but it was rogue and chaotic and not easy to control. It spread like wildfire through the new world, and the races within became entranced by the powers it offered them. Seeing the mortal races manipulating the magic, many of The Children of the Two became infuriated, for they were of the opinion that such magic was meant only for them.

Of all the mortal races, the humans seemed to benefit the most by the newfound magic. They learned they could perform extraordinary tasks—create fire from nothingness, heal a wounded comrade, even see into the future. The Children of the Two saw these humans, so young and bold, and some grew jealous. They sought to destroy the humans; the race they feared was the favorite of their Mothers.

War broke out between the races. It ravaged the mortal realm. The fighting went on for so long and with such ferocity it was thought all humans would die. The loss of life was immense and yet neither side would back down.

It was because of this bravery that some of the Children of The Two had a change of heart. They began to side with the humans and other mortal races. When such alliances were discovered, the war came to a peak. Battles, powered by magic and bloodlust, scarred the surface of the mortal realm and great cracks were torn into the world's crust. In these places, to this day, magic still bleeds through from the Otherealm, traces of the cataclysmic events of ages lost.

Gib raised his chestnut eyes toward his friend. "Do you think any of this is true?"

Joel shrugged. "I doubt we, as humans, will ever know all the answers. There is so much in this world which can't be explained." His eyes twinkled as he set his hands onto the open page. "But there is beauty in the unknown, is there not?"

Gib found himself staring at Joel's delicate hands. "I'm not sure I like not knowing what the future holds for me."

"Well," replied the mage trainee in a soft voice. "Whatever it is, I'm certain that you're destined for greatness, Gibben Nemesio."

Gib couldn't look the other boy in the eye.

Since the room had no windows, it was difficult to judge how long the two boys stayed in the library. The evening meal had to be close because by the time Joel announced they should leave, Gib's stomach was rumbling obnoxiously.

Joel started to collect the books scattered across the table, and Gib was quick to follow the mage trainee's example. "I'll help you put these away."

A trace of a smile came to Joel's lips as he stacked the books neatly in his arms. "All right. Follow me. I'll show you where they go so that if you ever come to the library alone, you'll know where to find them."

Gib nodded. He planned to come back as time permitted. He'd made admirable progress through *Tales of Fae*, despite being a poor reader. Joel had been there to help, offering to pronounce a word when Gib was unable to sound it out himself, but overall, he'd been able to muddle through the text without assistance. He would need several sessions at the library to finish the book, but Gib already felt an increase in his confidence. He, the uneducated farm boy, was actually reading. Who knew what else he could do if he set his mind to it.

"Will the library be open during Midwinter?" Gib asked.

"I believe so. Most of the local students go home for the celebration, but there are those who live too far away to make the journey—" The mage trainee's voice cut out without warning.

Gib glanced up and frowned when he saw that Joel had gone rigid in his place. "What's wrong?"

Another boy about their age stood in their path. His arms were loaded with books as well and his green eyes were wide and fixed on Joel like he'd seen a ghost. Gib couldn't be sure if the stranger had paled upon seeing them or if he was naturally so fair.

Joel's mouth moved but not a sound came forth. He took a sharp breath and turned his face away from this newcomer. "Uh—" Gib had never seen Joel so out of sorts. "I–I'm sorry," Joel finally managed to gasp.

Gib didn't know who the apology was directed at.

The other boy leapt back as if he'd been burned. Flattening himself against one side of the bookshelves, he allowed them to pass. Gib frowned. He and Joel weren't lepers. He didn't understand why the boy seemed so determined not to touch them. The boy's somewhat homely face was pinched, and he muttered some sort of undecipherable apology.

"Th–thank you," came Joel's stuttered response.

The mage trainee quickly sped past and Gib had to run to keep up—when Joel stopped suddenly they almost collided.

Gib made a noise somewhere deep in his throat. "*Chhaya's bane*, Joel. What is going on?"

Joel turned to look back at the boy they'd just passed, eyes brimming with cold resignation. He put a hand on Gib's shoulder. "I'm sorry if this becomes awkward. I just—I have to." The mage trainee didn't elaborate any further as he went back to the strange, cowering boy who had by now turned his back on them.

The boy turned to look Joel in the eye once more. Gib was sure he'd never seen that shade of crimson on a human face before. The boy flinched back and pleaded in a shrill voice, "Oh, can't you just leave?"

Gib stayed back a pace or two and listened.

"Syther Lais." Joel's voice was cold but sorrowful. "I was beginning to think you'd left Silver entirely."

The boy shifted under the weight of Joel's eyes. "I haven't gone anywhere."

"All the more suspicious I haven't seen you then." Joel's voice was bitter. "Where did you go, Syther, when I needed you most? Why did you choose to abandon me when I was most vulnerable? Was it something I did to you? Did I misuse you in some way?"

A rock formed in the pit of Gib's stomach. Oh. *Oh*. This boy must be the one who was—involved with Joel. And if he'd been involved then but not now, that meant—Gib clenched his jaw. It was odd how quickly the anger rose. He whole-heartedly disliked this boy, Syther Lais, but knew he was being unfair since he didn't know the boy's side of the story. Still,

Joel was his friend and had been wronged by this boy.

Syther squirmed back into the shelves. "You—you know why I had to leave." He glanced around. "You didn't even ask before you went and ran your mouth to everyone."

Joel gasped. "I didn't know you would leave me for that! I came back to my room, our room, and needed *your* support. You didn't even tell me you were leaving. I came back to an empty room and had no one to turn to."

Sweat had beaded up on Syther's forehead and he was looking around again, more desperately than before. Finally, the boy broke down into shuddering whispers. "I couldn't stay! People couldn't know about me."

"So I was to be a lone martyr? If I'd known that I may have reconsidered."

"*You didn't ask!*" Syther jumped and lowered his voice. "We don't all have rich families and noble names to fall back on, Joel Adelwijn. I have to pay to put myself through Academy and if I fail, I'm the one who ends up on the street. I can't afford to lose my job. I can't wait to find someone who will hire me despite my home life. I don't have that luxury."

Gib hadn't considered these possibilities while judging Syther. If this boy was from a more modest background, he couldn't chance being caught.

Joel hesitated. He sighed deeply. "I'm sorry. I didn't think about that when I—I was just so tired of hiding."

Syther glared at the floor. "Can I go now? I have work to do."

Joel's eyes were damp. "I'm sorry I bothered you. It won't happen again." He whirled around and stormed past Gib.

Gib hesitated before he followed. Syther's eyes went wide. He reached toward Joel for a fraction of a moment but withdrew his hand quickly. Then Syther lowered his scarlet face and slipped around the bend in the bookshelves.

Gib frowned. He didn't like Syther, but he hoped for a day when the boy wouldn't need to hide.

The following morning found Gib in a fog at his training class. He was going through the motions while sparring, but his mind was worlds away. He kept thinking back to his brothers on the farm and whether or not they'd be all right throughout the winter. He likewise continued to think about Joel and whether or not the mage trainee was faring well. After yesterday's run-in in the library, Joel was quiet. He pretended not to be crying, so Gib pretended not to notice. It seemed like the only civil thing to do.

Because his mind wasn't where it should have been, Gib failed to hear Kezra yelling at him or see Tarquin wince. The full length of Diddy's practice sword came crashing down on Gib's hand before he even knew what was happening.

Gib gasped for air and dropped his own practice sword, clutching the wrist of his right hand to his chest. Blinding white pain shot through the length of his arm. His wrist had made a wet pop followed by a crunch, and he wasn't entirely sure he could move his fingers.

Diddy dropped his sword and rushed to Gib's aid, the prince's face a flurry of emotions. "Oh, Gib, I'm so sorry! I thought you saw me coming at you. I didn't mean it—oh, where's the help?"

Otho Dahkeel, one of the assistants of Weapons Master Roland, jogged over and demanded to look at the injury. Gib had a difficult time pulling his good hand back long enough to let Otho see. The assistant determined additional help was needed, and a moment later Roland stormed over, his mouth set in a grimace as he eyed Gib's swollen hand. "All right, Nemesio, to the Healer's Pavilion. You know where it is?"

"Uh, no. I don't think so, sir."

Roland nodded toward his assistant. "Otho, take him there. That wrist is broken, I'd reckon, and needs a healer to have a look at it."

Eyes wide with horror, Diddy clapped a hand over his mouth. "I'm *so* sorry! I should have been paying closer attention. It's all my fault."

The Weapons Master rolled his eyes. "No, Didier, this is Gib's fault. Clearly he was the one not paying attention. This is unfortunate for him, but a good lesson to all." He raised his voice so everyone could hear him. "Don't think your enemy is going to wait for you to be ready! If you become distracted while on the battlefield, you'll die. Likewise, if your enemy becomes distracted then you need to act. Waiting for them to focus on you may be the polite thing to do, but such civilities are best left to the palace courts. 'Please' and 'thank you' don't win wars!"

Gib flinched, his face hot. He wanted to take his leave, but Otho hadn't offered to move just yet. The assistant, like everyone else, was focused on Roland. "I'm sure Gibben Nemesio will testify to the fact that it is better to not be distracted. Isn't that right, Nemesio?"

Gib fought to manage a response with all eyes on him. "Y–yes, sir."

Roland lowered his voice enough to no longer be quite so intimidating. "All right then. Off with you. If luck is on your side, you won't have to lift another sword until after the Midwinter break."

Gib bit down on his tongue and followed behind Otho. They walked in silence away from the training grounds. Once again, Gib had no idea where he was being led, and he nearly had to run to keep up with Otho's longer, quicker strides. They walked along the outside of the academy building, the side which overlooked the Tempist River. On the opposite riverbank Gib could see the bustle of Traders Row. People swarmed the street like an army of ants as they went about their business. He wondered briefly if Liza was out there, keeping the peace.

Gib's legs burned nearly as badly as his swollen wrist by the time the Healers Pavilion loomed into view. At first he had no idea they had arrived. When he thought of a pavilion, he pictured a small, open structure. This pale limestone building was grand, with multiple floors and wings. The uppermost landings on each branch stood wide open, with nothing more than pillars to support the tiled roof. He imagined the infirmed were allowed to catch fresh air in these places during fair weather, but for now, they lay barren.

Otho pointed Gib toward the door and left with no further instruction or farewell. Gib glared at the back of the assistant's head until he disappeared around the corner of the building. *All right. Apparently I'm to do this alone.* With a groan, he walked in the door.

The interior of the building was busy. Numerous students, all wearing the blue jerkins Kezra had mentioned, were attending to different people. Ailments seemed to range from minor sprains to one man who was bleeding quite heavily from his nose to a woman who looked as though she might be in labor. She was being led down the spacious corridor when Gib heard someone call to him.

"You there, sentinel student. Are you injured? Do you need assistance?"

Gib whirled around so fast he nearly lost his balance, and the act of catching himself caused a bolt of pain to shoot up his arm. With a wince, he righted himself and turned his eyes onto an older woman dressed in a simple blue tunic. "Y–yes. Master Roland Korbin thinks I may have broken my wrist."

The healer was a motherly looking woman with salt-and-pepper hair and gentle eyes. She stepped up to Gib and smoothed down his curls. "The sword got away from you, eh? All right, little one, follow me."

In a way, this woman reminded Gib of his own mother. She'd been dead for so long, but he suddenly wondered how she would have treated him had this sort of injury happened on the farm.

The farm. His chest tightened. What would he do if he couldn't tend the farm anymore? Surely this wouldn't be his end, would it? The healers must be able to help him, right? If his hand were to heal incorrectly, he wouldn't be able to lift a sword again either. What would he do if he couldn't be a soldier or a farmer? What would become of Tayver and Calisto? What would become of him? A million questions raced through his mind as the kind lady led him into a modestly sized room and seated him on a cot.

Again, the old woman ruffled his curls. "You stay here. I'll let the healer apprentice know you're waiting." When he didn't respond quickly enough, she reached out and cupped his chin in her work-rough hand.

"You'll be all right. Calm your nerves."

Gib nodded and did his best to wait patiently. But the sounds all around him put him on alert. Someone was groaning, pottery jars crashed in the distance, someone else was vomiting, a baby cried—Gib blinked and tried not to think about everything going on around him. His breathing was just coming back under control when the shuffling of feet indicated someone entering the small room. Gib glanced up and was met with a familiar face.

Nawaz Arrio's shocking blue eyes sparkled and a lopsided smile broke across his face. "Aren't you one of Diddy's friends?"

"Gib Nemesio." Gib started to offer his hand for a shake but his wrist made him think better of it.

"Gib. That's right. The farmer boy with the stout heart. I remember." Nawaz's attention zeroed in on the injured hand. He indicated the ailing limb with a nod and cock of an eyebrow. "Your bravery get you into trouble today, did it?"

"Master Roland thinks it may be broken," Gib replied. He blinked, taking a closer look at Nawaz's blue jerkin. "I didn't know you're a healer."

Nawaz carefully took Gib's aching hand and seemed to be giving it a thorough inspection. "Yeah, well, we all have to do something, don't we?"

"Healing is a rare gift, isn't it? I guess that means you have a secure job at least."

Nawaz's mouth slanted into a thin line. "I guess so, whether it's the job I want or not. How did you do this? You've got a couple different fractures here."

Gib's mouth was as dry as cotton. "Frac–fractures? Is that like a break? Will you be able to do something with it? I've got to be able to use my hands—"

"Might have to amputate it."

Gib stared at Nawaz with a gaping mouth. His heart had all but stopped inside his chest. "*Wh–what?*"

Blue eyes sparkled with mischief as the healer barked a laugh. "Relax! It was a joke. Just seeing if you were paying attention."

Gib's vision blurred. "A joke? I nearly died!" He groaned when Nawaz's only response was to continue laughing. "I thought you were being serious. You're terrible at this!"

"Yeah I am, but a rare gift must be utilized, right?" Nawaz wiped a laughter-induced tear from his cheek and cleared his throat as if to get down to business. "All right, so I'm going to get the bones set and started on their mending, then we'll get you a splint—"

"What's going on in here? I hear entirely too much laughter."

Gib did a double take when Dean Arrio stepped inside the small room.

He gave Gib a sideways glance and smiled. "Aren't you Liza's little brother? Gibben, right?"

Gib was unable to hide his surprise. He'd assumed being Dean of Academy would take most of the man's time. Then again, perhaps he needed a break from working with the likes of Diedrick Lyle. "Dean Marc? What are you doing here?"

Marc glanced down at his own healer's jerkin and nodded. "Oh right. I suppose this would be confusing to a newcomer. I was a healer first. Academy came later on. So whenever I get time or the pavilion has an excess of the sickly, I come over here to see if I can be useful. I can already tell I saved you just in time. This is Nawaz."

Nawaz folded his arms over his chest. "Yeah, yeah, save the introductions. He's friends with Diddy. I've met him before."

Marc gave Gib a sorrowful look in the eye. "You've met Nawaz before? I'm sorry."

Nawaz shot an ugly look at the dean. "Very funny. Anyway, Gib's got a couple fractures in his wrist cluster—the hamate and triquetral—so I'll make sure they're set and get them bonding. He'll need a splint."

Marc nodded along. "Light duty for a handful of sennights."

"Yeah, I'll get him a note for Roland and then he can get the hell out of here."

The dean pointed at Nawaz. "Remember to watch your mouth. You're at work!" When Nawaz rolled his eyes, Marc cuffed the back of his head. "Sorry, Gibben. I'm not usually so forward but I'm allowed to misuse my nephew a little more than the other trainees."

Gib nodded as the puzzle pieces came together. Marc Arrio. Nawaz Arrio. Both were loud and prone to laughter, though either could be goaded into outbursts if the situation called. They looked alike too. Both were tall and fair featured with dark hair and expressive eyes. "He's your nephew? I'm sorry."

Marc tipped his head back in laughter.

Nawaz narrowed his eyes. "Watch it, Nemesio. You're in my care now."

Gib smiled but declined to say more. He waited while Nawaz took the injured hand again and set to work on it.

"There's gonna be some tingling and warmth. That's normal. Let me know if the pain spikes."

Gib swallowed his nerves and nodded. "All right."

It took a moment for anything to happen at all. Nawaz seemed to be focusing intently. Gib swallowed as he waited. *Nothing is happening. It's not like my wrist can tell him what's wrong, can it?* But Nawaz seemed to know exactly where it was broken. Maybe the wound really could speak to him.

Healer-mages were known to call upon magic to aid with their healing. Perhaps Nawaz was using magic to help him right now. Gib decided to save his questions for Joel, who wouldn't laugh at them.

A moment later, the tingling set in just as Nawaz had said, but it was more intense than Gib imagined. Back on the farm, he'd sometimes slept wrong and had an arm or leg fall asleep. When he'd try to use the limb, it would feel like it was being engulfed in pinpricks and flame. This feeling was similar but more intense. He stiffened, a strangled cry escaping his throat.

Nawaz never broke his concentration. "Pain?"

Gib took a breath and thought. "N–No. Not really. Just hot and—odd."

Both Marc and his nephew nodded as if that were normal, and Nawaz didn't offer to let up. Despite the discomfort, Gib was mildly reassured—and determined to never need to be healed again.

He watched as Marc hovered over his nephew, observing every movement. If the dean's presence made Nawaz uncomfortable, he didn't show it. Marc frowned at one point and guided the younger healer. "Ground yourself. Remember to stay grounded."

Nawaz didn't look up from what he was doing but did manage to snipe back. "I *am* grounded. Will you just go get me a splint?"

Soon enough, Gib's bones had been set and started on their way to mending. He left the pavilion with a splint wrapped about his hand and a note detailing that he was not to resume heavy duty until further word was given from the healers. Nawaz and Marc had both assured him that he would regain full mobility of his hand and fingers. Gib hoped they weren't mistaken.

CHAPTER SIX

For the next several days, Gib found himself doing a lot of sweeping, feeding horses, and helping pick up the training swords and equipment—mostly one-handed jobs. Honestly, he wasn't sure if the "light duty" was any better than his actual training. He decided it was worse when Kezra began joking about his "lovely splint bracelet" and even Tarquin, Diddy, and Nage chuckled along.

On the last day of their training cycle before rest, Lady Beatrice from his Ardenian Law class came to ask Master Roland if she could borrow Gib. He was grateful. He turned a smug look back on his friends as they glared his way, their breath visible in the chilly air. He followed behind the professor, shedding his cloak as soon as they stepped inside the hall. Beatrice smiled, the smallest traces of wrinkles forming around her plump lips and olive-colored eyes.

"Could you deliver this for me?" She extended a letter to him.

Gib looked at the sealed envelope. "Yes, m'lady. Where should I take it?"

"To Dean Arrio's office. I expect when you're done with the task, it will be time for midday meal." She winked at him. "Let the others clean up after themselves for a day." She smiled.

Gib returned the gesture. He didn't mind pulling his weight, but it would be a lie to say he enjoyed the duties. He imagined he wouldn't make a very good servant.

"Thank you, Lady Beatrice."

"No, no. Thank you, Gibben. I'll see you in class later."

She dismissed him and he turned to make the trek to Marc's office.

It was odd being in the halls during class time. He was the only person there and his lone footsteps echoed off the high arches and limestone ceilings. An eerie feeling rose on the back of his neck, and he turned once or twice to be sure he wasn't being watched. Only the stone gargoyles which perched atop the pillars stared back at him, uncanny and unmoving. He hurried along.

As the dean's office door came into view, Gib nearly broke out into a full run to get to it. Red-faced, he rapped a fist on the maple wood and waited. The shuffling of feet came on the other side, and when the door opened, he forgot his manners and began to advance without permission.

"What is *your* business here?" The snide voice of Diedrick Lyle caught him unaware.

Gib cleared his throat. "Uh. I've been sent with a message for Dean Arrio."

The Instructions Master stuck his nose in the air, but Marc called out from further within. "Who is it, Lyle?"

"One of the students. He says he has a message for you."

Gib thought to look around Lyle but, true to the nature of any stubborn mule, the Instructions Master refused to move even a little. It was only when Marc gave the word that Diedrick rolled his eyes and stepped aside.

Gib squeezed through what little space had been given him. He could feel shrewd eyes on the back of his head as he made his way to the dean's desk. With a bow, he extended his arm, letter in hand. "Lady Beatrice asked me to bring this to you."

Marc hesitated for just an instant before saying, "What does my wife want? Couldn't she have come down here herself?"

"Your wife?" Gib almost dropped the letter but managed to grab it before the paper could slip through his fingers. "I didn't know Lady Beatrice was married to you. I would have never even imagined you—" Gib quickly tried to think of how to correct his blunder.

His words were met with laughter. "Yeah, I could see that. She's smarter than me. I got lucky. I'm still not sure why she said yes when I asked her to marry me."

"Well, I didn't mean—it's just that she's not—you seem more free-spirited than she." Gib gave up there and groaned. "Sorry. Forget I said anything." He handed over the letter.

Marc's dark eyes danced as he took it and waved toward one of the plush chairs. "Thank you, Gibben. Have a seat for a moment if you have one to spare. She may have requested a response."

The door slammed behind them and Gib was sure he heard Diedrick Lyle muttering under his breath about not being able to get any work done.

Doing as told, Gib ignored the Instructions Master and sat in the same chair he'd barely touched on his first visit to the office. Without looking up from his letter, Marc cocked an eyebrow and pressed coyly, "Ah, good. I see you've gotten over your fear of chairs."

Gib snorted a little. "It took some work, but yes. I've also grown accustomed to sleeping in an actual bed."

There was some sniveling from Diedrick's corner of the office, but Marc must have had years of experience in ignoring the Instructions Master.

Eyes still dancing, the dean smiled broadly at Gib. "Good to hear. How's your hand faring?"

"It doesn't hurt. I think it's healing well."

"Good. Apparently Nawaz can do something right when he applies himself." The dean glanced toward Lyle, who was not looking at them as he scribbled ferociously with his quill. Marc lowered his voice a little. "He's a little like me—lazy and unfortunately smart enough to get other people to pick up the slack for him. Sound about right, Lyle?"

The scribbling stopped abruptly, and the Instructions Master turned his pinched, scarlet face upward. "Is that funny to you?" His mouth gaped for a moment, and then he stabbed his quill into the inkwell, going back to work with more tenacity than ever. He muttered and spat under his breath about being undervalued and how not everyone would put up with such an insufferable supervisor.

Gib bit his bottom lip to keep from smiling.

Marc laughed. "Yes, yes, Diedrick. You're good for putting up with me. That's why you get to take extra time off as needed."

If the Instructions Master heard him, he made no indication of it.

Gib looked at the floor to keep from grinning. It really wasn't his place to laugh at someone so much older who held such authority, but it was difficult to be civil to someone so miserable.

Gib was glad when Marc dismissed him, not because he wanted to part ways with the dean but because he wasn't sure how much longer he could handle Diedrick's scalding glares without bursting into flame. Marc had no return message for Lady Beatrice, so Gib found himself in the same deserted hallway once more, meandering toward the dining hall. It wasn't time for the midday meal yet, but the bell was due to ring any moment.

As he passed through the corridors, another eerie sensation rose within him—not the feeling of being watched so much as the feeling of not being alone. He rubbed his injured wrist in an attempt to ward off the chill, but it did little to help. *I'm not running again.* He set his mouth in a firm line and refused to speed up.

"There you are. I was beginning to think you'd abandoned me."

Gib whirled around, but the empty hall was all that awaited him. *Where did that voice come from?* He started to call out but stopped short when someone else replied.

"So long as the pay hasn't been compromised, I'm still here."

Gib didn't know where either of the voices came from nor were the voices familiar. *I should keep moving.* As he took another step, the sentinel trainee realized a door stood slightly ajar to his left, which was where the two voices must have come from.

"Yes, yes. Don't worry about your pay. Worry more about whether I and the others trust you or not."

"Trust? You'd trust a murderer?"

Gib froze in place. *Murderer?* What were these two talking about?

"Watch your mouth," the first voice hissed. "There are eyes and ears everywhere."

"Soon there'll be all the more. Better make this quick, before the bell rings." The second voice was rougher, not as well trained as the first.

The first man snorted. "Then take this and be gone. You know where to go and when. Don't be seen."

Coins jingled, and the second man spoke. "This is only half."

"As agreed. You get the rest when he's dead."

"And the plan remains unchanged then?"

"Of course. Radek is overly confident. He's not as smart as he thinks he is. You do as we've agreed and you'll have free access to him."

Gib's stomach churned. *Radek? The royal family?* He glanced around, wishing the dean were there with him. Marc would know what to do.

The second man snorted. "I've never known a king to be unprotected."

The hall tilted and Gib wasn't sure he'd be able to catch his balance. *This is about the King? They mean to murder King Rishi?* A terrible humming rose in his ears.

The first voice leered, "Rishi Radek is unlike any king Arden has ever known. It's under his idiocy that women and commoners are able to lord around as if they're the equals of the learned men. It would be dangerous to leave him on the throne. His arrogance can be used against him."

Gib grasped the wall with his good hand. His knees felt weak. What should he do? He didn't know who was in the room and couldn't risk opening the door to look. He clutched at his side and tried to will away the panic.

The bells began to ring. The two men in the room stopped talking and Gib could hear their feet shuffling. His fear spiked when he realized they would have to come through the door he was standing beside.

Gib backed away knowing he would be caught if they emerged. A moment later, students swarmed the corridor and he looked for a teacher. He saw only students. Who could he tell?

He waited a moment more to see if the door would open, and when it didn't, his feet moved of their own accord toward the door. He could open the door and pretend he'd come to the wrong place. But at least he'd have seen their faces.

Gib's stomach knotted. He was likely to get a slit throat or gashed gut for his troubles, but he had to act quickly. Palms sweaty and breath held fast, he slammed his eyes closed and pushed the door open. The blood was rushing in his ears as he waited for whatever fate would befall him. Maybe they would bash him over the head or break his neck. Maybe they'd tie him up and drag him away to do something worse. Maybe they'd leave him there to die of heart failure.

Gib dared open one eye. Nothing. He opened the other. No one was inside the assembly hall. The room stood empty. Across from him, on the far wall, another door led outside. He could see through the windows that the outer courts were already teaming with people. He couldn't tell who the two men were.

Leaning back against the doorframe, he blew out a long breath. Was he lucky for having missed them and sparing his own life, or was he an idiot for not getting a glimpse of the traitors who were speaking about murdering the King? His mouth went dry. Who should he tell? He didn't know where to start. Who could he find who had connections to the King and would listen to him?

Joel. He turned and flew toward their room.

"Joel! Joel, I have to speak to you!" Gib didn't bother to knock before he threw the door open. "It's important!" His boots skidded to a halt when he realized his roommate wasn't alone. Hasain Radek was standing in front of the window.

Joel smiled from the edge of his bed. "Oh, Gib! There you are—" His smile fell away. "Are you all right? Is something wrong?"

Gib imagined he must look quite a sight. He knew he felt like he'd been through hell. He glanced back and forth between Joel and Hasain. Both of them scrutinized him carefully. "Hasain. You're here too."

Joel nodded. "You asked that I find him for you. You had questions about the draft. But are you all right? You look awful." He swept over, white mage robes fluttering as he moved, and placed a cool hand on Gib's shoulder.

The sentinel trainee looked up with wide eyes. "The King. The King is in danger but I don't know who or when—"

Crystal blue eyes went wide as the mage trainee put his entire arm around Gib. The embrace was warm and comforting despite Joel's harried words. "What do you mean? What is this about the King?" He led the younger boy over to the chair at their desk and sat him down before kneeling before him. "Gib, what are you talking about?"

Gib's mind was muddled and confused. He squeezed his eyes shut. "I brought a message to Dean Marc. When I was done there, I came down the hall and heard these voices. Two men. I don't know who and I didn't get a chance to see either of them. I–I'm sorry. If I'd been faster or braver I could have—"

Joel shook his head and behind him Hasain frowned. The mage student's voice was calming in the middle of all the chaos. "Just tell us what you know."

Gib tried to refocus. "Uh—they were talking about paying the killer. They even said it would be murder. I could hear the coins jingling. The one guy said he'd pay half now and half when the job was done. They were talking about how the King was bad for the country because he'd allowed women and commoners to work their way up in society."

Hasain waved one of his large hands in the air. "You said you didn't see them?"

"N–no." He couldn't look the King's son in the eye. "I'm sorry."

Joel glanced back at Hasain. The young Radek lord shrugged and stuck his nose in the air. "You said you heard this down by Marc Arrio's office? It was probably a disgruntled servant or teacher. I'm sure nothing will come of it."

"Don't you think you should at least warn King Rishi? What if it's something serious?" Joel asked.

Hasain narrowed his slim eyes further. "Joel, you've spent too much time with this farmer. It's as if you're new to the city yourself. You know how important my father is. The King receives death threats every moonturn. It almost always turns out to be someone of menial service or even a vagrant—typically the lazy people who feel they haven't been given enough privileges."

Gib clenched his good hand into a fist. "No, you're not listening. They were exchanging money, Hasain! Someone wants the King *dead*."

Hasain was as apathetic as ever. "As I already said, many people want the King dead. And perhaps money was exchanged. That is a fool's loss. Even if they carry out their attempt, they'll never get to my father. He's well protected and clever. They'll never take him."

Gib bit his bottom lip but knew when it was time to stand down. Joel glowered at his cousin. "I hope for your father's sake your arrogance is justified."

Hasain lifted one brow, smiling wolfishly. "I give you my word, for Arden's sake, my arrogance is justified." The young Radek lord turned and swept toward the door. "I have to go. There will be council sessions later and Father has asked that I attend. I'll let you know if I see any assassins." He waved coyly and left without waiting for even one more word.

Gib's jaw dropped. "Did that just happen? How can he not even care?"

Joel let out a deep sigh. "I know how it seems, but you have to believe me when I say that this is just Hasain's way. He's every bit as arrogant as his father and about half as smart." He winced as if he suddenly realized what he just said. "Half as *wise*. Hasain is young. We're all prone to mistakes when we're young."

"I'm young but I don't pretend anyone is invincible. I hope Hasain is right, of course." Gib clenched his jaw. "I also hope that some form of reality rides along and topples him from his high horse."

Joel laughed into his hands. "Gib! Manners."

"It's true," Gib replied as he rolled his eyes. "We could tell your father. Would Seneschal Koal have a chance to hear us?"

"He might." Joel hesitated. "It's just—"

"Hasain really was right, wasn't he? People threaten the King all the time." Gib couldn't force himself to believe it even as the words fell out of his mouth.

Joel pursed his lips. "I know how that sounds, believe me, I do. But—it's true. Without knowing who the men were or when or where they planned to strike I'm afraid there won't be much anyone can do. It would take more time and energy to look for these men, who may yet regain their senses and call the whole thing off, than it would to simply pay closer attention to where the King is at all times."

Gib threw his hands into the air. "But they could at least do that much!"

"I agree, but King Rishi is already as well protected as he'll allow himself to be." Joel elaborated with a patient sigh. "Our king is very stubborn. My father has gone around in circles with him for years. Queen Dahlia and the children are always guarded to the best of Arden's means but King Rishi himself—he prefers his freedom."

"But he could be *killed!*"

Joel took Gib's good hand and the sentinel trainee felt his stomach roll. "I promise to tell my father what you have told me. If you'd like, you could go speak with Dean Marc. He may be willing to speak to Father as well. I just don't want you to be terribly disappointed if nothing comes of it."

Gib groaned as he glared at the floor. "All right. If no one is concerned but me, I guess I'll let it go. Apparently in Silver, things like death threats are just another way of saying hello."

Joel's face creased and Gib wished immediately that he could take the words back. Joel didn't seem to take offense, however.

"I promise to do what I can. Now, you should go. Eat something and get to class."

"Yeah. All right." Gib headed for the door. He stopped at the threshold and looked back. His heart was hammering in his chest. "You should come with me. It isn't good for you to skip your midday meal just because of—what others may say."

Joel's fair face flushed in such a way Gib could scarcely look at him. He swallowed and seemed to look for words. "I—uh, th–thank you. I'll eat. I promise. You may still be able to find your friends."

"They could be your friends too. I know we're all younger than you and kind of bottom of the barrel scrapings, but we're all trustworthy, I assure you." When the young mage wrung his hands, Gib backed off. "All right. Not today. But consider it in the future."

Gib turned to leave and could only just make out the sound of his roommate's small voice. "Thank you."

The discussion at midday meal was so cryptic Gib wondered what he was getting himself into. On their eve away from training and responsibility, the group of friends decided to go out into the city to celebrate. Gib didn't feel like festivities after eavesdropping on the would-be assassin earlier that day, but Tarquin and the others were persistent.

"You haven't been to the Rose Bouquet yet?" Nage asked, mouth hanging agape as if it were some kind of huge scandal.

Gib shook his head. Clearly he was out of the loop yet again. "What is a Rose Bouquet?"

Tarquin and Kezra exchanged glances and snickered.

"It's only the most famous tavern in all of Silver!" Tarquin snorted. "Come with us. You'll have fun."

"They're accepting of everyone at the Rose," Kezra added. A wry smile came to her lips. "Even cripples such as yourself are welcome, Nemesio."

Gib rolled his eyes good-naturedly. He didn't know what could be so great about a dirty tavern full of drunkards, but he also didn't want to sit around his room all night, fretting about the assassin or Hasain's total disregard of his warning. He was also feeling strange around Joel. As pleasant as Joel could be, Gib always felt—*awkward* around the mage trainee.

So Gib agreed to meet his companions at the gates later that evening. He would give this Rose Bouquet a try. Perhaps after a round of ale, he would be able to forget about the worries plaguing his mind.

As the group of friends crossed over the crack-riddled bridge that spanned the width of the Tempist River, Gib blinked in sudden realization. Since arriving at Academy, he hadn't left the school grounds to venture into the city. Besides the time he'd ridden through with Liza, he'd never set foot in any other part of Silver.

Tarquin, Kezra, and Nage walked with the utmost confidence, suggesting that all three of them knew their way around—which of course, they did. Each of them had grown up in this city. Judging by the mansions lining both sides of the street, it was possible both Tarquin and Kezra had grown up along this very road.

Traders Row was nearly abandoned this late in the day. Indeed, nearly all the market stands that had lined the cobblestone path when Gib first arrived in Silver were missing. He ventured to guess little business was to be made once the sun went down. And who in their right mind would want to be out in this weather? Gib wrapped his fur cloak more tightly around his shoulders and sped up. It was downright bitter outside. He could see his breath in the chilled air. Surely it would begin to snow any day now.

"Almost there," Tarquin piped up ahead of him.

Gib squinted through the dimly lit streets and his mood improved at the sight of a large building on the corner ahead, with cheerful music and warm light radiating from behind the closed shutters. It was the only building in the entire city that seemed to have any life to it on this cold winter evening.

People were conversing on the front steps; some of them laughing boisterously and others talking in merry, spirited voices. Some of them were clad in armor, most likely sentinels of Arden who were off duty. Others appeared to be regular city folk, dressed in garments ranging from silken vests to drab linen tunics. It was a strange mix of wealthy and common folk.

Curiosity piqued, Gib followed at the heels of his friends, dodging between the strangers and doing his best not to accidentally bump into any of them. They seemed to be in fair moods, but Gib didn't want to take any chances of being the source of a drunken brawl.

As he approached the open door, Gib took in the scent of roasted meat, simmering stew, and ale. The winter breeze giving way to warmth lifted his spirits, and the sound of jovial music rang in his ears, beckoning him to come inside. Tarquin led the way through the door.

The interior of the tavern was more spacious than Gib would have imagined. Tables occupied most of the area and were packed tightly together, so close to one another it was possible to touch the person sitting at the next table. The tabletops were nothing like the finely crafted desks so frequently used at Academy. Made of rugged oak wood, these tables were cracked and chipped from rough handling and bathed in the scent of spilled ale and tobacco. Gib relaxed a bit—the etiquette encouraged at Academy wouldn't be enforced here.

At the rear of the tavern was a modest stage, elevated several feet. Standing on this platform was a trio of bards. One played a pan flute while the other two kept rhythm with a mellow sounding gittern and a set of hand drums. Many of the people gathered inside were clapping along to the light and joyous music. Some were even dancing. Gib blushed when he saw the scantily clad women twirling on tabletops. Clearly they were part of the entertainment, for even as Gib averted his eyes, one of the women leaned down to accept a coin from a patron.

To the side of the stage, a crowd of people gathered at what Gib assumed was the bar. Tavern maids carrying mugs brimming with ale made their way along the counter, stopping to deliver drinks or accept currency before scampering back into the kitchen. They were laughing with the customers, exchanging jokes and friendly touches as they worked. The crowd was boisterous in return, rowdy without being discourteous. Gib noted the discrepancies in clothing and social standing among the gathered patrons, yet no one seemed to care or even notice. He'd never seen such amity between perfect strangers. This place seemed to defy the laws that had for so long been engrained in his mind.

The group of friends chose a booth toward the back of the room, away from the bustle of the bar and music. A tavern maid brought each of them a tall mug of ale, smiling brightly as she worked, and accepted their coins.

Tarquin took a hearty pull from his tankard before turning his eyes to Gib. "So what do you think of the Rose Bouquet?"

"Uh, good." Gib also took a drink in an attempt to clear his thoughts. He didn't want to think about what had happened earlier. He didn't want to dwell on what may or may not befall the King. Clearly no one else was worried about it anyway. "So anyone can come here? Commoners and nobility alike?"

Tarquin nodded enthusiastically. "Yeah. As far as I know, anyone is welcome. My brother, Asher, told me all sorts of stories about the place."

Nage spluttered on his beer, setting his mug down with a loud thud. "Stories? You mean you've never been here before?"

True to his nature, Tarquin blushed a deep crimson and looked down at his hands. "You mean inside? Well, once or twice with my father. I've never been here on my own."

Kezra caught Gib's eye and they both grinned.

Tarquin puffed out his chest despite his blush. "I've had ale before! And I've travelled the Traders Row by myself plenty of times. I've just never had a chance to come here by myself."

Nage laughed and leaned across the table. "If you're so worldly, I dare ya to go and take a coin to one of the pretties over there. See what she'll do for ya in return."

Gib blushed almost as hard as Tarquin, knowing all too well the implications. Tarquin just about dove under the table at the suggestion. "I'm a gentleman!"

There was a good laugh at that. Nage slapped his hand on the table, but he didn't push it further. Instead, they all slipped into drinking their mugs and watching the sights. The music was changing and the dancing became more suggestive, slower and deeper. Gib winced and decided to focus on his drink, knowing he should have expected this when he agreed to come here. He just didn't expect to feel so uncomfortable.

Several moments passed before a loud whoop came from the tavern's entrance. Kezra and Tarquin both groaned, and Gib didn't have to look to know who it was. Nawaz Arrio swept through the door, closely followed by Hasain Radek. The two were almost instantly enveloped with giggling, scarcely dressed women.

Gib shifted uncomfortably once more and was sure he saw Tarquin do the same thing. They were both old enough to know what a brothel was and what was to be expected, but Gib felt out of place among his friends.

The music was picking up and still more people flocked inside. Gib found himself drumming his fingers on the tabletop and trying to find a polite way to excuse himself. He didn't want to spoil anyone's fun, but his discomfort wasn't lessening. It would be better to leave now rather than embarrass himself or someone else.

"Gibben Nemesio?"

Gib sank in the booth but knew it was too late. Nawaz Arrio had already jumped into one of their empty seats. "What are you guys doin' here? I was sure you'd all be tucked safe in your beds at this time of night."

Tarquin stiffened. "What's that supposed to mean? We have just as much right to be here as anyone else!"

Nawaz fixed the young lordling with a glazed-over stare. "You need to learn how to have fun, boy." He reached over and tipped the brim of Tarquin's hat down into his face. Tarquin spluttered but Nawaz had already turned back to Gib and lowered his voice. "Hey, Hasain told me about what you heard earlier."

"Did he scoff about how ignorant I am?"

Nawaz smiled crookedly. "Hasain thinks everyone's ignorant. You'll get used to it. For what it's worth, though, it's probably nothing to lose sleep over."

Gib rolled his eyes. "You too, then? All right. I guess I'll just sit here and drink ale *while our king's life is being threatened—*"

Kezra and Nage stopped their impromptu game of arm wrestling. She whipped her head toward them. "What was that?"

Before Gib could say another word, Nawaz had shot them all down with waving hands. "Hey! Shhh. Not here, okay? And trust me, this sort of thing happens a lot. It's probably nothing."

Tarquin, Nage, and Kezra shared dark looks among themselves but didn't press the issue.

Gib, however, was unsatisfied and shook his head. "I don't understand. Why would anyone dislike a king who has made it possible for everyone to do as they wish and make better lives for themselves? How could anyone be upset with the freedom of others? Won't it make our country stronger if more people are educated and more people are able to defend it?"

Nawaz smiled in a way that could almost be charming if he wasn't being loud and bothersome. "Not everyone sees it that way. There are people who fear they'll lose their power if others gain any. They fear equality."

Gib crossed his arms over his chest, careful to protect his splinted hand. "That doesn't make any sense."

Kezra jumped into the conversation. "You're right. It doesn't, but my own father is one of the ones who fight to keep commoners and women 'in their place.'"

Tarquin was blushing again as he regarded Kezra out of the corner of his eye. "My father says you're brave to be so defiant, Kezra."

Her own voice was stilted. "Uh, thanks. I suppose."

An awkward silence followed where neither she nor Tarquin seemed to know what to say. Nage snickered quietly and Gib wanted to smile despite the awkward lull.

Mercifully, Nawaz broke the quiet when he leaned back in his chair and waved Hasain Radek over to the table. "Hasain! Over here!" A mischievous smile flickered on his lips. "You babies up for some real fun? You know, drink some beer, play cards, watch a girl take off her clothes?"

Gib's insides were in knots, but the others all seemed to want to go along.

Nawaz laughed and tapped his fingers on the table directly in front of Gib. "Or I could send a servant to read you a bedtime story, if that's more your speed."

Gib bit his bottom lip, but the smile in Nawaz's eyes suggested that he meant no ill will.

Gib pushed past his discomfort. "Fine. What's your game?"

Nawaz produced a deck of cards from his pocket and moved over when Hasain showed up with two young women—one hanging off each arm. Gib tried not to notice how their dresses just barely covered their bosoms. He likewise tried not to look directly at Hasain, lest he glare and make it obvious he still wasn't satisfied with the lack of concern for their king.

Hasain, for his part, seemed equally dissatisfied. He stuck his nose in the air and addressed only Nawaz. "Why are we keeping company with the children?"

Nawaz rolled his eyes and began shuffling the cards. "You got a better idea? Make some friends I don't know about?" When Hasain only gave him an icy glare, the young lord nodded. "That's what I thought. Sit down. There's room."

The eight of them managed to fit around the table in their booth, and although space was limited, no one complained. Gib sighed and accepted the hand of cards he was dealt as Nawaz made his way around. Tarquin passed, saying that he'd watch the first round to learn, and the girls who'd accompanied Hasain opted out as well. They, instead, seemed more interested in ordering drinks and hanging off the older boys. Neither Nawaz nor Hasain seemed to take much note of them, tossing coins their way so they could drink their fill but paying them not even a glance other than that. Gib frowned but stayed his tongue.

The game was some form of gambling that Gib had never heard of before. He explained that he had no money to bet with. Hasain gave him a smug look but Nawaz only shrugged, saying it was just for fun. After that was cleared up, Nage also willingly joined.

They played ten rounds, and Kezra wiped the table all but three times. When Gib thought to harass her she only grinned back at him. Nawaz and Hasain likewise seemed impressed and laughed among themselves, even mentioning they were glad they hadn't bet money.

A little while later, a girl with dark hair and a scant outfit came up to their table. Gib assumed she was there to see if they wanted more drinks. Instead, she leaned over their scattered cards and half empty mugs to twirl a delicate finger in Nawaz's hair. "Hey there, lover boy. Were you watching me up there?" She indicated the stage with a nod of her head.

Nawaz looked up at her and offered a winning smile. "Jade! You know I was." He crawled out of the booth, past Hasain and his lady friend, to wrap his arms around her.

She glanced over at the table, specifically at the prostitute who'd been hanging off Nawaz earlier. "Am I ruining your plans?" She continued to run her fingers through his dark locks before leaning up to bite at his throat. "I don't want to share."

Gib shuddered uncomfortably and saw Hasain roll his eyes. The young Radek lord glared up at Nawaz and gave him a pointed reminder. "I paid for them tonight. Whether you take her or not, it's your turn to pay next time." Gib blinked. Was this conversation actually happening? And why wasn't the girl—prostitute or not—offended to be spoken of in such a way?

Nawaz waved off Hasain. "Yeah, yeah. Next time I buy. I get it."

"What are you going to do with her?" Hasain spoke of this person, this human being, like she was a play thing or a bauble. Gib glared at Hasain despite the fact that the girl didn't seem fazed in the least.

Nawaz wasn't paying attention any more. Jade was pulling him away from the table. He stopped long enough to look back at them and the prostitute. A wicked grin broke across his face, and Gib sank down in his seat when those piercing blue eyes fell onto him.

"That's a real shame, wasting such beauty on this cold night." His voice dripped sarcasm, his dangerous smile never wavering. Gib frowned and was about to jump up out of his seat, but as always, Nawaz was one step ahead of him. The young lord pointed to Gib before motioning to the lonely prostitute. "Here, have a gift."

Gib lifted both hands, not thinking of the one in the splint, and waved them. "No, no! That's all right."

The prostitute came over to him anyway, her own devilish smile fixed on him. When she touched his chest, the sentinel trainee fell back into his seat.

"Nawaz! Take her with you. I have to–to go back to Academy." His voice squeaked.

Nawaz made his getaway. "You can thank me later, boy. It's the only charity I'm giving you."

Gib turned his head, trying to call out once more, but already the prostitute was straddling his lap. Her hands were in his hair and her smooth voice caressed him gently, "What's the matter, little one?"

He was distantly aware of his friends laughing at him. Hasain was clearing the cards off the table as if nothing out of the ordinary was happening.

Gib looked up at her, realizing for the first time just how low-cut her dress was. Taking a deep breath, he tried to get his hands between himself and her. "I—really. I can't stay."

She laughed and put her mouth next to his ear, so close he could feel her breath. "It's okay. Everyone has to have their first time. Relax, I'll make you look good."

He tried to say something back, anything, but he couldn't even breathe. The knot in his stomach was wrapped so tightly his lungs couldn't expand. She was leaning down and pressing her lips to his neck. He tried to back away but the booth had him trapped. Kezra and Nage were making cat calls and telling him to relax.

The prostitute giggled as she licked his earlobe. "Close your eyes, little one. Think of whomever you want and pretend your friends aren't here."

Gib choked. He couldn't do that! He wouldn't do it. This was not what he'd wanted for himself for his first time, and he certainly didn't want to do it here, in front of his friends and Hasain.

Gib shook his head defiantly, but she closed in as if to kiss him, and he slammed his eyes shut on reflex. *Think of anyone you want and pretend no one else is here.* When her lips brushed his, Gib could think only of misty blue eyes and dark waving hair. Her small hands were replaced with slightly larger ones that were gentler and more timid. She whispered something in his ear about how well he was doing, but he couldn't hear her voice. He couldn't hear a woman's voice at all. All he could think of was Joel Adelwijn.

Gib gulped and spluttered, pushing her away with more force than he'd meant to use. She toppled back and he instinctively grabbed for her, knocking his splinted hand on the table in the process. The prostitute stared at him in shocked resentment, and he felt his cheeks go white hot. "I'm sorry," he gasped. "I'm sorry, but I can't do this."

The pain flared in his wrist, but he helped her stand anyway. The look of shock on her face made him wish he could curl up and die. Gib knew, in the back of his mind, that she was a prostitute and this was her job, but he couldn't imagine the rejection was any less jolting. "I'm sorry," he offered again, weaker this time. "It's not you. It's me. This isn't—I can't do this."

The table had gone quiet. Kezra scooted her way out from the booth, and Gib felt her tap him on the shoulder. Her voice was low but reassuring. "C'mon, Gib. I'll walk with you back to Academy if you want."

Tarquin scurried out to follow her, and Nage hesitated for just a moment more before also rising from the bench. The three of them lingered behind Gib, waiting, but he couldn't leave just yet. The sentinel trainee was distinctly aware of Hasain's eyes and the prostitute wrapped under the Radek lord's arm was glaring as well.

A horrible guilt rose in Gib's chest. He hadn't meant any offense to the woman, and he wanted her to know that. Swallowing hard, he tried one last time to get through to her. "Who are you? When you're not here, what do you do? What do you love? I don't even know your name."

The prostitute fixed her dark, wide eyes onto him. "My—my name? What do I love? I'm a whore. I'm here for your pleasure." She reached out and touched his cheek. "And you're too good for this place, little one. You should leave."

"Gibben Nemesio." He stood at his full height—still shorter than her—before bowing to her as any gentleman should bow to a lady. "My name is Gibben Nemesio. Please accept my apology and know it is sincere."

The prostitute seemed at a loss as she replied in a soft tone, "My name is Gwenth Fauve. I love music. And I know you're sincere." She smiled when he kissed the back of her hand.

Gib returned the smile. "Have a good night."

He left with his friends before he could think about what had just happened and how many pairs of eyes were watching his retreat. He chose not to think about the injustice of what life must be like for those who had only their bodies to sell. And he chose not to think about Joel Adelwijn's sapphire eyes and soft voice or why either of those things made his pulse race.

Gib's mood crashed down around him as they made their way back to Academy. No one said much of anything. Tarquin was especially quiet, though he stole glances at Kezra from time to time. If she noticed, she didn't say. Instead, she and Nage kept a light conversation going between them, warding off the deafening silence that might serve as an uncomfortable wedge between the friends.

Tarquin glumly looked at his feet, and Gib wished he could be there for his friend. As it was, however, all he could think of was Joel Adelwijn and his blue eyes, perfect smile, and hushed voice. His skin itched at the idea of the older boy's warm, firm hands touching him—Gib shook his head in an attempt to clear his wandering mind. How could this be happening? What was this? And how would he ever explain it to Joel?

His heart pounded the rest of the way. He was unsure how to feel when he returned to the room to find it empty. Relief? Disappointment? He climbed into bed but his overwhelmed thoughts wouldn't allow sleep. So many unanswered questions raced through his head and Gib found no solace as he tried to piece together what happened earlier at the Rose. What did any of it mean? The young prostitute had all but begged him to bed her—but when she'd touched him, he'd instead longed for Joel's soft fingers caressing his skin, his tenor voice whispering sweet words into Gib's ears—

Gib bit down on his lip until it stung. Did this mean he liked boys instead of girls? Or was he merely confused? Joel had been so nice. Perhaps it was only a sense of deep camaraderie Gib was feeling toward the mage trainee. Just because Gib had been uninterested in the prostitute didn't mean he wouldn't find some other girl attractive, right? Yet no girl had ever made his heart hammer the way Joel had.

Gib tried to calm his racing mind long enough to have one coherent thought. He felt no such attraction toward any girls in his class. Even Kezra, independent and wild as she was, would only ever be a friend. Gib knew it. Deep in his heart, he *knew*. Kezra didn't make his stomach flutter when she laughed or turn his face a dark shade of scarlet with a simple smile. But Joel did.

A desperate squeak made its way from between his pursed lips. He'd been attracted to Joel from the beginning—he just hadn't realized it until now. *By the light of Daya, no wonder I've acted so awkward around him. I didn't understand these feelings before now.* Gib's heart was beating rapidly in his chest as he lay in the darkness, trying to digest this new revelation about himself. He didn't know what he should do. Should he tell Joel? His friends and family? Perhaps he shouldn't tell anyone at all.

Gib's mind dwelled on the horrible things Annwyne had said, all the rumors and gossip that had been directed toward Joel, and the fear in Syther Lais' voice when the boy had defended his decision to remain veiled in secrecy. Maybe it would be wise for Gib to do the same. After all, Joel had been highborn, rich, the son of one of the most powerful men in Arden, and his confession had nearly cost him everything. What would Gib, a poor common-born farmer, stand to lose if people found out? If he simply kept quiet, no one would have to know.

The sentinel trainee glared at the ceiling, tears threatening to spill over from his chestnut eyes. *Why? Why this? As if being a poor fool wasn't bad enough. Even if I keep this a secret while I'm in Academy, even if I go to war and manage to survive, I'll still be expected to marry a woman upon my return. I just can't—I don't want to.* Gib wiped a hand across his cheek, catching the rebellious tear that dared fall. He was so confused. His heart ached and he wished there was someone he could talk to. *I could try to find Liza. She would listen.* But Gib had no idea where in Silver his sister was stationed. He didn't know how to locate her. That left only Joel. *I have to tell him. He's the only one who will know what to do. He's the only one who will understand.* Gib choked back a cry. *Chhaya's bane, how did I never know before?*

The entire room was beginning to spin. Gib slammed his eyes closed and rolled onto his side, bringing the blanket up to his chin as though by doing so, he could wrap himself away from the rest of the world. He wasn't sure how long he lay there, listening to the howl of the wind against the shuttered window. The gale outside was as brutal and violent as the one that raged within his heart.

Even though the blankets were stuffed thick with wool, the cold managed to seep through his clothing, under skin, and into joints and bones. Gib clasped at the splint holding his shattered wrist in place and winced as a tendril of icy pain shot up his arm. How was he ever to be expected to sleep under these conditions? His body and soul ached with terrible anguish. Gib had never missed home more than he did in that instant. He wished he was at the farm with a roaring fire in the hearth, spreading warmth throughout the cottage. Gib and his brothers would be curled up on straw cots in front of the flame, telling stories and laughing before falling asleep in the drowsy heat. There would be nothing to hide, nothing to fear. He wouldn't have to worry about who he was. Everything would be simple again.

The sound of a door hinge clicking into place stirred Gib from his restless slumber. The sentinel trainee blinked, but his eyes refused to adjust to the darkness. The candle beside his bed had long since burned itself out, the wax pooled and hardened at the bottom of the metal cup. It was impossible to know how long he'd been asleep. What time was it?

Gib remained still, pretending to sleep, but Joel must have heard him stir, for the mage trainee called out in a whisper, "I apologize. I didn't mean to wake you."

Gib's stomach was seized in unbearable knots. He opened his mouth to speak, but it took multiple tries to get the words to come forth. "It's okay," the sentinel trainee managed at last. "I couldn't sleep anyway."

Joel struck a match and a moment later, candlelight illuminated the room. Joel's mouth was titled downward as he turned his blue eyes on Gib. "Cold?"

Gib looked down at his own hands when he realized they were shaking. He didn't feel cold. "I, uh, only a little, I guess. I just had a long night. My mind refuses to keep quiet. And my wrist aches." He motioned toward the splint.

Joel pursed his lips before going to the chest at the end of his bed. He flung it open and emptied the contents. "I have some extra furs in here that you're welcome to borrow. On bitter nights like these, one can never be wearing too much clothing."

"Oh, you don't have to," Gib protested, cheeks going red. "I'll just— I'm fine, really. My blankets are plenty warm enough, I swear to you."

His roommate studied Gib narrowly before grabbing a cloak lined with soft rabbit fur. "At least take this." Joel marched over and gave Gib such a look that he didn't dare say no.

The sentinel trainee struggled with his one functioning hand to get the cloak around his shoulders, and his heart skipped a beat when Joel leaned down to help adjust it. Gib met the other boy's gaze for a second before tearing his eyes away. Joel's crystal orbs always managed to undo Gib, now more so than ever.

The mage trainee nodded his head toward Gib's bandaged wrist. "Might I have a look at it? Is the pain worse than before?"

"It just aches a little," Gib admitted. "I think I had too much fun earlier at the Rose."

The corner of Joel's mouth twitched. "You went to the Rose Bouquet? How did you like it?"

Gib kept his eyes on Joel's hands as the mage set his fingers atop the splint. "It was loud. The people there were—nice. It was refreshing to see the rich as well as the common folk all mingling under one roof." He winced when Joel pressed down a bit too hard on his thumb. "That's the spot that hurts. I think I bumped the side of my hand earlier."

Joel nodded but didn't remove his fingers. "It's swollen again. I can help ease the pain if you'll allow me."

"Can you Heal?"

The mage trainee shook his head. "No. But I can block the pain temporarily."

Gib swallowed. "More magic?"

"Mmm, yes. But don't worry, it's a fairly basic spell." Joel cradled Gib's injury in one hand while placing the other atop the splint. "All mage trainees are taught from a very young age how to shield themselves against outside forces, whether it be to ward against pain, emotion, or other magic. Some of us can extend our shields to include others. I can fool your mind into believing there is no pain."

The idea of magic—especially magic being directed toward him—still made Gib's nerves flare, but he wholly trusted Joel, so with only minor hesitation, the sentinel trainee nodded his consent. "All right, see what you can do."

Joel seemed to be concentrating on the injury, so Gib focused his own attention on steadying his heartbeat and ragged breaths. He hoped his roommate noticed neither. Gib's mind was racing. He wanted to confess his revelations discovered earlier that night, but an awkward silence had settled over the room and he couldn't think of a good way to initiate such a discussion.

For a while, the only sounds were the wind rattling through the shutters and the voices of doubt plaguing Gib's mind. He tried to relax but found the task impossible. *Daya, I need to talk to him. I need to be certain I'm not mistaken.* A horrible thought ran through his mind. *What if he doesn't even believe me? What if he thinks I just want attention?* Some kind of desperate noise made its way up his throat, and Joel glanced up at the sound.

"Do you feel anything now?"

Gib looked down. Joel's hands were radiating warmth as his fingers rested gently atop the splint. The sentinel trainee found himself focusing all his attention on those soft hands, admiring their graceful strength.

"Gib?"

He blinked. Had Joel just spoken? Gib's mind was so clouded he couldn't be sure. He dared to flash his eyes upward and felt his airway constrict. He couldn't breathe. Joel was looking back, fair features uncertain and brows knit in confusion. The mage trainee parted his lips as though to repeat whatever words he'd previously uttered, but Gib's own words came tumbling forth.

"When did you know?" Gib blurted out. When the mage trainee hesitated to respond—perhaps because he didn't understand the question—Gib went on to say, "When did you know you didn't like girls?"

Joel did nothing to conceal his shock. His grip on Gib's hand faltered, blue eyes wide with some obscure pang of emotion. "I—"

Gib dropped his face to the floor, feeling the heat rise from the back of his neck to his cheeks. "Wait. You don't have to answer that."

"No, it's all right." Joel's voice was only slightly strained now. The mage cleared his throat but didn't completely release Gib's hand. "I suppose I had seen my eleventh summer when I began to realize that I was—not like my peers. I wasn't yet old enough to enter Academy, so I spent a lot of my time being a nuisance by following Liro and his friends everywhere. He didn't mind so much back then though. Not at first anyway."

Gib raised an eyebrow. "Liro? Your brother, Liro?"

Joel smiled. "He used to be different. I know it's hard to comprehend." A deep sigh escaped his mouth. "There were little signs here and there, foreshadowing what would come to be known to me as I discovered myself. I remember Liro scolding me one time for playing with my sister's dolly. Another time, the older boys went swimming in the river and my father caught me spying on them while they were changing back into dry clothes. At the time, I didn't understand why Father was so upset—" Joel's pale cheeks began to flush with color as he spoke. "It wasn't until Liro started courting a young lady that I truly realized how different I was. Her name was Amara and even I can admit she was a beauty. Indeed, all of Liro's friends were quite infatuated by her perfectly placed features. They were all wooed, but I didn't understand it. Liro, of course, joked that I was still too young yet to appreciate women and in my innocence, I was inclined to agree with him. Until I met Amara's younger brother."

Gib's stomach was in knots as he remembered an incident that had taken place the previous summer. He was helping the Fadell family bring in their first crop of the year and their eldest son, Altair, was working side by side with Gib most of the day. The boy was nothing but pleasant, laughing and joking as he worked, yet Gib was uncomfortable the entire afternoon. He felt lightheaded each time Altair directed a smile toward him, and his pulse quickened when the boy accidentally brushed against him as they worked. *Oh Daya, I never realized it was attraction I was feeling toward Altair! It can't just be a coincidence. This has been going on longer than I thought. Joel didn't awaken these feelings. They've been there all along.*

"He was two wheelturns older than I, but that hardly mattered to me," Joel continued as if in a trance. "It was the first time I'd felt such infatuation for another person. Each time he smiled, a shameful blush came to my face, and every time he laughed, I felt as though my knees might give out. I knew it wasn't normal. My peers, my brother, my family—none of them acted in such a way toward one of their own. And so I told no one." A single tear escaped the mage's eye. "It happened again a few years later when I came of age to enter Academy. Only this time, the boy I longed for returned my affections, or so I thought. But you know that story already."

"I'm sorry." It was the only thing Gib could think to say at first. His mind was still a jumble of unanswered questions. It felt as though he'd been asleep for the past thirteen wheelturns and was just now waking up.

Joel blinked away his tears even as his voice finally cracked under the pressure he'd been holding in for so long. "I—It was just hard to go through alone."

Gib felt a sudden surge of bravery and reached out with his good hand to set it on top of Joel's. The older boy deserved better than how he'd been treated, and Gib felt compelled to show his support. "*No one should ever have to go through that alone. I can't even fathom how you must have felt. Joel, you're stronger than you think.*"

The mage trainee's eyes were shimmering in the candlelight, wet with emotion. "I'm tired of always having to be strong."

Heart aching at the weight of Joel's words, Gib couldn't catch his breath. He understood. He understood wholly. He, the poor farm boy, had been left to care for his younger brothers, tend a farm, and worry about whether or not his family would survive each winter. He'd been strong his entire life. His circumstances had forced him to be. But sometimes Gib wanted to break down and sob, cry until all the worry and sorrow bled from his soul. *Our situations were different but we're the same. Joel has put on a brave face just as I have. We're both fighting our battles alone, but we don't have to be.*

Gib dared to raise a trembling hand toward his companion, noting the pain in his injured wrist had faded away. Joel's spell must have worked. "You don't have to be strong all the time. You're only human." He touched Joel's shoulder gingerly. "I may not be as old or educated as you, but I do know the pain of suffering in silence. I know how awful it feels to think you have to keep your wits about you when all you want to do is fall apart."

Joel was looking at him now through thick, damp lashes. "If I fall apart, I may never be able to put the pieces back together."

"I can—I am—" Gib was struggling to get his words out. "I'm here for you, Joel."

The mage trainee quivered. "As I am for you." His voice trailed off into a forlorn whisper, but Gib was certain Joel had more to say. The older boy pursed his lips, and Gib could do nothing but wait—wait for the words that might change both their lives.

"Gib, there is something I need to ask you."

Gib's heart hammered in his chest. "You can ask me anything."

Joel lifted his face, mouth open just a little, as though he was trying to find the strength—

A sudden gust of wind tore through the window, flinging the shutters open with a bang. Gib promptly jumped out of his skin while Joel rose and ran over to the window. The mage trainee gasped as he reached the sill. "It's snowing."

Gib came back to his senses and went to assist his roommate. Sure enough, a silver misting of ice was being swept around outside and through the open window. Gib shivered as the bitter air met his skin. He looked to Joel but knew the moment was gone.

"Let's get this shut before we freeze to death." The mage trainee's voice suggested that nothing out of the ordinary had happened at all. His clever mask was once more impeccable.

Grudgingly, Gib lifted his good hand to help, and by the time the window was secured, Joel was more distant than ever. He immediately snuffed out the candle and climbed into his bed without another word, not even to wish his companion so much as a good night. It seemed yet again, Gib would be left to wonder what might have been.

CHAPTER SEVEN

Once the snow began to fall, it didn't stop. For three sennights, flurries of ice and slush cascaded down from the skies, burying Silver City under a catastrophic amount of dense, wet snow. Business in the city came to a grinding halt. The streets were impassible by horse or cart and most of the residents opted to stay inside, venturing into the weather only if the need was dire.

On the academy grounds, Gib's physical training class had to be moved inside. Even Weapons Master Roland admitted defeat and took the students out of the cold when they found themselves waddling around in waist deep snow. Gib's hand was on the mend, but he still hadn't been given permission from the healers to rejoin the class, so most of his time was occupied by cleaning armor, patching clothing, and doing other menial tasks that the sentinel trainee had become quite adept at performing over the past two moonturns.

His mind was likewise unable to remain idle. Damn Nawaz Arrio and his antics. If not for the stunt he'd pulled at the Rose Bouquet, Gib may have never realized his feelings and then none of this awkward business with Joel would have happened. Gib didn't know how or when, but he was determined to have it out with Nawaz the next time they met in private.

For his part, Joel made himself scarce again. They hadn't ever finished the conversation started on the night Gib returned from the Rose Bouquet. Gib wondered if Joel was really as busy as he said he was, or if he was purposely avoiding his roommate.

Another conversation still weighed heavily on Gib's mind as well—the one he'd heard between the two men plotting to kill King Rishi. Joel and Hasain seemed to have forgotten about the incident, but Gib found himself lingering in empty corridors, standing beside partially ajar doorways, listening for those terrible voices speaking of such unspeakable treason. But he heard nothing. He saw nothing. And eventually, Gib ceased trying to locate the would-be assassin. Perhaps Joel and Hasain had been right after all. Maybe it had just been an idle threat and nothing would ever come of it.

The snowstorm itself was a growing cause of concern, grating on Gib's frayed nerves. Every day it continued to snow was another day the roads couldn't be cleared. He planned to ride home with Liza over the Midwinter Festival to visit Tayver and Calisto, but now the journey would possibly be too dangerous to make. They hadn't seen their brothers in three moonturns, and this was the only chance to check in on them before Academy went on summer recess—four lunar cycles away. He couldn't wait that long to see them. He didn't even know how they were doing. Did they have enough food to make it through the winter? Were they starving to death? What if the roof collapsed? Or the cottage caught fire? A million different things could go wrong and Gib was not there to save them. Despair dragged him down and though Liza offered words of comfort, he felt helpless.

Gib was close to having a nervous breakdown by the time he returned to his room one evening, three days before the Midwinter Festival was set to begin. Everywhere he'd gone that day, students were talking about how happy they would be to go home for the festival. They gushed about being able to see their families and loved ones and about sleeping in their own beds. Gib wanted to cry. Traveling to Willowdale was a three-day journey under normal circumstances. He wouldn't be able to make the trek through three feet of snow.

Gib flopped down onto his bed miserably. He'd worked himself up so much his temples were throbbing.

"What's wrong?" Joel asked from his place at the writing desk.

Gib threw his hands into the air. "It's the snow! I'm not going to be able to travel home for Midwinter!"

The mage trainee grimaced. "I'm sorry. But it's true. The roads are far too dangerous for travel."

"I'm aware."

Joel shifted in his chair. "I'm sure your brothers will be all right, especially if they're as resourceful as you."

"I just miss them. It's my job to worry about their welfare." Gib reached up and began to massage his forehead. *Damn this headache.* "Not to mention all of the city-born students are going home to their families while I'll be stuck here, eating cold porridge three times a day and lamenting about the farm and everything else I have no control over."

Joel didn't immediately respond. Finally, the mage trainee got up and sat on the edge of Gib's bed, by his feet. "Hey, I have an idea. Why don't you come home with me? For the Midwinter Festival."

Gib was taken aback. He hadn't been expecting the other boy to suggest *that*. "Oh, I–I don't know—"

"I've told Mother all about you. She wants to meet you."

Gib blushed as he sat up. "Your mother does? Why?" He wrung his hands together. "I don't know—I wouldn't want to be in the way, and I'd be an extra mouth to have to feed."

Joel laughed, his eyes twinkling with amusement. "You wouldn't be either of those things. Trust me when I say my family always prepares *far* too much food for our Midwinter feast. I don't think there has been a year when the servants weren't sent out into the streets afterwards to give the homeless our gluttonous leftovers."

"Your father is Seneschal Koal. I don't think he would allow a common urchin like me to dine at the same table."

"You presume to know very much about a man you've never spoken to," Joel replied with a snort. "Father wouldn't mind."

Gib's face flushed even more as he searched for another excuse. "*Liro.* Your brother hates me."

Joel set a steady hand onto the sentinel trainee's shoulder. "It's entirely possible Liro won't partake in the feast. He hasn't been inclined to show up for family dinners as of late." He tightened his grip, squeezing Gib's arm gently. "Please come. I know my sisters and mother will adore you as much as I do."

"Adore?"

"I–I mean—admire. I admire you—*your*—I admire your courage." Joel dropped his hand to his side and looked away.

Gib was almost positive he saw a light shade of pink come to the mage trainee's cheeks. Joel's eloquence had abandoned him in that moment, which was uncommon for a person normally so well composed.

Gib spared his roommate the embarrassment and consented. "All right. I'll go with you."

Joel nodded and then said in a stiff voice, "I'll send word to Mother." He still couldn't look Gib in the eye.

Two mornings later, Gib found himself standing before the Adelwijn estate. The bitter wind cut through cloak, tunic, and skin as Gib stood in front of the wrought iron gate surrounding the perimeter of the property and waited for it to be opened. He shivered as a wet drop of snow found its way beneath his clothing and left a frigid trail down the back of his neck. He couldn't feel his toes—the slush had soaked into his boots almost as soon as he'd set foot outside—and his fingertips were in danger of suffering the same fate despite the leather gloves wrapped around his hands.

"*Daya,* Joel," Gib gasped. "I'm going to be an icicle soon if we don't get out of this weather."

Joel was fumbling with the latch. "Sorry, it's iced over." A moment later, the hinges groaned in protest and both of the boys pushed the gate open.

They entered the courtyard. Gib imagined during the summer, the space would be lush and filled with beautiful flora. But there was nothing except more snow now. Joel led him toward a towering door at the far end of the courtyard.

"Almost there," the mage trainee promised.

Gib gritted his teeth but elected not to respond. All his focus was on setting one frozen foot in front of the other. At least someone had taken the liberty of clearing a pathway inside the courtyard. He thought to ask about it, but they had already approached the door and his roommate was reaching for the brass handle. Gib swallowed nervously. Even the door, etched with beautiful carvings and fanciful paint, screamed of the wealth this noble family possessed. *What am I doing here? Who am I fooling? I'm common-born and they're all going to hate me for it.*

He thought to bolt, to go running back through the streets, all the way to his cold, empty room within the dormitory, but Joel opened the door and turned to grace him with another shy smile. "Come on. Let's get out of the cold." The mage trainee's voice was as smooth as silk.

Gib felt his heart quicken. *I can do this for him. Joel wants me to be here, even if his family discards me as unworthy.* He managed to nod. "Gladly."

Warmth hit his skin as soon as he stepped through the threshold, and before Gib could think to remove his cloak, a pair of servants was by his side, stripping him of the heavy furs. He gawked in awe, but Joel seemed nonchalant and greeted the pair warmly. "Hello, Otos, Tabitha."

The man, a wiry, middle-aged fellow with hair the color of straw and brown eyes, gave a small bow as he took Joel's cloak into his arms. "Welcome home, m'lord."

"Lady Mrifa is awaiting you," said the young girl, who couldn't have been much older than Gib. She was dressed in a simple frock made of cotton, and her dark curls were pulled back into a bun at the nape of her neck.

Joel gave them another warm smile. "Thank you both. I shan't keep Mother waiting then." He motioned for Gib to follow, and the two boys left the servants behind.

They made their way down a long hall. The ceilings were not as tall or as grand as those in the academy building, but this was undoubtedly a home suitable for nobility. Portraits lined the walls, illuminated by lanterns, the light casting an eerie glow across the paintings. The hair on the back of Gib's neck rose. All those faces seemed to be staring at him, judging him. *And rightfully so. What the hell am I doing here?*

Joel cleared his throat. "Mother insists on keeping the portraits despite the wishes of my father." The mage trainee smiled, turning to look directly at Gib. "Don't worry, I think they're uncanny too."

Gib barked a nervous laugh. "Yeah."

They came to an archway at the end of the corridor which opened up into a magnificent sitting room. The space was filled with plush, velvety furniture, and the largest rug Gib had ever seen before was laid down onto the white granite floor like a blanket. Tapestries clung to the walls and an immense pane of glass served as a window to overlook the courtyard outside. A roaring fireplace provided warmth to the area, but Gib hardly had time to see any of it before one woman and two girls about Gib's age entered the room from a separate hallway. The youngest adolescent squealed with excitement at the sight of them but was disciplined enough not to run forward.

"Gib, I'd like you to meet my mother, Lady Mrifa," Joel said, never missing a beat. His blue eyes flashed toward his family. "Mother, this is my roommate, Gibben Nemesio." Joel placed a hand onto Gib's shoulder.

Lady Mrifa came forward at once. A petite woman, she had the same mesmerizing blue eyes as her son but her locks were golden as opposed to Joel's dark hair. She wore a flowing ivory gown made of fine silk and had an intricately woven shawl wrapped around her shoulders to ward off the cold. Her oval face was adorned with powder, and jewels hung from her ears and neck. A delicate nose gave way to full, cherry-colored lips that were pulled upward into a welcoming smile.

"It is a delight to finally meet you, Gibben," Mrifa spoke at once. Her voice was as eloquent as any noble's but without the haughtiness commonly associated with such rank.

Gib gave a little bow. "Joel has told me so much about you, Lady—" He let out a startled gasp when Mrifa advanced on him without warning. She embraced the sentinel trainee around the shoulders like any mother might do to her own child.

Mrifa planted a kiss on his reddened cheek. "Welcome to our estate. Please make yourself at home." Before Gib could even think to respond to *that*, Mrifa turned and ushered the two girls forward. Both of them shared Mrifa's golden hair and blue eyes. "These are my daughters, Joel's sisters, Heidi and Carmen."

The girls introduced themselves, and Gib gave them each a gracious nod in return. He even managed to find his own voice. "It's a pleasure to meet you." He looked back at Joel, who gave him a smile of encouragement. Gib was surprised how easy it was to converse with Joel's family. "Joel has spoken of all of you many times, but I'm afraid he failed to mention just how lovely you were."

Heidi and Carmen both giggled and Lady Mrifa clapped her hands together. "Well, Joel failed to mention your charm to us, Gibben," she replied in a flattered, pleased tone. She winked at her son, lowering her voice a pitch. "Nor did he warn us of how handsome you are."

A deep blush rose to Joel's cheeks. "*Mother!*"

Mrifa laughed as she put an arm around her son's back. "Why don't you show Gibben around the house before midday meal? Tabitha is preparing a stew for all of us." She hesitated before pressing gently, "Shall

I also have the servants prepare one of the guest suites for your friend?"

Joel floundered, but Gib was fortunate enough to still be in control of his own voice. "Oh, you don't need to go through that trouble, Lady Mrifa. I'm perfectly content to sleep on a mat in Joel's room. We've shared a room at Academy for three moonturns now, after all."

"Are you certain?" Mrifa asked in a measured voice. "Surely you would enjoy some privacy."

Gib nodded his head adamantly. "Lady, truly, it is fine. In fact, I dare say I would be lonesome if I were to have a room all to myself. I shared a bedroom with two brothers until the day I moved into the dormitory with Joel. I think I would lose sleep if I were to suddenly be alone for the first time in my life."

"Very well," replied Mrifa. She smiled. "I'll have a cot and some blankets brought up to Joel's room for you."

Gib's eyelids fluttered open, his body bathed in heat as he lay upon the cot the family servant, Otos, set up for him the previous night. Sunlight poured in through the glass pane above his head, but it was hard to judge the time. *Well past sunrise, at the very least,* Gib wagered. At Academy, the sentinel trainee had always risen at dawn, just as the first traces of warm golden hues had begun to appear in the sky, but in this dreamscape world of marbled hallways and beautiful stained glass, it was easy to ignore the passage of time. No chores needed to be done or lessons learned. Gib wondered how the nobility ever found the motivation to leave the comfort of their own beds with so little responsibility in their lives. He pulled the quilted blanket Lady Mrifa insisted he use closer to his chin and turned onto his side.

Across the room, Joel slept peacefully, his slender body wrapped in blankets and dark hair wild and tussled. His mouth was set in a smile, as though he might be enjoying a dream. Gib couldn't help but smile too. Something about Joel Adelwijn caused Gib's pulse to quicken every time he laid eyes upon his roommate. Although Gib didn't understand these awakening feelings for his friend, he didn't want to suppress them. *I want to tell him. But I also don't want things to become strange between us. I've finally managed to get him to open up to me a little. Chhaya's Bane, I can't ruin that now.*

Gib was unsuccessful at holding back a yawn. Despite his restful slumber, the whirlwind of events from the day before had drained him. After introductions, he'd been taken on a tour of the entire Adelwijn estate. From the grand dining room to the private study and even the solar room on the second floor, a dazzling space where the roof had been replaced by glass and the flooring was a tiled mosaic masterpiece, he'd seen it all. Gib had been awestruck. If the academy building was magnificent, then the Adelwijn estate might well have been built for royalty. Never before had Gib been inside such an extravagant, beautiful home. *I still can't believe I'm here. This sleeping chamber alone is nearly bigger than the entire farmhouse and worth ten times it.* He yawned again, louder this time.

The sound caused Joel to rouse. The mage trainee let out a placid sigh as he turned onto his side. For a moment he remained still, but then he blinked twice and opened his blue eyes. His gaze landed on Gib almost immediately, and the sentinel trainee found himself blushing as he was regarded in silence through thick, dark lashes.

"Good morning," Gib called out, running a hand through his unruly curls in an attempt to flatten them.

Joel brought a hand to his mouth as he yawned. "Likewise. Did you sleep well?"

"Better than I have in a long time," Gib replied. "I don't want to get out of bed. It's so comfortable."

The older boy chuckled as he stretched his arms into the air. "Well, that's not an option, Gibben, unless you would like to skip your morning meal. Tabitha only serves breakfast until the seventh bell toll of the day. After that, you're on your own until dinner."

Gib groaned. "I don't think I can wait that long for a meal." As he rolled the blankets down the length of his legs and to his feet, Gib's stomach rumbled.

"Mother's rules." Joel stretched as he turned down the sheets on his own bed. "She has always roused my siblings and me early, even on days of rest. She says it makes us more responsible." The older boy cleared his throat, regarding Gib from the corner of his eye. "Thank you, by the way."

Gib turned. "What do you mean?"

"For coming home with me this week."

"Are you joking? I should be thanking *you*," Gib remarked with a snort.

Joel's face remained solemn. "I mean it, Gib. You're one of the only friends I have. It's been nice to spend more time with you." A fleeting smile passed over his lips. "And it will be nice to not have to face my eccentric family alone tomorrow during the feast."

Gib choked a nervous laugh. "Right. Bring the bumbling farm boy along to divert the attention away from you. You're so clever."

The mage trainee's eyes sparkled with amusement. "Fortunately, there is still a day of leisure before the feast. I was thinking perhaps we could go out on the town this morning. Despite the snow, Midwinter Festival is still in full swing. There is much to see. Is that something you'd be interested in doing?"

"You mean the nobility actually spend time outside during the winter?" Gib asked in mock jest.

A hearty laugh made its way from between Joel's lips. "Wait until you taste some of the food there. Then you'll understand what truly motivates us wealthy folk to brave the snow and ice."

"Food?" Gib asked, interest piqued.

Again, Joel broke down into fits of laughter. "Yes, lots of food. I'll even treat you to a freshly fried cinnamon fritter if you'd like. The bakery on Traders Row always sells them during Midwinter. Tell me, have you ever eaten a proper fritter before?"

The sentinel trainee shook his head. "No. Never."

Joel's eyes widened and he gasped in shock. "Oh, you *are* missing out. Fritters have to be one of the most delicious sweets in the world. Egg whites, cream, wheat, and ale mixed together and fried in a pan and then sprinkled with sugar and cinnamon. In the autumn, you can even find them made with fresh apples or raspberries."

Gib's mouth began to water. "That sounds wonderful."

"They truly are. We'll find some today at the festival. But first, baths and breakfast before Mother has our heads."

After baths and a hearty breakfast consisting of eggs, milk, and steaming bread, Joel and Gib prepared to venture outside. It quickly became apparent they wouldn't be allowed out the door until Lady Mrifa had bundled them inside wool cloaks and mittens, wrapped scarves around their necks, and plopped hats onto each of the boy's heads. Gib's mousy curls spewed out from beneath the hat as he adjusted it into place. He couldn't help but smile as he listened to Mrifa fret over her son.

"Joel, make sure you keep that hat over the top of your ears. It's bitter outside and I don't want you to come home with frozen extremities."

Joel sighed with impatience as his mother checked to be certain his cloak was properly buttoned. "I think you've forgotten, dearest Mother, this is the fifteenth winter I've seen. I'm at an age where I'm capable of donning proper clothing without guidance."

Mrifa smoothed her son's onyx waves, smiling sadly at him. "It's my job to be unbearable and overprotective. Let me fuss over you a little bit longer. You're the only son I have left who will allow it."

"Indeed," Joel replied with a roguish smile. "I'm sure it's been a long time since Liro allowed you to fawn all over him in such a way."

Mrifa's soft features pinched. "Your brother has been cold for some time now."

Joel set a hand on his mother's shoulder and uttered a quick apology. "That was out of line. I apologize."

"No, it's true," Mrifa responded, her voice sullen. "Your brother has treated you so unfairly. He isn't the same person he once was. It's sad that Liro's ambitions have become more important than kin." She leaned up to kiss Joel on the cheek. "He'll come around though. You'll see."

The mage trainee nodded stiffly and looked over to Gib. "We should go."

Gib shuffled his boots across the tiled floor as he made his way toward the door, where the servant girl, Tabitha, was already waiting to let them out. Joel followed closely.

"Now don't be gone too long," Mrifa warned from behind them. "There is still much work to be done before the feast tomorrow. Behave and don't eat so much that you make yourselves sick."

Gib nodded his head in acknowledgment and saw Joel do the same. Tabitha skirted in front of them and pulled the heavy oak door open just enough for the two boys to be able to slip past. Gib let out a startled gasp as a wave of frigid air slapped him hard in the face and caused every hair on his body to stand on end. *Oh, this was a grand idea. Really great.* He balked openly, but a moment later, he felt Joel's hands on his back, encouraging the sentinel trainee to move forward. He shivered. He wasn't sure if the spasm had been induced by the cold or the touch of the other boy.

Joel's voice was right behind him, in his ear. "Ready?"

Gib could barely force a nod. He pulled the scarf tighter around his neck and stepped into the blistering cold. He was almost immediately forced to squint his eyes to shield himself against the bright day. For the first time in sennights, the clouds had receded enough for the sun to peek through. The world was buried under a white, hardened glaze, and the sunlight reflected off the snow like a glass mirror.

Someone had taken the liberty of shoveling a fresh path through the courtyard—most likely one of the servants.

"Otos has been busy I see," Joel remarked under his breath.

Gib couldn't help but feel a twinge of guilt blossom in his chest. The Adelwijn family had been gracious enough to allow him to be a guest in their home and here he was, sleeping until an unacceptable time and being useless. Gib promised himself to help with chores when he returned from the festival. He didn't care if Joel balked at the suggestion.

The two boys left the Adelwijn estate behind, and for a while, the only sound was the crunch of their boots pressing into the snow as they walked. The drifts had transformed Silver City into a magnificent wonderland of sparkling towers and crystalized houses. Gib was grateful Joel was there to lead the way. Everything looked so different when it was buried under ice.

As they neared the famous street known as Traders Row, Gib was amazed at the sheer number of people who had chosen to come outside. Joel hadn't been joking when he'd told Gib the residents of Silver City refused to allow the snow to ruin their festival. People of varying social statuses lined the busy street. Fashionably dressed noblemen and ladies were strolling from one vendor to the next with a line of servants following, carrying the purchases for their masters. Even more common folk were present. Some of them were without mittens or hats, but their boisterous laughter and generously filled mugs of ale told Gib they were enjoying the festival despite the bitter temperature.

Joel set a hand on Gib's elbow and motioned toward a small group of men clad in armor who bore the Ardenian crest on their uniforms. "Be cautious of the sentinels," the mage trainee warned in a soft, measured tone. "You'll find those on duty tend to not be in the best of spirits. It's best we avoid them."

"Liza is a sentinel," Gib replied, his own voice sharp. "She'd never be mean-spirited—to us or anyone else."

"I wasn't trying to belittle your sister. I'm sure Liza is kind, but be that as it may, it would be wise to stay clear of any trouble while we're here. Festivities and mayhem tend to go hand in hand, and those soldiers ordered to keep the peace are always on edge. Sometimes they can overreact and a simple misunderstanding can become a dangerous situation."

Gib swallowed as he looked around with nervous eyes. "Chhaya's bane. You aren't making me want to stay here."

The older boy let out a short chuckle. "It'll be fine. Let's just be alert. If things start to get rowdy, it'll be best to make ourselves scarce before the authorities show up." Joel patted Gib on the shoulder and motioned toward one of the vendor booths. "Look. This is one of the bakery vendors I was telling you about."

Even before Gib turned to look for himself, the aroma of freshly baked bread and spices infiltrated his nostrils. The sight of the baker's stand was even more splendid. Rows of tarts sprinkled in sugar, breads of varying textures and shapes, and the fritters Joel raved about, glazed in honey and topped with cinnamon, were on display. Gib's mouth watered at the sight, and he was barely aware of his companion taking him by the arm and moving forward.

Shorter than Gib, the baker was a merry sort, with balding, peppered hair and a generous belly. He called out a greeting to Joel as the two boys made their approach. "Fair morning, young Lord Adelwijn. What brings you out to the festival?"

A smile played at the corner of Joel's mouth. "Only the best cinnamon fritters in all of Silver City, Master Baker Carbrey. I do believe I could smell them frying this morning when I awoke."

Hearty laughter filled the air. "That wouldn't surprise me. There's no limit on the capacity of a nose belonging to a young and hungry lordling. Tell me, how are your parents? It's been a long while since I've seen Lady Mrifa in my shop."

"My parents are well. Mother often sends the servants to fetch bread. The Adelwijn household hasn't lost our taste for your baked goods, Master Carbrey. I assure you." He placed a hand onto Gib's shoulder, moving him closer. "This is my friend, Gibben Nemesio. He's here to sample your famous fritters as well."

The baker bowed his head. "Well, you've certainly come to the right place, Lord Nemesio."

Gib was certain his face turned a hideous shade of crimson. The baker had just called him a lord. *He must think—he assumes because I'm here with Joel and wearing nice clothing I'm a noble.* The sentinel trainee opened his mouth but hesitated to speak. Would it be rude to correct the man? Would Gib stand to get in trouble if he didn't say anything? Surely it was against the law to pretend to be a noble.

Joel was there to save the moment, as always. "Gib is my roommate at the academy. He hails from beyond the city, from the farming village of Willowdale."

"Willowdale, eh?" The baker gave a second, more scrutinizing glance, but his eyes were still amicable. "That's a nice little ways from Silver, isn't it?"

"Uh, three days by horseback," Gib managed to respond, face burning. He couldn't quite look the baker in the eye. "I'm sort of hoping I dislike your baked goods. Three days is an awfully long journey to make if I develop an addiction for cinnamon fritters."

The baker's gut bounced as he laughed. "Well, I can't guarantee you won't, lad. You best hope you enjoy traveling."

Gib grinned from ear to ear. The awkward lull ended.

After both of the boys picked out a fritter and coins had been exchanged, they carried their snacks to one of the overpasses which spanned the width of the Tempist. Gib was amazed to see a section of the river cleared of all snow with dozens of people skating on the frozen water. He leaned against the stone masonry and watched the scene before him.

"Have you ever tried it before?" Joel asked. "Ice skating?"

Gib nibbled at his fritter for a moment before responding. "Never. I mean, my brothers and I used to go out onto the ice, but only in our boots." He laughed as he recalled memories of Tayver, Calisto, and him playing on the frozen pond behind their farm. "I feel as though the results would be disastrous if I were to try real ice skating."

A scandalous smiled stretched across the mage trainee's face. "Oh, you have to. I could teach you."

"*Now?*" Gib asked in a dubious voice, swallowing the bite of food. The sugared dough seemed to melt in his mouth. Joel had been right. The fritters were delicious.

Joel laughed, eyes afire with mischief. "No, not now, but at some point before the spring thaw. Skating is quite an entertaining way to pass the time during the long, boring winter cycles."

Gib raised an eyebrow even as he motioned toward his sore wrist. "I was only just allowed to remove the splint. Given my luck and lack of grace, I would step foot onto the ice and promptly have to go crawling back to the healers to treat another broken bone."

The mage trainee leaned in closer and Gib could feel a warm hand on the small of his back. "I'd never let you fall, my friend."

Gib's gut twisted as he stared into Joel's eyes—eyes so full of restrained emotion that Gib couldn't stand to look even a moment longer without losing the ability to breathe. His gaze fell to the ground, but his hands twitched at his sides longingly. He wanted to reach forward and touch Joel so badly it hurt. Gib wanted to show Joel that he wasn't alone, that he didn't have to face the tribulations of the world by himself. Gib started to raise a shaking hand, but the sound of a horn resonating loudly on the wind drew his attention.

A commotion was going on behind them. People were clustering at the far end of the street, many of them running to join the growing crowd. Children were being lifted onto shoulders, and noblemen and peasants alike were pointing and talking in excited voices. Gib furrowed his eyebrows and turned to Joel. "What do you suppose is going on over there?"

Joel was observing the crowd but didn't seem confused. His face remained calm. "Judging by the sound of the horn, I suspect a royal procession."

Gib's eyes widened. "*A royal procession?* Here?" He stood on the very tips of his toes, trying to get a better view, but he couldn't see through the horde of bodies.

"What, you think the royal family isn't allowed to partake in the festival?" Joel asked with a sly wink.

"N–no," Gib protested. "I was just under the impression it would be unsafe for them beyond the palace walls." He watched as a line of guardsmen, clad in ceremonial armor and each bearing a longsword on their hip, cut a path through the gathered crowd with only stern glances. "Then again, if I was being escorted by two dozen soldiers, I suppose I'd feel safe as well."

Gib watched as a carriage made of a smooth, dark wood and trimmed with golden details pulled by a team of four horses made its way through the congested street. Even the spokes of the wheels shone with a metallic gleam in the sunlight. The carriage windows were covered by velvet curtains that rustled in the breeze but didn't stir enough to allow a glimpse of whoever was inside.

"Do you suppose the King's in there?" Gib asked, squinting against the harsh sunlight.

Joel shrugged. "I wouldn't think so. The council would balk at even the suggestion of Arden's ruler leaving the palace. It's more likely to be the royal children and perhaps my Aunt Dahlia, the Queen. She comes into the city frequently to visit the local orphanages and to bring offerings to the Temple of the Two."

"What about Diddy? Is it possible he's here?"

"Perhaps." Joel motioned for Gib to follow and they moved farther down the street, away from the clutter of people. "But you have to understand that a different set of rules apply out here. Prince Didier can be your friend while you're in class with him, just as Queen Dahlia can be my aunt in private, but while under the scrutiny of the public eye, they're both members of the royal family and we're their subjects. Do you understand why that has to be?"

Gib gave a hesitant nod. He understood but didn't have to like it. It was no wonder Diddy hadn't wanted to reveal his true identity. Gib glanced over his shoulder and watched as the royal guardsmen formed a protective barrier around one of the food stands. The carriage door was open now, and Gib could see several people getting out, though he was too far away to see if Prince Didier was among them. All around, the city folk of Silver watched in wide-eyed awe as the royal family approached the vendor, but Gib found himself grimacing. Perhaps the comforts of palace living were not worth the price after all.

He turned to his friend. "Joel, I'm still worried about the royal family. Even if the conversation I overheard never amounted to anything, there must be other people out there planning similar attacks. What if something happens to Diddy or any of his siblings? They aren't protected as well as King Rishi."

Joel let out a sigh, his hand coming down to rest on Gib's forearm. "There will always be risk. That comes with being a royal. But they can't be forced to live in a cage either. Didier and his siblings are allowed so few liberties as it stands. To take away any more would be cruel. Besides, look at their escort. The royal guardsmen are well trained, and each of them would gladly lay down his life to defend the Radek family." Joel smiled warmly and motioned for Gib to follow. "Come on, I want to try to find some pastries to bring home for my sisters as a gift before we leave."

They spent the next half mark browsing the vendor booths set up along Traders Row. All kinds of goods were on display for purchase. Gib's mouth watered at the sight of steaming minced pies, fruit cakes garnished with little red berries, and sausage links that hung from strings above the stalls. Jewelry and clothing were also for sale—large hoop earrings made from silver, golden rings encrusted with gemstones, and pearl necklaces fit for any noble lady. Some of the vendor stalls were draped in clothing—fur cloaks and mittens, hats and woolen caps, and more scarves than Gib had ever seen in his life, and all were for sale.

"What is this?" Gib asked, pointing to a small evergreen plant which had been decorated with bells and fancy ribbon.

Joel issued a chuckle. "It's a kissing bush."

"Oh." Gib's cheeks went red. He'd never heard of it, but given the name, the implication was obvious enough. "I don't think I've ever seen such a thing before."

Joel paid no heed to the sentinel trainee's discomfort and went on to explain. "Often times during Midwinter, families will display such trees at the entrance of their homes. If an unwed lady or man is kissed while in sight of the kissing tree, it is believed good fortune will be bestowed upon them the following year."

Gib rubbed the back of his neck absently. "And what happens if they *aren't* kissed?"

The mage trainee snorted and made a ridiculous face. "Well naturally, shame and adversity will follow the poor souls whenever they go—so the legend says." Joel's handsome features constricted as he laughed. "It's quite a silly custom, I know."

Gib joined in a moment later, unable to conceal his shameless grin. "If we're supposed to kiss someone here and now, I guess both of us are doomed."

Joel choked as he laughed, eyes widening as he gave Gib a nudge in the chest. "Oh, stop. I am doomed. I'm sure a dozen young ladies would line up to have a go with you, Gibben Nemesio."

But what if I want you to be the one I kiss? Gib thought with despair. He focused his attention on the tree so he wouldn't have to look Joel in the eye. "I doubt that. I'm just a simple farm boy. I'd wager you'd have a longer line than I." He swallowed, too afraid to say the words truly on his mind. *I would stand in front of the kissing tree with you without a second thought if only you wouldn't turn me away.* Gib's breath caught in his throat when he caught Joel's gaze. The mage trainee's smile had fallen away and his eyes were inquisitive, questioning. Gib could tell his friend was seeking an answer to the unspoken question on both their minds.

Gib shifted his weight from one foot to the other. He could think of nothing to say, so to avoid another awkward lull, he changed the subject. "We should keep looking for those pastries. Heidi and Carmen will be upset if you don't bring them back a treat."

"Yes," Joel replied. The older boy blinked once, slowly, and Gib was certain he detected a trace of disappointment in his roommate's crystal blue eyes.

While Joel bartered and paid for a box of pastry desserts, Gib busied himself by pawing through a rack of brightly colored scarves at a nearby booth. Despite the sunshine and the festive atmosphere, his mood was glum. *I'm a coward. I've had ample opportunities to explain to Joel how I feel, yet I've managed to botch every chance due to my own idiocy. It's clear he isn't going to make the first move. Not that he should have to. He's been hurt already—deeply hurt.* Gib bit his bottom lip, tears of frustration threatening to spill over the crests of his eyelids.

"Halt there, boy!"

Gib was so caught up in his own emotions he barely registered the booming voice. It wasn't until Joel flew up nearby that the sentinel trainee noticed something was happening. Only a few paces from where they stood, a boy with wild, russet hair was being dragged into the street by a pair of sentinels. The boy was flailing his arms and trying to twist away from the guards. His tattered clothing clung to his emaciated body by threads. He had no hat or gloves, and the soles of his boots were so worn Gib imagined the boy's toes must be frozen inside.

The two burly sentinels marched the boy to where a hat vendor was standing with arms crossed over his squat chest and mouth pulled back into a fearsome scowl. One of the sentinels gave the boy a harsh shove, and the youngster crashed into the snow with a gasp.

"Is this the thief?" one of the sentinels asked.

"Aye," replied the vendor, sneering down at the alleged perpetrator. "That's 'im all right. He's the waif who stole a fur cap from my booth."

"I didn't neither," the boy cried, tears streaming down his dirty cheeks. "I didn't take nothin'."

The vendor balled his hands into fists. "Lyin' thief. I saw it with my own eyes. You took the hat and ran off without payin' even one silver for it." The vendor's caustic voice carried through the muted street. Indeed, business seemed to have come to a grinding halt as all eyes fell upon the confrontation.

"I didn't do it," the boy whined in a pitiful voice.

The sentinel turned to face his partner. "Search him."

The other guard nodded and began to roughly search the youngster. Only a moment later, he found a hat lined with rabbit fur stuffed into a sleeve. The boy wailed and once again tried to escape. He must have known there was no use denying the theft any longer.

The vendor's eyes widened. "That's the hat! That little bastard took my hat!"

Gib watched the scene unfold before him with a growing sense of pity. This poor boy couldn't have been any older than Calisto. What sort of desperation could the youngster be feeling if he needed to steal to survive?

"That settles it," the first of the sentinels remarked. Reaching down, he gripped the boy by the back of the neck and hoisted him to his feet. "It's off to the stockade for you. Maybe a couple days there will make you think twice about stealing again."

The boy's eyes were wide with terror. "No, please!"

The sentinel cuffed him on the back of the head. "Quiet, *boy*."

The vendor pointed a stubby finger at the boy. "Look to see if he's had previous offenses before you take 'im away," the vendor demanded.

The boy wailed as one of the sentinels held him in place while the other guard ripped the boy's tattered cloak away from his body and tossed it to the ground. The boy whimpered and tried to twist away, but the iron grip around his arm forced him to stand still. The other guardsman pulled the waif's tunic down, low enough to reveal his gaunt neck and shoulders. Gib stood close enough to see an angry, blistering welt branded into the boy's skin just above his left shoulder blade. All around, people gasped and whispered about the boy's fate being sealed.

The restraining sentinel growled as he spoke to his comrade. "He bears the mark all right. You know what that means."

"Please," the boy begged through his tears. "Let me go! I won't never do it again, I swear!"

"You won't be doing much of anything without hands!" the second guard snarled in response.

"We should leave," Joel hissed in Gib's ear. "I don't want to see 'justice' being enforced here." The mage trainee set a firm hand onto Gib's shoulder, trying to redirect his attention, but Gib was unable to turn away from the wretched scene as it played out before him.

The sound of metal scraping on leather rang out as one of the sentinels drew his sword. The blade gleamed dangerously in the sunlight. All the color drained from Gib's face as he realized what was about to happen. His brown eyes darted to Joel. "He's just a boy. Someone has to stop this."

Joel's eyes were filled with despair. He couldn't even meet Gib's gaze. "It's the law. There's nothing to be done for him. Come, let's leave. *Please.* Neither of us needs to see this!"

The young boy was being dragged, kicking and screaming, to a nearby vendor booth. People jumped out of the way, not wanting to be caught between the guards and their quarry. Gib took a step back as well, trembling as he watched one of the sentinels force the sobbing boy's arm flat against the wooden surface of the booth. The other sentinel prepared his sword, gripping the hilt between large hands. Tears streamed down the boy's cheeks as he begged them for mercy, but neither sentinel appeared to be in a forgiving mood.

The hat vendor was there too. His mouth twisted into a baleful smile as he pointed at the boy. "Carry out the punishment, gentlemen!"

Gib's stomach flopped as he tried to hold down the contents. *Oh Goddesses, they're really going to do it. Right here in front of everyone. They're going to cut off his hands and no one can stop it.* Joel was pulling Gib's arm, telling him to look away, but he was frozen in place. He watched in horror as the sentinel raised the longsword into the air, high above his head. Time seemed to stand still. The blade hung there, poised as though it was floating.

Gib slammed his eyes closed. He didn't want to see the weapon when it came crashing down—

"*Halt!*"

Down the street, one of the royal guardsmen had separated himself from the rest of the procession. He left his post in front of the carriage and was storming toward the two sentinels and the vendor. Gib's breath caught in his throat as he watched the pair of sentinels pause and exchange glances. He hoped this was some kind of intervention but was unsure if the royal guardsman was here to stop the madness or carry out the sentence himself. Ceremonial armor shimmering in the daylight and broadsword in hand, the royal guardsman glared down the length of his narrow nose at the sentinels, more intimidating than even Weapons Master Roland. Dark eyes glinted from within the helm.

The guardsman gripped his sword in one hand and pointed at the young boy with the other. "There's no need to carry out such a harsh punishment for a mere child. Hand the lad over to me. I'll see to it he's *properly* reprimanded."

The hat vendor issued a challenging snort. "Hand him over? On whose authority?"

The royal guardsman shot him a wry smile, but his words didn't contain even a trace of humor. "On the authority of Her Majesty, Queen Dahlia Adelwijn. The Queen commands you turn the boy over to the Crown of Arden."

Immediately, the two sentinels relinquished their hold on the boy, bowed their heads, muttered hasty apologies, and melted into the crowd.

The hat vendor's eyes bulged with rage. "It's written in the laws that this waif be punished for his crimes!"

The royal guardsman regarded the squat vendor for a moment before responding in a voice laced with superiority. "And so he will be, in a manner Her Majesty feels appropriate."

"B–but," the vendor floundered, face as red as a tomato. "The boy's been caught thieving already—he bears the brand on his shoulder as proof! This is his second offense! The law states he's to lose his hands so he can't steal again!"

The guardsman took the boy by the arm and began to guide him away but whirled back around to face the vendor. "Are you questioning the authority of Her Majesty, *your* Queen? I can very well escort you to the stocks if you're unable to quiet your foul mouth."

Jaw set into an ugly grimace, the vendor said nothing more. Gib smiled to himself. *He's smart enough to know when to shut up. A pity. I would've loved to see the royal guardsman drag the vile little man away.*

Joel cleared his throat. "I think it's best we leave."

Gib nodded, watching as the guardsman escorted the young boy in the direction of the carriage. "What do you think will happen to him? The

Queen won't—have his hands removed, will she? He's just a poor boy. It doesn't seem fair."

The crowd was dispersing around them. Joel sighed, keeping his voice low and measured. "I'm sure by now you've come to realize many of Arden's laws are unfair. I agree with you. It's an unjust punishment for a little boy who likely has no home or food and probably had been driven by the cold to steal that cap." Joel offered a smile. "For what it's worth though, I know my aunt, and I assure you, she would never let harm befall a child in her presence."

Gib's shoulders lost some of their rigidity. "That's good to know."

The mage trainee motioned in the direction of the royal procession. "It's likely tonight the boy will enjoy a warm meal and bed to sleep on for the first time in his life, if Queen Dahlia has her way. Before she was Queen, my aunt was a patron at the orphanage. She spent a lot of time and money there, and even after she accepted the role of Queen, she still feels it her duty to protect the children of Silver City."

"Well, now I know where Diddy gets his kind heart from," replied Gib as they made their way in the direction of the Adelwijn estate. He snorted a laugh. "If only all highborns could act with such compassion."

"Imagine that," Joel mumbled under his breath.

Gib furrowed his brow, a secondary thought crossing his mind. "Those sentinels—they were cruel too."

Joel's voice was flat. "Yes. You'll find that many abuse the power they've been given. This is why I warned you to stay clear of them today."

The two boys walked in silence. Gib was lost in his own thoughts. *Those sentinels—they could be me in a few years. I might very well be thrown into a similar situation. I don't think—no—I wouldn't be able to do something like that to a little, helpless boy. I couldn't. I don't care if it's the law. It's not right. That boy was starving and freezing. He needed a helping hand, not punishment.*

"I'm never going to be like that," Gib replied at last. "When I'm a sentinel, I'll uphold the values Seneschal Koal spoke about on that first day of class. I won't ever raise my sword against a child or anyone else who needs help. I'll serve justice if I must, but I'll never oppress."

Joel stopped, turning around so he was facing his roommate. A sad, sweet smile formed, sending a bolt of exhilaration surging through Gib's veins. "You, Gibben Nemesio, are a beautiful soul. Don't ever change. Ever."

CHAPTER EIGHT

The rest of the day whirled by in such a tangle of celebration and preparation that Gib lost track of time. When he awoke the following morning, his first thought was to look over at Joel, who was slumbering peacefully in his own bed. He looked lovely as always. It seemed a shame he would have to awaken soon.

The sentinel trainee's stomach rumbled as he became aware of the wonderful aromas hanging in the air. These were not normal breakfast foods. He could smell breads and pies, meats and spices. Gib's mouth watered and he wondered what could be waiting for them in the dining room.

Feet swinging over the edge of the cot, Joel sighed and blinked his eyes open. A moment passed when Gib couldn't look away. He was entirely transfixed by those misty blue orbs and began to wonder if he'd ever not be.

Joel rubbed his eyes as he sat up. "I'd thought I was dreaming at first. It took me a moment to realize you were actually sitting in front of me."

Gib glanced down at himself, still in the borrowed sleeping gown. He winced. "A good dream I hope." The sentinel trainee brought his hands up to his hair only to find that it was—as predicted—a wild mane that wouldn't be smoothed no matter what he tried to do. "I'm terrifying enough to be a nightmare right now though."

Joel chuckled as he rose from his own bed. "Gib, you don't know how wonderful you are." He smiled so genuinely that Gib could almost forget the broken, withdrawn boy from the start of the academic year. "I'd venture to say our baths are ready and then we may go eat."

"It smells like there's a feast down there."

"Oh, there no doubt will be. Mother always goes overboard with our Midwinter meal."

Gib found himself nodding, even though the concept of having too much food was lost to him. "I hope my brothers have plenty to eat today."

Joel's handsome face pinched as he winced. "I'm sorry they couldn't be here. Or that you couldn't be there. If it were within my power—"

"It's not." Gib tried change the subject. It had been a stupid thing to say. Joel shouldn't have to feel guilty for being born to a wealthy family.

Gib tried to right the situation. "Despite our modest means, my family has always done well enough for Midwinter—I didn't mean to make it sound as though I was being ungrateful. I miss them is all."

"I know." Joel's voice was soothing. "I'm sure they miss you as well. Perhaps when the caravan road clears you'll be able to send them a letter."

"I'll have to. I mean, I'm sure they know why I didn't make it home but still—" Gib put his hands in his hair and looked out the bedroom window at the snow. "Liza wasn't able to make it back to them either. She's on duty."

"I hope next year's festivities are more suitable to your family," Joel responded. The mage trainee had a hard time maintaining eye contact but his words were sincere. "I wouldn't know what to do with myself if I were to be separated from my loved ones on such a day as this."

Gib willed away the guilt and worry with a deep sigh. "They'll be all right. I'm sure of it." He turned back to his companion and offered the best smile he could muster. "Baths then?"

Joel nodded as he swept toward the door. "Yes."

Once they'd bathed, Joel offered Gib some fine garments to wear. The clothing was too short for Joel but still a bit long for Gib. Either way, the lush tunic and leggings were a vast improvement over Gib's worn-out clothes or the standard Academy uniform.

Gib looked at himself in the hallway mirror and barked a nervous laugh. He didn't recognize himself. "I hope your family has a sense of humor."

Joel smiled as he adjusted the long sleeves and pant legs. "You look fine. Just make sure not to fidget and it should hold." He took a step back to appreciate their joined efforts, giving a brief nod before going solemn. "My family will be here in the next couple of marks."

"Is everything all right?"

Joel forced a smile which Gib immediately disliked. The mage trainee's features were much better suited to honesty. The older boy cleared his throat and wrung his hands as though he was nervous. "Everything will be all right but—I feel I should warn you. You've already met Liro. You'll also meet my uncle today and he's much like Liro. I promise you everyone else will be favorable. They'll see you for what you *are*, not what you *are not*. Neetra, however—" He fished for words.

Gib acknowledged his understanding with a stiff nod. "Stay clear of Neetra and Liro. Got it." He offered a smile and hoped Joel would follow along, but it seemed his heart was heavy with worry.

"It's not fair and I'm sorry. They'll most likely ignore you, but even that is terrible."

"It's all right." Gib wanted to reach for Joel, to take his hand or touch his shoulder, but knew better. "Trust me, if Liro and your uncle ignoring me is the worst of it, I'll have a pleasant day."

Joel's smile was weak. He managed a nod and led the way down the stairs. "I'm sure there are things we can do to help. It will pass the time at least. And perhaps we should check on breakfast."

"I thought you'd never ask. Everything smells amazing."

"Unfortunately, you smell our midday meal. Breakfast this morning will be light, probably porridge with dates or toast. That way we will be more than ready to eat our fill when it's time."

Gib didn't mean to sound disappointed, but the emotion must have seeped through in his response regardless. Joel glanced back with a smile and assured him it would be worth the wait.

As soon as they walked through the dining room door, Gib knew he'd heard the truth. The smell of roasting ham, breads, sweets, gravies, and other wonderful foods bombarded his senses and made him want to beg at the kitchen door like a stray. It was with a heavy heart and watering mouth that he accepted his humble dish of porridge and took a seat next to Joel.

Across the large dining table sat Carmen, the youngest of Joel's sisters. She swung her feet back and forth beneath the table and picked the dates out of her breakfast one by one. Carmen kept her shrewd blue eyes on Gib. "How old are your brothers again?"

Gib smiled at her forwardness. She wasn't at all what he thought a highborn lady should be. He liked it. "Tayver is your age, twelve, and Calisto is nine. He'll be ten come spring."

Carmen nodded. "Will Tayver come to Academy next harvest? I'm going to go. Father says that if I behave myself I can even sign up to be a sentinel trainee." Having eaten all the dates, she began to pick at her porridge. "Are there any girls in your year? I heard there aren't many."

Gib swallowed a bite of his food and nodded heartily. "There are a couple of them. One of my good friends Kezra is a girl. She's one of the best in our class with a sword and shield."

Heidi, who was busy adjusting her dress, looked up. "Kezra Malin-Rai? Her elder brother was in my year when we went to primary school." She stuck her nose in the air. Heidi was *everything* Gib had expected a highborn lady to be. "Kezra was always rolling around in the dirt and getting into fights—most unbecoming of a lady."

Joel took a brief moment to scold his sister, reminding her that breakfast was getting cold. The four youths went quiet after that and ate without conversation. Just as their dishes were emptying, Mrifa came bustling out of the kitchen with a large pie in her hands. She set the hot pastry on the sill to cool before fixing a gaze on Joel and Gib. "Would the two of you be available to help move the furniture into place for our dinner?"

Gib jumped out of his seat to help. She'd been so kind to him already and he wanted to be sure he did all he could as a means of repaying such hospitality.

Mrifa laughed at his zealous reaction. "You're such a good boy, Gibben. With a work ethic such as that, you'll have no trouble in your future." She stopped for a moment to look him over with a narrower gaze. He thought to tug on his sleeves or straighten the tunic but he remembered Joel telling him to leave the clothing alone. Mrifa smiled as she touched his jawline. "I wish there was time to hem these clothes for you. Joel outgrew them so fast."

Gib turned his eyes downward, face growing warm with color. "No, Lady Mrifa, you've already done so much for me. I—thank you. For everything."

Her hand was gentle on his cheek. "No, Gibben. Thank you."

Gib didn't know what she meant and didn't have a chance to ask her. The servant, Otos, knocked and humbly entered the room. Joel and Gib were sent to follow, and the three of them set up the main hall so it was fit to accept their expected guests. So many stools and lounges were brought out that Gib began to wonder how many people would be visiting today.

When he voiced his question, Joel smiled. "Just be grateful this year it's only my father's brother who's coming. Last year it was my mother's family—her brother, sister, the in-laws, and all of their children."

Gib laughed and continued his work. "I forget how big some of the families are here."

The next few marks of the day escaped so fast that Gib had no idea where they went. All around was the bustle of food being prepared, the fuss over the girls to make sure they were "presentable," and the last-minute straightening up to be sure everything was in place for their guests. By the end of it, Gib was as worried about the way everything looked as Mrifa seemed to be. Part of him wished it was already over so he wouldn't have to think about it or stress any more. When he said as much, Joel laughed in agreement.

They were gathered in the front hall to receive their guests when Mrifa ushered Otos to the front door. The pie she'd set in the dining room sill was now carefully wrapped. Mrifa fussed with the servant's worn cloak a little as he put it on. When Otos was ready to brave the cold, she handed him the pie with a smile. "Say hello to your family for us and be careful in the cold. Are you sure you don't want to take a carriage? The ice is dreadful."

Otos kept his dark eyes cast toward the floor. His cheeks might even have shown a blush. "No, m'lady. I'll walk. It's not far."

Mrifa set her mouth into a thin line but nodded. "All right. Be safe.

Hurry along now. Enjoy your family dinner—we'll see you on the morrow."

"Yes, m'lady." Otos ducked through the door and was gone the next minute. Mrifa stayed at the open door for a moment or two and fretted about the weather. Gib smiled because even though Otos was a grown man, Mrifa seemed to brood over him as if he were one of her own children.

Gib nudged Joel with his elbow. "Is Tabitha going to leave as well?"

Joel shook his head, his features solemn. "No. She stays with us and takes her meal in private. Not everyone is so lucky to have a family."

"I see." Gib frowned, missing his brothers and sister terribly. He was going to be eating a fine feast without them, with no idea about their condition or whereabouts. He hoped Tayver and Calisto would have been invited to stay with the Fadells, but that wasn't for him to decide. And Liza—where was she to celebrate her Midwinter feast?

Heidi joined her mother, and the two women peered out the window. "Where are they? The soup will get cold."

Mrifa smiled and touched her daughter's shoulder. "Patience. Your father and uncle are important men. They can't drop their duties and leave on a whim."

Heidi nodded, but continued wringing her hands. "Does my dress look all right? My hair wouldn't do at all what I wanted it to."

Gib startled when both women cried out in unison to announce they saw the carriage. The Adelwijn children formed a quick line. Joel stood directly beside his mother while Heidi took the place next to him and Carmen capped the end. Gib stood awkwardly, wondering if he should join them—or possibly go somewhere else entirely.

Tabitha bustled to the door, readying herself to open it when the time arrived. Joel called out to Gib in a rushed voice. "Gib. Come stand behind Carmen so Mother can introduce you."

Gib leapt forward, wondering if it was normal for all highborn families to introduce themselves to their own kin. It seemed absurd to him, but then what did he know? His nervous hands sought to undo the work accomplished with his tunic, but he willed them down to his sides. Catching a sideways grin from Joel, Gib's face flushed with color.

The sound of people approaching made Gib's jaw clench. Tabitha opened the door and bowed her head as two men stepped through the threshold. Gib recognized the taller and broader of the two as Seneschal Koal Adelwijn. The seneschal was no less intimidating than he had been on the first day of class and was still dressed in his formal attire. His crimson cape blew back over his right shoulder in the cold winter wind.

Koal's companion was shorter and not as broad, yet he still bore a striking resemblance to the seneschal. With the same dark hair and fair features, their eyes were alike except for the color—brown as opposed to blue. Not unlike Liro, this man had the potential to be handsome if not for his sneer. Even before introductions could be made, Gib was certain this must be the uncle Joel had warned about.

Behind Seneschal Koal and his brother came a cluster of other family members. Two children, a boy and girl, looked to be about the same age as Calisto, and behind them were two other men. The first was busy keeping the children from tracking their wet boots through the house. His light chestnut hair was tied back, keeping his modest curls at bay, and his fair features were drawn in frustration. Green eyes flashed as he snipped at the children, who sighed and obliged him grudgingly while calling him by his first name—Bailey. As soon as their shoes were cleaned off properly, he stepped aside to help Tabitha collect cloaks, and Gib thought Bailey must be a servant as well.

The last man through the door was an all too familiar figure. Nawaz Arrio, dressed in a lush velvet doublet over an embroidered silk tunic, nodded curtly to Tabitha as she shut the door behind him. Gib noticed the young lord's typical smirk was nowhere to be seen and his eyes were sullen. Despite his fine attire and the upcoming feast, Nawaz seemed uncomfortable, even resentful.

Once everyone was inside and Mrifa had properly greeted her husband with a gentle embrace, she motioned toward Gib. "Welcome everyone. We have a guest with us for the holiday. This is Gibben Nemesio."

Gib cringed in his place as the entire flock proceeded toward him in an ordered line. As each person passed another, warm wishes were passed back and forth. Seneschal Koal hugged Joel and each of the girls on his way through and moved with such leisure that Gib had time to worry about how he must look. Had the seneschal even known Gib was invited to the feast? Would he be upset when he realized a common-born was present?

Gib wrung his hands as the seneschal came closer and caught a glimpse of Nawaz smirking darkly. *Of course that jackass finds this funny.* Memories of their escapade at the Rose Bouquet bombarded his mind. He remembered how he was left to fend for himself with an unknown prostitute and how his own thoughts had turned to Joel. Gib winced when he realized Koal Adelwijn was now standing directly ahead.

Koal was much like his son, except he was older and had flecks of silver in his dark hair. His misty eyes were intelligent as he studied the sentinel trainee. The seneschal's mouth was set in a thin line, but he didn't appear to be upset, only curious. He offered one of his large hands for a shake. "Seneschal Koal Adelwijn."

Gib's entire arm was numb as he lifted it to clasp hands with the seneschal. "Gibben Nemesio of Willowdale, sir."

Joel's uncle was right behind Koal. He glared down at Gib with an ugly sneer. "Who is *this* again? How does he know your son?" The whine in his high, fine voice was darkly insinuating. Gib fought to keep from shuddering, the full weight of the uncle's glare pressing down.

Koal withdrew his hand and turned to his brother. Gib thought he saw the seneschal roll his eyes as he replied, "They're roommates this year. Mrifa had told me he would be here but I'd forgotten. Apologies. It has been a long couple of days." He turned back to Gib and made a proper introduction. "High Counselor Neetra Adelwijn, this is Gibben Nemesio of Willowd—"

Joel's uncle stuck his pointed nose in the air and swept past them both. "Yes, yes. I heard the first time. I'm not deaf, brother."

Gib looked at the floor. He'd been warned of Neetra's foul personality but for some reason hadn't been prepared for the sting. Would there ever be anything he could do to win the councilor's approval? Gib looked up when he felt a hand rest on his shoulder.

Koal's mouth pressed into a tight line. "Apologies, little one." His voice was as kind as Neetra's had been condescending. "*I* am pleased to make your acquaintance." The seneschal bowed his head, and Gib immediately returned the gesture.

Mouth dry and wits failing him, Gib floundered for words. "I— Thank you, sir. It is an honor to be here." He wondered if the seneschal could even decipher the croaked words.

The seneschal took his leave with a small nod, and Gib had time to catch his breath as the children came through next. They were both dressed in finery, light blue silks and silver frills and cords. The girl curtsied and offered her hand, which Gib took despite his terror. Should he kiss it? She was highborn and he wasn't. It would seem to be custom, but he didn't want to make another gaffe.

Gib noted Nawaz giving Heidi's hand a simple peck. The young lord locked eyes with Gib just long enough for him to understand, and with a grateful nod, Gib did the same for the young girl. She bowed her head in response.

The young girl had the same dark eyes as Neetra but hers smiled with the rest of her face. "I'm Lady Inez Adelwijn, daughter of High Counselor Neetra Adelwijn."

Gib's voice was thick. "Gibben Nemesio of Willowdale. The honor is mine, m'lady."

Inez's smile was amused but not patronizing. She dropped her voice to a mere whisper. "Next time, introduce yourself first."

"Why?" The question rushed from Gib's mouth before he could stop it.

She took her hand from him to cover her giggling mouth. "Because we're the guests, silly." Inez picked up her lush skirt and moved over several steps to allow the second child access to Gib.

The boy who had entered with her came up next and offered his hand but didn't speak. He looked so much like Neetra that he must be the High Counselor's son.

Gib swallowed, wishing he could drop through a hole in the floor. He clasped the boy's hand. "G–Gibben Nemesio of Willowdale."

The boy flashed a bright smile. "Lord Inan Adelwijn, son of High Counselor Neetra Adelwijn. I'm pleased to make your acquaintance." He bowed his head.

"I—The pleasure is all mine."

Inan withdrew his hand, giggling softly. "Try not to stutter the next time, but you did well." He scurried to Inez, and they followed after their father.

Last to make his greeting was Nawaz. "Not too bad, really. Ya know, for a lowborn."

Gib sighed. A smile quirked at the corner of his mouth as he replied, "I never thought I'd be so happy to be introducing myself to you." He offered his hand.

Nawaz cocked his head to the side, considered, but ultimately rejected Gib's outstretched hand. "Nah, I've met you before. No need for introductions." An exasperated gasp escaped Gib's mouth. Nawaz laughed and mussed Gib's curls as he walked past. "You should know me well enough by now, boy. Your wrist looks good, by the way. You're welcome for fixing that."

Gib thought to argue with Nawaz or call him some nasty name. As it was, however, too many people were around.

Joel touched Gib's shoulder at that moment and all thoughts of avenging himself left his mind.

"You did well."

Warmth swelled in Gib's stomach as he turned to look into the mage trainee's eyes.

Joel's smile was apologetic. "I'm sorry I didn't think to step you through proper introductions. It never crossed my mind."

"Yeah. At least your cousins got a good laugh from it."

Joel's eyebrows shot straight up. "Oh, trust me, they must either like you or are on their very best behavior. Inan and Inez are both known to cause a fuss over the most ridiculous things."

Speaking of fussing, Gib could hear Lady Mrifa causing a small commotion as she followed Neetra's servant around. "Bailey, I insist you go seat yourself at the dining room table. You are a guest here!"

Bailey was shooing her away with a single, dismissive hand. "I'm a servant and this is what I do. Go attend your guests, m'lady, and don't worry yourself over me."

Mrifa groaned and tried to take a ladle from him. "I insist."

The servant narrowed his eyes and Gib thought he'd never seen such a thing. Neither Tabitha nor Otos dared speak to the good lady in such a light manner. Bailey's voice was crisp when he dropped it just low enough that those who were already in the dining room couldn't hear. "I swear to The Two, Mrifa, if I have to listen to that pompous windbag compliment himself one more time on his leadership skills, I'll break his scrawny chicken neck in two."

Mrifa raised her hand to her mouth but couldn't stop the incredulous laughter in time. "Bailey! That is your employer you're talking about."

Bailey nodded with a shrug. "I've told him as much myself but he still refuses to fire me. Pompous *and* daft, it would seem. Most unbecoming. I suppose it's a good thing he has me to raise his children to not be blathering idiots after himself."

Gib's jaw dropped and Joel laughed quietly, not that anyone would be able to hear him over his own mother's cackling delight. Joel leaned in closely to whisper in Gib's ear. "Bailey is unlike any other servant you'll ever meet. He's truly more a family member than hired help."

"I'd hope so, with a mouth like that." Gib still couldn't believe what he was hearing. "Has he been in Neetra's service long?"

Joel nodded and touched Gib's elbow, directing him to the dining room. "Yes. He's been a sort of nursemaid since before the twins were born. He bonded with Nawaz before his mother married Neetra. And more than that, Bailey's been King Rishi's dresser ever since the King took his place on the throne."

Gib was still at a loss. "A servant of the King *and* Neetra?" That seemed like more responsibility than he could comprehend. Another thought occurred to him. "Joel? Where is Neetra's wife?"

This question caused an instant lull in their conversation and Gib winced. He'd unwittingly overstepped some unknown boundary. Joel forced a tight smile and stopped Gib just short of entering the dining room. "She's no longer in Arden, though she and my uncle are still technically married. It would be best not to bring it up with anyone else here."

"I'm sorry. I didn't mean to pry."

Joel smiled and nodded toward the dining room. "It's all right. You'll find the highborn world is plagued with unmentionable truths and questions that can't be asked." He paused there for a moment. "I think I'd like your world better in that regard. Honesty should always be valued over shameful secrecy. Come, let's sit down to the feast."

Inside the dining room, the food had already been laid out. Gib's mouth watered at the sight of a giant roasted ham, placed in the center of the table. All around it were other fine things Gib had only dreamed of, for even the academy hadn't offered all of these delicacies. Boiled potatoes, gravies, breads of different colors and smells, roasted pheasant, pies, sausages, custards, and so many other things Gib had never seen before crowded the table. In all of his young life, he'd never imagined so much food could be served to one family.

Neetra and his children had already seated themselves with Joel's sisters and father. Koal had taken his place at the head of the grand table while the seat to his right remained empty, presumably for his wife. Neetra had taken the seat to Koal's immediate left leaving two empty spaces between him and his son, Inan. The three girls were all sitting on the opposite side. The two younger ones were giggling.

Joel touched Gib's shoulder. "Come sit beside me?"

Nodding, Gib followed at his friend's heels. Joel sat next to Inan, putting his cousin between himself and Neetra, and Gib took the next empty seat. "Are we waiting for your brother?"

Joel shrugged. "I'm really not sure. I suppose Mother will decide that."

"She won't want us to wait until the dinner is cold," Heidi remarked. She was exceptional at eavesdropping. "She and Bailey will be along any moment now." Her voice was impatient as she turned a narrow look onto Joel. "Have you seen Nawaz? Where did he go?"

Gib frowned and looked over his shoulder even as he heard Joel sigh. "I don't know, Heidi. Why don't you go look for him?"

She fixed her brother with a sour glare but before she could open her mouth, a commotion came from the front room. The servant, Bailey, was barking an order at someone. "Get in there and stop pissing around out here! You are under foot."

Less than a moment later, Nawaz slipped through the door and came into the dining room. His expression was grim, with his mouth pressed into a thin line and his spine rigid.

The councilor glared at Nawaz from behind a chalice and with voice raised just enough to carry through the room said, "Ah. There you are—looking like some displaced stray. Couldn't find anything useful to do?" He took a long pull from his cup before setting it down briskly. Nawaz remained silent the entire time, jaw locked and face pink. "Well, stop pouting. Sit down and appreciate your host's hospitality."

Gib held his breath, waiting for Nawaz to fight back. Memories of the young lord lifting Annwyne off the floor and yelling at her to shut her mouth came rushing back to him. Surely Neetra Adelwijn was no less deserving of such treatment as he sat there like a smug cat. Gib was sure that any moment, Nawaz would come to his senses and knock that gloating bastard end over end. When the highborn sank into the chair next to Gib without speaking back, Gib blinked in surprise.

Joel leaned around to give Nawaz a small smile. The young lord nodded, spirit dim. Indeed, he was barely recognizable. Gib let out a heavy sigh, his appetite waning even as the conversation around them began to pick back up.

Carmen and Inez chattered on about Academy and what they would do with themselves once they were done with their schooling. Gib found it peculiar to hear the dreams and ambitions of ones so young and privileged. Koal distracted Neetra with polite but uninspired conversation.

Heidi smiled warmly—an expression that looked out of place on her face—and leaned over her empty plate a little. "Nawaz, how is your internship faring? Are you looking forward to graduation?"

Nawaz didn't respond immediately, opting to fill his goblet with wine from a nearby pitcher. When he did answer her, the young lord sounded only half interested. "It's going as well as can be expected. I'm being forced to do it, and it will be done in a little more than a year's time."

Gib took the pitcher as it was passed to him and continued to eavesdrop.

Heidi didn't seem to catch Nawaz's icy reception. Instead, her eyes sparkled as she continued the conversation. "When you graduate you'll be able to get a fine job and buy a nice house. If you save for a year, or even two, you could buy something on this very street or the next one over." Nawaz grunted and drank while she tittered on. "And a year after you graduate I'll finish my schooling. It will work out perfectly."

"Hrm. Perfect." Nawaz refused to elaborate further, but her smile didn't falter.

When an uncomfortable silence grew around them, Joel stepped in to fill the void. "You know, Heidi, there's an old saying about chickens and counting."

She fixed angry eyes on her brother and opened her mouth but was stopped short when Mrifa came bustling through the entryway and announced they would be taking their soup now. Koal looked up from his conversation with Neetra long enough to ask his wife about their missing son.

Mrifa's mouth pulled down slightly at the corners. "I'm not sure, but you know Liro. He'll arrive when he deems it appropriate."

Joel snorted, rolling his eyes. Gib smiled and refrained from shaking his head. Who in their right mind would keep their family and this great feast waiting? He supposed Liro's sanity was debatable—

"Lady Mrifa Adelwijn, seat yourself," Bailey demanded as he swept through the room with Tabitha scurrying behind him. He set out the bowls more quickly than she could fill them, and Tabitha kept casting the male servant brooding looks.

Gib scrutinized the odd dish before him as he waited patiently for his soup to be served. The high gloss bowl was made from the purest white material and flaming phoenixes were painted along the sides. Smooth and cool, it was unlike any pottery he'd ever seen before.

Joel's voice was warm in Gib's ear. "It's porcelain—from Beihai."

"Isn't that far away?" Gib asked, so preoccupied with the details of the painting he barely heard Joel chuckle.

"It's as far east as you can go before meeting the sea."

Lady Mrifa piped up, settling her fine skirt as she took the seat next to her husband. "Oh yes. The phoenix bowls. They're lovely, aren't they? King Rishi gifted them to me several years back and I've only ever dared use them for special occasions." She smiled when Tabitha poured a ladle of soup into her dish before continuing. "If they were to break I would surely never be able to get a replacement."

When each bowl was full and Bailey finally sat at long last—per Mrifa's request and Neetra's command—they were allowed to enjoy the appetizer. Gib savored the rich broth, full of vegetables, wild rice, and chicken. Back on the farm, this would have been considered a meal on its own, but here it was meant to make him crave the main course even more. It worked like one of Joel's spells. The bottom of the bowl appeared all too soon, and Gib could scarcely wait for the next dish.

Koal began to slice the ham while other dishes were passed from hand to hand. Gib rolled his eyes when he heard Neetra snivel about having to fill his own plate. "Where is that servant of yours? Did she make off to be useless?"

The seneschal snorted, fixing his brother with a dark look. "Tabitha is taking her Midwinter meal in the other room. This is a holiday, after all."

Neetra stuck his nose in the air, and Gib saw Nawaz clench his jaw. Joel, Inez, and Carmen also seemed equally put off by the councilor's behavior. If Neetra noticed, he surely didn't care and promptly went back to his drink. The lull lingered before the others around the table ventured back to their prior conversations.

Nawaz bumped his elbow into Gib and passed him the gravy boat. "Maybe you can ask Lady Mrifa to save some of this for your friend Nage."

Gib froze for an instant, reminiscing. What an odd sight it must have been for the highborn to meet the two of them while they ate gravy straight from a bowl with nothing but bread to dip into it. A rebellious smile stole across Gib's face as he broke down into sobbing laughter.

Joel glanced up from his own plate, and one by one, the others around the table also stopped their conversations to look at Gib. When Lady Mrifa smiled and asked if he was all right, Gib nodded and poured himself some gravy before passing it on to Joel.

"Never better, m'lady. I swear it. Thank you for all of these wonderful foods."

She smiled warmly and bowed her head. Seneschal Koal might have even grinned a little as he handed out thick slabs of ham. The mood around the table lightened after that and the meal was enjoyed.

When everyone was close to being done with the main course and contemplating dessert, a commotion came from the front door. Lady Mrifa leapt to her feet at once and bustled out to see who it was. A moment later, her voice rang high and clear as she announced that Liro had arrived at long last. Gib's stomach lurched and he could hear both Nawaz and Joel sigh heavily. Even the other children fell silent.

Liro marched into the dining room a moment later, his mother virtually hanging off him. Without so much as a backward glance, he shooed her away with one hand as he came toward Koal and Neetra. Cloak still clasped around shoulders and dark hair speckled with snow, Liro was a formidable sight. As always, his mouth was pulled down into an ugly frown, and he glared around at all of them as though he disapproved.

"Father," Liro offered in greeting to the seneschal. His lofty voice carried across the quiet room as he bowed his head.

Koal tilted his own head downward in return. "Take off your cloak and sit down. What kept you?"

"Apologies for being tardy, I was unwell earlier." Mouth still pressed into a thin line, Liro unclasped his cloak and gestured to the empty space about him. "Where are the servants? There was no one to open the door when I arrived."

Lady Mrifa adjusted her skirt as she sat down for the second time. Her cheeks were flushed with color. She kept her voice even but the lack of warmth gave away her discontentment. "This is a holiday, Liro. Otos is with his family and Tabitha is taking her much deserved meal."

Liro groaned, annoyed. "A servant has a duty to see to the affairs of the house, Mother. I stood at the door, waiting. I even had to knock—at my own parents' door."

Koal leaned back in his seat and tilted his head to one side. "I'm sorry about that. Have you forgotten how the handle works?"

Liro's face pinched, and Gib bit his bottom lip to keep from laughing. Nawaz barked a laugh, drawing attention to himself. The elder Adelwijn son turned cold blue eyes toward their end of the table, and Gib sank down in his chair under the weight of the young lord's glare.

"I see we have—*guests*," Liro remarked. Nothing about his tone sounded pleasant as he removed the cloak from around his neck and folded it over his arm. "Mother, you're too kind, always taking in strays—and surely without a word of thanks."

Gib's face almost burst from the heat rising to his cheeks, and Joel instinctively jerked his hand toward Gib as if to protect him.

Seneschal Koal focused his sharp eyes onto Liro. "This is our guest, Gibben Nemesio of Willowdale. He's Joel's roommate and friend. You would do well to treat him with respect."

Liro paused and visibly recoiled as his gaze flickered to Gib. An evident note of shock could be heard in Liro's voice when next he spoke. "Oh, I see. I hadn't even noticed him, hidden as he was." Liro inclined his head in a mockery of a bow before pressing on. "I, of course, was referring to our good uncle's waif, Nawaz."

Nawaz flinched as though he'd taken a physical blow and sucked in his bottom lip. Joel gasped. Lady Mrifa and Bailey both turned a sharp look. Even Heidi, who had done nothing but twitter on mindlessly since Gib had first met her, whirled around to tell her brother to mind his mouth. For all of this, Liro only smiled. Gib shuddered as a jolt of cold resonated through his bones.

Koal frowned and shook his head. "We're not doing this, Liro. Our guests are—"

"Nay, brother." Neetra waved a dismissive hand and smiled in that same smug manner as before. "You do your son no favors by silencing him. The truth, no matter how unpopular, cares not who tells it. Liro's courage to speak honestly shouldn't be squashed."

This drew reprisal from Koal, Mrifa, and Bailey in unison. Despite the formality of their dinner, the heads of the house were at odds with their guests. Gib stared at his plate and stayed as quiet possible. The other children did the same. They had crossed into another of those unspoken guidelines which dictated how the highborn were to behave. So while the debate at the head of the table raged on, the rest of them sat in silence, waiting for it to ebb.

At one point Liro's voice separated from the others. "I only mean to say that proper respect and gratitude should be shown. My good uncle didn't have to take on a bastard and raise it as his own. Nawaz Arrio, despite his name, has been given all the fineries Lord Neetra has worked his life away for. Nawaz resides in the palace, has the finest schooling at his disposal, and even carries the crest of the Adelwijn family. Such great allowances should not be taken lightly."

The conversation grew even more heated. Gib could hear Nawaz's teeth grinding together. When the young lord cleared his throat and made to stand, Joel's hand shot out across Gib to grab Nawaz's wrist. "Nawaz, no. You needn't play into this." Joel's voice was hushed but all of the lordlings and young ladies could hear him.

Heidi's cheeks had gone a terrible scarlet under her powered face. "Joel is right. Liro knows what he's doing. Acknowledging him will only encourage this despicable behavior."

Gib agreed but felt it wasn't his place to say as much. Nawaz, however, seemed not to be swayed by their words. The young lord shook his head once, keeping his voice low and controlled. "Despite any of that, it is my duty to respond. If I don't, I'll be a coward as well as a bastard."

The twins had remained eerily quiet until now, but Inez broke her silence. "Nawaz, no. Let Father and Liro have their moment. It will pass and then we may—"

"Roll onto our backs, wag our tails, and hope for the best?" Nawaz shot back. No merriment entered his words; no glimmer in his eye suggested the analogy was a quip. Gib's guts churned as Nawaz stood and waited for an opportunity to speak.

The young lord cleared his throat to gain the attention of the adults at the head of the table, and though he spoke eloquently, his voice was raw and harsh. "I would beg forgiveness from my lord and high councilman, Neetra Adelwijn, as well as Lord Liro Adelwijn. If I've caused offence I assure you both it was not my intention." Every word grinded through his teeth like sand in a wheel cog.

Koal and Mrifa both opened their mouths as if to respond, horror etched across their countenances. Liro strolled closer, keeping his gaze fixed on his prey.

Pompous and overbearing, Liro closed in and his sinister voice dipped low as he replied, "Forgiveness granted, Arrio. It is good for every man to remember his place," Liro thrust his cloak at Nawaz, "which is why I'm sure you'll have no problem in hanging that up for me like a good lad."

Heidi shrieked her indignation. "Bad form, Liro Adelwijn!"

Joel gasped aloud, and Seneschal Koal flew to his feet. "That is enough! Liro, you can put your own damned cloak away! Nawaz, sit down."

Nawaz's eyes were bleary as he looked up from the cloak. The young lord began to nod, but Neetra's whine startled him, caused him to freeze in place.

"This is all nonsense. Liro is right, my stepson is rude. His privileged life has spoiled him and he often neglects to be sufficiently grateful. After all, were it not for the generosity of the Adelwijn family, he could just as well have wound up a Nessuno, working in the mines."

Bailey slammed his fist on the table so sharply that Lady Mrifa jumped almost as high as Gib. "Oh, this is ridiculous! Neetra Adelwijn, you pompous windbag, no wonder no one loves you." The servant rose to his feet so quickly he very nearly knocked into Liro. Bailey glared at the younger man without apology. "If the two of you are so determined to feel superior to someone then may I offer my assistance? *I'll* hang the damned cloak."

Liro paused, eyes flitting to his uncle. For the first time Gib had seen, Liro seemed to be in unfamiliar territory.

Neetra, however, overstepped his servant with little more than a grim look. "Bailey, sit down. This doesn't concern you."

Bailey waved toward Nawaz with a flourish and only won a more severe glare for his effort. "Well, it hardly concerns him either."

Neetra's voice clipped, his face angry and red. "Bailey, I will *not* be so considerate again. Sit down. This is between Nawaz and me."

The servant locked his jaw, an appalled look crossing his fair features. He only did as he was told when Inan reached up a hand and coaxed Bailey to take his seat once more. Gib's gut churned. It seemed as though Bailey, the servant of the King, was not used to being talked to in such a manner.

Neetra fixed his cold, dark eyes on Nawaz once more and issued a low hiss. "I've had enough of this humiliation, boy. You'll be gracious to our host or you'll leave."

Nawaz snorted, rolling his eyes. His smile was hollow and defeated and looked nothing like the young lord Gib had grown to know.

Unrelenting, Neetra kept his eyes locked on his stepson. "Are you not satisfied with the hospitality being shown us?"

The air in the room was thick and stale. Gib could hardly breathe. It took Nawaz a moment to respond. "Of course I'm satisfied with Seneschal Koal's hospitality."

Neetra's dark eyes flashed as he pointed a finger toward the cloak. "Then the least you could do is show it. *Take this and be gone!*"

Gib's gut clenched. Something sinister and familiar about Neetra's voice came to him just then. Perhaps it could be blamed on Diedrick Lyle for being so foul to everyone. But Gib felt it was something deeper than that. Some dark foreboding, something unfair that had pressed itself upon him or others like him who were utterly powerless at the time. He didn't want to dwell on this uncomfortable feeling.

Koal threw his hands into the air. "Oh, for the sake of The Two, Neetra, leave the boy alone! Let's be done with this."

"He's hardly a boy anymore. More a thorn in my side, and it is high time he began to act like a man."

Gib bit down on his tongue as Neetra Adelwijn's words sliced through the air like a sharpened knife. Gib had never known poison to be so bitter or cold. Out of the corner of his eye, Gib noted Nawaz wincing.

Seneschal Koal opened his mouth but Nawaz spoke first, directly to Neetra. "You're right, my lord. I've been impolite." He turned to Koal and offered a deep bow. "Apologies, Seneschal Koal Adelwijn. Please forgive this undeserving waif for not properly thanking you for your hospitality." He folded Liro's cloak tightly over his arm and refused to look any one person in the eye. The effort was in vain—if Gib could see his wet eyes, then surely so could everyone else. "I'll gladly take care of this for Lord Liro Adelwijn." Nawaz turned on his heels to leave.

Heidi stamped her foot from under the table and fixed her elder brother with a glare so icy it burned. "You, Liro Adelwijn, are a snake!"

Neetra frowned at her in a disapproving way. "Niece, it is impolite for a lady to criticize a lord so openly. What are they teaching you in those finishing classes if not how to behave and spare your family public shame?"

Joel locked his eyes onto his uncle. "Lineage. And it has become apparent Liro has inherited his forked tongue from some branch of the family tree."

Neetra physically reeled from the insult, his mouth agape. "I beg your pardon?"

Shoulders tense and pale face screaming of terror, the mage student pressed on bravely. "It's about time you did, Uncle. It would be the most polite thing you've done since your arrival."

Liro sneered at his brother, and Neetra's face was a mask of rage as he spun to look at Koal. "Are you going to allow him to speak to me like that?"

The seneschal drank from his goblet before responding. With a small, upward curl on one side of his mouth, Koal shifted his eyes to meet Neetra's terrible gaze. "Oh, shut up and sit down. He's only said what the rest of us have been avoiding." When Neetra didn't immediately respond, Koal's smile fell away entirely and he lost any hint of jovialness. The seneschal gave both Liro and Neetra a stern look. "Both of you, sit and be pleasant—or leave. That's the last I'll say on any of it."

Dark and brooding, both Liro and Neetra sat down, side by side. When Mrifa grudgingly offered desserts, the rest of the company tried to feign interest but everyone knew the merriment was over. Gib humbly accepted both pie and custard which were both delicious, but he couldn't find it within himself to enjoy either. His eyes kept darting back to the monsters who sat at the table, and he couldn't help but feel the cool of the empty seat beside him.

As soon as each person was done eating, they asked to be excused. Carmen and the twins asked if they could go play for a while before Neetra and his family had to leave. Heidi made some lame excuse about not feeling well. Bailey jumped up and immediately began clearing the table which, of course, caused Mrifa to join him, begging for him to stop and sit back down.

When they were the last at their end of the table, Joel touched Gib's shoulder gently to indicate it was time to leave. Gib pushed down the fluttering in his stomach and joined his roommate. Joel excused the both of them and Koal nodded. They received narrow looks from both Neetra and Liro, but Gib had expected as much.

As soon as they were out of the dining room, Joel looked around and wrung his hands. "I wonder where Nawaz has gotten to."

Gib scuffed his foot across the floor and couldn't bring himself to look his friend in the eye. "Joel? Is Nawaz—all right? Does Neetra always treat him that way?"

Joel paused, and Gib scratched the back of his neck. He knew before he asked that surely such a question would be taboo but wasn't able to help himself. Gib couldn't imagine a father approving of his son, adopted or not, any less than Neetra appeared to.

Joel's voice was cautious. "I'm sorry you had to see that."

"I'm sorry Nawaz had to be there for it."

"Yes." Joel glanced around, eyes alert in the event anyone should be listening to them. "My uncle isn't a generous man. I have no doubt you've figured out as much on your own. He doesn't give anything more than required, and he doesn't show respect for anyone who is 'beneath' him. When I was a young child, Neetra married a woman who already had a child though she'd never been married before. I was too young to understand then, but I understand now why Father and Mother never required me to call her aunt or speak to her any more than in passing. They knew even then that she wouldn't be a permanent addition to our family."

Gib blinked. "Why not? Did they know she planned on leaving Arden?"

Joel smiled, but it held no warmth. He hesitated, and Gib could tell the mage trainee was holding back information. Gib was determined not to push, but he couldn't deny his wish to understand more.

Joel finally conceded and hung his head as if admitting something terrible. "They knew the marriage was a ruse. Neetra was twenty-three when he married—and he only did it at all because it raised his credibility as a politician. There is no law that keeps unmarried men from joining the royal council but it's just not done that way. The councilors are supposed to set an example for the rest of the country. The appearance they desire is for the councilmen to all be married with children while also being wealthy and successful."

"That doesn't make any sense. Why marry just for the sake of furthering your career?"

Devastated blue eyes met Gib's own. "I would agree, but Neetra is— ambitious. He was willing to sacrifice his own happiness for success. Unfortunately, in his greed to paint a portrait of perfection for himself, Nawaz, Inan, and Inez were pulled into the mix."

Gib grunted. He was trying to understand, but some things were just beyond his ability to comprehend. "I guess it's a good thing Nawaz and the twins have Bailey then."

Joel nodded. "Oh, yes. Father begged and the King reassigned Bailey to work fewer marks for him so he could take care of the children for my uncle. Father and King Rishi were so concerned for the wellbeing of the children that they even agreed to pay Bailey extra as an incentive not to abandon them like their mother had done—though I doubt Bailey could ever find it within himself to leave Nawaz and the twins now." He glanced around. "I'm not supposed to know any of this, so you must keep it a secret."

The more Gib heard, the less he wanted to know, yet morbid curiosity and the sense of injustice drove him on. "Are the twins as mistreated as Nawaz?"

"No. They're Neetra's own flesh and blood. He has always favored them. It's just Nawaz. He'll never be good enough. It's like how the lowborn are treated. Or women. Or—" He paused and Gib knew where this was going even though Joel couldn't bring himself to say it. "—anyone who is different for any reason. People like Neetra and Liro will never respect them. They'll always only be servants, labor animals, soldiers for war."

"The King won't allow that, will he? I mean, the boy at the festival—"

Joel shook his head. "That was one person. King Rishi can only do so much without the council's backing."

The pieces clicked together and made Gib's stomach turn sour. "So as long as there are people like Neetra on the council, the King's hands are tied."

"I'm afraid so. It has taken King Rishi's entire reign to make any real changes and there is always the fear of falling back into the old ways."

Gib nodded, full of melancholy. He didn't know what else he could say and also knew he could do nothing to help change the situation. He was one farmer, an insignificant child compared to these learned men who ran the world around him. Gib sighed and stared down the length of the darkened hallway. "Should we—go find Nawaz?"

Joel forced a tight smile. "I would like to. I feel he needs to be reminded that not all Adelwijns are created monsters."

They parted ways, hoping to find the shunned lord faster for their joint effort. Joel swept away toward the sitting room, and Gib wandered back toward the kitchen and storage areas.

His footsteps fell lightly as he crept past the dining room. The three men inside were still deep in conversation, and Gib shuddered at what was being discussed. Even now, Neetra and Liro were both going on about how servants shouldn't be allowed to take rest on holidays. They talked as though these servants weren't people. Gib frowned as he stormed past the door and toward the pantry leading into the other side of the kitchen. He hesitated when he heard soft sobbing.

Surely that couldn't be Nawaz—could it? A nurturing voice cut through the silence from within the pantry.

"Heidi, calm yourself. This fuss won't do you any good." It was Lady Mrifa. Her tone was low and sweet. "Your father isn't going to make any rash choices. You know that."

Heidi sniffled. "I know, but Father doesn't like Uncle Neetra. And if Neetra continues to be so foul, Father will surely say no to the marriage."

Gib blinked. *Marriage? Marriage to whom?* Guilt bubbled up inside him. He shouldn't be listening to this. He was supposed to be looking for Nawaz, after all. He began to creep away, but Bailey's voice piped up.

"Seneschal Koal is a good and wise man, Heidi. He'll choose whether or not the two of you should be married based on Nawaz's merits. Not

Neetra's. Besides, dearling, there is still at least a year's time before a lady in your position should be worried about marriage. How are your classes going?"

Gib decided to scuttle away while he was still unnoticed. A smile crept across his face at the thought of Nawaz, who was perfectly comfortable bedding prostitutes and drinking the night away at The Rose Bouquet, marrying straight-laced Heidi.

Laughter and tumbling footfalls spilled down into the empty hall from upstairs as Gib passed by. He could make out the soft giggles of Carmen and Inez as they whispered back and forth about finding hiding places. Gib smiled even wider when he realized he could also hear Inan counting and wondered once more what Tay and Cal might be up to. Would they have time for such simple games this holiday? Or would they be busy trying to stay warm and pushing snow from the roof to keep it from collapsing? He hoped they could be children for at least one day this year.

He wandered back toward the sitting room and stopped short when he heard more laughter, this time from a woman. Gib glanced in the direction he'd heard it and startled when Tabitha came bounding toward him, an empty dish in her hand. No doubt she was done with her meal and was making her way to the kitchen to help clean up. Upon noticing Gib, she stopped long enough to give him a courteous bow and inform him that Joel and Nawaz were waiting on the far end of the sitting room. Gib thanked her and moved forward.

As he drew closer, he could make out their voices. Nawaz and Joel were just beyond the bend of the hallway which led to the servants' rooms. Gib opened his mouth to announce his arrival but fell silent when he heard his name.

Nawaz sounded tired but jovial, his voice dipping lower than typical. "So how are you and Gib getting on?"

A moment passed before Joel cleared his throat, and Gib could imagine his roommate wringing his hands. "We're getting along well. Why do you ask?" Another pause, this one heavy with insinuation. Joel's voice raised an octave. "Don't give me that look! Say what you mean."

Laughter blossomed from the other young lord. "You know damned well what I mean. Don't think I didn't catch the two of you sending doe eyes back and forth."

Gib's face went hot as he listened to Joel's stammered response. "We—I have no idea what you're talking about. Gib and I are friends. That's all. I'm fortunate to have found such a pleasant roommate."

"Enjoying one another's company then?"

The question itself could have been innocent if not for the tone. Nawaz knew exactly what he was saying and Gib's face went from hot to scorching. Why would the young lord say such things? *Have I been so obvious?*

If Nawaz figured it out then Joel must surely know. The floor tilted beneath Gib's feet.

The mage trainee gasped. "Stop it with your crude insinuations! You hardly have any room to speak, seeing as I just caught you in Tabitha's room." Joel gave a nervous laugh. "Gib and I are only friends."

Nawaz chuckled. "Hey, Tabitha invited me in. And besides, you wouldn't be turning so pink if I weren't right." Another silent lapse entered the conversation while Gib wondered how badly Joel was floundering. Nawaz filled the lull for them. "How serious is it?"

Gib pressed his face against the wall as he listened. *Serious? Serious about what? There's nothing to be serious about. We're friends! Nothing more—*

Joel's voice was unsure. "Truly, we're only friends—and I know it should stay that way. It's just—" He stopped there. If the lump in Gib's own throat was so caught in place he could hardly imagine how Joel must feel. "It's lonely being so different."

The sound of clothing rustling made its way to Gib's ears. Someone was moving. Gib took a step back. He didn't want to be caught spying. He never intended to eavesdrop. He heard a patting sound, one of them clapping the other on the back. An embrace, perhaps?

Nawaz's gentle voice lent itself well to Gib's theory. "Not as different as you imagine. Gib is a good boy. I like him and I'm sure he'd be good to you but—he's thirteen. And you're fifteen. I just want for you to be careful."

Gib's head was swimming. Nawaz was right. The two students were just that, students. Both old enough to be considered men by law but neither so experienced they knew of the world and its workings. Any relationship would be difficult at their age. But—had Joel admitted his attraction? Gib's heart hammered, but he was unsure if he was excited or nauseous or a combination of both. If his feelings were his own, he could contain them, pretend they didn't exist, but if Joel felt the same way, what would happen then?

Gib jumped back when Joel and Nawaz rounded the corner, nearly getting run over. Gib had been so preoccupied with his own thoughts that he hadn't heard them coming. Nawaz made an ungraceful sound and Joel froze in place.

"G—Gib! How long have you been—what are you doing here?" the mage trainee clamored, face red and eyes wide.

Gib's own racing heart took its time slowing. "I—Tabitha sent me. I ran into her in the hall."

Nawaz cocked an eyebrow, white teeth visible as he grinned. "You're pretty damned good at eavesdropping, aren't you?"

"I didn't mean to, I swear! I was only trying to find the two of you." Gib thought to spare Joel—and himself—some embarrassment. "I only just arrived. You two startled me as badly as I startled you."

Joel smoothed down his hair, loosening his rigid stance. Glancing around, the mage trainee's face evened back to its natural color. "Sorry about that."

"No, no. It's fine." Gib stood awkwardly, wishing he could think of something to say or do. His mind was blank. Any wit he normally possessed had abandoned him. Joel likewise seemed at a loss.

Nawaz broke the silence. Storming past Joel and Gib, he shook his head. "Pffft. A fine couple you make. Ask Lady Mrifa for a kissing bush, why don't you?"

Joel shot a poisonous look at his cousin. "*Nawaz!*"

The young lord turned back, a mischievous grin in place, and mocked a quick bow. "No, no! There's no need to dismiss me. I know when I'm the third wheel. You two have fun." He wagged his eyebrows at them before bolting out of sight.

Gib's knees wanted to give out and he wondered if this was what it felt like to die, with his heart pounding and lungs working overtime. His vision blurred around the edges but he could still make out Joel's blush.

"I suppose we should join the others," Joel said, clearing his throat. He was avoiding any sort of eye contact.

Gib's voice jittered as he forced himself to speak. He didn't want to ask the burning question, but he just couldn't stop himself. He had to know if his feelings were returned. "J–Joel?"

The mage trainee held up both of his hands as though he were deflecting a blow. His voice was hushed and quivering as well. "I'm sorry, Gib, for all of that. Nawaz means no harm, but it still must be— uncomfortable to be accused of—" He trailed off, unable to say it. Gib raised a hand, reaching for his friend, but Joel took a step back and diverted to go around Gib altogether.

"It was inappropriate and I apologize." The older boy raced off before Gib could respond.

Gib pulled his hand back to himself. So this was it then? He was destined to remain quiet and, therefore, alone. Why did his voice fail him when he needed it most?

The fire bathed Gib in drowsy heat. His eyelids were heavy as bricks, yet every time he started to nod off, the roaring flames would issue a crackle and he would be jarred alert. He raised a hand to his mouth as a yawn escaped his lips and tried to focus on the letters on the page before him.

It was late. The guests, Neetra Adelwijn and his family, had long since bid their farewells. Koal had returned to the palace shortly after, stating he had work to finish there, and that snake Liro had managed to slip away without so much as a goodbye. Gib had helped Tabitha and Lady Mrifa wash and put away the fancy porcelain dishes used during their meal and then he and Joel had retired to the sitting room to study.

Joel graciously declined to bring up anything pertaining to their relationship, and Gib had been more than content to sit in silence. He needed time to process the events from dinner and thereafter, especially the conversation he'd unwittingly stumbled upon between Joel and Nawaz. Was it true? Was Joel harboring feelings for his roommate?

Gib let loose a sigh. He tried again to focus on the book which sat in his lap but his attention seemed to be everywhere else. *My feelings for Joel aside, I really need to work on my reading. I'm so far behind the rest of the class.* He swallowed. It wasn't exactly his fault. He'd been busy with chores and sentinel training, but now that he had some free time he had no excuses for not dedicating time to his studies.

Joel stirred from across the room. "I'm going to retire for the night." His tone was as aloof as it had been for marks now.

"I think I'm going to stay up a little longer," Gib replied, watching out of the corner of his eye as the mage trainee stood and stretched his arms. "Lady Beatrice says I need to practice my reading."

"All right," Joel answered with a nod. "Be sure to snuff the fire on your way out. Goodnight." Joel excused himself, and Gib was left alone, listening to the soft sound of the older boy's footfalls as he retreated.

Gib turned back to the book in his lap and focused on the whimsical words in front of him. A smile crossed his lips. Joel had found a copy of *Tales of Fae* buried in the family's study and had given it to Gib to read while he remained at the Adelwijn estate. *Joel is always thinking of everyone else's welfare instead of his own. What would I do if I didn't have him?*

Gib wasn't sure how long he read, but the fire had nearly burnt itself out when the sound of a door opening caught his attention. He shifted wide eyes to gaze down the corridor, muscles tense. Who would be here so late? Surely not a thief of any sort? After all, what kind of criminal would be bold enough to use the front door? Gib glanced at the fire poker and wondered if he could reach it before the intruder made his way down the hall.

The soft steps didn't shuffle or hesitate. Even in the dark of the home, the person seemed to know where he was going. The churning in Gib's stomach subsided a little. Perhaps it was Otos returning. Gib had almost persuaded himself of this when the footfalls grew louder. The person was coming for the sitting room. The fire must have alerted him. It had to be Otos. A shadow fell across the room, and Gib knew he was no longer alone.

Gib sank into his seat, ice in his guts. It wasn't Otos. It wasn't a thief either. Seneschal Koal Adelwijn came into the room and went straight for the fire, muttering something under his breath—no doubt lamenting the flames being left unattended. He hadn't appeared to notice Gib, who played with the idea of trying to sneak away. It wouldn't work, of course, but it was tempting. He didn't want to be a bother—he likewise didn't want to be thought a deviant.

Gib opted to clear his throat. At the sound, Koal whirled about, his crimson cape billowing around his shoulders. Gib was pretty sure his own face was the same shade of red as he jumped back in his seat and stammered a polite greeting. "G–good evening, Lord Adelwijn. I'm sorry if I gave you a fright—"

Koal relaxed his tense stance when he seemed to recognize Gib. "Likewise. Apologies, little one." The seneschal's voice was tired but not unpleasant. "I didn't realize anyone would still be awake this late." Bringing a hand through his short raven hair, Koal stepped closer, the light cast by the fireplace illuminating the small creases around his mouth and eyes. "It's Gibben, right?"

The sentinel trainee nodded. "Yes. Gibben Nemesio, sir."

"Is Joel awake as well?"

"No, sir. He retired a bit ago. I was just practicing my reading."

One of Koal's dark eyebrows twitched. He motioned toward the book in Gib's lap. "Is that *Tales of Fae*?"

"Oh, uh—yes," Gib replied. He winced when realizing it was possible the seneschal didn't approve of him "borrowing" the Adelwijn family's possessions. "S–sorry, Joel said it would be all right if I read it while I'm here. I can put it away if—if you'd prefer, sir."

Koal raised both hands in front of him. "Oh, I wasn't implying you stop. By the light of Daya, you have to be the only first-year student I've seen practicing his studies outside of Academy." The seneschal fixed Gib with a warm smile. "I was merely curious. It has been several years since any of my children have dusted the cobwebs off that book."

"Joel wanted to help me with my reading." Gib blinked with surprise when the seneschal settled down into a cushioned chair across the room but continued on tentatively. "As you might imagine, I, uh—I didn't have much time for reading before I came to Silver City."

"You hail from Willowdale, yes?"

"My family's farm is within a dozen leagues of the village, sir." *Is he going to stay and talk to me?* Gib fidgeted in his seat. It seemed odd that someone as important and busy as Koal Adelwijn was taking the time to chat with him.

Clever eyes gleamed in the waning light as the seneschal took his time replying. "I recall Willowdale being quite charming, as most farming communities tend to be. It's been a long while since I journeyed through those parts of Arden though." Gib was surprised to hear a soft chuckle rise from the seneschal's chest. "Of course, it's been a long while since I've journeyed beyond the inner walls of Silver City. I sometimes feel as though I may as well pitch a tent inside the palace for as much time as I spend there."

Gib didn't know what to say, so he opted to stare at the floor. What could he say? What could he possibly have in common with the seneschal of Arden, the second most powerful man in the realm? Why was Koal even bothering to converse with him at all?

"I'm sorry you weren't able to make the journey to see your family," the seneschal continued before the silence had a chance to overwhelm the room.

Gib's stomach churned. "I miss them."

"I'm sure they miss you as well." Koal leaned forward in his chair, and Gib noted how the seneschal's eyes sparkled the same as Joel's. "Your mother and father must be proud of you for being so brave."

Gib grimaced, his eyes boring into the marbled floor. "Ma and Pa are both dead. It's just my sister, two younger brothers, and me left."

Koal's face pinched. "I'm sorry to hear that." After an uncomfortable pause, his tenor voice came again softly. "Both of my parents died while I was still a boy as well. I was all of fourteen when my father made the journey. My mother followed behind him only three cycles thereafter. At the time, my brother was all of six wheelturns and my sister had only just seen her second Naming Day ceremony. I know how difficult it can be to be left in charge of younglings."

Gib wasn't sure if he was overstepping his boundaries, but the words slipped from his mouth before he could stop them. "I didn't want to leave my brothers to fate! It's the draft—I mean, uh, not that I don't want to serve Arden, but—"

Koal held up a hand, shaking his head. "No, no. You don't have to explain yourself to me. Serving in the army is no menial task and the decision to do so should not be taken lightly—nor should it be forced upon anyone."

Gib looked down at his hands to hide his shame. "I truly mean not to complain, Seneschal. I know the safety of Arden is a concern for any who live within its borders. If only my brothers weren't so young and alone—" He stopped there, not wanting to bother Koal. Surely the seneschal had many other worries, far grander than this, concerning him.

Koal leaned back in his chair and set his mouth in a thin line, eyes reflecting deep thought. "It would be cold comfort to you, if any at all, but I promise there are people who support you. There are several of us, myself and the King included, who agree the draft is set at too young an age. Rishi ventures as far to say that it is entirely unnecessary—" He seemed to catch himself there and sighed. "Forgive me. *King* Rishi."

Gib swallowed. "Sir, do you know if the law is going to change? Will my brother also be called to fight?"

Koal frowned and shifted his eyes to the side. "I would like to tell you no, but the truth is that I don't know yet. It is unlikely considering how hard the King is fighting against it and many of us stand with him, but I've seen many unfair things come to pass. I'm sorry."

The truth was like a stone in Gib's stomach. He tried to swallow but couldn't. He tried to speak but nothing would come out. He could think of nothing but how he should be there with Tayver and Calisto. If only Gib could do something for them. He sighed and closed his book.

Koal looked over at the noise, his face lined with trouble. "Apologies. It was not my intention to put you off from your studies."

Gib shook his head. "No. I should be off to bed anyway. Joel will no doubt tutor me tomorrow." He didn't know what else to say and was sure both of them knew the words were a lie. He wanted to go to bed so he could worry in private. However, Gib had been unprepared for the way Koal's eyes lit up when his son's name was mentioned. If Gib's father were still alive, would he have looked the same when Gib's name was mentioned? Would the same instant and undeniable pride flash behind his father's eyes?

Gib decided to linger a moment longer. "Joel has been a lot of help. I'd never have been able to find my way around without him."

"I'm glad to hear that." Koal paused, leaving his mouth slightly ajar. "Forgive me for having to ask, but how *is* Joel faring? I'm afraid I don't get to see any of my children as much as I would like, least of all my two eldest."

Warmth blossomed on Gib's cheeks, but he didn't hesitate to respond. "Joel is doing well. We've become good friends. He's one of the kindest people I've met."

"It's good he has opened up to someone. After what happened last year, I feared he—" Koal swallowed, jaw set in a firm line. "I feared he wouldn't recover."

"Joel is stronger than most men. To face such adversity and still be willing to extend hospitality to a poor, uneducated farm boy is a testament to that."

The seneschal gave a stiff nod. "Adversity, from his friends and family, nonetheless. It is unjust how Joel has been treated."

Gib winced, but what could he say? It was all true. If the hurtful words spoken by Liro and Annwyne were any indication of the tribulations Joel had endured the previous year—

Koal sighed, turning his stark eyes toward the fire. "I feel it is my duty to apologize to you for the behavior displayed by my brother and eldest son during the feast."

"Oh, you don't need to apologize, sir," Gib protested. "Regardless of what happened, I'm grateful for the hospitality you showed by allowing me to dine at your table."

Koal shook his head as he replied, "No. It was wrong of them to be so callous. I wish I was able to say you caught them both on a bad day, but I'm afraid Liro and Neetra are very much the coldhearted highborns you were no doubt cautioned to avoid." His voice caught.

Gib wasn't sure how to respond. He didn't want to come across as rude, but the seneschal's words were true. Gib tried to keep his tone respectful. "I, uh, not all highborns are the same, sir. Just as all lowborns aren't either. I'm quickly finding that each man earns his own merits."

Koal nodded. "Very good. You are wise beyond your years."

"I've had a lot of growing up to do, sir." Gib's breath was ragged, and he made a conscious effort to calm it. "As has Joel. Perhaps that is why he and Liro are so different." Gib winced at his own buffoonery. What possessed him to be so presumptuous?

Koal's voice came out in halted, reserved bouts. "They're terribly different. We weren't always so broken, you know. We were a family once—before Liro began to pull away." He rubbed his face, the fine lines suddenly more prominent. "I don't know where I went wrong with him."

Gib's knuckles hurt as he belatedly realized he was wringing his hands. How long had he been doing that? Probably from the moment he'd realized he was in over his head and about to keep talking when he should shut up. "It's not your doing, Seneschal. Each man earns his own merit, after all. You set the best example you could for your children."

Koal shook his head with a wry smile. "You presume a lot, young one."

Gib bit his lower lip. The rational part of him knew he should fall silent or apologize for being so forward, but the rational part of his mind seemed to have been put out to pasture as of late. "No. Joel, Carmen, and even Heidi have treated me with nothing but kindness. If you and Lady Mrifa had fallen short even a little, they wouldn't all be so wonderful."

The seneschal turned to look at the flames as they guttered and danced low.

Gib took to his feet as quietly as he could. "Would you like me to put out the fire, sir?"

Koal startled. His blue eyes were haunted when he looked upon Gib. "Do you remember the lessons of your father? Did he help make you who you are? Or your mother? Did she mold your honest heart?"

Gib swallowed and looked at his feet. "My mother—I barely remember her. I was only four when she made the journey but I remember my father, yes. He wanted me to be the best person I knew how. 'Listen to people, Gib,' he'd say. 'Don't pretend to know who they are because even when they tell you, they only tell you the part they want you to hear. You can't know their strengths, weaknesses, joys, pains until they show them to you.' It's one of the things I remember most from him."

Koal's sad smile sought to undo Gib. "Your wisdom is his, I see. You had a fine teacher."

Gib nodded and wiped at the sudden droplet rolling down his cheek. "Yes. But I remember his temper too. I remember the times when he lost hope, when he'd despair. I remember when he'd mutter about 'those people born with a silver spoon in their mouth.'" Gib paused long enough to catch his breath. "Those weren't his finest moments, and I remember them but, sir, it's my choice to earn my merits. I've chosen to listen to people, to respect them, to help when I can. And even when I fail to do so, I don't forget what I've been taught. So I think it's worth your thought to consider that Liro also remembers what good you've done for him and others. And one day he may choose to follow that example."

Gib's insides shook so terribly he didn't think he could say another word. Koal stared into the dying embers. At long last the seneschal stood. He patted one of his large hands across Gib's shoulder and ducked to eye level. "Thank you, Gibben, I can see why Joel has grown so fond of you. Now go on. I'll quench the fire."

Gib bowed before retreating into the corridor. His mind was swimming as he attempted to digest the fact that he'd just sat across from the seneschal of Arden and, furthermore, had actually *spoken* to him. It seemed like a strange dream he'd surely wake from at any moment.

The grand entrance room stood dark and vacant as he passed through. Gib crept toward the stairwell, trying to remain as quiet as possible despite the noise his boots made each time they hit the marble floor. The family's sleeping quarters were on the second level of the house, but he knew Tabitha slept downstairs.

Gib had just set foot on the first rung of the stairway when a deafening banging noise arose behind him. He almost fell over. He whirled around, grasping the banister of the stairway for balance. *What the hell?* The thudding noise sounded again, and after a moment, he registered it as someone knocking on the door. No—not knocking—*pounding*. Someone struck the oak wood as if his life depended upon it.

Gib froze in place. He didn't know what to do. Should he answer the call or run up the stairs and pretend he didn't hear it? Even as he opened his mouth to call for the seneschal, Koal flew into the room. Glancing at Gib, the seneschal waved his hand in a stay back motion. With one hand on the hilt of his sword, Koal drew the door open just enough to peer outside.

"Seneschal Koal Adelwijn!" A young page shivered on the step, his face drawn and pale. "His Highness King Rishi Radek has sent me for you."

Koal looked around, his face contorted with confusion. "At this time? What is it?"

"The King, sir, he's been attacked!"

Koal threw the door open all the way. "*What?* Is he all right?"

The boy nodded. "Yes, sir, but he commands you come to the palace at once. They can't find the attacker and don't know how he got in." His narrow chest heaved as he dropped his voice to a hushed whisper. "They tried to kill him, sir. They tried to kill our king."

CHAPTER NINE

The next couple of days were torturous as Gib waited for more details about the royal family. Joel suggested they tell the seneschal what Gib had heard in the hall that day, but Koal didn't come back to the Adelwijn estate before the two students had to return to Academy. The only good to have come from this whole dirty business was that Gib and Joel had gotten back on good speaking terms again. During the chaos surrounding the assassination attempt, they had no time to ponder their friendship or its status.

As they made their way into the dormitory, the halls were abuzz with rumors about what had happened. Word had gotten out—whether it was supposed to or not. Gib and Joel made it to their room without any incidents.

Once inside, Joel locked the door and flopped on his bed. "This is insanity! Did you hear the ridiculous things people were saying?"

Gib tossed his rucksack aside and sat down on his own bed. "I know. Do you think the assassination attempt was made by the person I overheard? Should I tell someone?"

Joel's face went blank. At length, he sighed and muttered more to himself than to Gib, "I don't know. It might be the same person, but it may not. I wish I could speak with Father."

"Do you think you could find him? Let me speak to him?" Gib whispered. He was shaking.

Joel shook his head. "I don't think so. Not right now. He must be going out of his mind trying to sort this out."

"It might be important." Gib kept his voice neutral despite his churning stomach. He didn't want to push so hard that Joel lost patience with him.

A long, uncomfortable silence fell over them while Joel merely glared at the floor. Various emotions played behind his eyes but were not allowed to steal over his face.

When Gib thought he could take no more of the suffocating stillness, a pounding came on the dormitory door.

Joel managed to get to his feet. "Who is it?" he asked as he reached for the latch.

"Let me in!"

Gib recognized the muffled voice of Hasain Radek immediately, and Joel threw the door open. Hasain, pale and sporting dark rings beneath his eyes, strode in and marched straight to Gib. The sentinel trainee shuddered under the scrutiny of those dark, troubled eyes.

"All right, Nemesio, you have my attention now. What do you know?"

Gib's mouth fell open. "I—uh, well I heard two men in the academy hallway near Dean Marc's office—"

Hasain dragged the stool from the desk and sat heavily before Gib. "I know that already. But what was said? Tell me as well as you can remember it."

Gib slammed his eyes shut in an attempt to concentrate. *What had been said?* "Give me a moment."

Hasain's voice was dark. "I don't have a moment."

Joel hovered beside the bed. "Do you think it was the men he heard then?"

"I don't know for sure, but it's better to rule them out if I can."

Gib swallowed and forced his breathing to calm as he thought back to the day in the hallway outside of Dean Marc's office. He'd been walking toward the dining hall and a voice had gotten his attention. "The first man said he was worried the assassin had abandoned the mission. And the second man, the killer, said he wouldn't so long as he was paid. The first said he wasn't worried about the money. He was worried about whether he and the others could trust the assassin."

"Others?" Hasain demanded. "The conspirator wasn't acting alone?"

Gib frowned, keeping his eyes closed. "There were only two people there. The assassin and the one paying him. They didn't mention the others again." He grasped for more details but could only think of jingling coins. "He paid half the fee. The conspirator said he'd pay the other half when the job was finished." Gib opened his eyes in time to witness Hasain lock his jaw.

The young lord seethed in silence. "So this is still an open job—and he has others backing him." He gave a great sigh and locked his dark eyes on Gib. "You are positive they were talking about the King?"

Gib nodded so hard his curls bounced. "Yes. The conspirator mentioned how—forgive my directness, he said it, not me—Rishi Radek is overconfident. That he isn't as smart as he thinks he is and they could use that against him."

Hasain's face constricted into an ugly, red mask. He flinched backward, nearly causing the stool to topple. "Traitor! This common lowlife thinks he may speak of my father, our king, without title or respect?"

Joel put a hand on Hasain's shoulder. "Perhaps it's someone who knows King Rishi well. It would make more sense for them to speak lightly of someone they know."

"A snake."

There was a pause. Joel bit his bottom lip, his next words chosen carefully. "One of possibly many snakes, Hasain—and if there are more than one, the others could still be poised to attack. We must warn the King."

Hasain was on his feet so fast Gib nearly fell back onto his bed. The young lord was already at the door before he stopped to look back at them. He pointed one long finger at Gib and growled through gritted teeth, "Say not a single word, Nemesio, until I tell you to. We have no idea where these snakes may be lying in wait."

Gib rose to his feet but found his knees shaking. He understood what Hasain was saying, but the weight of his secret was already crushing him. "There must be someone I can tell! Someone who can protect the King."

Joel snapped his fingers. "What about Dean Marc? He and my father are like brothers and they both work hand in hand with King Rishi—"

Hasain waved the mage trainee off. "No. Both are with the King and his trusted council now. No precaution is being spared for the royal family. Gib will have to wait until I can speak to the King or someone trustworthy." He opened the door and leveled Gib with another dark glare. "Silence, Nemesio, absolute silence."

***

Gib found himself tossing and turning the entire night. What if the assassin came back? What if King Rishi's life was taken this time? His heart pounded at the thought of Arden crumbling. Who would lead the country if the King were to die? What would happen to poor people like Gib and his brothers? Or girls and women? Would the King be replaced by someone cruel, like Neetra or Liro Adelwijn? Gib sat up, gasping for air. *Chhaya's bane, why me? Why did I have to be the one to overhear those men? It should have been someone with power. Someone who knew what to do. If it had been someone braver, they could have stormed into the room and unveiled the assassin and none of this would have happened.*

"Gib?" Joel's voice was soft as he sat up as well. The moonlight played over his dark hair. "You must try to get some sleep. Hasain is on your side now. You'll be able to tell your story soon."

"What if the assassin gets the King tonight?" Gib blurted, unable to remain quiet. "What if he hurts the royal family before Seneschal Koal and the others can figure out who he is?"

"It's frightening, I know, but you have to understand that the King and his family are better protected than anyone else in Arden." Joel paused and, even in the dark, Gib could see his roommate grimace. "King Rishi has a bodyguard who never leaves his side. And the entire family has the best trained and most loyal guards in all the land. Not to mention the Blessed Mages. Believe me, the King and his family are well protected."

Gib tried to find conviction in those words. The rational part of his mind knew Joel was probably right. He would voice his concern if there were any to be had. Likewise, the mage trainee wouldn't lie and say he was confident in the protection offered to the royal family if he truly wasn't. Gib knew these things, but he just couldn't get his mind to calm, so he settled on a reference Joel had made. "Blessed Mages? Is that an elite faction of magery?"

"No, not exactly." Joel laughed, a whisper of sound in the otherwise silent room. "The Blessed Mages are rumored to be a gift from The Two—Father says the rumors are ridiculous but he's never fully explained where they came from either—and their power is unlike anything any mortal mage possesses. The Blessed Mages are loyal to King Rishi and his family. Have faith in them, if no one else."

The story had merit, fantastical and otherworldly merit as it may be. It should have been able to calm Gib's nerves but even as he lay back down, he knew sleep was a lost cause.

When the first light of day crept over the horizon, he drew himself out of bed and prepared for his bath. Joel stirred, and Gib tried to comfort the older boy back to sleep with promises to wake him after Gib's bath was finished.

The mage trainee frowned. "You didn't sleep at all, did you?"

"A little here and there." The lie tasted bitter, but Gib knew the truth would cause his friend even more grief. "Please sleep a bit more. I'm sorry for waking you."

Joel didn't say any more and lay still as if he were going to try to rest, but Gib was sure this was also a lie. The sentinel trainee left for the bathing chamber, trying not to feel guilty for waking his friend.

Gib was unable to enjoy his bath with so much melancholy floating in his head and the secret still pressing on his conscience. When the morning bell rang, he made his way to the dining hall for breakfast. Perhaps a hearty meal would help clear his mind.

As soon as he arrived, Gib knew keeping his silence was going to be hard. The entire hall was packed tight and all around him he could hear whispers about the royal scandal. Theories abounded, each crazier than the last, and Gib locked his jaw to keep from pointing out how ridiculous these students were making themselves sound. With tray in hand, he went about trying to find an empty seat.

"Nemesio!"

Kezra flagged him over to where she and his other friends had managed to hunker down.

"Thanks." Gib could think of nothing else to say as he sat down beside her.

Tarquin lost no time in leaning across the table to interrogate Gib. "You must have heard the news about the King! What do you think?"

Gib took a drink from his goblet in an attempt to buy time, but he wasn't any good at stalling. When he couldn't shake the three sets of eyes on him, he shrugged. "I heard, yeah, but I don't know—maybe speculations should be left to people with more authority." His answer sounded feeble, even to himself.

Kezra cocked an eyebrow. She was entirely too clever for this game. Her sly voice suggested she wasn't fooled at all. "You don't think it has anything to do with what you overheard before Midwinter, do you?"

Gib's face burst with uncomfortable heat. Why was she looking at him so narrowly? And why were the others focused on him as well? Shouldn't they all be eating their breakfast and preparing for class? "I, uh— I don't know. I guess it's a good thing the King is well protected."

Nage nodded. "It's true. He has the best guards in all of Arden at his disposal. But someone almost got through them once already. If I were the King, I'd be looking for some better guards."

Tarquin balked and pointed out the soldiers who protected the royal family were the best trained. He went on about the honor of such a respectable position and that Nage had no idea what he was saying. Nage fired back and the two descended into a heated discussion about it. Gib wasn't interested in anything they had to say, but at the moment he would give anything to be included in the argument. Their conversation would be easier to handle than Kezra's hard glare.

Gib deliberately avoided her gaze, but she wouldn't relent. Leaning across the table and keeping her voice low, Kezra skewered him. "If I were you, I'd tell someone."

He nodded and took another sip from his chalice. Gods, he wished she'd stop looking at him. "Yeah. I mean, I guess I could. Maybe if I have time later."

Kezra leaned back into her seat. Her critical look was all he needed to know she knew he was being dishonest. Gib wished he could speak to her—to all of his friends even—but mostly Kezra. He wanted to tell them about the conversation with Hasain and how he's been sworn to silence, but he couldn't trust Tarquin to keep his big mouth shut and Nage was unlikely to have any helpful advice.

Silence, Nemesio, absolute silence.

Hasain's words echoed in his mind like a sinister threat. No. He couldn't tell her. Could she not see it in his face? Gib pleaded with her, silently, and Kezra finally withdrew just a little.

"I hope you know what you're doing."

Gib wanted to thank her. He truly wished he could. Instead, he nodded toward her plate. "You'd better eat, Kez. Practice is sure to be brutal after having so much time away."

The space which served as the training arena during the winter months was so packed with students that Gib squeezed himself against the wall to enter the room. Kezra, Tarquin, and Nage stayed close by.

Gib groaned. "Well, this is lovely. Why isn't everyone in formation? Master Roland is going to make us all run laps outside in the snow."

"I don't see him," Kezra replied, her green eyes darting around the room.

Tarquin stood on his toes, craning his neck as he looked for their instructor. "Roland's the Weapons Master so maybe he's at the palace because of—well, you know."

Nage coughed. "Speaking of missing persons, has anyone seen Diddy? He wasn't at breakfast and he ain't here either."

Diddy. Gib's guts were as tight as ever. What was going on? What if they were trying to figure out who the assassin was and Gib's information could help them? What if they didn't call on him, and because of that Diddy or one of the other members of the royal family were hurt—or killed?

His anxiety must have shown. Kezra was glaring at him with no remorse. "Rethinking this vow of silence yet?"

Gib opened his mouth but only a shuddering gasp would come out. He was supposed to wait until Hasain returned to him with further instruction. "I–I can't. Kezra, you have to believe me."

Hunter green eyes narrowed into threatening slits. Kezra jabbed a finger into Gib's chest and spat, "If your silence causes more harm, Gibben Nemesio, you'd best pray I don't get my hands on you."

The sentinel trainee shuddered, knowing it was no idle threat. Kezra always meant what she said. "I know. If–if anything changes, I'll find you. I just can't say—" He took a breath, wishing he could make her understand. "My silence is taking all the faith I have. Please try to have as much faith in me."

Kezra frowned. "I put no faith in men."

A hush fell over the trainees as their instructor approached. Otho Dakheel, the assistant to the Weapons Master, stepped forward. Raising both hands, the young soldier demanded silence and the trainees conformed. Only a couple years older than Gib, the assistant commanded respect with his intimidating poise and eerie pale eyes.

"You've all heard of the attack on the King." Otho spoke quietly, though he didn't need to raise his voice. The arena had fallen into complete silence. "Our Weapons Master is otherwise engaged until further notice. You'll be taking your lessons from me."

No one questioned this pronouncement. They fell into formation and followed each command as though it had come from Roland himself. Otho ordered them to find their normal sparring partners, even stopping long enough to put Gib with Tarquin and Kezra. "Your partner isn't here. Join up with these two."

Gib nodded. "Y–yes, sir. Uh, Otho, sir? Is Diddy all right? Do you know why he isn't here?"

Otho's odd yellow-green eyes speared the student. "Fall in, Nemesio. You're behind in your training."

Gib bit his tongue and followed along with the other two, despairing when he realized the words were true. He did have a lot of catching up to do. Even though he'd been close enough to see most of the new drills, he hadn't had the practice of his fellow students due to his injury. Spirit dim, he nonetheless raised his wooden sword. He had only one way to improve—by practicing—even if he wasn't in the mood to do anything besides fret about his current predicament.

Tarquin did his best to show Gib how to properly do the new moves. Kezra, on the other hand, was relentless. Gib was so caught up with avoiding her angry sword strikes that he failed to notice a pair of newcomers entering the arena. Tarquin broke formation to look at the guests, and Gib finally realized they were being watched—or rather, *he* was being watched.

Two royal guards, dressed in fine plated armor, were speaking to Otho and pointing in Gib's direction. He winced as horrible thoughts flashed through his mind. *I didn't say a word! Are they here to arrest me anyway? Oh Goddesses, where is Hasain—*

Otho trotted over, flanked by the guards. Gib drew back but had nowhere to run, no place he could escape or hide from them. He was vaguely aware of the other students in the room shuffling out of the way—all except Tarquin and Kezra. If anything, his two friends moved closer. Were they trying to protect him? He didn't have time to ponder it as Otho opened his mouth to speak.

"Gibben, you've been summoned."

He blinked. *Summoned? Summoned where?*

Otho motioned for Gib to follow the royal guardsmen. The sentinel trainee looked back to Tarquin and Kezra for assistance, but the look on his friends' faces told him they could do nothing.

Gib straightened his back and put on the bravest smile he could muster. "O–okay. I'm ready." *No, I'm not ready. I don't even know where I'm being taken.*

He wasn't sure if his words were decipherable, meek as they were, but the royal guardsmen must have heard him, for they turned on their heels and marched toward the door in perfect unison. Gib had to run to keep up with them. As he left the arena, the sentinel trainee was painfully aware that *all* eyes were on him.

Gib was surprised to find Hasain and Joel standing in the corridor outside. Hasain was frigid as always, but Joel offered a faint smile in greeting. It was clear the two young lords had been waiting for Gib.

"Hasain? Joel? W–what are you doing here?" Gib dared to ask.

Hasain turned a shrewd eye. "We're going to Seneschal Koal so you can tell him everything you know."

Gib's heart was pounding in his chest so viciously it hurt, but he had no time to ask further questions as Hasain had already turned on his heels and begun to stride away. The two guardsmen followed behind the young Radek lord, ominous and silent.

Joel set a hand against Gib's trembling arm. "It will be all right. You aren't in trouble," the mage trainee assured. "We're going to Marc's office. Follow."

Gib nodded, keeping one eye on the guardsmen. If he wasn't in trouble then why did he need soldiers to escort him? The sentinel trainee glanced at Joel, who gave a gentle nod. It was a small comfort.

All too soon, they were standing in front of Dean Marc's office. Gib swallowed. He wasn't sure if he was relieved to be there or terrified of what questions he might be asked once they went inside. Hasain struck the heavy door, echoes jumping off the stone walls around them as they all waited for a response.

The door opened, and Dean Marc poked his head through the crack. The scowl contorting his fair features quickly retreated. "Thank the Two. I thought you were Diedrick Lyle, returning early from his midday meal." His dark eyes darted back and forth across the corridor before opening the door fully and standing aside. "Come in, come in!"

Hasain nodded curtly, sweeping inside, and Gib hurried along behind the young lord, vaguely aware of Joel's hand offering silent support on Gib's shoulder. Marc ushered the three boys into the office, closing the door behind them. Gib blinked in the dim light, unsure of what—if anything—he should do or say.

"Gibben Nemesio, have a seat."

Gib reeled when he realized Seneschal Koal Adelwijn had spoken. How had Hasain convinced the right hand of King Rishi to come away from his duties long enough for this? A hard knot formed in the pit of Gib's stomach as he followed orders and sat down.

Koal swept over from the depths of the shadows near Diedrick Lyle's desk, his features grim. The Instruction Master's desk was occupied by Roland Korbin whose sharp eyes focused on Gib.

Marc sat on the corner of his desk and folded his arms over his chest. His voice pressed, but he wasn't condescending. "Gibben, it has been brought to our attention that you may have valuable information about the recent attempt on our king's life. Is this true?"

Gib's heart was pounding. "Y–yes. Well—I mean, I don't know if it's valuable or not."

The seneschal was pacing across the marbled floor but stopped long enough to give Gib a withering glare. "Damn it. Don't you realize the importance of the royal family's safety? Keeping silent in such a situation is punishable as treason."

Oh. He hadn't considered—was he a traitor? Would he be hung or beheaded for such a terrible lapse in judgment? Gib's mouth fell open but no words came out.

To his right, Joel stiffened and started to raise his voice—only to be cut off by Hasain.

The young Radek lord took a deep bow before leaping in. "Apologies, Seneschal. The fault is mine, not Gibben's. He came to me on the day in question, but I discredited the threat as that of a disgruntled servant or teacher. It was my lack of judgment that may have—" His smooth voice shuddered there as he sucked in a breath of air. "—caused my father harm."

"Or cost him his life," the seneschal spat. Gone was the reserved gentility of the worried father Gib had spoken to three nights past. This Koal Adelwijn was more terrible and frightening than anyone the student had ever seen. No one in the room dared to move under the seneschal's heavy glare.

Even Hasain, who had seemed so powerful and in control only moments before, kept his head low. His voice was weak. "I know. I'm sorry. I wasn't thinking. I let my pride cloud my judgment."

A stretch of uncomfortable silence fell upon them until Dean Marc cleared his throat. "Gibben, please, time is of the essence. What do you know?"

Insides churning, the sentinel trainee managed to open his mouth a second time. The words spilled forth like a flooded river. Gib told them where he'd been and why. He tried to recollect every detail and answered each question to the best of his ability. Koal pressed for details about who the two men may have been while Roland spoke up to ask about what sort of plans may have been discussed. It was frustrating to have so few answers for them, and the men seemed to grow upset as well.

When the questions began to repeat themselves, and Gib's breaths were shuddering, Marc waved his hands. "All right, enough. The boy is too shaken to continue. Besides, I think he's told us all he knows."

Koal nodded stiffly as he continued to pace the overcrowded office. "Yes. For all we know, these may not even be the same people. No actual plan was mentioned." He rubbed his chin, deep in thought.

"Yeah, not much to go on for what sort of weaponry or tactic they'll use," Roland grunted. "From what I've gathered so far, I'm expecting long range attacks or planned encounters. They're not opportunists. They'll organize something else."

Marc let out a deep sigh, stress lines gathering around his dark eyes. "I suppose you're dismissed, Gibben. And you as well, Joel. Go back to your classes."

Both boys bowed low and turned to leave. However, Gib found his feet refusing to move. His tongue lay heavy in his mouth; a question had been killing him since that morning. *Diddy. I need to know if he's okay.* Gib wasn't sure which of the men to address, so he shared his gaze among all three. "Uh, sir? Is–is Prince Didier all right? He wasn't in class. I just— he's my friend."

The three men shared guarded looks and after what felt like an eternity, Koal graced Gib with a response. "It's only because you've been nothing but an exceptional man, Gibben, that I share this information with you. Likewise, I would expect your discretion in sharing it with others. Prince Didier is fine. He's within the palace walls for his own protection."

Gib bit his lower lip, holding back further questions. Did this mean Diddy wouldn't be coming back to class? *Ever?* "Thank you, Seneschal Koal," he replied, doing his best not to forget his manners.

Koal nodded and waved for Gib to be on his way. Joel was already waiting by the door, and Gib went to join his roommate. He felt no resolve. Few of his questions had been answered, and he'd done little to aid Seneschal Koal and the other men. This entire meeting seemed to have been a giant waste of everyone's time—

"Wait," Roland grunted.

Gib paused, his hand resting on the brass door handle. "S–sir?"

The Weapons Master stood, motioning with one large hand for Gib to stay where he was. Hazel eyes flitted in the direction of the seneschal. "Koal, Gibben is one of the classmates Prince Didier specified he wanted. Gib is the prince's sparring partner in my morning class. They work well together."

The hair on the back of Gib's neck began to rise. Diddy had mentioned him by name?

"Two classmates then?" Koal asked, frowning. "Are you sure that is necessary? I would think Joaquin's son would be better matched with Didier, and with safety to keep in mind—" The seneschal furrowed his brow.

"The prince asked for both of them—and Gib's a good lad. He'll work hard," Roland replied. "Give the young man a chance."

Gib's mouth fell open. *Give me a chance? Has Roland lost his mind?* In that moment, Gib was certain the Weapons Master must be delirious. He'd never been prone to such kind words in the past.

The seneschal folded his arms over his chest. "Barely men, either of them. This will be to the King's discretion. He'll have to approve—"

"He already has," Roland interjected. The Weapons Master pulled a sealed scroll from his pocket and waved it under Koal's nose. "He told me to find the right trainees for the job."

Koal frowned, snatching the document up. "He never tells me anything! How am I supposed to keep him and his family safe if—" His words passed off into quiet, if angry, resolve as he read the parchment.

Cowering in his place, Gib couldn't breathe. He latched onto Joel's arm for support. What was this about? Was he in some sort of trouble? Why were they discussing his training?

With a groan, the seneschal rolled the document and turned his attention to Gib. "Gibben Nemesio." Koal's heavy gaze threatened to suffocate Gib. "You are to take your midday meal and then report to the palace."

Clinging to Joel for dear life, Gib felt the floor sway beneath his feet. "The palace?" He wasn't sure his voice was audible. "W–why?"

Koal narrowed his eyes and slammed the scroll into Roland's hand. The Weapons Master sneered as he took the liberty of answering Gib. "For weaponry lessons. You are behind and will benefit from the additional lessons as much as Prince Didier."

The sentinel trainee's voice quivered. "The prince?"

"Yes. It seems as though he needs sparring partners—and since he isn't allowed to leave the palace for the foreseeable future, *you* must go to *him*."

A mark later Gib found himself standing at the edge of the grounds belonging to the academy. He stared across the cobblestone bridge that spanned the width of the Tempist River and eyed the wall of mortar and stone on the far side. Built along the river, the rampart circling the palace towered ominously above Gib's head, and even from a distance, he could see sentinels walking along the top of the wall, armed with crossbows as they watched vigilantly for intruders. *They won't shoot me down before I have a chance to explain myself, will they?*

Gib fumbled with the badge given to him by Weapons Master Roland. He'd instructed Gib to show it to the guards at the gate to gain access inside. *Daya, I hope he wasn't mistaken.* Gib glanced down at his drab cloak and simple tunic. *I don't look like anyone who belongs inside the palace walls.*

What if they don't believe me? He sucked in a deep breath. The air was cold and stung his lungs.

Mustering up what little courage he could find, Gib took a step onto the bridge. The snow crunched under his boots as he walked and was the only sound to be heard. His eyes flashed toward the gatehouse, a higharched break in the wall where a wrought iron gate had been constructed. A grizzly looking sentinel stood at attention there, tall and intimidating in his plated armor and fur cloak.

Is this who I'm supposed to talk to? Gib held back the urge to groan. Why did everyone always expect him to know where to go and what to do?

The soldier drew his sword as soon as Gib stepped off the opposite side of the bridge. "Halt! What is your business?"

Gib fumbled for his badge. His hands trembled so badly he nearly dropped the damned thing before he could hold it up for examination. His voice likewise shook as he tried to remember why he was there. "I, uh—my name is Gibben Nemesio. Weapons Master Roland Korbin summoned me. I—" He was unsure if he should continue or not. "I'm to report to Prince Didier within the palace."

The soldier sheathed his sword and took the badge, turning it over to examine it. His shrewd, hard features studied Gib before curling a lip to reply. "You are a sentinel trainee?"

Gib nodded so hard his curls fell over his brow. He was painfully aware of the sentinels on the wall above moving closer. They were scrutinizing him just as closely as the guard on the ground, though none of them had raised their crossbows yet. "Y–yes, sir."

"Who are you and what was your year of birth?" the guard demanded.

Gib's mind went blank. Why did his Name Day matter? "Uh, I, um, I'm Gibben Nemesio of Willowdale, born in the Ardenian year of five hundred twenty-five."

The soldier still didn't seem convinced. "You are thirteen years old? You hardly look—"

"Gibben Nemesio. I was beginning to think you were never going to arrive."

Hasain Radek strode up behind the gate, black robe billowing around him as he moved. The young lord wore his typical smirk and his haughty poise made Gib want to roll his eyes. *Was he waiting for me?*

The sentinel straightened his back. "Good day, Lord Hasain."

Hasain stuck his nose in the air, gesturing toward Gib. "Gibben is a sentinel trainee. He's old enough—just short."

Gib clenched his jaw but said nothing. He wasn't particularly excited to see Hasain, but if the young Radek was here to assist Gib, it was to his benefit to mind his manners.

Hasain's presence alone seemed to be enough to convince the guard Gib was telling the truth. The sentinel handed the badge back to Gib and signaled for the men on top of the wall to raise the gate. The sound of iron squealing offended Gib's ears as the gate was raised just high enough for Gib to slip under.

Gib bowed to the guard as he passed beneath the archway, keeping his eyes trained on Hasain. "Are you here to show me the way?"

"Oh? You don't know where to go?" Hasain's words dripped with mockery, and if the situation were any different, Gib would have thought to find his own damn way. As it was, he couldn't afford to be late.

Gib gritted his teeth. "I've never been in the palace before."

"No, I should think not." The young lord chuckled, but the sound generated was unkind. "Follow me."

Gib gaped as he turned and got his first clear view of the royal palace. It was the largest structure he'd ever seen—even the three wings of Academy were dwarfed in comparison to this building. Marble columns taller than trees supported the stone walls which rose four stories above the ground and stretched nearly two furlongs in length. The roof was made from terracotta and gilded with golden powder that shone as brightly as the midday sun, and great window panes of stained glass towered over an open courtyard.

Gib forced his legs to move, but he couldn't take his eyes away from the splendor in front of him. Hasain's expression was nonchalant, as though the young lord were approaching the home of a peasant. *I don't understand. I could look at this every day and it would never lose its magnificence.*

It took the two young men some time to cross the sprawling courtyard, greater than even the largest crop field Gib had seen in Willowdale. Two fountains carved from alabaster stone stood on each side of the path, and though no water flowed through them due to the frigid weather, he imagined the view would be spectacular in the summer cycles.

Hasain cleared his throat, motioning for Gib to follow through an arched doorway. A pair of sentries stood dutifully beside the entrance, but they did little more than nod toward Hasain as the young lord passed by.

Inside, the palace corridors were long and narrow. Some of the walls were covered in decorative stucco while others were bare marble. Light poured through tall glass windows, illuminating the hallways and warming the stone architecture.

Hasain led Gib through corridors and up several stairwells. To keep up with Hasain's longer strides, Gib had to trot. If he were to get lost in such a big place, he'd never be able to find his way. He had lost all sense of direction by the time they reached their destination.

Hasain stopped before a large door made from polished oak. The Crest of Arden had been etched into the wood with intricate detail—some artist had been paid a hefty purse for such detailed work, no doubt. Gib swallowed, feeling out of place.

"Stand up straight," Hasain commanded in a somber, lofty voice. "If any of the officials address you, be sure to bow to them before you respond. If the servants address you, don't bow—it will embarrass and confuse them. You are a guest of the royal family while you're within the palace walls and you'll conduct yourself as such. If you have any questions, it would be best for you to ask Didier since he already knows you and is least likely to be offended by your ignorance."

Gib took a deep breath, head spinning. How did anyone expect him to be able to do this? There were probably a thousand ways to offend the highborns who walked these halls, and he was sure to figure out each and every way. Leaning against the wall, the sentinel trainee managed a garbled response. "Are you going to stay?"

Hasain stuck his nose in the air. "No. I'm far too busy. I must go to council with my father to discuss what other measures are to be taken against these traitors."

"*You're* on the High Council?" Gib had imagined the royal council would consist only of old politicians—men who cared little for individual peasants and a lot for the size of their own purse. Hasain seemed to be too young for such a position. *Though in another twenty years, he may fit in perfectly.*

The young lord narrowed his eyes. "Not yet, but my father is the king. I'm being trained to give council to our future king, my younger brother, Crowned Prince Deegan. There will come a day when I'll sit in the council chamber and those old men will all take orders from *me*."

Gib chuckled at the absurdity of the idea. "I wouldn't want that job. Too much pressure."

Hasain didn't laugh, but his mouth twisted into a thin slant. "I wouldn't worry about that if I were you. It's not the place of a peasant to sit on the chair of a decision maker." No more courtesies were exchanged after that. With a deep frown, Hasain pushed the heavy door open and motioned for Gib to go inside.

The sentinel trainee froze at the sight of the finest arena he'd ever seen. Lined with polished weapons which—to Gib—had no name and conjured images of brutal death and warfare, the space was more than twice the size of the indoor sparring area in the academy.

Foreboding washed over the sentinel trainee as he took in the hard lines of the marbled architecture and tiled floors which weren't covered by mats. A person falling here risked cracking his skull in two. The bare feel of dread was scarcely softened by lush velvet curtains and paintings decorating the walls. The arena was like a gallows where the nooses were made of silk.

"Gib! I'm glad you were chosen to come!"

Gib was so taken with the sights and splendors around him that it took a moment to realize he was being spoken to. He blinked out of his reverie only to realize Diddy was standing nearby, dressed in splendid finery much like the first day they'd met one another.

"Diddy—" Gib winced, remembering Hasain's warning. *Conduct myself as a guest of the royal family. All right.* "I mean, Prince Didier. I, uh, I'm honored to be here." He bowed, just in case anyone else was around to see them.

A solemn, grave look passed across Diddy's brown eyes. "Arise, Gibben Nemesio. The honor is mine." The prince's voice was formal, stifled, and nothing like the friend from class Gib had grown accustomed to.

Gib stood to his full height, glancing around. He didn't like having to be so formal but was glad he'd erred on the side of caution. He and Diddy were not the only people in the room.

Hasain had joined a group of three men on the opposite side of the arena—one of which Gib recognized as Weapons Master Roland. Of the other two, one was tall with dark, braided hair and a red cape similar to Seneschal Koal's except that it hung from his right shoulder instead of the left. He was fitted with a fine linen doublet and heavy fur cloak beneath his cape to ward off the cold. The other stranger was the opposite of the first, small of stature, with red hair and a patch covering his right eye. Gib could only assume this stranger had no reason to leave the palace for all he wore were a pair of boots and a kilt. Both men stood beside Roland and six royal guardsmen waited nearby, still as statues.

As Gib observed them, he pondered whether this lesson would be a spectacle for all these gathered strangers to see. It was bad enough when he made a fool out of himself in private.

The men talked quietly among themselves, stealing glances in Gib's direction now and then. Roland even gestured toward Gib at one point. He shrunk back a pace, doing all he could to keep from wincing. *Are they talking about me? Do they disapprove of a commoner training with the prince? What if they send me away?*

Diddy's voice was soft and reassuring in his ear. "They're learning your name and face—a safety measure, nothing more."

Gib forced himself to nod, though he had little idea what was happening or who any of these strangers were. *But when do you ever really know what's going on? Just nod your head and pretend you're content.* "Fair enough."

Diddy began to pull the velvet cloak from his shoulders. "We should start practicing. It won't be long until the lesson commences."

The prince unclasped the golden button that held his cloak in place, and almost immediately, a young attendant slipped from behind a pillar and scampered to Diddy's side. "M'lord, Prince Didier, can I take your cloak?"

Gib blinked in surprise. He recognized the boy with russet-colored hair at once as the waif who had been caught stealing the fur cap from a vendor during Midwinter Festival—the same boy who had nearly lost his hands until Queen Dahlia herself had ordered the sentinels to stand down.

The royal guardsmen had taken custody of the youngster—and now he was here at the palace?

Diddy turned toward the boy and gave him a small smile of gratitude. "Yes, Gideon. Thank you. Gib, you may give your cloak to him as well. I assure you Gideon will take good care of it."

The boy took their cloaks, bowing as he stepped out of the way. Gib noted the youngster looked to be in good health. He'd been half-starved and wearing rags less than a moonturn ago and now he was dressed in a clean tunic and appeared to be receiving regular meals. *Joel did say his aunt has a soft spot for homeless children. Queen Dahlia must have offered him a job as a servant.* He thought to ask Diddy about the young boy later—now was hardly an appropriate time.

Diddy smiled as he turned his attention back to Gib. "We're only waiting for Tarquin now."

"Tarquin is coming?" Gib asked.

"Yes. He was also chosen to train with me. I requested Kezra and Nage as well, but I fear they were overlooked for being a girl and a peasant."

"I'm a peasant." Gib didn't mean for his voice to sound so strained, but he couldn't correct it once he'd started talking.

Diddy's dark eyes went wide even as his pale cheeks flushed with color. The prince stumbled over his next words in perhaps the most ungraceful display he'd ever shown Gib. "I didn't mean—apologies, Gib. I–I only meant that I believe Kezra and Nage weren't given fair treatment when it was decided who would come to the palace. The fact that you were chosen speaks highly of your skill and the trust Master Roland has bestowed upon you."

Guilt blossomed in Gib's stomach. He knew he and Nage wouldn't be judged so harshly—or Kezra either for that matter—but all he could think of were Hasain's arrogant words in the hallway only moments before he'd entered the room. The young Radek lord had been so condescending and cruel. Still, it was unfair for Gib to vent his frustrations on Diddy. "I'm sorry. I know what you meant."

Diddy opened his mouth to speak but stopped when the large door opened again. This time Tarquin and an older man with dark hair stepped through. No introductions needed to be made. The man was clearly Tarquin's father; they looked exactly the same except for their coloring. Tarquin's white blond hair and ivory skin must have been inherited from his mother.

Diddy was once again a prince, taller, intimidating, and perfectly reserved. "Greetings, Councilor Joaquin Aldino and Lord Tarquin Aldino."

Tarquin and his father both bowed low and made their greetings, and once Diddy had commanded them to rise, Tarquin's father went to join the other grown men across the room.

Tarquin wrung his hands as he looked around the arena with wide eyes. "I never dreamed I'd be here." He turned a full circle. "Imagine the kings of old training in this very spot—" His voice faded into hushed awe.

Diddy's smile seemed much more genuine now that the three friends were alone again. "You don't mind too terribly being taken from your afternoon classes?"

"No!" Tarquin laughed. "To have the honor of training within the palace—" He froze as he looked toward Hasain, the pack of royal guardsmen, and the other adults. "Are they—?"

"They're here to learn your faces," the prince explained for the second time since Gib had arrived. A rueful smile stole across his lips. "I was instructed to pretend they weren't here at all."

Gib snorted. "The guards? Who could ignore them?"

Tarquin gave him a confused glance, his face a flustered shade of pink. "N–no. I meant—"

"*Stand at attention!*"

The Weapons Master's voice rang clearly off the high stone walls and caused all three boys to jump. Roland strode over in full armor with his sword pulled and at the ready. Gib winced. Apparently it was time to begin.

"Tarquin and Gibben, you've been chosen from your peers. It is your duty and honor to serve by training with our prince. Lessons will commence at once and henceforth until the King himself determines otherwise." Roland pointed to a selection of swords on a nearby rack—real, steel swords, not the wooden ones Gib had expected to train with. "This class is no small matter. No mistakes will be tolerated here. Armor up and find the weapon that suits you." Roland's smile was wicked and fearsome. "No one leaves the arena until he cries for mercy."

Gib returned from his lesson at the palace, tunic drenched in sweat and bruises the size of chicken eggs already darkening his skin. His arms and legs were afire despite the cold winter air. Weapons Master Roland had pushed the three boys hard. Even Tarquin and Diddy had been gasping for reprieve by the time the lesson was over. Gib groaned aloud at the prospect of having to return the following day. He'd reminded himself—if only to keep from crawling into a hole in the ground and never coming out—that it was an honor to train in the splendid arena inside the palace walls and in such company as a prince of Arden. He was supposed to be *grateful* for the beating he'd endured.

By the time Gib bathed and ate dinner, his muscles ached so terribly that all he wanted to do was curl up on his mattress and sleep. As it was though, the sentinel trainee hadn't worked on his studies since returning to Academy and with an exam looming in his Ardenian Law class, Gib knew rest would have to wait.

Forsaking his warm bed, the sentinel trainee went to his desk instead and began to read. It was hard to focus on the words with so many thoughts running through his head. Despite the assurance that every necessary precaution was being taken, Gib couldn't help the feeling of terror in his gut. The assassin who attacked King Rishi hadn't been found—how could everyone be so confident no second attempt to take the King's life would occur?

A faint scratching noise at the door caught Gib's attention and the irrational fear that somehow the assassin had come for Gib raced through his mind. The sentinel trainee's head shot up, brown eyes wide, any number of awful scenarios traversing his thoughts. *What if the assassin figures out I provided Seneschal Koal and the other officials with information? What if he comes to shut me up for good?*

"Gib? Are you all right?"

Joel's tender voice brought Gib back to his senses. The older boy was standing in the doorway like a beacon of light in the middle of the night, a pillar of strength among the chaos. His raven hair shimmered in the candlelight and his eyes were as bright as a cloudless summer sky. Gib's breath caught in his throat. He'd never wanted—no, *needed*—Joel more than right now.

Gib forced his lips to move. "I'm okay. It's been a long day." His heart hammered in his chest as he watched the mage trainee sweep into the room. *Daya, I need to tell him. I've kept this a secret for too long.* Joel's smile was wistful as he closed the door, sliding the bolt into place. The click of the lock was like thunder in Gib's ear. *Alone. We're alone. I'll never have a better chance than now—*

"It's been a long day for both of us," Joel replied. "I'm sure you can imagine the gossip I had to endure in my classes today. I suppose I should be grateful I wasn't the topic of discussion for once, but—being son of the seneschal has its disadvantages. Everyone kept expecting me to know what was going on. You should have heard some of the questions I was being asked." Joel flopped down onto his bed with a sigh. "How was *your* day? Was the royal palace everything you dreamed it would be?"

Gib groaned. He welcomed the light conversation despite his heavy, tumultuous thoughts. "Let me tell you about that. Or I could just save my breath and show you the bruises."

Joel laughed as he rolled onto his side, propping himself up by the elbow. "I take it Master Roland was hard on you?"

"It was worse than group class."

"You should know many students would gladly pay for that kind of one-on-one attention from the Weapons Master."

Gib's eyebrows creased as he contemplated Joel's words. "I would have to say such students are insane."

Light laughter echoed off the walls. "Perhaps they are." Joel cleared his throat pointedly as he sat up on his bed. "How was Didier faring when you saw him this afternoon?"

Gib could feel the mage trainee's eyes. "Given the circumstances, Diddy seemed to be okay. He was happy to see me and Tarquin." Gib sighed, closing the book he hadn't really been studying anyway, and went to his own bed. "That doesn't change the fact that I've been worried about him all damn day. I'm worried about his entire family." Gib rubbed the back of his neck. "I've been so stressed."

Joel frowned and immediately rose to his feet, crossing the space between their beds. He sat next to Gib and gave him a gentle tap on the shoulder. "Hey, I know you're afraid for Diddy and the others, but it will be all right. You need to try to get some sleep tonight. I'm sure you're tired."

Gib nodded. "I'm exhausted, but—" He bit his lip as he carefully debated his next words. Yes, he was worried sick about the safety of the royal family, but in this moment, all he wanted to do was share the truth about the way he felt about Joel. *Goddesses, give me strength.* Gib let out a stifled breath of air. "There is something I need to say to you." With uncertain, shaking fingers, Gib reached out to take hold of the other boy's hands.

Joel started to pull away, to retreat into his shell of indifference and isolation, but this time Gib had anticipated it and was ready. He tightened his grip around his roommate's hands before he could escape. "Wait."

Joel stiffened his shoulders, panic flittering across his beautiful face. "Gib, I—uh—"

"Talk to me, Joel," Gib pressed, before his courage abandoned him. "I can't keep pretending like there's nothing going on between us."

The mage trainee's voice was weak. "O–oh, if this is about what Nawaz said after the Midwinter feast, I already said his behavior was less than appropriate and I'm sorry—"

"Nawaz spoke the truth. He was right about everything."

Joel paled. "The truth about what?"

"*Us.* You and me." Gib's voice threatened to catch in his throat. He shut his eyes, willing his nerves to settle. "You're my best friend, Joel. But it's not enough. Not anymore. I–it's time I tell you exactly how I feel."

"What do you feel, Gib?" Joel asked, his voice a silken whisper.

"I–I feel—" Gib paused for a gasp of air. "I feel like you're the most wonderful, caring person in the world. I want to be around you, hear your laughter, see your smile. When you're near, I'm not alone in this giant, frightening place that is so different from everything I've ever known. I'm not afraid of what dangers may befall us or our friends—you give me hope that everything will work out the way it's supposed to. And you make me feel—whole, complete. I've realized who I am and it's because of you." Gib dared to reach forward and touch his fingers to the older boy's onyx locks.

The sentinel trainee's heart leapt in his chest when Joel raised his own hand to cup the side of Gib's face in a tentative way. "I—you—I feel—" All of Joel's graceful mannerisms seemed to have abandoned him in that moment. His voice was timid, even shy. "I feel the same, Gib." The mage trainee brushed an unruly curl away from Gib's cheek, hand trembling against Gib's skin.

Joel's lips were so close, so soft and inviting. "I want to kiss you," Gib murmured, leaning closer. He could feel Joel's hot, jagged breath.

"I'm scared," replied the older boy, voice shaking as surely as his hands.

"I'd never hurt you."

Joel's eyes were clouded and his chest was heaving. "I know that, but I—I don't want you to get hurt either."

Gib frowned, not understanding. It seemed a silly thing for Joel to even suggest. "I know you'd never hurt me."

"If—if we—are to be more than just friends, I can't protect you from the rest of the world. I can't stop the rumors, the unkind words, the sideways glances. People are cruel, Gib. You must know the consequences of this decision. You'll be labeled forever. I don't want you to regret it after it's too late. People will never forget."

Gib shook his head adamantly. "This is who I am. I'm the same as you, Joel. You speak of me regretting this decision—well I will sooner regret continuing to pretend I don't feel this way about you. I want this." Joel tried to look away, but Gib slipped his hand beneath the mage trainee's chin, forcing their eyes to meet. "I don't care what people think. This is what I want. *I want you.*"

Joel's eyes were wide with unmasked emotion. His lips parted—he might have even whispered some kind of garbled, indecipherable response—but it was all lost to the sentinel trainee as Joel leaned forward and pressed his mouth to Gib's. *Oh Gods.*

Gib returned the kiss as though his life depended upon it. All the confusion, all the sorrow, all the fear—every last bit of it drained from his body like an open wound that was finally beginning to heal. In that instant, the only thing that mattered was the present. The now. And right now he and Joel were kissing. Gib squeezed his eyes closed, lost in the moment.

Joel's lips were as soft as silk and tasted of sweet despair. Gib deepened the kiss, searching for a place where he could find a trace of the proud, confident boy Gib knew was hidden inside, suppressed by harsh words and unfair judgments. It wasn't fair—everything the young highborn had endured—but he no longer had to face the world alone.

Gib's eyes fluttered open as the older boy ended the kiss. Joel was staring at Gib, handsome features lined with uncertainty. The mage trainee suddenly looked so young and vulnerable. He clutched Gib's face as though fearing he might flutter away like the end of a wonderful reverie.

"I—I fear this is a dream." Joel's words were hushed.

"If it's a dream," Gib replied, pausing to touch his lips to the mage trainee's forehead. "Then we can dream together."

Joel's eyes brimmed with tears. "You are too wonderful, Gibben Nemesio. I don't—I don't even know what to say—" His voice cracked, and he lowered his face.

Gib stroked the older boy's hair, running fingers through silky, raven waves, smoothing the strands which refused to lay flat. The younger boy parted his lips, meaning to offer words of comfort, but Joel's stark crystal eyes stole away the words with just a single glance. With gentle caresses, Gib rested a hand against Joel's cheek, wiping away the single tear which had formed in the corner of the mage trainee's eye.

Joel leaned into the touch, his own voice silenced by the weight of the emotions they both were feeling. He let out a sobbing gasp before his entire body crumbled against the sentinel trainee. Gib held the older boy as he cried, offering gentle words and soothing touches. Joel rested his face against Gib's neck, tears streaming down and pooling on the front of the younger boy's tunic.

Time seemed to stand still. Gib wasn't sure how long they sat together, but when Joel next spoke, the candles had burned low. The mage trainee raised his head. His face was red and stained by tears, but the crushing despair that once clouded his eyes was gone. Now his sapphire orbs sparkled with renewed hope.

"My heart—it finally feels at peace. You've brought so much happiness into my life," Joel whispered. He took Gib's hands. "That is why I didn't want to say anything. I didn't want to ruin our friendship. I couldn't be sure if you felt the same way, and I couldn't risk losing you. You know what happened the last time—"

Gib leaned forward to rest his forehead against the older boy's. "I'm not going anywhere and I won't ever abandon you. I *promise*."

"As do I." Joel's smile was agonizingly beautiful as he caressed the sentinel trainee's hands. "I can't think of anyone else I'd rather face the world with, Gibben Nemesio. You are one of the most compassionate, bravest people I've ever met and—I cherish you."

Gib parted his lips, meaning to reply, but his words fell by the wayside when their mouths locked together once again. Electrifying emotion surged through his body as they shared another kiss, and somehow—despite the many challenges facing him—Gib knew everything was going to be all right.

CHAPTER TEN

Three days later Liza paid Gib a visit. His relationship was still so new and he was in such a fog that he barely heard the light tap on the door. Even as he went to let Liza inside, the sentinel trainee's thoughts kept drifting back to Joel.

Chhaya's bane, I haven't been able to focus. What is wrong with me? He'd never experienced such emotions before. An intoxicating sense of euphoria would overwhelm him each time he and Joel touched. It was even more exhilarating when they kissed. Gib blushed every time as he promptly melted into a sappy, love-struck mess, unable to catch a breath of air or think of anything witty to say. Joel would laugh in response. His light and flirtatious chuckles did nothing but cause Gib's knees to tremble—

Stop. Focus. Gib sat down, his head clouded. "I've missed you, Liza."

"How are things going with your roommate—Joel, is it?" Liza asked as she closed the door. The question was innocent, yet almost immediately heat rushed to Gib's cheeks at the mention of the mage trainee's name.

Motioning for Liza to take a seat, Gib replied, "That's right. Joel Adelwijn. Son of—"

"Seneschal Koal," his sister finished. Liza chuckled as she sat on the edge of his bed. "I didn't forget *that* part. Who would have thought my little brother would be roomed with the son of the second most powerful man in all of Arden?"

Gib wrung his hands. "Joel is wonderful. He's my best friend." The sentinel trainee dared to meet his sister's questioning gaze. The truth was churning inside his stomach, begging to be told, but Gib bit his tongue. He wasn't sure if Joel wanted their relationship to be known by anyone else. Gib cleared his throat. "Any word from Tay and Cal?" he asked, directing the conversation elsewhere.

"Yes. That's part of the reason I'm here." Liza reached into a pouch clinging to her belt and pulled out a crumpled piece of parchment. "I got this from the boys yesterday morning."

Gib took the paper into his hands at once and unfolded it. He recognized Tayver's handwriting immediately, and if Gib wasn't mistaken, his brother's penmanship was more crisp than it had been the previous summer. Was Tayver getting lessons? Gib focused on the words, hoping his younger brother had fair news to report.

Dearest Liza,

The Fadells have been kind to us. During the snowstorm, they shared their Midwinter Feast. Sorry you and Gib were not able to come home. Me and Cal miss you. I want to come to the city in the summer and live there. I'm old enough now to do apprentice work so I won't be in your way. I've been practicing my writing at the temple and the priests say I'm better at reading than any of the other children here. It is really hard for me and Cal to run the farm without you and Gib. Altair has said that Cal can stay on his farm and be a hand until he turns thirteen. I think it is time to let the farm go. Life is taking us all in different directions and I think Pa would have agreed. Please write us soon.

May the Two bless you,
Tayver

Gib handed the letter back to Liza, knitting his eyebrows. "Huh."

"That's Tayver for you—blunt as always." Liza chuckled. She gave Gib a gentle pat on his shoulder. "If anything was seriously wrong, he would have said so. Though it does give us some things to think about."

Gib nodded, worried for his brothers. This winter had been kind to them. But luck could be devious and theirs was certain to run out sooner than later. "Tayver is right, Liza," he stated. "With both of us in Silver, we can't maintain the farm. Tay and Cal can't do it by themselves either. I think—I think it's time to sell the farm." It was hard to admit, even to himself. All he'd wanted to do was make his father proud by keeping the farm afloat and now everything seemed to be falling apart.

Liza nodded, a pained grimace on her face. "You knew it might come to this, Gib. We can't keep them at the farm all alone. Tayver can apprentice, and we'll figure out what to do with Cal."

"I feel like I failed them both. And Pa."

"No, Gib." Liza's voice was firm as she squeezed her brother's shoulder. "It's the best thing to do. The boys are proud of you. And Pa would be too, if he could see the young man you've become."

Gib turned to look at her. "You really think so?"

"I *know* so." She paused long enough to wrap her arms around his back. "There is something else I came here to tell you."

Gib winced at her ominous tone. "O–oh?"

Liza caressed his curls absently. Her eyes were distant as she stared across the room. "I've been reassigned to Winterdell, due to the growing tension with Shiraz. My unit's been ordered to reinforce Arden's eastern border. I leave in one sennight."

Gib's stomach flopped. "H–how long will you be there?"

"I'm not sure," Liza admitted with a shrug. Her nonchalance didn't fool either of them. They knew how dangerous it was to be stationed along the border Arden shared with Shiraz. "I'll be there half a wheelturn at least."

"*Half a wheelturn?*" Gib didn't mean for his voice to spike, but the shock hit him like a rock to the face. "I'm sorry, it's just—how am I going to figure out what to do with the farm if you're gone? And the boys—I don't even know—" He bit his bottom lip and glared at the floor. *Liza doesn't need to hear me complain. She has enough to worry about without me blathering on.*

"I'm sorry, too," Liza sighed, hugging him close. "I'm sorry that life hasn't gone as planned. But our family is strong—you, me, Tay, Cal—we'll be all right. No matter what fate decides to throw at us next, we'll get through it. And when the time comes to make a decision about the farm, you'll do the right thing, Gib. The boys trust your judgment, as do I."

Gib swallowed the lump that formed in the back of his throat. His eyes burned, tears threatening to spill over his eyelashes, but with a shuddering sigh, he blinked them away. Things could always be worse, much worse. It looked as though Tayver and Calisto would survive the winter, Liza was alive and well even if she was being sent into danger, and Gib had a warm bed to sleep in, friends to laugh with—and Joel Adelwijn. *Deep breaths, everything is going to be okay.*

Gib turned to look Liza in the eye with renewed resolve. "I'll try to make you proud, Liza. I promise."

His sister gave him a small, knowing smile. "You always do, Gib. Always."

The next two sennights were hell on Gib's body and mind as he tried desperately to keep up with the demands Weapons Master Roland placed. The private lessons were brutal, and each night Gib had to drag himself back to his room. It wouldn't have been so bad if he could have simply gone to sleep upon his return, but he had to study for his other classes. He became reliant on Kezra and Nage to give him pertinent information each morning at breakfast from the previous day's lesson.

Nights were spent studying and practicing his reading and arithmetic skills. Joel was wonderful about helping as much as possible, but still Gib feared this extra strain may hurt their blooming romance. How long could these extra lessons possibly last? He wasn't sure he could continue this way until the end of the academic year, still three moonturns away.

At practice, Tarquin pulled his chosen sword from its holster on the wall and gave Gib a small nod. They'd missed each other after midday meal today and had each walked to the palace alone. The boys' faces were known well enough now that they were rarely stopped other than to show their badges to the sentries posted at the gate. Didier was running late and Gib wished he'd brought a book. He could have been practicing his reading while he waited for the prince.

Tarquin took off his hat. In the enclosed arena, he didn't need protection from the sun. "Want to drill with me until they show up? I want my muscles to loosen up a little before—"

"Before Master Roland beats us to death?" Gib offered wryly.

Tarquin snickered. It was easy enough to joke now, but in a few marks none of them would be in any mood for merriment. They took their starting stances and were prepared to begin sparring when the door behind them opened. Didier hurried through, followed closely by his newest servant, russet-haired Gideon.

Diddy trotted over to them. "Master Roland isn't here yet?"

"No," Gib grunted, keeping a close eye on Tarquin. They had begun to circle each other now, each boy looking for an opening to strike. "We're just warming—" Tarquin launched himself and Gib darted aside, grinning at his improved speed. "—up."

The prince was entirely inattentive as he paced across the tiled floor. "I wonder if he's still with Father. They were in deep discussion earlier." Gib had a hard time listening and watching Tarquin at the same time. The sentinel trainee opted to save himself from receiving any more broken limbs. Diddy didn't appear to be talking to him anyway.

After Gib had worked up a sweat, the arena door swung open again. He and Tarquin stopped long enough to see who had joined them. Weapons Master Roland came through the arched doorway, barely casting a glance in their direction. He was invested in conversation with the same tall, dark-haired man who had supervised the boys' first private lesson. Roland and the stranger were followed by a handful of royal guards, and all the men swept off to the viewing auditorium without a single word to the students. Gib glanced at Tarquin, who merely shrugged.

Gib heaved a sigh. "One more drill before certain death?"

Tarquin chuckled. "Yeah. Let me get a drink quick." He holstered his weapon and went over to a bucket set aside for drinking. Lifting the ladle, the young highborn took a long gulp of water. Gib considered doing the same. Once they began their training, they would find no time for drinks. With a grunt, Gib holstered his blade as well and went for a drink.

Tarquin turned to look at Diddy as they shared turns with the ladle. "Something has Diddy up in arms. What do you think they're talking about up there?" He nodded in the direction of the gallery.

Gib shrugged. "Something to do with the safety of the royal family maybe? Perhaps there's been news."

Tarquin snorted and rolled his eyes. "It's just not like Diddy to be so preoccupied."

At length, Roland strode away from the other men and came upon the trainees. His face was set in a grim mask and Gib's stomach flopped. "Gibben, Tarquin, to me. You as well, Your Highness, if I may." The three approached in unison and waited in tense silence for further instruction.

Roland glanced over his shoulder, and Gib followed the gaze. The tall, dark-haired stranger and royal guards were waiting in icy silence, all eyes on the arena. It was an eerie feeling to be under their scrutiny.

The Weapons Master spoke mainly to Diddy. "They want to see your progress, Highness. The three of you need to be at your best. Show them everything you've learned. This will determine whether these private lessons continue."

Diddy nodded, his face grim.

Roland's eyes were apologetic, though his voice remained rough and authoritative. "Prepare yourself, Highness. We wait for one other and then you'll begin."

Gib waited until they had moved out of Roland's earshot before questioning the prince. "What's going on? Why would they stop the lessons?"

Gideon was already helping Diddy remove his fine cape and restrictive doublet. The servant would fetch the sword in a moment, as he did each day, and Diddy would thank him despite what Hasain had said about not needing to thank the servants.

Diddy looked back at the men in the auditorium. "It has been suggested that lessons with you and Tarquin may be risky. The High Council says either of you could be spies or informants for the assassin." Tarquin balked and Diddy gestured for the young lord to keep his voice low. "I know it's ridiculous and Father thinks the same, but we have to prove that I've made adequate progress or the risk will be deemed too high. So please, be serious about this, friends."

Gib frowned. "What will happen if they decide you haven't progressed enough?"

Diddy's eyes were wide and hopelessly lost. "I won't be able to go to class anymore. In the future, even when this danger has passed, I'll be given a tutor and forced to stay within the palace walls."

"That doesn't make any sense. What does your progress here have to do with you taking other classes once the danger is gone? You won't have to lift a sword for your history lesson or law lectures."

"I know," Diddy sighed. "But the politics of Arden run deep. There are those on the High Council who have always questioned Father's judgment on allowing his children to be schooled with lesser nobles and commoners at Academy. They believe royalty should not mingle with anyone who is 'beneath them.' Of course, Father is defiant and has always fought against this, but in light of recent events, the idea has gained support within the council. They would use my performance today as an excuse to pull the royal family away from outside influences."

Gib shook his head. It all seemed more confusing than it needed to be—confusing and dirty. But such matters were not up to a lowborn to decide. "If you should fail this today then you'll be tutored? Is that such a terrible thing?"

Diddy's eyes shone with unshed tears as he looked to the marbled floor. "I must sound a spoiled brat to you. It's just—Father indulges our dreams of leaving the palace. I've always been taught outside of the palace and the thought of being tutored feels like I'm being sentenced to prison. I leave so rarely as it is—" The prince stopped there, head hung low. Gib would have never considered the palace to be a prison but now, in context, he thought he understood Diddy's dilemma.

They had no time to discuss it, however. The arena doors flew open a final time and Seneschal Koal stormed through. The look on his face showed he was in no mood for merriment, and a moment later the sentinel trainee understood why. High Councilor Neetra Adelwijn followed just behind the billow of Koal's red cape.

Neetra's face was set in a foul sneer. Pointed nose in the air, he didn't wait to be acknowledged before climbing the steps to the auditorium. Gib watched as Koal took a stance on the far side of the dark-haired stranger, putting the man between the seneschal and his brother. Gib watched with growing apprehension as Neetra bowed stiffly to the tall stranger. Who in hell was this man if the high councilor—arrogant and lofty as he was—had bowed to him?

Roland was bearing down on the trainees. No time was left to ponder the stranger's identity.

"Formation!"

Roland's voice filled the arena. Gib had no time to think about anything besides following the command. Falling into position, he shared one last meaningful look with the prince and Tarquin. They all knew everything rode on this performance.

At Roland's command, they commenced. Gib and Tarquin advanced as they would on an enemy. Diddy was no longer their prince and close friend. He was an obstacle to overcome, and the prince had to prove he could undo them both. In whirling steel and clashing blades, Prince Didier proved himself to the gathered men. If Gib hadn't known any better, he would have sworn the trio of boys had rehearsed this performance beforehand. He hoped Neetra didn't accuse them of as much.

They pressed on until Gib's shoulders were on fire and he could barely catch a breath of air. He had no idea how Diddy was continuing with two opponents trying to best him. Tarquin was likewise flushed and gasping for air when Koal finally raised a hand into the air.

Roland called them to halt, and the three students gratefully complied, only just managing not to drop their weapons on the floor. It took all of Gib's reserve to hang his sword back where it belonged before kneeling to take a rest. Diddy handed his weapon to Gideon, but the young prince remained standing, anxiously watching the men in the gallery as they deliberated.

From the distance, Gib couldn't hear their words, but he could see Neetra's scowl. Likewise, Koal and the tall, dark-haired stranger with the long braid frowned and waved their hands as they argued with one another.

After a heated few minutes, the man whom Gib didn't know flagged a hand, catching Roland's attention. The Weapons Master barked a single command for the three students to follow him and they fell in line behind the instructor.

Tarquin's eyes were wide as he rubbed his sweating palms across his leggings. He examined the occupied auditorium, and Gib felt one corner of his mouth turn up. He kept his voice low. "Seneschal Koal isn't so bad. He was very hospitable when I met him before. High Councilor Neetra, on the other hand—"

The puzzled look on Tarquin's face should have been a bigger clue. "I'm more concerned about the King."

Gib's stomach seized. *The King?* "Why? Are we going to meet him too?"

Tarquin didn't have time to respond. They were too close to the group of men now. The sentinel trainee swallowed hard, a knot in his stomach. The sparkle in Tarquin's eye suggested he was amused about something—only Gib couldn't figure out what he'd overlooked.

Standing before the panel of judges, Gib bit his bottom lip and remained silent. The tall man who'd called them over addressed only Roland. "Weapons Master, how fares the prince with his lessons?"

Roland bowed to the stranger and as he did, a sickening realization began to dawn on Gib. Roland's voice sounded a hundred leagues away as he responded, "Prince Didier is doing well for his age and build. The areas he needs to work on are—"

Gib wasn't listening any more. How had he never realized this stranger looked so familiar before now? Tall and slender, he bore a striking resemblance to Hasain Radek. His dark, almond-shaped eyes, olive skin, and braided onyx hair—albeit silver dusted with age—were all testament to the truth now so painfully obvious. Save for the thin mustache resting above his lip, he looked so much like Hasain that no one could say this man wasn't the young lord's father. And if he was Hasain's father then— Gib swallowed to keep from throwing up his midday meal. *Goddesses! How could I not know?*

Neetra's high whine needled its way into Gib's consciousness, drawing his attention back to the conversing men. "Yes, yes. The prince performed well against his peers, but how would he do against a true enemy? A full grown man?"

Roland's eyes were sharp. "Not as well. It would be unfair to pit him against a grown man."

The high councilor threw his hands into the air. "I didn't ask whether it would be fair or not. I asked how he would do! Surely you don't think the enemy will concern themselves with being fair?"

"Of course an enemy won't fight fair. Politicians, each one of them," Roland replied through gritted teeth.

Neetra's mouth fell open, aghast. He narrowed his eyes as if to respond but the tall stranger who so closely resembled Hasain cut the councilor off. "Roland Korbin, tell me the truth. Will the prince benefit from training with the royal guards? Should these two students be dismissed?"

"No. The prince is not so tall or built as fully trained soldiers. He wouldn't stand a chance—"

Neetra snorted. "Then perhaps your training is little more than a waste of time and resources, Master Roland."

Roland's mouth pulled back into an ugly sneer. "With all due respect, High Councilor, how many soldiers have you trained? How many of Arden's wars were won by troops you taught?" Neetra fell into angry silence. "I've dedicated my entire life to Arden's defenses. I assure you all that I've taken the utmost precaution with Prince Didier."

"Roland, what is your suggestion?" asked the tall, dark-haired man.

The Weapons Master scrutinized Gib and Tarquin for a long moment. "I would keep the students I've selected. And if you would like, I can bring in a couple of the older boys to train with Prince Didier as well. Nawaz Arrio, Otho Dakheel, and Lord Tular Galloway would be suitable. All are taller and stronger than the prince and will give him a good comparison for fighting a grown man."

The stranger—who Gib was now sure was no stranger at all—nodded his head as if his thoughts were deep. Diddy took the opportunity to step forward, bowing low. Tarquin did the same, and Gib was quick to follow. He couldn't breathe. This was proof. Who else would the prince ever need bow to?

"Please, Sire, if I may request my friends stay, I would." Diddy's voice was eloquent as he took a deep breath. "I wouldn't be caged now, having been free for so long. Please."

Gib's head was swimming. He feared his knees might buckle right there. The King of Arden looked over the three boys in silence. The weight of his dark eyes was enough to crush Gib's lungs without so much as a touch.

"I'll allow it, Didier," King Rishi responded at length. "Unless there comes a time when the danger is too great. If and when such a time should come, I'll do what I must to keep you safe. There are worse prisons than this palace."

"Thank you, Sire." Diddy stood slowly, the trace of a smile gracing his lips.

It wasn't until King Rishi told them they may rise that Gib and Tarquin straightened their backs. Gib was so flustered he could barely tell which way was up anymore. *The King! I just met the King of Arden!* Diddy had a full-fledged smile while Tarquin was doing his best not to grin—and failing miserably. As Gib watched the King and his entourage depart, he began to shake his head slowly. *How did I not know?*

CHAPTER ELEVEN

The sennights sped by quickly after that, and before Gib knew it, the ice and snow covering Silver City began to recede. Cold rain fell in its place, sometimes for days on end, leaving the streets in muddy disarray. The rain was hardly any more tolerable than the snow, but at least an end to the bitter winter was within sight. Spring was just around the corner.

Gib had settled into a steady routine. In the mornings, he attended weaponry class with his peers. He would then scarf down his midday meal and report to the palace for training with Diddy. For Gib not to be tardy to his afternoon classes, he would then have to sprint from the royal grounds back to Academy and hope he arrived before Lady Beatrice began the day's lesson. Nights were spent catching up on his studies with Joel.

Gib stayed so busy he had little time to think about the assassination attempt, and after a couple of moonturns, it seemed like everyone else had forgotten about it too. It was possible that after one botched effort, the assassin was too scared to act again. *Possible*, but nothing was ever certain.

The King never returned to watch Diddy spar, but other members of the royal family frequented the arena. The students' daily training sessions were becoming quite the spectacle within the palace walls. Diddy introduced Gib to all the visitors as they arrived—cousins, siblings, family of family—it was all difficult for Gib to keep track of and he didn't pretend to understand the different titles and ranks they associated with themselves. However, after two moonturns of training inside the palace, Gib certainly had learned how to bow correctly. He realized a gracious bow could spare an awkward conversation in situations where he simply didn't know what to say or do.

"You gonna make it through class, Nemesio?"

Gib jumped to attention. He hadn't realized he'd been slouching so low in his seat that his chin was resting on his chest. In fact, the sentinel trainee was so out of sorts that it took him a moment to remember he was sitting in his Ardenian Law class.

Gib held back a yawn and blinked his heavy eyelids fully open as he turned toward Nage. "Sorry. I'm tired."

Nage clasped him on the shoulder. "I can tell."

"We could hear you snoring," Kezra snorted. She sat on the opposite side of Gib. "Better not let Lady Beatrice catch you sleeping in her class or there'll be hell to pay."

Gib grimaced. He believed it. "Lady Beatrice isn't here yet. I can't get into trouble if class hasn't begun."

Tarquin issued a groan, leaning around Nage to address Kezra. "Gib and I have to sneak in naps whenever possible. Training once a day with Roland is brutal enough. You guys try doing it twice in the same day and let me know how you feel by nightfall."

Kezra's green eyes speared the young highborn. "Spare me your whining, Aldino."

The assembly hall was filling quickly; students poured through the open door in droves. A group of young, well-dressed ladies passed by, and Gib caught part of their conversation.

"—having a new gown tailored just for the celebration," one girl squealed in an excited voice.

A second girl giggled. "My mother is allowing me to wear her fine golden jewelry. It'll be sure to catch the attention of the young men in attendance."

"Oh, I can't wait for the dancing. The royal palace is the perfect place to hold such a glamorous ball—"

The rest of the conversation was lost as the two girls moved away. Gib furrowed his brow. "What do you suppose they were going on about?"

Kezra rolled her eyes. "Oh, just mindless twitter about the ball."

"Ball? What ball?"

Kezra and Tarquin exchanged amused glances before the young lord elaborated further. "The ball held at the palace every year to celebrate Aithne."

Gib froze. *Aithne. Daya, how could I forget?* Had he lost track of time so completely that he'd forgotten the most important holiday on the Ardenian calendar was less than a moonturn away?

Aithne was the celebration marking the day, some five hundred years ago, that Arden had won its independence from the Northern Empire. Like a phoenix emerging from the ashes, the people had risen against the tyranny of the Empire and fought for their freedom. The price of such freedom had been immense and many had lost their lives. Each year since, bonfires were lit in every village, town, and city to honor the sacrifice Arden's ancestors had made for their children to be free.

But Gib had never heard of a ball to commemorate Aithne. Of course, he'd never spent time in Silver City either—among highborns who seemed to thrive on wealth, possessions, and extravagant celebrations.

"It must be a pretty spectacular event if it's hosted at the royal palace," Gib replied.

"Ha!" Tarquin spat, sarcasm lacing his tenor voice. "One would think so."

"It's not?"

Now it was Kezra's turn to groan. "It's awful."

Tarquin echoed her sentiment. "Completely dreadful. It's so boring. My father makes me go every year."

"Mine too," Kezra lamented. "He says it's the 'duty of every highborn' to celebrate Arden's independence in the presence of the King."

"King Rishi goes?" Gib asked curiously.

"Yes," Tarquin answered. "The whole royal family attends. And they always look just as bored as the rest of us. The whole thing is a waste of time!"

Nage let out a snort, shaking his head. "You highborns have it so bad," he teased. "Being bored at some stuffy party with the King of Arden sure seems *awful*. You should try spending the holiday in the streets of Silver, scrounging for food and a warm place to sleep. I've had to do it a time or two in my life." The lowborn boy turned a sly grin onto Gib. "It's all right, Gib. While these two are enjoying the ball with the rest of the social elite, me and you can head over to the Rose Bouquet and have a real party, eh?"

The sentinel trainee frantically tried to think up an excuse for why he couldn't accompany Nage to the tavern, but luck was with him as Lady Beatrice strolled through the door and announced class was beginning.

Gib returned to his room still pondering everything his friends had talked about during class. He'd never heard of such a thing as the Aithne Ball before—but then again, the residents of Willowdale were too poor to hold great feasts or festivals for any of the major Ardenian holidays. Families had always celebrated Aithne alone, in the privacy of their homes. Gib remembered his own family setting a candle in the windowsill each year and taking time to say a word of gratitude in tribute to the ancestors who had sacrificed so much for the country. But no splendid parties or grand dances had occurred.

Joel greeted him warmly as Gib came through the door. "Hey. You're back early."

"Yeah, Lady Beatrice dismissed us. The highborn students were restless today. She told us that if no one was going to focus then we all should get out of her assembly hall." Gib grinned, though at the time, it hadn't been the least bit funny. Lady Beatrice was known for her patience and kind heart, but even a woman of such petite stature could be intimidating when bellowing at her unruly students.

"Oh?" Joel asked, raising an eyebrow. He extended a hand to the sentinel trainee.

Gib graciously accepted the silent invitation. Taking the offered hand, he was pulled closer by the older boy. "Yeah, they were all going on about the ball—"

"Ah yes," Joel interjected, smiling wistfully. "To commemorate Aithne. I should have known. In the highborn world, Aithne is the biggest celebration of the year."

"Well, my friends didn't seem very excited to go. Tarquin and Kezra were complaining all through class."

Joel chuckled, stroking long fingers through Gib's hair. "It can be dreadfully stifling. Being an event held for the social elite, I'm sure you can imagine the proper decorum and mannerisms that need to be followed. It's certainly not like the party your friends took you to at the Rose Bouquet."

The sentinel trainee grinned and relaxed against Joel's sturdier frame, enjoying this private moment. Life had kept them so busy lately. "Will you be going?"

"Unfortunately it is expected of me." Joel rested his chin on the top of Gib's head, sighing into his curls. "People will take notice if the son of the seneschal is absent, and rumors will ensue. Of course, people will talk even if I do go. It seems as though I'm destined to be the subject of nasty gossip everywhere."

Gib took hold of the mage trainee's hand. "I'm sorry. I wish there was something I could do to stop it. No one deserves to be slandered in such a way—least of all you."

Joel's eyes were sad as he leaned his forehead against Gib's. "I appreciate your words, but it's my own fault. I should never have said what I did."

"You shouldn't have to hide."

"No one should."

Gib gave the older boy a gentle smile. "Maybe someday things will be different."

Joel remained quiet for some time. His eyes were far away, as though he were caught in some momentous reverie. At last, the mage trainee spoke. His voice sounded a hundred leagues away, hushed as it was. "Gib, this might sound like a foolish request, but how—how would you feel about attending the ball with me?"

"Lady Mrifa, you really don't have to go through the trouble—"

"Oh, nonsense! I don't want to hear any of it," Lady Mrifa lamented as she circled around the young seamstress who was taking Joel's and Gib's measurements. Her eyes were attentive, as though she were truly concerned the tailoring apprentice might overlook something. "I insist you have custom-made attire for the ball."

Gib looked to Joel for help, but the mage trainee only shook his head and snickered. "Don't. It's not worth the argument."

"I'll have to work a lifetime to be able to repay this!" Gib protested, unable to quiet himself. The seamstress huffed for him to stand taller, and with a wince, the sentinel trainee jumped to do as he was told.

Mrifa scoffed. "My brother, Joran Nireefa, is Headmaster of the Tailoring Guild, and he owes me a favor or two. There will be no need to repay me, Gibben." She smiled, blue eyes twinkling with warmth as she set a hand against Gib's face. "Besides, truly it is I who am indebted to you."

Gib met her gaze with shy, uncertain eyes. "I'm afraid I don't follow you, m'lady."

Mrifa sighed, her own eyes flickering to Joel for a moment. "This world can be so cruel. For a while, I believed my son would never recover from the scorn he was made to endure, only because he was—different." She stroked the sentinel trainee's cheek. "It wasn't until you came into Joel's life that I could once again hear his laughter or see a trace of a true smile. You brought him back to us, Gibben. And one silly outfit will never be enough to repay you for that." Mrifa leaned forward, pressing her lips to Gib's forehead as a mother might do to show affection for a child.

His cheeks were as hot as iron rods. "I–I, uh, it's easy to like Joel. You raised a wonderful son." Gib stole a glance at his roommate. Joel was smiling shyly back. "I'm honored to be able to call him a friend."

For a moment afterward the room was silent, and the seamstress took advantage of the lull by clearing her throat and announcing her work was complete. "All done with the young lords, Lady Mrifa. Will you be needing measurements taken today as well?"

Mrifa turned away from Gib, dismissing the girl with a wave of her hand. "I assure you, my brother has made enough dresses by now to have dedicated my measurements to memory, and I haven't grown—taller or otherwise—since Carmen's birth nine wheelturns ago." Mrifa laughed as she helped the seamstress collect her belongings. "If you could inform Master Joran to have Joel and Gibben's outfits delivered to their dormitory room when they're completed, it would be most appreciated."

"Of course, my lady." The seamstress clutched her satchel between her hands and offered a low curtsey. "I'll return to Master Joran at once."

"I'll see you to the door," Mrifa replied. She gave Gib a scandalous wink as she passed. "Try not to grow any more between now and Aithne. There isn't enough time to make a second garment for you."

The sentinel trainee couldn't stop the crooked grin from spreading across his face. "I'll do my best not to, m'lady." Mrifa patted him on the shoulder as she departed, following at the heels of the young seamstress.

As soon as the two women left the room, Joel stepped down from his pedestal and swept to Gib's side. "Well, I'm certainly glad *that* is out of the way." The mage trainee took hold of Gib's hand, weaving their fingers together. "Thank you for your kind words."

Gib nodded as he stared at their interlaced fingers, lost in a trance. It was still hard to believe they were finally together. "Is your mother having fine garments made for *all* of your siblings?"

"I'm sure she is." Joel let out a deep sigh. "We highborns tend to go above and beyond for these kinds of celebrations, especially ones where the royal family is promised to be in attendance. My family's attire will be modest in comparison to some, no doubt. You'll see what I mean."

"I still can't believe I'm allowed to attend," Gib replied. "You're sure they won't take one look at me and bar me from the palace?"

Joel's lips curled in a dashing smile. "You'll blend in by the time you're dressed in my uncle's finery. Uncle Joran is the best tailor in the city. He can make a pauper look like royalty. Besides," the mage trainee leaned down and rested his forehead against Gib's. "You are my family's guest—my guest—and no one would dare turn away the company of Seneschal Koal's son."

Gib chuckled lightly but couldn't think of anything to say. It was nearly impossible to believe that he would be attending a grand ball. Of course, if someone had told him a year ago that he would join the Arden Sentinels, train with a prince, fall in love, and meet a *king*—all within the next six moonturns—Gib would have laughed until he'd turned blue in the face. *At this point, I shouldn't have even been surprised when Joel asked me to go. Tay and Cal won't believe me when I go home and tell them I've been to a grand ball at the palace. Or when I say my friend is a prince and I got to stand in the same room as the King of Arden!* He smiled to himself. It all sounded absurd, even to him.

Gib's thoughts lingered on the royal family and for the first time in sennights, the sentinel trainee found his mind troubled.

"Joel," he began. "Do you think it's a good idea for the royal family to be present at the ball? I mean, I know there haven't been any threats made on King Rishi since Midwinter, but—with so many people in the palace for the celebration and the royal family in attendance, don't you think it would be the perfect time for the assassin to strike again?"

The mage trainee's smile was grim. "It would be unwise to rule out the possibility of such a thing happening, I won't deny it—but Gib, you've been to the palace enough times to know how well protected the royal family is." Joel squeezed the younger boy's shoulder. "How many royal guardsmen were with King Rishi the day you met him?"

"I know, but—" Gib tried to keep his voice level despite his churning stomach. "Why not just cancel the ball? Is the safety of our ruler really worth the risk for some petty highborns to gather and exchange gossip with one another?"

"They can't just cancel everything. Life can't come to a grinding halt just because some terrible person tried to murder the King three moonturns ago. It simply can't be." Joel sighed, his mouth set in a straight line. "Besides, if the Aithne ball is cancelled, people will question King Rishi's strength as a ruler. Some might even go as far as to call him a coward."

Gib made a horrified sound. "That seems unfair."

"It is. King Rishi is no coward, of course, but you have to realize that danger is unavoidable for a king. The High Council would never allow the Aithne ball to be cancelled anyway. The patrons who keep all those old men's purses filled would balk too much." Joel's voice grew lighter as he rubbed Gib's tense shoulders. "Don't worry yourself over all of this, Gib. I would have you enjoy the ball, if possible. I've never seen a student handed as much responsibility as you and not crack beneath the pressure. You deserve a night of frivolity."

"Yeah," the sentinel trainee replied. "I'll try not to worry." Despite Joel's reassurance that things would be all right, Gib wasn't entirely convinced he would be able to have a good time. The entire situation screamed of unnecessary peril—

And something else unrelated was weighing down on his mind as well.

Joel was giving him a measured look. "Is something else bothering you?"

Gib nodded slowly. *He knows me too well.* "Yes. It's about—us. I need to know before I go with you to this ball." He dared to meet the older boy's gaze as the words began to pour out with no reserve. "What are we, Joel? What are we to each other? And to other people? Are we lovers in our dormitory room but only friends the moment we step outside? What about when I tell my brothers about the wonderful person I met in Silver? Am I to introduce you as a friend—or something more? Are you going to tell your family or is this whole thing supposed to be a secret? Or have I gotten the wrong impression about everything? Are we only *just* friends?"

Shock registered on the mage trainee's face. Joel lifted delicate hands into the air, holding them in front of his body as though deflecting a physical blow. "Slow down, Gib."

Gib winced, biting down on his lower lip until it hurt. "I'm sorry. I just—I need to know."

Joel allowed a moment of silence to pass between them before he took hold of the younger boy's hands once again. "No, you're right. We haven't had time to discuss such things." Joel swallowed and a deep sigh escaped his lips. "You're my best friend, my partner, the person I trust above anyone else. There is no other person I'd rather spend my time with. I—cherish you. But—" Joel paused there. His voice was a pitch lower when he next spoke. "—but you have to understand that—for now—we have to keep our relationship private. I can't afford to cause another scandal within my family. I need time to figure this out."

An uncomfortable knot sat in Gib's stomach. "I understand."

"It's not only my family's reputation I worry about. I want to protect you as long as possible. I can bear the gossip and cold words, but you don't have the protection of being a highborn or the Seneschal of Arden's son to fall back on. You stand to suffer from more than only words if people find out. So for now, tell only those close to your heart." Joel slipped his arms around Gib, holding him close. "You don't know how badly I wish to announce our love to the world."

"Yes I do. I know because I feel the same way."

They shared a tender kiss before leaving the room together.

"Try not to fidget. You'll wrinkle your sleeves."

Gib put his busy hands to rest at Joel's gentle prompting. His soft voice was a testament to the mage trainee's patience after having to issue so many reminders. Gib didn't know how the highborns did it. He felt wedged into his woolen tunic and fine doublet. Everything fit well, like a second skin, but he was unaccustomed to such finery. At least when he'd taken the midwinter holiday at the Adelwijn estate he'd had reminders that he wasn't from their world. Joel's hand-me-down outfit had been lush and comfortable but too long in the sleeves and legs.

This outfit, tailored specifically for him, got under Gib's skin and threatened to make him forget where he came from. These clothes made him blend in, and the highborn society would accept him at face value—but what would happen if he was called upon to speak? If anyone could mess up a simple response, Gib was sure he could.

His heart leapt into his throat as the carriage rolled to a stop. *Are we here already?* He'd never ridden in a carriage before and the distance to the palace had flown by. No more than a quarter of a mark could have passed since he'd stepped into the carriage with Joel's family to start their journey from the Adelwijn estate to the palace gates. Gib's stomach twisted into tight knots. He flinched when a gentle hand touched his arm.

Joel gave him a soft smile. "We've arrived." The mage trainee looked handsome in his blue and silver mage robes.

"What if I trip? Or say something I shouldn't? I don't know if I—"

"Don't be silly. You'll be fine." Heidi offered reassurance as she fussed with her flowing lace skirt.

Carmen nodded. "It's mostly just boring old people talking. You'll be all right. Just stay with Joel or one of us."

"Carmen! *Manners!*" Lady Mrifa covered her laugh with one gloved hand. "Those 'boring old' people are the leaders of our country. They're politicians and they help decide our laws."

"It's boring," Carmen replied with a shrug. "I'll go find Inez and Inan. That way I won't be under foot."

Seneschal Koal chuckled. "Under foot? Who would have told you that?" His eyes twinkled. The seneschal gave his daughter a quick hug before the carriage door swung open.

A wiry footman waited outside. "Seneschal Koal. I'm honored to serve your family."

The seneschal stepped out of the carriage and stood aside as the footman proceeded to lend his arm to Lady Mrifa, Heidi, and Carmen. Joel touched Gib's shoulder to let him know it was his turn, and the sentinel trainee breathed a sigh of relief when the footman stepped back to allow Gib to step down on his own. Likewise, Joel was offered no help.

"Is it because the women's dresses get in the way when they dismount?" Gib asked before he could think to censor himself. His face instantly burst into a hot blush. He wished he could take the silly question back.

The footman smiled, turning to close the coach door. Joel pressed his lips together in a valiant attempt not to smile. Koal, however, chuckled as he took Mrifa's arm. Voice low, the seneschal looked around to be sure they were alone. "Yes, but they also help put drunk men back into the coaches later."

Mrifa giggled and cuffed her husband's arm even as the footman coughed politely to cover his own laugh. Koal led the way down the stone path which cut through the palace courtyard, the trace of a smile gracing his lips the entire way to the door.

As the family passed through the grand archway that led inside the palace, a pair of door attendants stood waiting to take their cloaks. Gib lifted his hand to the clasp around his neck, meaning to unfasten it, but hesitated when he heard Joel clear his throat. The mage trainee gave a single head shake and Gib dropped his hand. Sure enough, when the attendant came within reach, the man unhooked Gib's cloak and removed it.

"Thank you," Gib muttered, face red. The attendant faltered for an instant before moving along as if nothing had been said. Gib swallowed. He kept forgetting he wasn't supposed to thank the servants. When Joel made eye contact, Gib apologized. "I forgot. Sorry."

"Don't be. It's likely the only thanks he'll get all night."

Mouth set in a thin slant, Gib wandered forward with the Adelwijn family. How was he ever going to make it through the night? He couldn't even get through the door without asking awkward questions and forgetting protocol. He wished he could ask Joel to leave before faltering even more. If Gib caused Joel's parents embarrassment, he didn't know how he'd be able to live with the shame.

"Gib." Joel leaned closer to whisper when they reached another sprawling archway. "We're going to be announced. When we come through the ballroom door, it's important not to leave the belvedere until your name is called. That way the other guests will know who you are."

"What? They're going to call my name?"

Joel nodded. "Everything will be all right. Follow my lead."

The panic rose in Gib's throat like bile as the family moved through the entranceway.

The announcer rang a gong and called out Koal's full name and title as well as Mrifa's. Next were Heidi and Carmen, who were both given the title of lady. Joel was called a lord. Gib couldn't breathe as he waited. Would the announcer even know to call his name? What if he got it wrong? If his name wasn't called, would he have to stay outside? It might be more comfortable out there anyway—

"Gibben Nemesio of Willowdale!" proclaimed the announcer.

Gib touched the railing for balance and descended slowly down the red velvet stairway. Never had a mere five steps seemed so treacherous or steep. With all eyes on him, he felt as though his ears would burst into flame along with the rest of his face. What if he tripped? As his feet hit the floor, Gib managed to raise his eyes and get a good look around.

The ballroom was the most extravagant thing Gib had ever seen. The floor was a mosaic masterpiece of tiles made from tiny colored stones and topped by velvet carpeting. Portraits, sparkling chandeliers, and silken tapestries graced the walls, and no less than a dozen marble pillars supported a ceiling dusted in gilding. The golden paint shimmered in the candlelight. Gib gawked as he stared up at the second and third levels of the chamber—two darkened balconies stacked atop each other, high above the party. An ominous feeling swept over him. He squinted in his attempt to peer into the shadows of the galleries above, but the gloom was too thick. *It would be so easy for someone to go unnoticed up there, lurking in the darkness.*

Ladies in corseted gowns and frilly lace skirts twirled around the room on the arms of men, dancing to the beat set by a musician tapping on a hand drum. The mellow timbre of a harp resonated on the walls and a lute and reed flute flirted back and forth with one another, each lending a unique sound to the song. The music was as warm and inviting as the galleries above were cold.

As Joel had assured, royal guardsmen lined the room, standing vigilant and unmoving. In their armored finery, it was almost as though the sentinels were just another splendid decoration in this already opulent chamber.

In the center of the ballroom, a pyre of stacked tinder sat upon a giant pedestal, unlit. Gib imagined at some point tonight the wood would be set to flame in honor of Arden's fallen heroes. *I'm sure some flashy ceremony will ensue. Gods know, the highborns can't do anything without causing a scene.*

Joel placed a hand on Gib's shoulder. "See? That wasn't so bad. You did well."

Gib took a jagged breath and closed his eyes for an instant. The ballroom was twirling around him. "I never thought my bravest moment in life would be walking down a set of stairs."

The smile that broke across Joel's face reminded Gib of all the reasons he'd decided to come here. The mage trainee deserved support and if he asked Gib to walk down a million steps, then so be it.

"You're doing fine," Joel praised. "Don't be too hard on yourself. There is much to learn when it comes to the formalities of high society."

Gib nodded. He supposed it was true. The highborns themselves must have dedicated their entire lives to learning each detail of the many rules of their society.

"Seneschal Koal Adelwijn, Lady Mrifa, welcome."

Gib turned to see Hasain Radek bowing his head as he spoke to the seneschal and his wife. Koal nodded in response and Mrifa offered her hand. Hasain's manners were impeccable as he kissed her fingers. He paid the same respect to Heidi and Carmen.

Nawaz Arrio stood beside Hasain and followed the same guidelines as his friends, bowing to Koal before kissing each of the ladies' offered hands. When the young lord got to Carmen, who was trying valiantly to hold back her giggles, he deliberately blew air through his pursed lips onto her hand, making a loud spluttering noise.

Carmen shrieked a laugh. "Nawaz, stop!"

Nawaz stuck out his tongue. "Your hand tastes funny."

"You're a clown!"

Lady Mrifa cleared her throat pointedly. "Carmen, manners."

Carmen fell silent, her smile lost, but Nawaz stood to his full height and shook his head. "No, no, my lady. She's right." He winked at the youngest Adelwijn daughter. "But the proper term is 'politician.'"

Lady Mrifa gasped. Joel laughed and Hasain frowned hard at his friend. Gib found himself grinning despite being pretty sure the joke would be considered in poor taste here.

Nawaz didn't seem to care even a little as he made his way over to Joel and Gib. "Well, look what the cat dragged in. How do you keep gettin' dragged to these things?"

Gib's smile covered his entire face. At least Nawaz wasn't like the others here. If Gib slipped up or said something stupid, Nawaz would laugh with him, not scorn his ignorance. "Joel invited me. I could hardly say no to the seneschal's son."

Nawaz chuckled with a raised brow. "No, I suppose not." He looked at Joel, mischief dancing behind his terrible blue eyes. "Bringin' your friend along to every formality? Careful, he'll run at his first chance once he sees what these things are like."

"Gibben Nemesio?" Hasain's eyes shot wide open as he took notice of Gib's presence for the first time. "Is that you?"

A humored grunt escaped the back of Gib's throat. "Yeah. I'm afraid to move in these clothes, but it's me." He tugged on his sleeves a little and was scolded by Joel.

"You could pass for highborn."

Gib wasn't so sure about that, but he was trying his best to play the part. "You think so? You must not have seen my entrance then."

"They announced you?" Hasain looked at Nawaz in utter disbelief. "How did I miss that?"

Nawaz shrugged. "I told you he cleans up good. At the Midwinter feast he looked like he'd always been a noble."

Hasain opened his mouth, but the sound of horns blowing stopped his words before they could escape his lips. The music ceased and everyone in the room turned toward the blaring noise. Gib craned his neck, trying to see.

Joel leaned down and whispered, "The royal family is making their entrance now. You'll get to see them up close."

"All of them?" Gib didn't know why the thought made his stomach flutter. He wasn't likely to speak to any of them, but until now they'd merely been characters in a legend. In person, would they all be as human as Diddy?

The horns grew louder and several of the ladies of the court made oohs and aahs of appreciation. Gib couldn't yet see what held their attention, but from the wondrous looks on their faces, he was sure it must be them—the family he'd only heard fables about. A few breathless moments later, two figures came into view.

King Rishi was as tall and slender as Gib remembered from the last time they met. His onyx hair was woven into a long, thin braid down his back and his crown cleverly disguised the silver flecking around his temples. Face set and expressionless, he walked arm in arm with a lovely woman with dark hair and eyes. Her gown was immaculate but not as elaborate as Gib would have guessed. The simple, silken folds fell elegantly about her curved frame.

"You've met King Rishi." Joel's words were hushed and perhaps just a little proud. "She's Queen Dahlia."

Gib smiled. "She looks almost young enough to be the King's daughter." As soon as the words were out of his mouth, he winced. "S–sorry. I shouldn't have said that, right?"

Joel shook his head gently but didn't scold Gib. "She's my father's younger sister. Here come the royal children. You know Prince Didier."

Gib looked back to the procession and saw Diddy keeping pace just behind his mother and father. The young prince held his head high and was wearing a simple circlet wrapped around his head. "He seems to resemble his mother, not the King."

Joel pressed his lips together and Gib stopped talking. "The next one is Crowned Prince Deegan, the future king of Arden."

Gib watched the boy, probably about Calisto's age, as he strode stiffly behind Diddy. He looked determined and perhaps nervous. Gib understood the feeling. Having so many eyes on one so young must have been difficult.

"And the young girl is Princess Gudrin." Gib looked up to see a little girl being carried by the red-headed man with the eye patch and kilt who'd visited the arena on Gib's first day of training with Diddy.

"Who's that carrying her?" Gib asked.

"His name is Aodan Galloway. He's King Rishi's personal guard and one of his most trusted advisers."

Gib frowned. "Personal guard? He's hardly any taller than me—"

"Manners, Gib, manners."

"Manners are killing me. I never know what's going on."

Behind the adviser and princess came a pair of white-robed figures, a man and a woman. Both had raven hair, dark skin, and strange violet-colored eyes that sparkled with mysterious, otherworldly intellect. They looked so much alike Gib thought they had to be twins.

"Those are the Blessed Mages," Joel answered before Gib could even open his mouth to ask the burning question. "The ones I told you about. They're charged with protecting the Radek family."

The royal family ascended from the ballroom to a dais, where a table and benches sat. They took their seats, but still no one in the room dared move or speak. Only after all members of the family were situated and the strange mages had taken post behind the table did the King raise a large hand into the air. "You may continue."

The music picked up where it left off, and the guests went back to their previous conversations.

A servant came through, a platter topped with chalices balancing in one hand. "Would any of my lords or ladies like wine?"

Gib glanced at Joel and was met with a smile. They each asked for a glass.

"We don't even have to get our own drinks? What wonders." Gib looked around at the high arches of the ceiling and the fine paintings all around them. Even if he absorbed every detail he'd never be able to do the ballroom justice when he described it to his brothers. "This place is truly a dream."

"More like a nightmare," Nawaz groaned.

Gib was sure he hadn't heard him correctly until he realized Heidi was coming for them.

Nose in the air and skirt flaring impressively around her, she marched up to Nawaz in a huff. "You haven't even asked me for a dance yet. Have you forgotten your manners entirely?" Heidi offered her hand.

Nawaz grudgingly reached for her. "Maybe."

Hasain broke into a wide, fierce smile showing dimples for the first time. Gib realized he hadn't seen Hasain smile without mockery or sarcasm before. The young Radek lord was typically as well guarded as the palace walls. Hasain pushed Nawaz's arm. "Yes, go dance. Stop being rude."

Terrible blue eyes skewered Hasain as Nawaz handed his chalice to Joel and followed Heidi onto the ballroom floor. She could be heard needling Nawaz about his lack of manners and how a lady should never have to ask for a dance.

Gib could no longer contain himself and started laughing in earnest. A moment later Joel joined him while Hasain smiled in a smug manner.

"I almost feel bad for him," Seneschal Koal said with a sigh. He watched his daughter as she continued to talk the ear off of her chosen lord. Nawaz nodded curtly, never once offering to interject. "It looks like he's learned not to interrupt. That's a valuable lesson."

Lady Mrifa cuffed her husband's arm. "That is *not* funny. Heidi is clearly smitten with him."

Koal frowned. "He doesn't appear to feel the same way for her." When Mrifa gasped, he patted her hand gently. "In time, maybe—but let's not preoccupy ourselves with matchmaking tonight. They're both still young and I would see her finish her studies at Academy." He took his wife's arm. "Let's go see my sister and the children."

Mrifa intertwined her arm with his. "Yes, all right. Gudrin and Deegan both look as though they've grown since last I saw them."

The seneschal chuckled. "I was talking about the King and his adviser, but we can see the actual children too."

Mrifa swiped at his chest as they walked toward the dais. Gib watched as people parted for them almost as if they were royalty themselves. In a way, Koal and Mrifa were like a Tale of Fae on their own. He imagined theirs was a beautiful romance. They looked like two halves of one whole, destined to be together as if written in the stars. He wondered if he and Joel would look like that someday. Would it ever be safe to show their affection so openly?

Hasain sighed. "I'm going to take my leave as well." The young lord nodded to Joel and Gib before he passed by them and went to mingle with the other guests.

"Well look at you. Gibben Nemesio, as I live and breathe, I never thought I'd see such a sight."

Gib turned toward the familiar voice and grinned. Tarquin Aldino strode closer, dressed in formal finery with a rather lovely girl by his side. They contrasted nicely: him, pale and clothed in pastels, and her, dark and draped in vibrant reds, oranges, and gold.

"Uh, yeah. Here I am," Gib called out in greeting. "When did you get here?"

The young lord laughed. "Long before you. My father always likes to be early to these things. We'll also be some of the last to leave. He and mother are both terrible gossips."

Gib grinned. Tarquin must have gotten his mouth from his parents. He paused, turning to look at the lovely, exotic girl who had accompanied Tarquin. Gib nearly jumped out of his skin when he recognized her face. "*Kezra?*"

Kezra folded her arms over her chest. "Really, Nemesio?"

Eyes wide, he couldn't stop staring at her. He'd never seen her in anything but her training tunic and breeches. Now, in her scarlet dress, golden jewelry, and shimmering makeup, she was unrecognizable. The sentinel trainee's face burst with warmth. "You look like a girl."

Kezra's shrewd eyes narrowed into slits. "I hate to break it to you, but I *am* a girl."

Gib floundered, hands waving wildly. "I know that! I mean, you don't usually look like a girl—" Wait. That still didn't sound right. He opened his mouth but didn't know how to fix it. "I mean to say, the dress and jewelry—"

Kezra rolled her eyes and gestured down toward her body. "This is a sari from my mother's native country, Shantar. They really don't teach you anything in Willowdale, do they?"

"There's more than one kind of dress?" Gib winced at her poisonous glare and struggled to find something more to say.

Joel clucked softly in his ear. "I think now would be an excellent time to apologize and stop talking." Tarquin and the mage trainee both laughed.

Gib wished a hole would open up in the floor beneath him and swallow him. "Chhaya's bane. I'm sorry, Kezra."

"You're an idiot."

Gib took a long drink from his chalice. "Yeah. I think so."

"Best only take one glass. It's strong," Kezra warned, eyeing the wine chalice.

"Strong but delicious!" called out another newcomer.

Prince Didier was making his approach. The group of friends bowed to the prince.

Diddy blushed. "Oh, rise. All of you. I wish you didn't have to—we're friends. I hate that you have to bow to me."

Joel chuckled and put a hand onto his cousin's shoulder. "Formalities. You can't change them. They've been around forever."

"I know. Father tried once but apparently the council shot him down."

Joel laughed, taking a sip from his goblet. "My father told me King

Rishi also tried to get rid of his crown once—the council out-voted him then too."

The prince smiled and absently touched his own crown, a thin silver band around his head. "He told me. Though Father wears his more now to cover his graying hair." The two cousins laughed.

Gib found it surreal to hear of the King in such informal terms and took another drink from the chalice. "It was odd to see your family just now. It's like meeting the characters from a story."

Diddy turned his expressive, dark eyes onto the sentinel trainee. "Oh, Gib, you must meet them in person. I've told them much about you. They would like to meet you, I'm sure."

A lump rose up into Gib's throat. Him? Meet the royal family? "O–oh. I don't know. Aren't they busy? Surely they have more important guests to attend to."

"Nonsense! My mother has asked about you more than once. You must meet them. Come with me, please? All of you!"

Gib looked around at the others but found no help. Tarquin was hanging off every word Diddy had to say, and Kezra seemed to have no opinion whatsoever. Gib could tell he had no polite way to decline so grudgingly began to follow. He stopped only when he realized Joel had hung back. "What about you?"

Joel's smile was not entirely convincing. "I've met my cousins before, Gib. I'll stay here with Nawaz's drink until he manages to escape Heidi." His laugh sounded hollow. "Besides, you're entitled to your friends. You needn't drag me along with you."

It felt like a slap in the face, and Gib physically reeled. "I like doing things with you."

Haunted blue eyes drank him in. "I know, but Liro is across the room, just there." Joel nodded vaguely, his voice a ghost of a whisper. "He's been watching us and—I think it would be good for your image if you were to enjoy the company of your friends for a while."

Gib locked his jaw. He didn't dare look for Liro. He nodded hesitantly. "All right. But I'll be coming back for you."

Joel's smiled was pained. "I'll be here." Gib wished he could kiss the older boy.

The sentinel trainee followed his friends, mind in a fog. He hated the politics of highborn life. Were they always watching? Did they sit and plot whom they would tear apart next? Was banishment how they punished others for being anything less than perfect? Was this what it meant to be highborn? He frowned and followed Diddy, taking note of how the people parted for the prince and his friends.

As they approached the dais, a servant came to attend Diddy, and Gib wondered belatedly where Gideon was. Perhaps he wasn't well enough trained to be present for such a formal event. Diddy dismissed the servant and instead went before the table where the King and Queen were seated. The prince bowed low, and Gib followed suit even as Tarquin and Kezra did the same. They rose only when the King told them to do so.

"My King and Queen," Diddy began in a poised voice. He spoke to them as though they were not his parents, but complete strangers. "I would speak openly if you would allow it."

King Rishi nodded and waved a dismissive hand. "Speak."

As soon as permission was granted, all pretenses melted away. The prince morphed into the boy Gib had met in class on their first day. Smile wide and crooked, Diddy made his introductions. "Mother, these are my friends from class, Lord Tarquin Aldino, Lady Kezra Malin-Rai, and Gibben Nemesio of Willowdale. They are the ones I've spoken of."

Queen Dahlia's dark eyes sparkled when she smiled, and Gib found himself liking her. "Didier has told me so much about you. I thank you all for being hospitable to him."

Who wouldn't be hospitable to a prince? Any laughter Gib might have had died in his throat when he realized the Queen's eyes had landed on him. Dahlia continued to smile. "Gibben Nemesio and Tarquin Aldino, you're the two who train with Didier regularly, aren't you? You both deserve praise for your sacrifice. You give much to spend time that could be used on your studies."

Tarquin responded without missing a beat. "Oh no, my Queen. It is an honor to assist the prince. You are too kind." Gib nodded in turn, hoping the gesture was a suitable response.

King Rishi glanced toward Koal, who was sitting to his right. "The short one is your son's roommate?"

Gib's mouth fell open as Seneschal Koal bit back a smile and replied, "Yes. Gibben. He's one of the ones you met in the arena."

The King waved Koal into silence. "I know that." He frowned. "The kitchen should feed him more. Maybe he'll grow if they feed him."

Diddy's face twisted in horror. "We'll take our leave now, Your Highness." The edge to his voice reminded Gib of what embarrassed children used with their parents. King Rishi smiled like a wolf, incisors sharp and eyes narrow, as he dismissed the youngsters.

"I'm so sorry, Gib," the prince apologized as soon as they moved away from the dais. "He's like that with everyone. He doesn't care if I'm embarrassed or not—"

Gib laughed. "It's all right. Really."

"No, it's not. His behavior is abominable. Just because he's the king—" Diddy sighed. "I'm so sorry."

No more was said as the four walked away. Gib tried looking across the ballroom to see if he could spot Joel, but too many people were dancing. He noted that Nawaz and Heidi seemed to have moved on. They were nowhere to be seen on the floor.

Gib glanced around and didn't see anyone else their age on this side of the ballroom. These were all learned men with careers—politicians and masters. Highborn elite. A sinking sensation settled in his gut. Someone here was bound to notice he wasn't what he looked like in these fine clothes.

Tarquin's pale face screwed down into a frown. "Kezra, my father is talking to your father."

Kezra looked up, eyes narrowing into dangerous slits. "What does Anders want with your father?"

"I have no idea, but we're being called over."

The tall, sturdy man Gib recognized as Tarquin's father was motioning for his son to approach. A second man stood nearby, engaging him in conversation. "Tarquin! There you are, son. Come here for a moment."

Gib thought to sneak away but couldn't think of any way to excuse himself without sounding rude. Grudgingly, he followed behind Tarquin, Kezra, and the prince.

As the group of friends closed in, both men stopped their discussion long enough to bow to Diddy. The prince told them to rise and bit his bottom lip. Gib thought he'd also feel tired of being fawned over if people bowed to him everywhere he went.

Straightening, Tarquin's father picked up where he'd left off. He was speaking to another tall man with dark hair and eyes. "Tarquin, this is Councilor Anders Malin-Rai, your friend's father." He gestured vaguely toward Kezra, who frowned and folded her arms over her chest.

Gib looked up at Anders. The councilor's pale, drawn face and cold eyes brought to mind Neetra Adelwijn's foul personality. Gib glanced at Kezra, only to find her backing away. Her typically shrewd eyes were low and clouded. She reminded Gib of a wild animal, trapped by hunters, as she looked around as though contemplating escape.

Tarquin's tenor voice brought Gib back to the moment. "Greetings, Councilor. I have the honor of training with Kezra daily."

Anders Malin-Rai stuck his nose in the air as he scowled. "The honor? You would call it an honor to play at sword fighting with a girl? Kezra has forgotten her place."

Gib's stomach clenched into knots. So many things made sense now. Kezra's tough exterior and no nonsense approach to her lessons were *defensive* in nature. She was strong willed, yes, but Gib had never considered that perhaps she wasn't supported by her family. After all, she was highborn. He'd thought highborn privilege allowed them to do as they wished without facing scorn—but then again, Joel was also persecuted for not fitting in.

Tarquin locked his jaw and his face went a blotchy crimson. His voice, however, remained regal. No doubt he'd been trained his entire life how to remain polite in awkward situations. "I assure you, Councilor, Kezra plays no games in the training arena. I've carried the bruises to prove it."

Anders only narrowed his eyes further. "Then perhaps it is you who needs more training."

Tarquin's father shook his head. Like Tarquin, his voice was as even and polite as ever, but his frown suggested his displeasure. "Actually, Tarquin is one of the selected students who has been training with Prince Didier."

At the older man's prompt, Diddy jumped into the conversation. "Yes. I owe much to your son, Councilor Joaquin. He has taught me quite a bit."

Gib smiled smugly, glancing back to Kezra. Surely this would be enough to silence her father. But she was still looking at the ground and fidgeting with her hands. His smile fell away. He'd never seen her so out of sorts.

Anders Malin-Rai seemed undaunted by the high recommendations of Tarquin and his daughter. He swilled down the last of the drink in his goblet and rolled his eyes. "With all due respect, Prince Didier, it was the opinion of some of the council that you should have been trained with grown men. What can fellow students teach you?"

The prince was even better at keeping his temper where it should be. He smiled. "The King felt it best to allow Weapons Master Roland to train me in the way he fashioned. I think you'll agree that Master Roland's experience is unquestionable. I'm in the most capable of hands."

Unmoved, Anders shoved his empty cup at a passing servant. "Fill that," he ordered. Fixing his cold eyes on Diddy, the councilor continued. "Were I you, I would pray the King made the right choice. The loss could be great if he were to—miscalculate."

The blood rushed to Gib's face. How could this man, noble or otherwise, get away with speaking so lightly of the King?

Joaquin Aldino cleared his throat. "Well, out with it anyway, Anders. Why did you want me to call my son over?"

"To get a look at him," Anders snorted. "He's of the right age to begin thinking of marriage. I have too many daughters to count. What say you, Joaquin? Have you made a match for him yet?"

Tarquin's mouth fell open, but he closed it at the severe look from his father. Without missing a beat, Joaquin lifted a goblet from another beverage tray as it passed by, handing it to Anders. "Marriage? Tarquin only turned fourteen last moonturn. He still has three years of schooling ahead of him. He wouldn't make much of a husband yet." The two politicians headed away after that and the air instantly felt less stifling.

Tarquin glanced to Kezra, his brow knit tight. "S–sorry about that."

She didn't meet his eyes. "I'm used to Anders being himself. It's you who is unaccustomed to his foul mouth."

Gib wished he had something comforting to say to her but his words had dried up like a shallow well in the heat of summer. He could say or do nothing to take back what Kezra's father had said. Doubtless, he didn't know about many things she'd experienced. How many slights had been made over time by a father who clearly disapproved of his daughter? Gib doubted he could say anything to ease the pain of such rejection.

"Didier, there you are."

Hasain had found them again. He walked with Nawaz and Joel flanking either side. Gib smiled but clenched his hand at his side when instinct told him to reach for the mage trainee. Joel was strictly off limits while under the scrutiny of the public eye.

The young prince nodded to his elder brother. "Here I am. Is everything all right?"

Nawaz took a long pull from his goblet, grinning from ear to ear. "The lighting ceremony will be starting soon. He wants to make sure you don't get lost between now and then."

"What are you doing over here amongst the councilors, Diddy?" Hasain pressed. "Shouldn't you be dancing or drinking?"

"Tarquin's father called us over. It wasn't our original intention to stay here."

Hasain frowned. "Father wants you to come back to the dais. The entire royal family needs to be present for the ceremony. You know that."

"I suppose," Diddy sighed, voice sullen.

"Muttering is most unbecoming for a prince, Your Highness."

Gib jumped as the distinctive whine of Neetra Adelwijn's voice cut through the air like a sharpened blade. The high councilor fixed them all with a stern look as he drew nearer. As if Neetra's presence wasn't bad enough, his understudy, Liro Adelwijn, stood at the councilor's side. They approached together, a pair of snarling wolves looking for easy prey.

"The same could be said for a councilor eavesdropping." Kezra's voice was low but not so quiet to go undetected. Neetra gave her a narrow glare.

Nawaz turned an incredulous look on Kezra. "Kezra Malin-Rai? I didn't recognize you in your—" He stopped awkwardly and a pink blush rose on the lordling's fair cheeks.

Neetra was not amused. "Yes, it would seem Lord Anders managed to get her into a dress for such a formal occasion—but that wicked tongue testifies to her unruly and disrespectful nature. She lacks respect for our traditions." He stuck his nose in the air, speaking directly to Kezra now. "I pity your father for being saddled with such a shamefully errant daughter."

Kezra locked her jaw, fists balled at her sides. For a terrifying moment, Gib feared she might say something she would come to regret. Neetra was not a man to be trifled with—

Joel's tender voice rose to her defense. "It will be to your discredit, Uncle, should Kezra become a warrior of renown in the future. I've heard nothing but good things about her training and progress. Perhaps it is time for some of our old traditions to be laid aside."

Gib couldn't breathe. *How do I manage to find myself in the middle of these altercations?*

Liro raised an eyebrow and Gib tensed as he prepared for the acid sting of the young lord's venom.

"I suppose you would be the one to set these new standards for us, brother? Tell me, where would your country be with an army of women to defend it and male brides keeping the homes? Would you pay out of your pocket for every street urchin to be schooled? Who would grow the crops for this backward utopia of yours? And who would be the king? You?" Liro made a noise that Gib belatedly realized was supposed to pass for a laugh. "Perhaps 'Queen' would be a more appropriate title."

Joel eyes were wide. Gib stepped forward and opened his mouth before he realized what he was doing. "Do women in the army scare you because you fear they can't do the work or because you think they can? Are you afraid you'll have to take a male bride, or are you scared that others will do so out of their own free will? Do the poor terrify you, or are you really just afraid that if there were no poor people then you would be seen as less? How will the world know you're rich and powerful if no one is poor and weak? What is it you want, Liro Adelwijn? Do you fight to defend Arden or keep it in the shadows?"

The silence was so thick it settled like fog around them. Gib felt a solid thump on his back, support from someone—Nawaz. Tarquin was nodding his approval and the fire had returned to Kezra's defiant eyes. Joel had turned to look at Gib and wore a dazed and lovely smile. The blood pounded so hard in Gib's ears that he wasn't sure he'd be able to hear Liro's response even if the lord chose to grace them with one.

Diddy lifted his chin, measuring Liro. "A good and gracious ruler would reflect on all of this. What is your opinion, cousin?"

Liro's face pinched. He pointed savagely to Gib. "You're that filthy lowborn farmer, aren't you? Joel is still spoiling you, I see. He must be polishing you to be his new bauble to play with. I can hardly imagine what he's seen in you other than easy prey."

Joel gasped and Gib clenched his fist. *How dare he—*

"I would remind you to consider your words carefully, Lord Adelwijn." Hasain's voice had dropped to an eerie lilt. "Gibben Nemesio is a guest of Seneschal Koal Adelwijn and a trusted friend of Prince Didier Adelwijn—therefore under the protection and gratitude of King Rishi Radek. You would do well to treat him with such respect."

Liro's eyes flashed as he gritted his teeth and hissed back. "Big words for a bastard son. No authority is given you, Hasain Radek."

Hasain's frown was every bit as intimidating as Liro's. "Is my status yet one more thing to frighten you? Does it infuriate you to know that I've been given the privilege of a king's son when I don't have the title? Does the knowledge that I'll always be your equal make you feel slighted in some way?"

Neetra snorted. "Equal indeed. Liro is the product of a good and decent marriage between two people of noble standing. You were the slip up of an overconfident fool with a servant. There is nothing fair or just about the leisure you've been given, and one day change will come."

"I would agree. Change is needed in Arden. Perhaps no titles are needed anymore. Perhaps we would all be better off as equals." Hasain was lofty, though even Gib knew the young lord wouldn't appreciate the loss of his title. Gib was still comforted to hear his feelings echoed by someone else.

Before anyone else could say anything, the gong rang one last time. "Dean of Academy Marc Arrio and Lady Beatrice," called out the announcer. Gib glanced over as the dean and his wife made their belated entrance.

Neetra lifted his goblet then and nodded to the ragtag group of friends. "I suppose that's enough chatter for now. Here's to the inevitable change." He took a drink and turned his cold eyes on Diddy. "My prince, if I'm not mistaken, it's time for you to rejoin your family. The main event for the evening will commence soon. We wouldn't want anyone to miss it." The councilor smiled darkly.

The hair on the back of Gib's neck stood on end. A smile had no place on Neetra's face for *any* reason.

Diddy looked back at his friends and nodded an apology. "I'm afraid it's true. I must go."

Gib didn't feel it was fair. Neetra and Liro were walking away as if they hadn't said anything terrible or hurt anyone with their cruel words. They should be made to apologize—to Kezra and Joel and Hasain, even himself—but it appeared no one was going to stop them.

Joel leaned a bit closer, his voice bitter and subdued. "Would you like to get out of here for a while, Gib?"

The sentinel trainee nodded as he glared at Liro Adelwijn's back. "Yes. I'd like that very much."

The grand hallway outside the ballroom was abandoned save for a lone sentry posted at the door. He paid Gib and Joel little heed as the two boys passed. They moved beyond the immediate passageways surrounding the ballroom, and the corridors began to grow dark and eerily quiet. No lighted torches or beautiful chandeliers illuminated their path here.

"I'm glad we snuck away," Gib whispered as they walked. "I really needed a breath of fresh air." *And time to clear my head. That was all too much to absorb at once.*

Joel let out a frustrated sigh. "I'm sorry. This whole night has probably been awful for you."

"No it hasn't. I was enjoying myself until Diddy and Tarquin led me over to where all the councilors were congregating." Gib laughed nervously.

"My uncle's behavior was deplorable," Joel replied, jaw set in a straight line. "Liro's too." He shook his head in disgust, his eyes overtaken by defeat. "I'm truly sorry."

"There's nothing to be sorry about. It's not your fault." Gib dared to reach out, taking hold of the mage trainee's hand. "I could never be mad at you."

Joel's shoulders tensed, but he didn't immediately pull his hand away. Instead, the older boy stopped to squeeze Gib's fingers, caressing his calloused palm. Joel's voice was soft as he replied, "Thank you for standing up for me back there. I—Liro always manages to fluster me so horribly that I can't speak."

"I'd say it all again, in a heartbeat."

"You're too wonderful." Joel released Gib's hand with a sad smile and took another step. "Come. I want to show you something."

Gib followed, curiosity piqued. He was led through another corridor and then up a set of winding stairs. Gib stumbled once or twice in the dark, but he managed to reach the top step unscathed. A second stairway loomed ahead, and Gib couldn't help but curse under his breath as the mage trainee headed toward it. "Chhaya's bane, Joel! Where are you taking us?"

Even in the dim light, Gib could see Joel's eyes sparkle. "The view will be worth it, trust me."

By the time they had ascended the second stairwell, Gib's lungs were on fire and he was glaring daggers at Joel's back. *Nothing can possibly be worth this effort. Nothing.*

The corridor was dimly lit up here, though the sentinel trainee couldn't figure out the source of the illumination—but as they went forward, passing through an arched doorway, the narrow walls opened around them and Gib knew where he'd been led. It was one of the galleries that loomed above the ballroom. Weak light filtered up from the chandeliers below, casting shadows along the sculpted marble curvatures above.

"I thought maybe we could watch the bonfire lighting ceremony from up here," Joel said. He went to the edge of the balcony, his mage robes flowing around his feet with so much grace he appeared to be floating.

Gib followed at length, setting a cautious hand on the stone railing that ran along the outer edge of the balcony. His stomach lurched when he realized just how far up they were. He knew it was silly and irrational, but the fear of toppling over the ledge and crashing to his death kept him from moving any closer.

"It's perfectly safe," the mage trainee assured, smiling as he patted the sturdy marble banister with one hand.

"Daya, Joel. We could have started out with the lower gallery and then worked our way up. I'm not used to being up so high." Gib laughed nervously.

Joel leaned against the balcony, resting his forearms on the smooth stone. He nodded down. "Have a look."

Following the older boy's gaze, Gib shifted his eyes downward to watch the celebration. People swayed and danced far below. Adorned in silk dresses and perfectly tailored doublets, they all looked more like stringed marionettes than real people. Music filtered up to Gib and Joel, as did the jolly laughter and chatter of the patrons. Removed from the party as they were, Gib could almost forget the harsh words and unfair judgments many of these highborns placed onto their peers. It was possible—just for a brief moment—to admire the beauty of the world below, despite the lies within its immaculate foundation.

His brown eyes found the dais where the royal family's table was positioned, and from his vantage point, Gib could see them all: the King, Queen, and royal children. Diddy had rejoined his family. The young prince sat between his mother and younger brother and appeared to be in good spirits based upon the crooked grin on his face.

"Joel," Gib asked as a sudden thought dawned on him. "Why isn't Diddy's last name Radek?"

The mage trainee turned to look at him. "What do you mean?"

Gib hesitated. "Earlier, Hasain addressed him as Prince Didier Adelwijn. Forgive me, but if King Rishi is his father, then why is Diddy's last name Adelwijn? Shouldn't he be a Radek?"

Joel coughed and looked around as though to be certain they were alone. He lowered his voice to a soft hush. "Because when the King first met my aunt, Didier was already a toddler."

The sentinel trainee blinked. He didn't comprehend Joel's delicately phrased words at first. *Oh. Diddy has his mother's last name because—* "You mean Diddy isn't really King Rishi's son?"

"Didier was raised as the King's son. King Rishi recognizes him as his child—but they aren't of the same blood." Joel stared down at the festivities below. "My aunt was ostracized for being young, unwed, and with a child whose father she refused to name. I was too young at the time to remember any of this, but I've heard it was quite the scandal."

Gib smirked. "It seems as though scandal runs deep in your

bloodline."

"Yes. My father was worried Aunt Dahlia's life would be ruined. You have to understand how serious it was—and still can be—for a highborn lady to have a child but no husband. Fortunately, King Rishi didn't care. He married my aunt despite her shameful predicament."

"Somehow that doesn't shock me."

Joel chuckled. "You'll quickly learn that *all* Radeks bear a healthy disregard for rules and tradition. But no, Didier will never be in line for the throne, for he's not of Radek lineage. The burden of the crown will rest on Prince Deegan."

"I wouldn't wish that burden on anyone."

"Nor would I." Joel paused, his smile pained. His silvery-blue eyes flitted toward Gib. "Thank you for coming with me tonight. You'll never know how much it means to have you by my side. The scorn is—easier to brush aside."

Gib's heart panged with emotion, and he was reaching for the older boy's hand before thinking otherwise. "I'm glad you invited me and I—I would stand by you even if it meant feeling the scorn of every highborn in Silver City."

Joel's smile was dazed and lovely, but as he parted his lips to respond, the sound of blaring trumpets from below caught their attention. A moment later, the other instruments in the ensemble had joined in the fanfare.

"Is the ceremony starting?" Gib asked, peering over the balcony ledge.

All the guests were crowding around the pyre, and up on the dais, the members of the royal family had all risen to their feet and began to make their way to the center of the room. King Rishi walked arm in arm with the Queen while the two princes and young princess trailed closely behind. The strange Blessed Mages and red-headed bodyguard watched from the dais but made no move to follow the family.

"Gib. I don't want to hide anymore."

Joel's tender voice was like silk in Gib's ear. It cut through the resounding music below, through flesh and bone, piercing Gib's very core. The sentinel trainee turned away from the pyre and toward the voice which always managed to undo him so completely. Joel's eyes were beautiful and devastating as he reached out with both hands, pulling Gib close, wrapping him in a desperate embrace. A moment later, when he felt the touch of Joel's lips against his own, Gib melted against the older boy.

"What about the guards? What if they see us?" Gib asked through shuddering gasps, his own hands weaving their way into Joel's smooth waves.

The older boy sighed against Gib's mouth, his fingers coming to rest at the base of Gib's skull. "Let's hope they're as occupied watching the ceremony as the highborns." Joel kissed him a second time, just as feverishly as the first. "I think I'm in love with you, Gibben Nemesio."

A strained squeak made its way up Gib's throat as the words hit him like a hammer in the center of his chest. His knees wobbled feebly and he found himself leaning against Joel for support. Cupping the older boy's face in his hands, Gib clung to him for dear life. "I love you, too."

The two boys held each other, the only sound the procession below. The celebration might as well have been a thousand leagues away. Everything else faded into nothingness and for a brief moment, they were the only two people in the world.

Joel's fingers worked through Gib's hair, caressing his curls. "We should watch King Rishi light the pyre," the mage trainee murmured softly.

Gib was more than content to absorb every detail of the older boy's face instead, still lost in a dream—but then Joel pulled away without warning or reason, and Gib's reverie came to a grinding, gut-wrenching halt. He blinked. "J–Joel? W–what is it?"

Joel raised a hand, demanding silence. "Something is wrong." The mage trainee's eyes were fixed on something beyond Gib.

Swallowing the lump in his throat, he turned to see what held Joel's attention. Down the corridor, Gib could only see a fallen candelabrum, nothing more. "It must have been knocked over by someone. What's so wrong with that?"

Joel shook his head. "There's a sentry posted on every floor of the palace. Surely he would have heard it fall."

As the pieces clicked into place, a harrowing feeling settled over the sentinel trainee. "If the guard investigated the sound, you'd think he would have picked it up." Joel nodded but was already making his way down the hall.

Every hair on the back of Gib's neck was on end as they neared the end of the corridor. The candelabrum had been toppled onto its side and lay haphazardly in the middle of the hallway, and a pool of dark liquid stained the marble floor just beyond. At first, Gib thought it was spilled candlewax, but as he moved closer, a sickening realization began to rise from the pit of his stomach. He latched onto Joel's arm. "Is that—?"

"Blood." The mage trainee's voice was devoid of emotion.

Joel stepped around the candelabrum, and still clinging to the older boy's arm, Gib was forced to follow along. A shuddering gasp escaped his lips when he saw the blood was not contained to a single location—a path of ugly red smeared the corridor floor and disappeared around a pillar several paces in front of where they stood.

Gib froze. He knew, somehow, what kind of horror waited around the corner. He wanted to turn and run away, to get as far from this dark, wicked place as he could, but even as Joel lurched forward, Gib found his own legs moving. His logical mind screamed at him to flee, but he couldn't.

He had to know—

As they rounded the pillar, he heard Joel issue a chilling gasp. It was a sound that would haunt Gib for the rest of his life. He was only a pace behind, so a moment later he could see it as well—

His eyes went wide and his hand shot up to his mouth, stifling a cry of his own. *Goddesses, help us.*

Gib's stomach heaved at the sight of the royal guardsman, cold and motionless on the floor with his throat slashed wide open.

CHAPTER TWELVE

"He's dead," Gib croaked, leaning against the marble pillar for support. His heart raced in his chest. "Oh Gods, he's dead."

The celebration in the ballroom blared on beneath them, but the sounds were lost to Gib. His pulse was like thunder inside his ears, and he struggled to take gasping breaths into lungs burning from lack of air. He tried to look away from the horror strewn across the corridor floor in front of him, but his eyes refused to turn from the bloodied body.

Joel knelt down beside the fallen sentry, dark crimson soaking the bottom of his mage robes. He touched the side of the guard's neck, searching for any sign of life. "The sentinel's armor is missing." Joel's words shook as uncontrollably as Gib's knees.

Gib realized it was true. The sentry's fine uniform had been stripped off his body. Only his woolen undergarments and boots remained intact. The man's broadsword also lay haphazardly by his side. A shiver made its way up Gib's spine like a shard of ice. "Joel, it's the assassin. It has to be! He killed this man and now he's on his way to—" Gib choked, unable to finish.

The mage trainee stood, his features contorted into a mask of fury. "He's going to attack the King when he lights the pyre!"

Gib moved without words or thought. He lurched forward, bending low to take the sentinel's discarded broadsword into his hands, scooping the weapon off the floor in one fluid motion. He gripped the hilt between his hands. The blade towered above his head like a tree trunk made of steel.

"What are you doing?" Joel asked, eyes wide and frightened. "We have to call for help."

Gib shook his head. "Even if you go over to the balcony and scream as loud as you can, no one will hear you above the crowd."

"Then we'll run for help. We'll warn them—"

"There isn't time, Joel! *Look!*"

Far below, cheers rose from the crowd as King Rishi stepped away from the rest of the royal family. One of the royal guardsmen held a burning torch in one hand and was approaching the King—

"We have to find the assassin now." Gib peered down the length of the dark corridor, head spinning. The killer could be hiding anywhere. How would they ever find and stop him in time? "It will be faster if we split up." The sentinel trainee could barely form words through his chattering teeth. He pointed down the corridor. "You go one way, I'll go the other. We'll flush the assassin out in the middle."

Joel shook his head. "No, that's a bad idea. We're just the two of us—a half trained mage and first-year sentinel trainee. This is a skilled killer. We should stay together."

"*Go!*" Gib demanded. "The King is about to light the fire!"

Joel locked his jaw but nodded his head in dubious agreement. "Be careful." The older boy turned on his heels and sped down the corridor.

Gib's feet carried him in the opposite direction, back toward the stairwell. He tried not to think of the danger King Rishi was in—or the peril he and Joel also faced. Instead, the sentinel trainee concentrated on placing one shaking foot in front of the other. His breaths shot forth from between pursed lips in jagged spurts, and cold beads of sweat now threatened to drench the entirety of his tunic. The noise of the celebration below was a dull humming in his head, but Gib could barely hear it over his pounding heart.

Gib kept the broadsword raised and at the ready. His forearms screamed in agony, the weight of the heavy steel bearing down on his muscles. Gib could almost hear Master Roland's sharp words in his mind. "*Gibben Nemesio, you dolt! That sword is meant to be wielded by a man twice your size and height! What do you plan on doing when you have to swing it at an enemy?*" What other option did he have? Time was running out.

Gib glanced over the balcony again, and a swirl of color within the shadows of the gallery below caught his attention. His blood ran cold. *Someone is down there.* Gib swung around, looking for Joel, wanting desperately to call to him—but the mage trainee was already out of sight.

It might be a sentry, Gib told himself. *Joel said one patrolled each floor of the palace.* He craned his neck to look over the balcony ledge once more. The shadowy figure moved along the corridor beneath Gib, silent and lethal, like a predator stalking its unsuspecting prey. The tiny hairs on the back of Gib's neck stood on end and suddenly he *knew*—without a doubt—this was no royal guard. This was the man he'd overheard that day in the hallway. The same man who had already once attempted to take King Rishi's life.

Gib swung around and dove into the stairwell that led to the lower gallery. His footfalls were a flurry as he descended the winding stairwell, and the sound of his boots against the marble steps echoed off the narrow walls. The steps that seemed to have taken eons to climb flew by in seconds as the sentinel trainee ran down the flight of stairs.

He burst through the passageway that led into the lower gallery with the broadsword still gripped between his hands and body crouched low against the corridor wall. *Use the shadows. Stay hidden within them.* He took a trembling step forward, knowing full well the danger he was in. The sentinel trainee focused on keeping his breaths steady and making certain his eyes never veered away from the dark hallway ahead.

Gib nearly went tumbling to the floor when his feet were entangled by an unknown entity. He grasped the wall with one hand to regain balance and jerked his head down to see what was blocking his path. All the courage he'd mustered drained from his body at the sight of the second guardsman—as cold and lifeless as the first.

The ill-fated victim lay on his side, with the shaft of an arrow wedged into the space between the plated armor covering his neck and chest. The shot had been precise, and the lack of any evident struggle confirmed the sentry had died swiftly. Gib leaned against the wall, chest heaving and eyes wide. His hands shook so badly he nearly lost his hold upon the broadsword, but the rest of his body was frozen in fear. *Two. He's already killed twice. How many more people will lose their lives before the night is over? Will I be one of them?*

The music and cheers of the crowd below reached a crescendo. Gib managed to turn his head away from the sentinel long enough to see King Rishi take hold of the flaming torch. As the King approached the pyre and began to lower the torch into the bundled tinder, Gib realized with a bolt of despair that he'd run out of time. *I failed. I failed them all. I didn't find the assassin in time and now the King is going to die—*

Movement caught Gib's eye. He pressed his back to the wall, wishing he could melt into the shadows. A figure materialized from within the gloom, further down the corridor. Gib gritted his teeth together, begging his arms and legs to stop trembling. He slammed his eyes closed. *Here he is. And what real chance do I have against him? He killed two trained men. I'm just a student. Goddesses, help me.* Gib sucked in a harsh breath of air and opened his eyes.

The assassin stood about fifteen paces ahead. Shadows concealed the man from below, but from Gib's vantage point on the balcony, he could see everything—the plated armor and flowing cape, stolen from the sentry, and a small wooden crossbow by the man's side. The killer stood rigidly as he cast his gaze downward, surveying the crowd like a bird of prey.

And then the man shifted within the dark, drawing nearer to the balcony's ledge, as he watched King Rishi throw the torch onto the pyre. The tinder crackled, flames jumping to life, even as the killer made his move to end the King's—

Gib held back a gasp when the assassin raised the crossbow, aiming the deadly weapon down into the ballroom—fixing it onto King Rishi's chest. *Oh Goddesses, he's going to shoot the King! Move! Do something! Now!*

Letting out a shrill battle cry, Gib launched forward, sword raised above his head as he charged the assassin. Seconds before the sentinel trainee reached his foe, he heard the snap of the crossbow releasing and a rush of air as the arrow was set free. Screams of shock and horror rose from the ballroom a moment later, but Gib had no time to dwell on whether or not the arrow had met its mark.

He swung the broadsword with all his strength, aiming for the assassin's throat, but the man managed to thrust the empty crossbow between himself and Gib at the last moment, using the weapon as a shield. The broadsword crashed into it, sending shards of wood splintering through the air. The assassin uttered an angry cry as Gib's momentum sent them both tumbling to the ground in a flurry of tangled limbs.

Gib struggled with the weight of the sword, trying to regain control of the weapon, but the assassin knocked it away, sending the blade spiraling across the corridor. Gib immediately dove for it, but his foe was much faster. The assassin pinned Gib to the floor, a growl rumbling from between gritted, yellow teeth.

Gib grunted when the man's elbow made contact with his nose but barely had time to register the pain before the assassin's fist crashed into his jaw. It felt as though a sharpened rock had been thrown against his face. He let out a gasp of pain, his head reeling to the side. A moment later, the killer's hands fastened around his neck like a steel vice.

Gib saw stars as the pressure on his throat increased, cutting off the airflow to his lungs. He fought to break free from the iron grip, digging blunt fingernails into the flesh of the assailant's hands, but the pressure didn't lessen. Darkness swept across his vision and a dull hum rang through his ears. Gib tried to scream, but his voice was dampened by the hands around his neck.

In one last desperate attempt to free himself, Gib reached for the broadsword, but it was still just out of reach of his grasping fingers. His lungs burned, crying for precious, vital air. The sentinel trainee's consciousness began to slip away even as he fought against it. *He's going to strangle me. I'm going to die—*

Gib's heart leapt when he reached, one last time, and could feel the hilt of the broadsword brush his fingertips. He clutched the leather-bound grip in one hand, knowing the sword was his last lifeline and if he dropped it again, he would die. He turned defiant, feral eyes onto the assassin, and with all remaining strength, bashed the steel pommel against the side of the man's head.

The assassin wailed furiously and teetered back, releasing his hands to cradle the side of his face. Blood trickled from the man's ear, a trail of bright crimson down his neck. Gib took in a deep, gasping breath and used the opportunity to escape. He rolled away from the assailant, putting distance between them.

"You little bastard!" the assassin jeered as he recovered from the blow. His voice was the same rough, grating voice Gib had overheard outside the academy lecture hall.

Gib raised the broadsword, keeping the weapon poised between the killer and his own body, hoping the sight of the blade would deter the assailant from advancing. Angry shouts could be heard all around, resonating off the stone walls. The sounds were like sweet music to Gib's ear. Help was arriving.

Gib glared at his opponent. "The Royal Guard is coming. You'll soon pay for the lives you've ended."

The assassin hissed a curse at Gib but must have decided slaying the trainee wasn't worth the risk of being captured. The man leapt to his feet and dashed away, vanishing into the shadows. Gib dropped the sword and collapsed to the marble floor. He was completely spent.

In the next instant, royal guardsmen had swarmed through the stairwell opening and out to the balcony. Gib forced himself into a sitting position, face throbbing and teeth chattering. He lifted a shaking arm and pointed in the direction the assassin had fled. "That way! He's getting away!"

Four of the soldiers immediately turned to take chase—but one hung back, his dark eyes suspicious as he fixed a sharp look on Gib. The sentinel trainee realized belatedly how bad this entire scene must have appeared. Here he was, alone, with a stolen sword and crossbow in the place where the King had been shot—Gib paled. *The King! Did the arrow hit its mark? Is King Rishi dead?* As he stumbled to gain his feet, the royal guardsman pulled his blade from its sheath.

"No, no, *don't.*"

Joel's frail voice bounced off the high ceilings as the mage trainee ran forward and took to his knee. He glared at the guard from his spot beside Gib. "I swear to you, he had nothing to do with this. We were trying to find the assassin!"

The soldier hesitated but lowered his blade. "You are the son of the seneschal. I'll heed your words, but neither of you may leave my sight until I have further orders."

Joel turned back to Gib, worry lining his beautiful face. "Are you hurt? Look at you—"

"The King," Gib gasped. "How is the King?"

"Marc is with him." Joel paused to stand and look over the edge of the balcony. "I think he'll be all right."

"He went down? He was hit?"

The devastation in the mage trainee's eyes was enough to undo Gib. "Yes, he was shot—but you did all you could to stop it. The King is in the greatest of care. Marc is the very best healer I know."

Gib swallowed his despair, the taste of blood in his mouth. His face hurt and his eyes wouldn't stop watering. "I failed the King. I should have been able to stop the assassin."

More voices echoed through the corridor as royal soldiers continued to pour into the gallery. The boom of Seneschal Koal's voice could be heard above the others. He shouted for the guardsmen to spread out. "Search every room, every shadow! Find the criminal and bring him to the King so justice may be served!"

As the seneschal rounded the corner, Gib and Joel got to their feet. The soldier who had found them bowed and cleared his throat. "Seneschal Koal, these two boys were with the assassin's weapon."

Koal fixed a terrifying glare on the empty crossbow before responding to the guard. "Send for Aodan. He'll want to inspect the weapon. Touch nothing and allow no one to disturb anything until he arrives."

The sentinel nodded. "Yes, Seneschal."

Koal turned his attention to the trainees. "What are the two of you doing up here? And what happened to Gib's face?" His features softened just a little as he took Joel under one arm. "Are you both all right?"

Gib winced. His face did hurt. Gingerly, he touched his nose and lip. A sick knot formed in his guts at the feel of warm blood. *Chhaya's bane. That bastard did a number on my face.* "I–I saw the man who attacked the King. H–he was standing right here. I tried to prevent it but—he elbowed me when I tried to stop him." Nausea swept over him. "Is the King going to die?"

Koal kept his voice low. "No. King Rishi is wounded, but Marc is with him. He was complaining about being forced to sit as I left the ballroom. He seemed to be himself." The seneschal set one large hand on Gib's shoulder. "This man, the assassin, what did he look like? Was he working alone?"

"Y–yes, he was the only one. He was sort of tall, compared to me anyway. He was wearing stolen armor from—" Gib paled. "—from the guardsman he murdered. I can't remember any other specifics. I–I didn't get a good look at him, sir. It all happened so fast. He took off running just before help arrived. I'm sorry."

"Did you see which way he ran?"

Gib nodded, trying to get his foggy mind to form coherent sentences. "He ran toward the opposite stairwell. I think he was trying to escape to the upper level." He watched as the seneschal's mouth fell into an even deeper scowl. "Will they be able to find him? He's dressed like one of the royal guardsmen."

"The Royal Guard all know one another. When they see his face, they'll know he's not one of them," Koal replied, tone angry. The seneschal opened his mouth to fire another question but stopped short as an angry command was bellowed from above.

Gib sucked in a breath of air, a chill making its way up his spine. He would recognize that menacing voice anywhere. Liro Adelwijn.

Joel's face went grim. "What is Liro doing up there? Why is he giving orders?"

Koal also looked up. "He's acting on behalf of Neetra. The High Councilor has delegated this task to his understudy. The King was—preoccupied and voiced no command otherwise."

The sound of shouts and scuffling could be heard overhead. Gib flinched, and Joel and his father froze. A loud clang brought to mind more toppling candelabrum and the angry cries of guardsmen caused Gib's stomach to heave. Had they found and cornered the assassin?

"Seneschal Koal!" someone was shouting from the stairwell. "We have located the assassin—"

Before the soldier could finish his call, Koal sped away from Gib and Joel with a single command for them to stay. The severity of his tone was enough for neither of them to question further. Joel held up one hand as his father disappeared around the corner. "Be careful." The words were so soft Gib barely caught them.

"He'll be surrounded by the soldiers," Gib reassured, wishing he could take Joel's hand. "He'll be okay."

Liro's voice rose above the din upstairs. "He's one man! Catch him and hold him d—"

The unexpected break in his words caused both students to stiffen and share a concerned glance. Without a word, they rushed to the edge of the balcony and looked up, hoping to catch a glimpse of what was happening above them. Through the darkness, it was difficult to see anything until—

Gib grabbed Joel, yanking him back from the railing. An ear-piercing scream rippled through the air as a body plunged from the third story balcony. It barely missed the students on its descent. A sickening squelch of bone and flesh came as the body hit the stone floor below, and more voices cried out in horror.

"*Oh Goddesses.*" Joel stood frozen, eyes wide with terror.

Gib held up a hand for his friend to stay. The older boy didn't need to see the body if it was Liro or Koal—Gib took a deep breath and forced himself to peer over the railing.

Below, the body of the assassin lay in a tangle of unnaturally positioned limbs and the twisted cape of the dead soldier. King Rishi was on his feet, bleeding arm cradled to his chest, and glaring upward. For a terrifying second, Gib thought the King was looking at him—but, no, he was looking farther up.

Gib craned his neck and saw the hard, cold face of Liro Adelwijn as he stood at the third story balcony with not a single hair out of place nor bead of sweat on his brow. He was the deadly eye of the storm.

"Tell me it wasn't Father or Liro." Joel's voice was a broken gasp.

Gib whirled around. "No. It was the assassin. He's dead."

Joel put his hands over his face and sobbed openly. "Oh, thank the Two. I thought—for a moment—" The mage trainee shook his head, unable to continue speaking through the tears.

Gib came to Joel and put an arm around his shoulders. "No. It's all right. Your father and brother are alive. I could see Liro above."

Joel shuddered and wiped at his face. He took a step back from Gib. "Thank you."

Gib wished he could offer more comfort, but now was not the time or place. A moment later, Koal had raced back down the stairs, Liro right behind. The seneschal's face was set in a hard scowl as he interrogated his eldest son. "You had no choice? You're sure of it?"

Liro's soft voice dripped with venom. "Father, an armed assassin launched himself at me. What was I supposed to do? Fall victim? In the struggle, he toppled. There is nothing more to tell."

Koal glared hard. "He should have been questioned! You'll have the King to answer to for this."

"Your concern for my welfare is overwhelming. Really, I must insist you keep your head."

The seneschal stopped short and turned to look over his son at length. With a sigh, he asked, "Are you all right?"

"So fatherly of you to inquire. I am fine."

Joel ventured a step closer as the two adults approached. "I'm glad to see you're not hurt, Liro. When the body fell, I feared the worst—"

Liro shot his younger brother a cold glare. "Yes. It would have been a tragedy for you, wouldn't it? With me dead, you would be eldest and in line for the entirety of the Adelwijn estate." He rolled his eyes. "Wipe your face, you child, before you bring any further disgrace upon us."

Koal balked and Joel winced. Gib opened his mouth, trying to think of something to say in defense of his friend. Before any of them could retort, Liro waved them off and continued toward the stairwell to the ballroom. "Save your breath, all of you. It's my duty to report to the King, seeing as preserving my own life cost the assassin his."

Koal sighed and motioned for the two students to follow him down the stairwell. "Come. You both may have to explain what you saw to King Rishi as well." Joel bit his bottom lip and dutifully shadowed behind his father. Dumbfounded, Gib had no choice but to do the same. He trailed his roommate in silence.

By the time they reached the ballroom, Joel had dried his face and gotten his breathing under control. Gib continued to glare at Liro's back, hating how the elder brother made Joel feel and hating even more how nothing could be done for it.

The ballroom stood cold and deserted, save for a group of men gathered around a very irate and injured King Rishi. He stormed back and forth, face in a fearsome grimace with his bloody right arm hugged to his chest. A ragged hole in his uniform showed where the arrow had pierced him. All the other guests had been sent home and the cheerful music which had resonated off the marble walls was replaced by muted voices and nervous whispers.

Koal gave Joel and Gib a severe look before stopping long enough to speak to them. "You boys stand back. I have to speak with the King. Don't move from this spot." Neither said anything as they halted next to a pillar and watched the seneschal march away to join the other men. Not a word was exchanged between them and though neither drew attention to the fact, they both pointedly looked away from where the assassin's body lay in a ruined heap on the opposite side of the room.

Instead, Gib focused his attention on the King and his council. Would Gib have to speak to him? Or worse—would he be questioned by the King directly? Gib didn't know if he'd be able to answer. Neetra and Liro Adelwijn were standing close by, as were Diedrick Lyle, Anders Malin-Rai, and Joaquin Aldino. The other men who lingered were probably also council members. Gib didn't know if he could speak in front of these learned, powerful men.

The youngest royal children and Queen Dahlia were already gone, no doubt swept off to safety. The strange Blessed Mages had disappeared as well. Hasain was the only other Radek present, his features pale and drawn. Dean Marc hovered beside the King, muttering none too politely about how difficult it was to work on a resistant patient. Paying no heed to the healer's laments, King Rishi paced and fired questions at Liro and Koal.

"Who is this man? Does anyone recognize him? Is there any evidence of who he works for or if he acted alone?" The King narrowed his dark eyes at Liro. "He should have been brought to me alive for questioning, damn it!"

Gib bit his bottom lip and leaned against the pillar. Liro shouldn't have looked so collected and confident. He should have been nervous. Gib knew that in the same position, he would have been desperately trying to explain himself. Instead, Liro seemed apathetic. He also appeared to be backed by no less than half the royal council—Neetra the loudest supporter of them all.

"My understudy acted as any rational man would, were they being attacked by an armed assassin," the High Councilor replied. "Liro committed no crime by defending himself."

A commotion erupted in the arched entranceway and a moment later King Rishi's personal guard, Aodan, barreled into the ballroom. His face was pulled into a fearsome scowl as he nearly flew down the steps with the assassin's battered crossbow under one arm. His voice was loud, and he came at Liro with such ferocity that Koal stepped between the two of them.

"What the hell happened up there? Why did ya throw him over?" Aodan demanded.

Liro didn't even flinch. "The assassin came at me. I tried to stop him, but in the struggle he toppled." He fixed the red-headed man with a cold glare. "How many times will I be asked this same question?"

Aodan pointed and snarled back, "Why were you up there anyway? Who called fer this whelp to be involved with security?" His one good eye glared around at the council.

Neetra stuck his nose in the air. "That was me. Liro is my understudy and I sent him to act on my behalf—"

"Yer a coward, Neetra Adelwijn, and this was a ploy to save your own neck." Aodan aimed the crossbow, albeit empty, at Neetra and growled, "You sendin' that boy up there has cost us our perpetrator. Who will we question now?"

Neetra's high whine grated Gib's nerves. "How dare you point that weapon at me! I could have your head, you filthy—"

"Damn it, Aodan, drop the bow!" Koal interjected. "And Neetra, calm yourself. We need to discuss this as rational men—"

"Enough!" King Rishi ordered. All the other men fell into grudging silence around him. The King's word was final. Rishi pointed at the lifeless body still sprawled upon the ballroom floor. "We need to figure out who he was and who he worked for."

Gib took a shuddering breath and couldn't help but glance at the disheveled body lying motionless on the white marble floor. Three guards were posted around it, as if the deceased were going to jump up and go somewhere.

The sentinel trainee looked to Joel. "Are they going to—cover his body or something? They won't just leave it there, will they?"

"No. They'll get him moved," Joel reassured. "His body will be cleaned and put in one of the common tombs." Gib could feel the mage trainee's eyes but lacked the strength to meet them. "If no one claims his body, that is."

"I know it must sound foolish, and I mean no disrespect to the King but—the assassin was still a person. He should be buried like a human being."

Joel's hand was warm on Gib's shoulder. "You're right. And I promise you, the assassin's body will be treated with proper respect. King Rishi wouldn't allow for him to be defiled."

Dean Marc spoke next as he crossed the room toward the two students. "Of course he wouldn't!"

Gib jumped and turned to look up at the dean. Marc's typical good humor was nowhere to be seen and his dark eyes held not a trace of a sparkle. In this moment, he looked like a worried father. Concern etched every fair feature of his face.

Laying a hand on Gib's free shoulder, Marc dropped his voice down low. "It would be bad form to disrespect the dead. Joel is right. The King won't allow for that. The assassin will be buried after they examine his face and clothing for evidence about his origin."

Gib tried to find comfort in this but just couldn't bring himself to stop feeling so—empty.

Marc squeezed Gib's shoulder. "You need to come with me now. Both of you. The King has questions."

Gib was certain he wouldn't be able to lift his feet to cross the ballroom floor, but he found his body moving of its own accord. He and Joel shuffled in silence as they approached the King and all of his advisers.

A hush fell over the room—even the gathered councilors dared not breathe. Gib swallowed, feeling oddly hollow. He should have been panicking by now. His breaths should have been growing rapid—but he felt nothing inside. He'd saved the King from death and watched the assassin fall to a gruesome demise, yet it was an empty void that ate away at the sentinel trainee's heart. Was this what it felt like to be a soldier, exposed to death and danger each day? If so, would he ever feel anything again?

They came to a full stop before the men, all of them giants in the moment. King Rishi scanned the students with dark eyes before focusing his attention on Gib. "You were there with the assassin?"

Gib scarcely recognized his own meek voice. "Yes."

"What were you doing in the gallery?"

"We wanted to watch the pyre from above." When the King raised an eyebrow, Gib thought to explain better. "Joel and I. We were both up there."

The King turned his dark eyes to the mage trainee, and Joel immediately bowed. A hazy tingle in the back of Gib's mind warned him that he should probably bow too, but he couldn't quite relay the message to the rest of his body. King Rishi asked Joel something, but Gib's ears were ringing so loudly he couldn't decipher the words.

Joel answered, voice heavy with emotion. "On the third floor. I wanted Gib to have a good view of the lighting ceremony. He's not from Silver and had never seen a lighting before."

"How did you come upon the assassin?"

Joel's face went pale. "We found the body of a royal soldier. We wanted to yell down to you and the others, but the ceremony was too loud. I thought to get help, but Gib said there wasn't time." Joel took a shuddering breath. "He was right. If Gib hadn't found the assassin when he did then—" He didn't seem able to finish the sentence.

The King nodded and turned back to Gib, who shrank into himself. "What happened to your face, little one?"

Gib's lip trembled. "He hit me. When I tried to stop him—I tried to make him stop but he fired at you anyway." Gib stared at King Rishi through thick, damp lashes. The sight of the blood on the King's uniform was nauseating. Where was the arrow? Who had removed it? The King must have been in pain. "I'm sorry! You could have been killed and I just— I couldn't—"

A hand patted the back of his neck and Marc's gentle voice filled Gib's ears, soothing his frazzled nerves. "Deep breaths. You're doing well."

The sentinel trainee nodded but couldn't seem to catch his breath. Why was he so overwhelmed? He'd dealt with raising his brothers by himself, bringing in crops, cold winters with little food, and even coming to this strange city alone. The death of one enemy shouldn't have been enough to undo him so thoroughly. King Rishi glanced around before stepping away from his councilmen, impossibly tall as he approached Gib. The sentinel trainee tipped his head back, trying to maintain eye contact.

A moment later, the King had taken to one knee, meeting Gib face to face. Up close, Rishi looked like a person, just another man, and not so much a king. His dark eyes weren't warm and compassionate like Marc's, but they weren't cynical either. The man looked so much like Hasain that it seemed odd he didn't point his nose in the air when he spoke.

"Yes, as Marc has said—breathe easy and know you've done all you could." The King paused before pressing in a gentle tone. "How did you know to act? What made you look for the soldier's killer?"

Gib blinked. He wasn't sure where to start.

Koal, who had been quiet until now, swept forward. The seneschal kept his voice quiet as he leaned over King Rishi's shoulder. "This is Gibben Nemesio of Willowdale—the boy who overheard the plot."

King Rishi's eyes came into sharp focus. "*You're* the one who overheard the assassin? *And* you happened to be in the right place at the right time tonight?"

Gib nodded. He couldn't think of anything to say. Looking back on it now, he supposed his story would sound incredible, maybe even unbelievable—

As if the High Councilor could somehow read Gib's thoughts, Neetra Adelwijn tore away from the group of advisors and came at them. "Who is this boy? Why are we wasting our time with him?"

Koal narrowed his eyes and whirled around to face his brother. "Gibben has valuable information about what has happened tonight and possibly how the event was planned. You would do well to hold your tongue."

Neetra's face contorted and his shrill voice rang off the high ceiling.

"Don't speak so lightly to me, Seneschal! I represent the Royal Council of Arden and my questions are their questions. Now, I demand some answers."

The King rolled his eyes but nodded. His attention flitted back to Gib. "Tell my council what you overheard."

Gib looked around at the shrewd faces watching him. His lungs threatened to seize again until he found Hasain within the sea of strangers. The young Radek lord met Gib's gaze and offered silent encouragement with a simple nod.

"When I broke my wrist before the first snow, I was running a message to Dean Marc." Marc's hand squeezed just a little—more encouragement. "On my way back, I heard two men talking about killing the King." A collective gasp came from several of the councilors.

The King seemed unfazed. "Continue."

Gib's breaths were choppy, but Hasain kept eye contact and Marc's touch was reassuring. Joel was by his side and Seneschal Koal nodded as well, encouraging him to continue. He wasn't alone. "They were in one of the empty lecture halls in Academy. It was during class time, so I was the only one in the halls. They spoke of killing you, Sire, and I heard coins jingling."

A wry, wolfish smile crossed the King's face. "Someone wanted me dead badly enough to pay this man?" He turned a devilish look onto his council. "My reputation precedes me!"

In general, his grin was met with rolling eyes or no reaction at all. Neetra alone winced and took an unwilling step back. His thin face was blank.

When the High Councilor managed to recompose himself, crimson stole over his fair features and he shrieked, "Are we really going to believe the words of this one peasant child? If he heard this news so many moonturns ago then why is he only telling us now?"

Murmurs rose from the councilmen. Gib's stomach twisted painfully. *Not this again.* He slammed his eyes closed, trying not to think back to when he'd been questioned in Dean Marc's office after Midwinter.

Hasain cleared his throat, voice meek. "He told me." Still pale and wringing his hands, the young lord cast his eyes to the floor when everyone directed their attention toward him. "Gibben voiced his concern to me on the eve he overheard the plot."

An outcry came from several of the councilors at once, namely Anders Malin-Rai and Diedrick Lyle. They fired questions and accusations about Hasain's lack of action.

Hasain shivered and took a step back. "I was wrong! I'm sorry, Father. I thought you were too well protected to worry. It's my fault you weren't informed sooner." His face was crimson and drawn into an ugly grimace.

King Rishi looked over his shoulder and Gib could see no trace of anger or disappointment there. He looked like a father, like Gib's own Pa when the children had made mistakes. The King's voice was level as he replied, "Calm yourself, Hasain. Apologies can be made later. Keep your head while in council."

With a deep breath, the young lord nodded once and seemed to regain control over himself.

Neetra didn't seem to be satisfied by Hasain's apology. "So then, really, this is the bastard's fault." His words scalded and even Gib flinched. "Had he not been so errant in his assumptions then this whole thing may have been avoided!"

King Rishi rose from his knee with only the slightest wince as he cradled his injured arm. Standing to his full height, he strode over to Neetra as silently as any shadow might cross a floor. Indeed, the High Councilor didn't realize he'd drawn the King's wrath until Rishi was closing in. Neetra's shrill words fell off, and he lifted an arm as if to shield himself.

Gib sucked his bottom lip into his mouth and wished he could take Joel's hand. He didn't want to see any more violence tonight.

The King's unscathed arm shot out and his hand clenched the front of Neetra's doublet, bringing the miserable gnat within an inch of the ruler's face. King Rishi's voice was a dangerous whisper. "If you *ever* call my son a bastard again, I'll rip your wagging tongue from your mouth."

The High Councilor's face went white. His typically sharp and prolific vocabulary left him, and all he could do was nod. The silence fell so thickly that Gib's chest heaved from the weight of it.

King Rishi shoved Neetra back hard enough that he stumbled. No one moved to help him. No one dared speak. Under the iron curtain of quiet, time stood still. Only when the King began to pace did life seem to lurch forward once more.

"Enough of this for tonight. Go home, everyone. At first light, there will be a meeting." King Rishi turned to look at his councilmen. "All of you will attend and we will figure out what to do about this."

The next three days blurred together. Gib had a hard time recalling what he'd said when he was called upon to go before the King and his council for a second time. He was grateful Joel was also there. The two boys were questioned yet again, more thoroughly than the night of the incident. Neetra and his supporters fired all manner of demeaning questions as if they felt Gib and Joel could have been involved with the assassin. The bile and terror rose within Gib until he could no longer speak and only then did the King stop the interrogation to remind his council the students were heroes, not enemies.

Life at the Adelwijn estate was barely any more comfortable while the two boys awaited the final few sennights of Academy. Carmen and Heidi watched the boys' every move, concern and something else—perhaps pity—etched into their faces. However, the girls did their best to respect Gib and Joel's space and never once asked a single question about the assassin. Indeed, they barely spoke at all other than to offer a cup of tea here or some other form of comfort there. Gib found himself wringing his hands, wishing to go back to the dorm room and the solitude it offered.

A rider arrived the day before they were due to return to Academy. Nawaz Arrio's voice boomed from the door as Otos ushered him inside. Joel looked up from a scroll he was studying, and Gib locked eyes with the mage trainee. They shared a smile and bolted for the stairs.

Lady Mrifa and Heidi made it to their guest first, but Nawaz took it all in stride, even showing the good grace to kiss Heidi's hand and console her twittering concern for his welfare. Gib caught the young lord rolling his eyes, but all in all, the smile never fell from his face, even as he excused himself to speak to Gib and Joel.

As soon as the three of them were alone, Nawaz put his hand over his face and laughed. "How do the two of you put up with her? I've never known someone to fret like Heidi does."

Joel cut a shrewd look at the healer trainee and folded his arms over his chest. "I assure you, Heidi doesn't fret over anyone else nearly as much as she does for you."

Nawaz grunted. Rolling his eyes, he flopped onto one of the lounges in the study and fixed his crystal stare on Gib. "How you feelin', Gib? Both of you, really."

Gib forced a smile as he sat in a chair near the fireplace. "Fine. Why do you ask?" He fought not to cringe at the sound of his own voice. He was a terrible liar and could only hope Nawaz was stupid enough not to see. Of course, the young lord wasn't, and Joel was having none of Gib's denial anyway.

The mage student cleared his throat and looked directly at Gib. "He's having nightmares. He can't sleep. Is there something you can do for him?"

Gib opened his mouth to protest but was cut off by Nawaz, who jumped to his feet and flashed a wide grin. "Marc is busy tending to the King—who's the worst patient ever—so you're stuck with me."

His long stride brought him across the room in an instant and he was looking into Gib's face as if it could give all the needed answers. Nawaz's hands were heavy on Gib's shoulders and the genuine look of concern was nearly enough to undo him on the spot.

"Specific nightmares or something more vague?"

Gib thought to lie and press that nothing was wrong—but Joel knew the truth and Nawaz was sure to know as well. Hanging his head, the sentinel trainee heaved a sigh. "I—it's always about the assassin. I mean, it's only been the last two nights but each time it's the same thing."

Nawaz nodded and his mouth set into a thin line. "All right. Have you talked to anyone about the dreams? Or about your experience with the assassin?"

Not this again. Gib folded his arms over his chest. "I've spoken until I was blue in the face! What good could more talking do?"

The healer stood back to his full height. He was nothing but giving, listening to Gib's answer and objecting about nothing. Gib didn't know why but it frustrated him. Shouldn't Nawaz have something sharp to say? Shouldn't his eyes sparkle with mischief and delight as he proclaimed Gib a weakling and the dreams simply the young man's overactive imagination? Shouldn't Nawaz dismiss Gib as foolish?

"Death is no glamorous thing. It tends to haunt people who are inexperienced with it—"

"My parents are both dead. I have experience with it." Gib flinched at the way his voice grated. He hadn't meant to be so foul.

If Nawaz noticed he didn't bring attention to it. The young lord continued to be gracious and took a seat in the sill opposite Gib. "You were there when they died? You felt to blame?"

Jittery, angry panic rose up within Gib's guts. "I'm not to blame for the assassin! There wasn't anything more I could do. The King said so—" He took a ragged breath. If that were true then why did he still shake at the thought of it?

Nawaz was on his feet and at Gib's side before the sentinel trainee noticed the difference. Taking one knee, Nawaz looked Gib in the eye, and he flattened against the back of his chair.

The voice which was usually so crisp and full of humor was soft and crystal blue eyes were nonjudgmental. "The King is right, but do you realize that? Do you understand how fortunate you are to be alive? The assassin was a grown man, a trained killer, and you faced him alone. If not for you, the King would be dead."

Gib flinched.

"Death is jarring. There was nothing pleasant about seeing that man's broken body on the floor, but there was nothing to be done for him. With all of the King's men there—the best trained soldiers in our entire land— there was nothing to be done. None of them were failures and neither are you."

Gib's mouth had gone dry and his eyes were so wide they hurt. He was distantly aware of Joel's arm around his shoulders. Nawaz remained on his knee, not touching Gib, but still close.

The trainee's heart pounded so hard he could scarcely hear his voice over it. "I was right there when he fell. I should have grabbed him or something. What if it had been Koal or Liro who fell?"

Joel squeezed Gib, whispering words of comfort into his hair. Nawaz shook his head vaguely. "No. Even if it had been Koal or Liro, if you had reached for them then you would have fallen. You'd be dead too. There was nothing you could do."

A tear burned its way down Gib's cheek. He jumped to wipe it away. Why did he have to feel like this? His head knew there was nothing more he could have done, but his heart—a sob broke free from within his throat and he buried his face in his hands.

"I–I have to be strong. Always. I have to care for Tayver and Calisto. They're all I have left, but I couldn't even protect someone I didn't love. What would happen if one of my brothers were hurt? Or Liza?" He gasped for air, reeling for some purchase on the real world. "I couldn't help Ma, I was too young. And Pa didn't take me with him the day he died." His anguish swelled into rage. "I should have been there! I could have helped him!"

Joel's lips were still in Gib's hair. "Oh, Gib, no—there are terrible things in the world. You can't undo them all." The mage trainee somehow squeezed in beside Gib on the chair and was holding him close. "You're a hero, but no hero can save the world on his own."

Gib fell against Joel and cried. The sentinel trainee couldn't do anything else. A mark ago he hadn't known he felt any of these things and now they were crushing and tearing him apart.

Nawaz patted Gib's knee and said something to Joel about departing to allow them privacy. The young lord made mention of leaving something for Gib on the study desk. He couldn't even look up, but he could hear Joel thanking Nawaz. The study door clicked shut so softly Gib was unsure he heard it over his sobs.

"Are you ready for this?" Joel's words were a quiet hush in Gib's ear. He did his best to nod and not think about what likely lay ahead for him.

Ascending the steps into Academy, Gib thought it was odd how the building looked so much smaller. When he'd first arrived in Silver, the architecture had astounded him into silence. Had he truly grown so accustomed to it already?

The halls were as busy as they ever had been, but he and Joel encountered no trouble navigating the corridors. Was it Gib's imagination or were people parting for them? Were they whispering as well? The noise level had dropped to a low murmur. Gib was sure he wasn't imagining it. People were staring and talking about *him*.

He met Joel's icy blue eyes. "Don't pay them any mind. Come with me."

Gib's heart hammered in his chest. "They're watching us."

The mage trainee kept his face down. "I know. Let's get to our room."

Gib's nerves were wound so tight that when a hand grabbed his shoulder, he did the first thing that came to mind—he whirled on one heel, fist at the ready. He stopped only when he recognized the familiar hunter green eyes.

Kezra cocked a brow and smirked, voice dropping low. "Nice to see you're in a fair mood, Nemesio."

Gib breathed a sigh of relief. "I'm sorry, I thought—"

Kezra shook her head, wild hair tumbling around her shoulders. "Nah. I shouldn't have grabbed you." She looked around at the multitude of students as they stared and raised her voice just enough to draw their attention. "If I were under such narrow examination I would have kicked an arse or two by now."

At once people scuttled away, affording the three at least a small amount of breathing space. Tarquin and Nage were the only others who surfaced from the crowd and stayed close. Gib smiled, happy to see them all.

Joel cleared his throat. "Perhaps we should make to our room." The mage trainee bowed modestly to Gib's companions. "Civil company, of course, would be welcome."

Nage and Tarquin shared a half smile before the Nessuno admitted, "I'm not sure how civil our company is, but we'll try."

Inside the dorm, with the door left slightly ajar—to avoid speculation about their female companion—the friends took various seats and a comfortable quiet settled. Gib didn't know what to say and none of them seemed to be pushing. So it went for a time.

Finally, from his seat at the foot of Gib's cot, Nage turned and asked, "Hey, you hear anything from Diddy? You think he's gonna come back to class?"

Gib caught Joel's expectant look. Shifting in the seat, the sentinel trainee reached for his rucksack and pulled out a folded piece of parchment. "I, uh, I got a letter from him. Nawaz dropped it off to me."

"Well, are you gonna read it? Or at least tell us what it says?" asked Nage.

Gib stiffened. He could, but he didn't want to. Despite his mending heart and the support of his friends, he just couldn't summon the will to fumble over the eloquent words right now. He searched around, imploring mercy from someone, anyone. He heard Joel shift on his own bed, but Kezra had already risen and crossed the room to stand before him. She held out a hand.

"I'll do it, if you want."

Gib could barely meet her eyes. "Thanks. I'm just—tired."

She nodded but offered nothing more as her eyes fell over the script. After reading it first to herself, she cleared her throat and spoke aloud for the rest of them.

"*Dearest friend Gibben,*

I hope this letter finds you well. Proper words cannot express my gratitude for your actions three nights past. You are a hero for the entire country, my friend, as I'm sure you have been told countless times. I must thank you from the heart of a son. Thank you for saving my father. You risked your life so that he may live and I will forever be at your call, for anything you may need.

I wish also to bid a farewell to you and the others—Tarquin, Kezra, and Nage. I will not be allowed to attend class again. Mother fears for my safety and, for once, I agree with her. Father is likewise grudgingly admitting defeat. He is displeased with having to 'cage' me but insists he must do whatever it takes to ensure the family's safety.

I miss all of you dearly. Thank you for accepting me as myself and not merely a prince. You may never know what that has meant to me.

Lastly, I wish to settle an account with you on behalf of Queen Dahlia Adelwijn of Arden. She declares you a hero, not only of Silver City, but of all of Arden. As such, she would implore you to take a gift of our gratitude—anything you may need or desire. I know it is not in your nature to accept such a reward, but she feels you deserve it. You do deserve it. Please let us know what you would consider payment for your services and understand that nothing you could ask for would ever be enough to express our gratitude.

Sincerely, Prince Didier Adelwijn of Arden"

Kezra's wistful smile let Gib know she was touched. Everyone else had fallen silent. Nage and Tarquin each blinked in disbelief.

"Well, what are you going to ask for?" Nage pressed.

"I don't know." Gib took a deep breath and tried to calm the rushing in his ears. "I can't take something from the royal family! I only did what anyone would do, and it's not like I saved the King completely. He still got shot. I can't ask for a prize—"

Joel lifted his hands with an exasperated groan. "For the love of The Two, Gib, you're being too modest!"

Kezra snorted as she handed the letter back to Gib. "Right. If not for you, the King would be dead. I'd say you've earned something—especially if they're offering."

Gib tucked the parchment away. "No. A good deed doesn't require repayment. It was hardly a good deed anyway. I didn't have time to think. I just acted."

Tarquin pointed. "You acted and could have died. Not everyone would choose to act the way you did. Don't sell yourself short."

"I don't know." Gib folded his arms over his chest and looked at his feet. "What would I ask for anyway? A riding cloak and new clothes for the boys? The Queen would laugh at me. There isn't anything else I need."

Uncomfortable silence blossomed and Gib was determined to keep his eyes down. No one was saying anything, but he was sure they were all thinking the same thing. *I'm a poor farmer with nothing. What else do I need? Everything. But I won't ask for it. I can't.*

Kezra cleared her throat. "It's a damn long walk back to Willowdale." She put her fists on her hips and gave him a sly look. "Ask for a horse, you fool."

A lump settled in Gib's stomach. A horse? He could use a horse. But how would he feed it? He'd never had one before and though Liza's had seemed to be easily cared for, he had no firsthand experience. His family had never been well off enough to afford their own. He swallowed. It would be nice not to have to walk back to Willowdale. "I suppose I could—"

Nage clapped his hands together. "You're damned right you could. Your own horse, Gib! What would your brothers say to that?" He laughed.

Gib smiled for what felt like the first time in ages. Some of the weight finally lifted from his chest. He could breathe again. He could see his brothers now, especially little Calisto. Their eyes would shine with wonder and their chests would puff out when they could brag their brother was one of the only farming men in Willowdale to own a horse.

"No one will ever believe how I came to have it," Gib heard himself say. "I'll have to tell the neighbors I found it and nursed it back to health or something."

Joel laughed. "Nonsense. The Queen herself will most likely write a scroll for you. If anyone should question your ownership, you will have the royal seal to say otherwise." He paused before lowering his voice, a blush dusting his fair cheeks. "Then they'll know you for the hero you are."

Gib shook his head. Nothing felt real anymore, yet it somehow was *perfectly* real. He chuckled. "I suppose a horse is all fine and good, but maybe the Queen could gift me something to keep everyone from staring at me in the halls and whispering behind my back."

His friends laughed at that. Tarquin waved a hand. "I don't think you have to worry too much. Kezra will protect you."

Nage nodded. "Right. No one is scarier than her."

Another round of laughter. Kezra only grinned. Gib found himself smiling too as he enjoyed a deep, refreshing breath of air. The nightmares would soon pass. He didn't know how or why, but everything was going to be all right.

Gib sighed as he folded the last tunic and placed it into his rucksack. The bedding had already been stripped from his mattress and placed into a bin for the servants to collect, and everything else that wasn't a personal belonging had been removed from the chamber earlier in the day. As Gib looked around the empty dormitory room, the realization that he was leaving struck him hard in the chest.

It was difficult to believe the school year was at an end, and in a few short marks, he would be on his way to Willowdale—home. The sentinel trainee's stomach churned. He'd been away from his brothers for so many moonturns he was almost afraid to see them again. Had they grown as much as he had? Would he even recognize them—and would they recognize him? Gib certainly didn't feel like the same shy, oblivious boy who had walked into this very room for the first time six moonturns prior. Would he be viewed as a completely different person to Tayver and Calisto as well?

The events of the past half-year had changed him. When he'd arrived he hadn't known anyone, and his only goal had been to live long enough to go back to the farm. But then he'd met Nage, Tarquin, Kezra, and Diddy. Each of them had played a vital part in his growth. He'd learned so much from them all and their diverse circumstances.

Gib had said his goodbyes to each of his friends earlier. Tarquin tried his best at stoicism while Nage and Kezra had given Gib nothing but grins and thumps on the back. He would see all of them when the new academic year began, and in time, the four of them would earn their shields and swords together.

Gib's heart hurt when his thoughts brought him to the farm. He still wasn't sure what he was going to do about it. He'd been raised there and all his childhood memories were tied to that place—but after being in this grand city and meeting so many new and intriguing people, Gib didn't know if he could go back to existing as he once had. He'd met royalty and politicians. Some of them had even surprised him with their kind souls and generosity. He'd seen some of the finest events the country had to offer, attended the Aithne Ball, eaten at the seneschal's dinner table over Midwinter, and trained in the royal palace. He'd met Joel—

Gib's face blushed so hot it hurt. *I'm going to miss him the most.*

Joel cleared his throat from across the room just then. The mage trainee's possessions were stacked neatly beside him on the bed, but he hadn't packed anything yet. He'd been withdrawn all day, and Gib had a pretty good inkling as to why.

Gib set his rucksack aside and crossed the room. Without a single word, he sat down next to the older boy, placing an arm around Joel's shoulders. If he needed support, Gib would sit there until Joel could admit to it.

Joel didn't immediately respond; at first, the mage trainee chose to stare out the open window, his eyes lost and brimming with emotion. A moment of silence passed between the two roommates as they seemed to contemplate what the other might be thinking. At last, Joel's shoulders lost some of their rigidity and he leaned his body against Gib's.

"Must you leave?" The words were breathless and pained.

Gib winced as he stroked his palm against the older boy's soft hair. "You know I have to."

Joel raised his face long enough to cast a forlorn smile in his companion's direction. "You could stay at the Adelwijn estate for the summer. I know Father wouldn't mind, and Mother would be more than thrilled to accommodate you—"

Gib shook his head. "I can't do that, as much as I want to. I have to go see my brothers, Joel. They need me."

The mage trainee whimpered deep in his throat. "I need you too."

Gib took hold of Joel's hands, squeezing them desperately, trying to make him realize how difficult all of this was. "I know what you mean, but it will only be for a few moonturns, I promise. I need to figure out what to do with the farm—and my brothers. And then I'll be back."

Joel gave a weak nod, sitting up a little taller. "I understand. You do need to go. I would do the same for any of my siblings. It was selfish of me to ask you to stay, but I just—it will be hard not to see you every day."

"I'll think of you more than is probably good for me," Gib replied with a light chuckle. "And I'm sure Tay and Cal will be sick of hearing your name by the time the summer is through."

The mage trainee issued a strained laugh. The sound made Gib's heart jump in his chest. *I'm going to miss hearing that laughter more than I yet realize.*

Gib pressed on, determined not to break down. It had been hard enough to say goodbye to his friends earlier. He wasn't sure how he was going to bid farewell to Joel. "We can be roommates again when the new semester begins—if you want to, that is."

"I would like that very much." A smile stretched across the older boy's face as he leaned closer. His voice lowered to a soft whisper. "Will you promise not to forget about me, Gibben Nemesio?"

"Never in a million moonturns could I forget you. That's not even possible."

A tear slipped down Joel's fair cheek. "I love you."

Gib wrapped his arms around the other boy, pulling him close, reveling in the warmth their bodies shared and knowing how much it would be missed. *Daya, give me strength.* A single sob escaped Gib's lips, even as he felt Joel break down in silent tears of his own.

"I love you too, Joel Adelwijn. I love you with everything I am."

They shared a tender kiss, both knowing it would be their last for quite some time—but despite that knowledge, they also understood everything was going to be all right. The strangest of circumstances had brought them together, and neither time nor fate would ever pull them apart now that they'd found themselves in one another's arms.

Lifting the rucksack over his shoulder, Gib gave the closed door to his dorm room one last look. It seemed unreal this should be the last time he would see it for the next few moonturns. Despite its cramped quarters and impersonal feel, it had become his home. Despair rose in his chest. *I'm going to miss it all.*

At least as he walked away from one home he could comfort himself with the knowledge he was heading toward another. Tayver and Calisto were sure to have grown since last he saw them. A smile touched his lips as he wondered if their clothes would be too short in the arms and legs now.

He and the boys would have to write Liza. He hadn't heard from his sister since her relocation to Winterdell, but he refused to give in to the fear of her demise. She was clever. Surely this brewing war wouldn't be her undoing, not when she still had so much to give the world. It was his hope, one day, to stand at her side wearing a sentinel uniform. They could protect Arden together.

Who was to say what the future held? Gib surely had no idea. All he knew was that he'd grown to love Silver City, and in his heart, things would never be the same if he tried to leave it all behind.

"Gib! Gibben Nemesio! Stop! I finally found you!"

Sucking his bottom lip into his mouth, Gib stopped in his tracks and turned to look over his shoulder. Dean Marc waved as he bustled down the busy hall after the student. Gib's guts churned. What now? Couldn't he just go home in peace? The doorway was *right* there. He could see it. "Yes, Dean Marc?"

Marc clambered over and waved his hands as he bent to catch his breath. "Just Marc is fine. The school term is over." He gasped for air. "I need to get out of that office more. Look at me." His ragged breathing was comical, but Gib did his best not to smile.

At length, the dean stood to his full height and recomposed himself. "I feared I'd missed you. I need you to come to my office for a moment before you leave. Do you have time to spare?"

He wanted to say no. If he got on the road while it was still morning he could make good timing on his homeward journey to Willowdale—all thanks to the lively young mare Queen Dahlia had given him as a reward for thwarting the assassin's plan. Grudgingly, Gib gave in. The dean had been nothing but gracious to him. Gib supposed he owed Marc the favor. "Sure. I suppose."

Marc slapped Gib on the back, smiling widely. "Great. Follow me."

Gib followed in silence as they traversed the crowded halls. He looked around, scouring passersby for familiar faces but saw none. Many of the dorm rooms already stood empty. It was sad, somehow. Before he knew it, they were at the dean's office.

"This way, Gib. Take a seat." Marc opened the door and ushered him inside.

"Thank you, sir. Could I ask what this is about—"

Seneschal Koal stood by the window behind Marc's polished desk, his back to them. "You could, but you're going to have to wait a moment to be told the answer."

Gib froze. "Uh, h–hello, Seneschal. What brings you here?" His mouth was as dry as parchment. Surely Koal wasn't here to ask Gib to come back to the Adelwijn estate. Gib could think of no way to refuse the Seneschal without being offensive. Surely Koal, of all people, would understand how badly Gib needed to go home and see his brothers, wouldn't he?

Koal turned from the window, his face a guarded mask. "We have much to discuss," came his cryptic reply.

Marc put a hand on the sentinel trainee's shoulder. "Have a seat. This may take a little while."

A cold rock settled in Gib's stomach. Certainly if the seneschal was present, this meeting couldn't be about his grades, could it? He knew his reading scores weren't the best, but he'd tried his hardest. He'd also missed several sennights of physical training, but surely his private lessons with Diddy had more than made up for that. "Is something wrong?"

"That is yet to be decided."

The office door swung shut and behind it stood King Rishi, as tall and intimidating as ever. The wolfish smile that cut his face in two did nothing to calm Gib's nerves. What was this? Was he going to be questioned more about the assassin? He had no idea what else he could tell them. They knew everything he did and they'd analyzed every word at length. What more could he say?

"Sit down," the King commanded.

"Y–yes, Sire."

Gib sank into the chair which was typically so comfortable. Today, it offered no comfort. His mind raced as the three men paced the office and finally came to rest along different surfaces—Koal against the sill, Marc in the chair beside Gib, and the King atop Marc's desk.

Quiet overtook them for a time and Gib waited on the edge of his seat. A million different ideas ran through his mind, none of them bringing clarity to their current situation. When none of the men offered to break the silence, Gib heard his own shaking voice come out. "Is–is this about the assassin? I've told you all I know. I don't remember a name being mentioned, or an accent. No places were spoken of, not a town or a country—"

Koal shook his head. "No, no. This is nothing to do about any of that. It was determined the assassin was of Ardenian origin. He had a couple of prisoner brands on his shoulder—petty crimes mostly. We didn't get a name for him and no one claimed him so his body went to a common tomb." The seneschal frowned. "I don't suppose we'll ever figure out who he worked for."

Marc shuffled a couple of papers in his lap. After what felt like an eternity, the dean cleared his throat. "Ah, here we are. I have your marks here. Have you reviewed them yet?"

Gib shook his head. "I, uh, didn't know where to find them. I didn't think to ask." He tapped his fingers along the arm of the chair. *So this is about my grades? Why is the King here for this?*

Marc listed off each score, reading aloud what the professors had to say. A warm blush stole over Gib's face at the sparse praise from Weapons Master Roland. Lady Beatrice commended Gib on his progress in her law class. Indeed, reading was his only real shortfall—though he'd managed to pass. Barely.

Koal folded his arms over his chest. "What are your plans for the future, Gib? You're not getting any younger. You must have some plan."

His mind reeled. *Plans?* He'd never had a plan before. Before Silver City it was plant the crop, harvest the crop, sell the crop, don't freeze to death, repeat. He hadn't dedicated much thought to it before now, but it would be a lie to say he hadn't enjoyed this past year.

"I–I'm not sure, sir."

Koal tilted his head to the side. "Where is your heart, Gib? Do you long to go back to the farm one day or do you think you could be happy here, in Silver?"

Gib wrung his hands together. "It's not that simple. If it were just me, I'd stay here I think. But I've got two brothers. They still need me."

Koal nodded. "There are many opportunities in Silver. Your brothers could come to the city if they choose."

"We've already thought of that." Gib looked out the window at the green blooms and smiled. "Tayver is old enough to find apprentice work. And Cal has had an offer from our neighbor to be a farm hand until he's old enough to apprentice or enter Academy too. But I still need to talk to both of them about it." It dawned on him that he still had no idea where any of this was going. "Why, sir?"

Marc shifted in his seat and glanced at the King, who nodded once. Gib sucked in a deep breath and waited. The dean flashed a large smile. "Gib, it is Academy's decision to recommend you for the scholarly program. This line of training takes four years to complete instead of two, and once you're fully trained you'll be able to rise to the highest ranks within the Arden Sentinels or become a politician. One day you could find yourself wearing a red cape or sitting at the royal council table, if you work hard enough."

Gib's mind went blank. What? They wanted him to take the advanced courses? Those classes were reserved for students with exceptional grades or who came from nobility. He was neither a star student nor a highborn. They couldn't be serious. Gib issued an incredulous laugh. "I, uh, I appreciate the recommendation, sir, but I can't afford those classes. I'd never be able to pay—"

The King had remained quiet until now, content to listen to the conversation and observe them all, but now he raised his voice to interject. "We didn't recommend you *pay* for the classes—only that you take them."

"I could take a job, Your Highness, but I still could never repay—"

The King's frown managed to be even more intimidating than his smile. King Rishi leapt to his feet and paced around Gib's chair, as graceful as ever, even with his right arm in a sling beneath his cape. "Enough of this job nonsense. You won't have time for a job with these new classes. Your studies will be much more difficult now—so much you'll probably question why you agreed to them." He flashed a wicked grin at Gib's slack-jawed wonder. "But seeing as you won't have a job, you should be able to keep yourself at the top of your class, correct?"

"Y–yes, Your Highness!"

King Rishi smiled devilishly as he walked to the door. "Good. I would expect nothing less from a self-made hero, Gibben Nemesio of Willowdale. Don't disappoint those who have put their faith in you." And without a single word of goodbye, he left, the door banging shut behind him.

Mouth ajar, Gib could think of nothing to say. *What just happened?*

His confusion must have been apparent, for Marc barked a laugh. "Well done, Gib! The King is rarely so open with anyone. He must truly like you."

Gib swallowed. "I would never have guessed."

More laughter met his ears and Koal came to him a moment later to clap a hand on his back. "You needn't worry for the cost of the classes, Gib. I stepped forward to sponsor you, and after the events from the Aithne ceremony, King Rishi offered free tuition for you anyway. There is nothing else you need do. Just show up when planting is done and resume your classes."

Gib's head swam. Looking at Koal, he wasn't sure he was really seeing the seneschal. He wasn't sure if any of this was real or merely a figment of his imagination. When he came back to Academy, he'd be on the same career path as Tarquin. Gib couldn't imagine what his other friends—Kezra, Nage, Diddy, Joel, and everyone else—would have to say. "Th–thank you. I don't—I—thank you."

Koal smiled. "No, thank you. We'll see you in a couple of moonturns, Gibben Nemesio."

FINAL WORD

With war imminent and the High Council of Arden and King Rishi Radek at odds with one another, what will become of Gib and his friends? Find out in **Nightfall: Book Two of the Chronicles of Arden**. Available now on Amazon here; http://www.amazon.com/dp/B00X1UTEBW

If you enjoyed *A Call to Arms*, please consider leaving an honest review on Amazon.com! It would be extremely appreciated.

Please sign up for the mailing list;
http://www.shirilunanott.com/mailinglist.html

Shiriluna's Goodreads page;
https://www.goodreads.com/author/show/9757614.Shiriluna_Nott

'Like' us on Facebook;
Shiriluna Nott's Author Page;
https://www.facebook.com/authorshirilunanott
and
SaJa H.'s Author Page
https://www.facebook.com/pages/SaJa-H/794070493991829

Follow us on Twitter;
@ShirilunaNott and @SaJaH_ofArden

Official Website
http://www.shirilunanott.com

Printed in Great Britain
by Amazon